THE YELLOW SIGN

AND OTHER STORIES

THE YELLOW SIGN

AND OTHER STORIES

ROBERT W. CHAMBERS

Disclaimer

Throughout the text readers may find that some of the language used and sentiments expressed are offensive and unacceptable by today's standards. These reflect the attitudes and usage common at the time the book was written. In no way do they reflect the attitude of the publishers.

This edition published in 2021 by Arcturus Publishing Limited
26/27 Bickels Yard, 151–153 Bermondsey Street,
London SE1 3HA

Cover design: Peter Ridley
Cover illustration: Peter Gray

AD008448US

Printed in the UK

CONTENTS

INTRODUCTION

Robert William Chambers (1865–1933) was both an artist and a writer and one of the pioneers of weird fiction.

He was born in Brooklyn, New York, into a wealthy family. His father, William P. Chambers, was a famous corporate lawyer and a direct descendant of the founder of Rhode Island. In this family, everyone was expected to excel. His brother, Walter Boughton Chambers, became a leading architect and helped to establish New York's skyline as we know it today.

Chambers studied at the Brooklyn Polytechnic Institute before turning his attention to painting, which he studied at the Art Students' League. When he was 21, he traveled to Paris and spent seven years at the École des Beaux Arts and the Julien Academy. The first exhibition of his work occurred in 1889, and when he returned to New York a few years later, he found himself in high demand as an illustrator. Soon, you could find his work in such popular magazines as *Vogue, Life,* and *Truth.*

Around this time, Chambers turned his attention to writing. His first book, *In the Quarter* (1894), dramatized his experiences as a student in Paris, and its success encouraged him to continue writing. In 1895 he published the book that he would always be remembered for: *The King in Yellow.*

This collection of short stories focused on the mythical play of the same name that would drive anyone who read it mad and the terrifying strange city of Carcosa. Stories like "The Yellow Sign" and "The Repairer of Reputations" drew on the imagery of the bohemian lifestyles he had seen firsthand in Paris and New York and were filled with the hedonistic fatalism that characterized the growing Decadence Movement of the 1890s. Yet they also were undeniably influenced by gothic literature in general and the works of Edgar Allan Poe in particular. Simultaneously a satire on contemporary culture and a tale of unnerving dread, the stories of *The King in Yellow* have an unyielding hold on all who read them.

In this collection you will find all of the stories originally published in *The King in Yellow*, as well as two other horror stories by Chambers that demonstrate the wild terrors that haunted his imagination: "The Maker of Moons", a story filled with cosmic horror and glimpses of madness which proved to be a pivotal influence on H. P. Lovecraft's "The Whisperer in Darkness;" and "The Harbor-Master," a bizarre and disturbing tale of aquatic monsters that would have fit perfectly into Lovecraft's Cthulhu Mythos.

Chambers' ventures into the world of weird fiction were short-lived, however. He soon turned his hand to more conventional novels and wrote a series of popular society romances, including *The Fighting Chance* (1906) and *The Streets of Ascalon* (1912). These achieved great commercial success and enabled him to live the opulent lifestyle he so desired, but they left critics unimpressed: H. L. Mencken described him as the "Boudoir Balzac."

During the interwar period, popular tastes changed and the once-thriving market for his novels quickly declined. From 1924, he focused on historical fiction for the magazines, but his work never again reached the heights of *The King in Yellow*. In 1933, at the age of 68, he passed away after undergoing abdominal surgery.

The legacy of Chambers' fiction is remarkable. His work influenced writers like Robert E. Howard, H. P. Lovecraft, and Karl Edward Wagner. As many as 14 of his books were adapted for cinema and more recently his writing inspired the HBO television series *True Detective*. As Lovecraft noted, he "could so easily have become a recognized master" if only he had continued to write horror. Instead, we are left to enjoy his small but brilliant output in the genre.

THE REPAIRER OF REPUTATIONS

"Ne raillons pas les fous; leur folie
dure plus longtemps que la nôtre....
Voila toute la différence."

I

Toward the end of the year 1920 the Government of the United States had practically completed the programme, adopted during the last months of President Winthrop's administration. The country was apparently tranquil. Everybody knows how the Tariff and Labor questions were settled. The war with Germany, incident on that country's seizure of the Samoan Islands, had left no visible scars upon the republic, and the temporary occupation of Norfolk by the invading army had been forgotten in the joy over repeated naval victories, and the subsequent ridiculous plight of General Von Gartenlaube's forces in the State of New Jersey. The Cuban and Hawaiian investments had paid one hundred per cent and the territory of Samoa was well worth its cost as a coaling station. The country was in a superb state of defence. Every coast city had been well supplied with land fortifications; the army under the parental eye of the General Staff, organized according to the Prussian system, had been increased to 300,000 men, with a territorial reserve of a million; and six magnificent squadrons of cruisers and battle-ships patrolled the six stations of the navigable seas, leaving a steam reserve amply fitted to control home waters. The gentlemen from the West had at last been constrained to acknowledge that a college for the training of diplomats was as necessary as law schools are for the training of barristers; consequently we were no longer represented abroad by incompetent patriots. The nation was prosperous; Chicago, for a moment paralyzed after a second great fire, had risen from its ruins, white and imperial, and more beautiful than the white city which had been built for its plaything in 1893. Everywhere good architecture was replacing bad, and even in New York, a sudden craving for decency had swept away a great portion of the existing horrors. Streets had been widened, properly paved and lighted, trees had been planted, squares laid out, elevated structures demolished and underground roads built to replace them. The new government buildings and barracks were fine bits of architecture, and the long system of stone quays which completely surrounded the island had been turned into parks which proved a god-send to the population. The subsidizing of the state theatre and state opera brought its own reward. The United States National Academy of Design was much like European institutions of the same kind. Nobody envied the Secretary of Fine Arts, either his cabinet position or his portfolio. The Secretary of Forestry and Game Preservation had a much easier time, thanks to the new system of National Mounted Police. We had profited well by the latest treaties with France and England; the exclusion of foreign-born Jews as a measure of self-preservation, the settlement of the new independent negro state of Suanee, the checking of immigration, the new laws concerning naturalization, and the gradual centralization of power in the executive all contributed to national calm and prosperity. When the Government solved the Indian problem and squadrons of Indian cavalry scouts in native costume were substituted for the pitiable organizations tacked on to the tail of skeletonized regiments by a former Secretary of War, the nation drew a long sigh of relief. When, after the colossal Congress of Religions, bigotry and intolerance were laid in their graves and kindness and charity began to draw warring sects together, many thought the millennium had arrived, at least in the new world which after all is a world by itself.

But self-preservation is the first law, and the United States had to look on in helpless sorrow as Germany, Italy, Spain and Belgium writhed in the throes of Anarchy, while Russia, watching from the Caucasus, stooped and bound them one by one.

In the city of New York the summer of 1899 was signalized by the dismantling of the Elevated Railroads. The summer of 1900 will live in the memories of New York people for many a cycle; the Dodge Statue was removed in that year. In the following winter began that agitation for the repeal of the laws prohibiting suicide which bore its final fruit in the month of April, 1920, when the first Government Lethal Chamber was opened on Washington Square.

I had walked down that day from Dr. Archer's house on Madison Avenue, where I had been as a mere formality. Ever since that fall from my horse, four years before, I had been troubled at times with pains in the back of my head and neck, but now for months they had been absent, and the doctor sent me away that day saying there was nothing more to be cured in me. It was hardly worth his fee to be told that; I knew it myself. Still I did not grudge him the money. What I minded was the mistake which he made at first. When they picked me up from the pavement where I lay unconscious, and somebody had mercifully sent a bullet through my horse's head, I was carried to Dr. Archer, and he, pronouncing my brain affected, placed me in his private asylum where I was obliged to endure treatment for insanity. At last he decided that I was well, and I, knowing that my mind had always been as sound as his, if not sounder, "paid my tuition" as he jokingly called it, and left. I told him, smiling, that I would get even with him for his mistake, and he laughed heartily, and asked me to call once in a while. I did so, hoping for a chance to even up accounts, but he gave me none, and I told him I would wait.

The fall from my horse had fortunately left no evil results; on the contrary it had changed my whole character for the better. From a lazy young man about town, I had become active, energetic, temperate, and above all—oh, above all else—ambitious. There was only one thing which troubled me, I laughed at my own uneasiness, and yet it troubled me.

During my convalescence I had bought and read for the first time, *The King in Yellow*. I remember after finishing the first act that it occurred to me that I had better stop. I started up and flung the book into the fireplace; the volume struck the barred grate and fell open on the hearth in the firelight. If I had not caught a glimpse of the opening words in the second act I should never have finished it, but as I stooped to pick it up, my eyes became riveted to the open page, and with a cry of terror, or perhaps it was of joy so poignant that I suffered in every nerve, I snatched the thing out of the coals and crept shaking to my bedroom, where I read it and reread it, and wept and laughed and trembled with a horror which at times assails me yet. This is the thing that troubles me, for I cannot forget Carcosa where black stars hang in the heavens; where the shadows of men's thoughts lengthen in the afternoon, when the twin suns sink into the lake of Hali; and my mind will bear for ever the memory of the Pallid Mask. I pray God will curse the writer, as the writer has cursed the world with this beautiful, stupendous creation, terrible in its simplicity, irresistible in its truth—a world which now trembles before the King in Yellow. When the French Government seized the translated copies which had just arrived in Paris, London, of course, became eager to read it. It is well known how the book spread like an infectious disease, from city to city, from continent to continent, barred out here, confiscated there, denounced by Press and pulpit, censured even by the most advanced of literary anarchists. No definite principles had been violated in those wicked pages, no doctrine promulgated, no convictions outraged. It could not be judged by any known standard, yet, although it was acknowledged that the supreme note of art had been struck in *The King in Yellow*, all felt that human nature could not bear the strain, nor thrive on words in which the essence of purest poison lurked. The very banality and innocence of the first act only allowed the blow to fall afterward with more awful effect.

It was, I remember, the 13th day of April, 1920, that the first Government Lethal Chamber was established on the south side of Washington Square, between Wooster Street and South Fifth

Avenue. The block which had formerly consisted of a lot of shabby old buildings, used as cafés and restaurants for foreigners, had been acquired by the Government in the winter of 1898. The French and Italian cafés and restaurants were torn down; the whole block was enclosed by a gilded iron railing, and converted into a lovely garden with lawns, flowers and fountains. In the centre of the garden stood a small, white building, severely classical in architecture, and surrounded by thickets of flowers. Six Ionic columns supported the roof, and the single door was of bronze. A splendid marble group of the "Fates" stood before the door, the work of a young American sculptor, Boris Yvain, who had died in Paris when only twenty-three years old.

The inauguration ceremonies were in progress as I crossed University Place and entered the square. I threaded my way through the silent throng of spectators, but was stopped at Fourth Street by a cordon of police. A regiment of United States lancers were drawn up in a hollow square round the Lethal Chamber. On a raised tribune facing Washington Park stood the Governor of New York, and behind him were grouped the Mayor of New York and Brooklyn, the Inspector-General of Police, the Commandant of the state troops, Colonel Livingston, military aid to the President of the United States, General Blount, commanding at Governor's Island, Major-General Hamilton, commanding the garrison of New York and Brooklyn, Admiral Buffby of the fleet in the North River, Surgeon-General Lanceford, the staff of the National Free Hospital, Senators Wyse and Franklin of New York, and the Commissioner of Public Works. The tribune was surrounded by a squadron of hussars of the National Guard.

The Governor was finishing his reply to the short speech of the Surgeon-General. I heard him say: "The laws prohibiting suicide and providing punishment for any attempt at self-destruction have been repealed. The Government has seen fit to acknowledge the right of man to end an existence which may have become intolerable to him, through physical suffering or mental despair. It is believed that the community will be benefited by the removal of such people from their midst. Since the passage of this law, the number of suicides in the United States has not increased. Now the Government has determined to establish a Lethal Chamber in every city, town and village in the country, it remains to be seen whether or not that class of human creatures from whose desponding ranks new victims of self-destruction fall daily will accept the relief thus provided." He paused, and turned to the white Lethal Chamber. The silence in the street was absolute. "There a painless death awaits him who can no longer bear the sorrows of this life. If death is welcome let him seek it there." Then quickly turning to the military aid of the President's household, he said, "I declare the Lethal Chamber open," and again facing the vast crowd he cried in a clear voice: "Citizens of New York and of the United States of America, through me the Government declares the Lethal Chamber to be open."

The solemn hush was broken by a sharp cry of command, the squadron of hussars filed after the Governor's carriage, the lancers wheeled and formed along Fifth Avenue to wait for the commandant of the garrison, and the mounted police followed them. I left the crowd to gape and stare at the white marble Death Chamber, and, crossing South Fifth Avenue, walked along the western side of that thoroughfare to Bleecker Street. Then I turned to the right and stopped before a dingy shop which bore the sign:

HAWBERK, ARMORER.

I glanced in at the doorway and saw Hawberk busy in his little shop at the end of the hall. He looked up, and catching sight of me cried in his deep, hearty voice, "Come in, Mr. Castaigne!" Constance, his daughter, rose to meet me as I crossed the threshold, and held out her pretty hand, but I saw the blush of disappointment on her cheeks, and knew that it was another Castaigne she had expected, my cousin Louis. I smiled at her confusion and complimented her on the banner she was embroidering from a colored plate. Old Hawberk sat riveting the worn greaves of some ancient suit of armor, and the ting! ting! ting! of his little hammer sounded pleasantly in the quaint shop. Presently he dropped his hammer, and fussed about for a moment with a tiny wrench. The soft clash of the mail sent a thrill of pleasure through me. I loved to hear the music of steel brushing against steel, the mellow shock of the mallet on thigh pieces, and the jingle of chain armor. That was the only reason I went to see Hawberk. He had never interested me personally, nor did Constance, except for the fact of her being in love with Louis. This did occupy my attention, and sometimes even kept me awake at night. But I knew in my heart that all would come right, and that I should arrange their future as I expected to arrange that of my kind doctor, John Archer. However, I should never have troubled myself about visiting them just then, had it not been, as I say, that the music of the tinkling hammer had for me this strong fascination. I would sit for hours, listening and listening, and when a stray sunbeam struck the inlaid steel, the sensation it gave me was almost too keen to endure. My eyes would become fixed, dilating with a pleasure that stretched every nerve almost to breaking, until some movement of the old armorer cut off the ray of sunlight, then, still thrilling secretly, I leaned back and listened again to the sound of the polishing rag, swish! swish! rubbing rust from the rivets.

Constance worked with the embroidery over her knees, now and then pausing to examine more closely the pattern in the colored plate from the Metropolitan Museum.

"Who is this for?" I asked.

Hawberk explained, that in addition to the treasures of armor in the Metropolitan Museum of which he had been appointed armorer, he also had charge of several collections belonging to rich amateurs. This was the missing greave of a famous suit which a client of his had traced to a little shop in Paris on the Quai d'Orsay. He, Hawberk, had negotiated for and secured the greave, and now the suit was complete. He laid down his hammer and read me the history of the suit, traced since 1450 from owner to owner until it was acquired by Thomas Stainbridge. When his superb collection was sold, this client of Hawberk's bought the suit, and since then the search for the missing greave had been pushed until it was, almost by accident, located in Paris.

"Did you continue the search so persistently without any certainty of the greave being still in existence?" I demanded.

"Of course," he replied coolly.

Then for the first time I took a personal interest in Hawberk.

"It was worth something to you," I ventured.

"No," he replied, laughing, "my pleasure in finding it was my reward."

"Have you no ambition to be rich?" I asked, smiling.

"My one ambition is to be the best armorer in the world," he answered gravely.

Constance asked me if I had seen the ceremonies at the Lethal Chamber. She herself had noticed cavalry passing up Broadway that morning, and had wished to see the inauguration, but her father wanted the banner finished, and she had stayed at his request.

"Did you see your cousin, Mr. Castaigne, there?" she asked, with the slightest tremor of her soft eyelashes.

"No," I replied carelessly. "Louis' regiment is manœuvring out in Westchester County." I rose and picked up my hat and cane.

"Are you going upstairs to see the lunatic again?" laughed old Hawberk. If Hawberk knew how I loathe that word "lunatic," he would never use it in my presence. It rouses certain feelings within me which I do not care to explain. However, I answered him quietly:"I think I shall drop in and see Mr.Wilde for a moment or two."

"Poor fellow," said Constance, with a shake of the head, "it must be hard to live alone year after year poor, crippled and almost demented. It is very good of you, Mr. Castaigne, to visit him as often as you do."

"I think he is vicious," observed Hawberk, beginning again with his hammer. I listened to the golden tinkle on the greave plates; when he had finished I replied:

"No, he is not vicious, nor is he in the least demented. His mind is a wonder chamber, from which he can extract treasures that you and I would give years of our life to acquire."

Hawberk laughed.

I continued a little impatiently: "He knows history as no one else could know it. Nothing, however trivial, escapes his search, and his memory is so absolute, so precise in details, that were it known in New York that such a man existed, the people could not honor him enough."

"Nonsense," muttered Hawberk, searching on the floor for a fallen rivet.

"Is it nonsense," I asked, managing to suppress what I felt, "is it nonsense when he says that the tassets and cuissards of the enamelled suit of armor commonly known as the 'Prince's Emblazoned' can be found among a mass of rusty theatrical properties, broken stoves and ragpicker's refuse in a garret in Pell Street?"

Hawberk's hammer fell to the ground, but he picked it up and asked, with a great deal of calm, how I knew that the tassets and left cuissard were missing from the "Prince's Emblazoned."

"I did not know until Mr. Wilde mentioned it to me the other day. He said they were in the garret of 998 Pell Street."

"Nonsense," he cried, but I noticed his hand trembling under his leathern apron.

"Is this nonsense too?" I asked pleasantly, "is it nonsense when Mr. Wilde continually speaks of you as the Marquis of Avonshire and of Miss Constance—"

I did not finish, for Constance had started to her feet with terror written on every feature. Hawberk looked at me and slowly smoothed his leathern apron.

"That is impossible," he observed, "Mr. Wilde may know a great many things—"

"About armor, for instance, and the 'Prince's Emblazoned,'" I interposed, smiling.

"Yes," he continued, slowly, "about armor also—may be—but he is wrong in regard to the Marquis of Avonshire, who, as you know, killed his wife's traducer years ago, and went to Australia where he did not long survive his wife."

"Mr. Wilde is wrong," murmured Constance. Her lips were blanched, but her voice was sweet and calm.

"Let us agree, if you please, that in this one circumstance Mr. Wilde is wrong," I said.

II

I climbed the three dilapidated flights of stairs, which I had so often climbed before, and knocked at a small door at the end of the corridor. Mr. Wilde opened the door and I walked in.

When he had double-locked the door and pushed a heavy chest against it, he came and sat down beside me, peering up into my face with his little light-colored eyes. Half a dozen new scratches covered his nose and cheeks, and the silver wires which supported his artificial ears had become displaced. I thought I had never seen him so hideously fascinating. He had no ears. The artificial ones, which now stood out at an angle from the fine wire, were his one weakness. They were made of wax and painted a shell pink, but the rest of his face was yellow. He might better have revelled in the luxury of some artificial fingers for his left hand, which was absolutely fingerless, but it seemed to cause him no inconvenience, and he was satisfied with his wax ears. He was very small, scarcely higher than a child of ten, but his arms were magnificently developed, and his thighs as thick as any athlete's. Still, the most remarkable thing about Mr. Wilde was that a man of his marvellous intelligence and knowledge should have such a head. It was flat and pointed, like the heads of many of those unfortunates whom people imprison in asylums for the weak-minded. Many called him insane, but I knew him to be as sane as I was.

I do not deny that he was eccentric; the mania he had for keeping that cat and teasing her until she flew at his face like a demon was certainly eccentric. I never could understand why he kept the creature, nor what pleasure he found in shutting himself up in his room with this surly, vicious beast. I remember once, glancing up from the manuscript I was studying by the light of some tallow dips, and seeing Mr. Wilde squatting motionless on his high chair, his eyes fairly blazing with excitement, while the cat, which had risen from her place before the stove, came creeping across the floor right at him. Before I could move she flattened her belly to the ground, crouched, trembled, and sprang into his face. Howling and foaming they rolled over and over on the floor, scratching and clawing, until the cat screamed and fled under the cabinet, and Mr. Wilde turned over on his back, his limbs contracting and curling up like the legs of a dying spider. He *was* eccentric.

Mr. Wilde had climbed into his high chair, and, after studying my face, picked up a dog's-eared ledger and opened it.

"Henry B. Matthews," he read, "book-keeper with Whysot Whysot and Company, dealers in church ornaments. Called April 3rd. Reputation damaged on the race-track. Known as a welcher. Reputation to be repaired by August 1st. Retainer Five Dollars." He turned the page and ran his fingerless knuckles down the closely-written columns.

"P. Greene Dusenberry, Minister of the Gospel, Fairbeach, New Jersey. Reputation damaged in the Bowery. To be repaired as soon as possible. Retainer $100."

He coughed and added, "Called, April 6th."

"Then you are not in need of money, Mr. Wilde," I inquired.

"Listen," he coughed again.

"Mrs. C. Hamilton Chester, of Chester Park, New York City. Called April 7th. Reputation damaged at Dieppe, France. To be repaired by October 1st Retainer $500.

"Note.—C. Hamilton Chester, Captain U.S.S. 'Avalanche', ordered home from South Sea Squadron October 1st."

"Well," I said, "the profession of a Repairer of Reputations is lucrative."

His colorless eyes sought mine, "I only wanted to demonstrate that I was correct. You said it was impossible to succeed as a Repairer of Reputations; that even if I did succeed in certain cases it would cost me more than I would gain by it. Today I have five hundred men in my employ, who are poorly paid, but who pursue the work with an enthusiasm which possibly may be born of fear. These men enter every shade and grade of society; some even are pillars of the most exclusive social temples; others are the prop and pride of the financial world; still others, hold undisputed sway among the 'Fancy and the Talent.' I choose them at my leisure from those who reply to my advertisements. It is easy enough, they are all cowards. I could treble the number in twenty days if I wished. So you see, those who have in their keeping the reputations of their fellow-citizens, I have in my pay."

"They may turn on you," I suggested.

He rubbed his thumb over his cropped ears, and adjusted the wax substitutes. "I think not," he murmured thoughtfully, "I seldom have to apply the whip, and then only once. Besides they like their wages."

"How do you apply the whip?" I demanded.

His face for a moment was awful to look upon. His eyes dwindled to a pair of green sparks.

"I invite them to come and have a little chat with me," he said in a soft voice.

A knock at the door interrupted him, and his face resumed its amiable expression.

"Who is it?" he inquired.

"Mr. Steylette," was the answer.

"Come tomorrow," replied Mr. Wilde.

"Impossible," began the other, but was silenced by a sort of bark from Mr. Wilde.

"Come tomorrow," he repeated.

We heard somebody move away from the door and turn the corner by the stairway.

"Who is that?" I asked.

"Arnold Steylette, Owner and Editor in Chief of the great New York daily."

He drummed on the ledger with his fingerless hand adding: "I pay him very badly, but he thinks it a good bargain."

"Arnold Steylette!" I repeated amazed.

"Yes," said Mr. Wilde, with a self-satisfied cough.

The cat, which had entered the room as he spoke, hesitated, looked up at him and snarled. He climbed down from the chair and, squatting on the floor, took the creature into his arms and caressed her. The cat ceased snarling and presently began a loud purring which seemed to increase in timbre as he stroked her. "Where are the notes?" I asked. He pointed to the table, and for the hundredth time I picked up the bundle of manuscript entitled—

"THE IMPERIAL DYNASTY OF AMERICA."

One by one I studied the well-worn pages, worn only by my own handling, and although I knew all by heart, from the beginning, "When from Carcosa, the Hyades, Hastur, and Aldebaran," to "Castaigne, Louis de Calvados, born December 19th, 1877," I read it with an eager, rapt attention, pausing to repeat parts of it aloud, and dwelling especially on "Hildred de Calvados, only son of Hildred Castaigne and Edythe Landes Castaigne, first in succession," etc., etc.

When I finished, Mr. Wilde nodded and coughed.

"Speaking of your legitimate ambition," he said, "how do Constance and Louis get along?"

"She loves him," I replied simply.

The cat on his knee suddenly turned and struck at his eyes, and he flung her off and climbed on to the chair opposite me.

"And Dr. Archer! But that's a matter you can settle any time you wish," he added.

"Yes," I replied, "Dr. Archer can wait, but it is time I saw my cousin Louis."

"It is time," he repeated. Then he took another ledger from the table and ran over the leaves rapidly. "We are now in communication with ten thousand men," he muttered. "We can count on one hundred thousand within the first twenty-eight hours, and in forty-eight hours the state will rise *en masse*. The country follows the state, and the portion that will not, I mean California and the Northwest, might better never have been inhabited. I shall not send them the Yellow Sign."

The blood rushed to my head, but I only answered, "A new broom sweeps clean."

"The ambition of Caesar and of Napoleon pales before that which could not rest until it had seized the minds of men and controlled even their unborn thoughts," said Mr. Wilde.

"You are speaking of the King in Yellow," I groaned, with a shudder.

"He is a king whom emperors have served."

"I am content to serve him," I replied.

Mr. Wilde sat rubbing his ears with his crippled hand. "Perhaps Constance does not love him," he suggested.

I started to reply, but a sudden burst of military music from the street below drowned my voice. The twentieth dragoon regiment, formerly in garrison at Mount St. Vincent, was returning from the manœuvres in Westchester County, to its new barracks on East Washington Square. It was my cousin's regiment. They were a fine lot of fellows, in their pale blue, tight-fitting jackets, jaunty busbys and white riding breeches with the double yellow stripe, into which their limbs seemed moulded. Every other squadron was armed with lances, from the metal points of which fluttered yellow and white pennons. The band passed, playing the regimental march, then came the colonel and staff, the horses crowding and trampling, while their heads bobbed in unison, and the pennons fluttered from their lance points. The troopers, who rode with the beautiful English seat, looked brown as berries from their bloodless campaign among the farms of Westchester, and the music of their sabres against the stirrups, and the jingle of spurs and carbines was delightful to me. I saw Louis riding with his squadron. He was as handsome an officer as I have ever seen. Mr. Wilde, who had mounted a chair by the window, saw him too, but said nothing. Louis turned and looked straight at Hawberk's shop as he passed, and I could see the flush on his brown cheeks. I think Constance must have been at the window. When the last troopers had clattered by, and the last pennons vanished into South Fifth Avenue, Mr. Wilde clambered out of his chair and dragged the chest away from the door.

"Yes," he said, "it is time that you saw your cousin Louis."

He unlocked the door and I picked up my hat and stick and stepped into the corridor. The stairs were dark. Groping about, I set my foot on something soft, which snarled and spit, and I aimed a murderous blow at the cat, but my cane shivered to splinters against the balustrade, and the beast scurried back into Mr. Wilde's room.

Passing Hawberk's door again I saw him still at work on the armor, but I did not stop, and stepping out into Bleecker Street, I followed it to Wooster, skirted the grounds of the Lethal Chamber, and crossing Washington Park went straight to my rooms in the Benedick. Here I lunched comfortably, read the *Herald* and the *Meteor*, and finally went to the steel safe in my bedroom and set the time combination. The three and three-quarter minutes which it is necessary to wait, while the time lock is opening, are to me golden moments. From the instant I set the combination to the moment when I grasp the knobs and swing back the solid steel doors, I live in an ecstasy of expectation. Those moments must be like moments passed in Paradise. I know what I am to find at the end of the time limit. I know what the massive safe holds secure for me, for me alone, and the exquisite pleasure of waiting is hardly enhanced when the safe opens and I lift, from its velvet crown, a diadem of purest gold, blazing with diamonds. I do this every day, and yet the joy of waiting and at last touching again the diadem, only seems to increase as the days pass. It is a diadem fit for a King among kings, an Emperor among emperors. The King in Yellow might scorn it, but it shall be worn by his royal servant.

I held it in my arms until the alarm in the safe rang harshly, and then tenderly, proudly, I replaced it and shut the steel doors. I walked slowly back into my study, which faces Washington Square, and leaned on the window sill. The afternoon sun poured into my windows, and a gentle breeze stirred the branches of the elms and maples in the park, now covered with buds and tender foliage. A flock of pigeons circled about the tower of the Memorial Church; sometimes alighting on the purple tiled roof, sometimes wheeling downward to the lotos fountain in front of the marble arch. The gardeners were busy with the flower beds around the fountain, and the freshly turned earth smelled sweet and spicy. A lawn mower, drawn by a fat white horse, clinked across the green sward, and watering-carts poured showers of spray over the asphalt drives. Around the statue of Peter Stuyvesant, which in 1897 had replaced the monstrosity supposed to represent Garibaldi, children played in the spring sunshine, and nurse girls wheeled elaborate baby carriages with a reckless disregard for the pasty-faced occupants, which could probably be explained by the presence of half a dozen trim dragoon troopers languidly lolling on the benches. Through the trees, the Washington Memorial Arch glistened like silver in the sunshine, and beyond, on the eastern extremity of the square the grey stone barracks of the dragoons, and the white granite artillery stables were alive with color and motion.

I looked at the Lethal Chamber on the corner of the square opposite. A few curious people still lingered about the gilded iron railing, but inside the grounds the paths were deserted. I watched the fountains ripple and sparkle; the sparrows had already found this new bathing nook, and the basins were covered with the dusty-feathered little things. Two or three white peacocks picked their way across the lawns, and a drab-colored pigeon sat so motionless on the arm of one of the "Fates," that it seemed to be a part of the sculptured stone.

As I was turning carelessly away, a slight commotion in the group of curious loiterers around the gates attracted my attention. A young man had entered, and was advancing with nervous strides along the gravel path which leads to the bronze doors of the Lethal Chamber. He paused a moment before the "Fates," and as he raised his head to those three mysterious faces, the pigeon rose from its sculptured perch, circled about for a moment and wheeled to the east. The young man pressed his hand to his face, and then with an undefinable gesture sprang up the marble steps, the bronze doors closed behind him, and half an hour later the loiterers slouched away, and the frightened pigeon returned to its perch in the arms of Fate.

I put on my hat and went out into the park for a little walk before dinner. As I crossed the central driveway a group of officers passed, and one of them called out, "Hello, Hildred," and came back to shake hands with me. It was my cousin Louis, who stood smiling and tapping his spurred heels with his riding-whip.

"Just back from Westchester," he said; "been doing the bucolic; milk and curds, you know, dairy-maids in sunbonnets, who say 'haeow' and 'I don't think' when you tell them they are pretty. I'm nearly dead for a square meal at Delmonico's. What's the news?"

"There is none," I replied pleasantly. "I saw your regiment coming in this morning."

"Did you? I didn't see you. Where were you?"

"In Mr. Wilde's window."

"Oh, hell!" he began impatiently, "that man is stark mad! I don't understand why you—"

He saw how annoyed I felt by this outburst, and begged my pardon.

"Really, old chap," he said, "I don't mean to run down a man you like, but for the life of me I can't see what the deuce you find in common with Mr. Wilde. He's not well bred, to put it generously; he is hideously deformed; his head is the head of a criminally insane person. You know yourself he's been in an asylum—"

"So have I," I interrupted calmly.

Louis looked startled and confused for a moment, but recovered and slapped me heartily on the shoulder. "You were completely cured," he began; but I stopped him again.

"I suppose you mean that I was simply acknowledged never to have been insane."

"Of course that—that's what I meant," he laughed.

I disliked his laugh because I knew it was forced, but I nodded gaily and asked him where he was going. Louis looked after his brother officers who had now almost reached Broadway.

"We had intended to sample a Brunswick cocktail, but to tell you the truth I was anxious for an excuse to go and see Hawberk instead. Come along, I'll make you my excuse."

We found old Hawberk, neatly attired in a fresh spring suit, standing at the door of his shop and sniffing the air.

"I had just decided to take Constance for a little stroll before dinner," he replied to the impetuous volley of questions from Louis. "We thought of walking on the park terrace along the North River."

At that moment Constance appeared and grew pale and rosy by turns as Louis bent over her small gloved fingers. I tried to excuse myself, alleging an engagement uptown, but Louis and Constance would not listen, and I saw I was expected to remain and engage old Hawberk's attention. After all it would be just as well if I kept my eye on Louis, I thought, and when they hailed a Spring Street horse-car, I got in after them and took my seat beside the armorer.

The beautiful line of parks and granite terraces overlooking the wharves along the North River, which were built in 1910 and finished in the autumn of 1917, had become one of the most popular promenades in the metropolis. They extended from the battery to 190th Street, overlooking the noble river and affording a fine view of the Jersey shore and the Highlands opposite. Cafés and restaurants were scattered here and there among the trees, and twice a week military bands from the garrison played in the kiosks on the parapets.

We sat down in the sunshine on the bench at the foot of the equestrian statue of General Sheridan. Constance tipped her sunshade to shield her eyes, and she and Louis began a murmuring conversation which was impossible to catch. Old Hawberk, leaning on his ivory headed cane, lighted an excellent cigar, the mate to which I politely refused, and smiled at vacancy. The sun hung low above the Staten Island woods, and the bay was dyed with golden hues reflected from the sun-warmed sails of the shipping in the harbor.

Brigs, schooners, yachts, clumsy ferry-boats, their decks swarming with people, railroad transports carrying lines of brown, blue and white freight cars, stately sound steamers, déclassé tramp steamers, coasters, dredgers, scows, and everywhere pervading the entire bay impudent little tugs puffing and whistling officiously;—these were the craft which churned the sunlight waters as far as the eye could reach. In calm contrast to the hurry of sailing vessel and steamer a silent fleet of white warships lay motionless in midstream.

Constance's merry laugh aroused me from my reverie.

"What *are* you staring at?" she inquired.

"Nothing—the fleet," I smiled.

Then Louis told us what the vessels were, pointing out each by its relative position to the old Red Fort on Governor's Island.

"That little cigar-shaped thing is a torpedo boat," he explained; "there are four more lying close together. They are the *Tarpon*, the *Falcon*, the *Sea Fox*, and the *Octopus*. The gun-boats just above are the *Princeton*, the *Champlain*, the *Still Water* and the *Erie*. Next to them lie the cruisers *Faragut* and *Los Angeles*, and above them the battle ships *California*, and *Dakota*, and the *Washington* which is the flag ship. Those two squatty looking chunks of metal which are anchored there off Castle William are the double-turreted monitors *Terrible* and *Magnificent*; behind them lies the ram, *Osceola*."

Constance looked at him with deep approval in her beautiful eyes. "What loads of things you know for a soldier," she said, and we all joined in the laugh which followed.

Presently Louis rose with a nod to us and offered his arm to Constance, and they strolled away along the river wall. Hawberk watched them for a moment and then turned to me.

"Mr. Wilde was right," he said. "I have found the missing tassets and left cuissard of the 'Prince's Emblazoned,' in a vile old junk garret in Pell Street."

"998?" I inquired, with a smile.

"Yes."

"Mr. Wilde is a very intelligent man," I observed.

"I want to give him the credit of this most important discovery," continued Hawberk. "And I intend it shall be known that he is entitled to the fame of it."

"He won't thank you for that," I answered sharply; "please say nothing about it."

"Do you know what it is worth?" said Hawberk.

"No, fifty dollars, perhaps."

"It is valued at five hundred, but the owner of the 'Prince's Emblazoned' will give two thousand dollars to the person who completes his suit; that reward also belongs to Mr. Wilde."

"He doesn't want it! He refuses it!" I answered angrily. "What do you know about Mr. Wilde? He doesn't need the money. He is rich—or will be—richer than any living man except myself. What will we care for money then—what will we care, he and I, when—when—"

"When what?" demanded Hawberk, astonished.

"You will see," I replied, on my guard again.

He looked at me narrowly, much as Doctor Archer used to, and I knew he thought I was mentally unsound. Perhaps it was fortunate for him that he did not use the word lunatic just then.

"No," I replied to his unspoken thought, "I am not mentally

weak; my mind is as healthy as Mr. Wilde's. I do not care to explain just yet what I have on hand, but it is an investment which will pay more than mere gold, silver and precious stones. It will secure the happiness and prosperity of a continent—yes, a hemisphere!"

"Oh," said Hawberk.

"And eventually," I continued more quietly, "it will secure the happiness of the whole world."

"And incidentally your own happiness and prosperity as well as Mr. Wilde's?"

"Exactly," I smiled. But I could have throttled him for taking that tone.

He looked at me in silence for a while and then said very gently, "Why don't you give up your books and studies, Mr. Castaigne, and take a tramp among the mountains somewhere or other? You used to be fond of fishing. Take a cast or two at the trout in the Rangelys."

"I don't care for fishing any more," I answered, without a shade of annoyance in my voice.

"You used to be fond of everything," he continued; "athletics, yachting, shooting, riding—"

"I have never cared to ride since my fall," I said quietly.

"Ah, yes, your fall," he repeated, looking away from me.

I thought this nonsense had gone far enough, so I brought the conversation back to Mr. Wilde; but he was scanning my face again in a manner highly offensive to me.

"Mr. Wilde," he repeated, "do you know what he did this afternoon? He came downstairs and nailed a sign over the hall door next to mine; it read:

MR. WILDE,
REPAIRER OF REPUTATIONS.
Third Bell.

"Do you know what a Repairer of Reputations can be?"

"I do," I replied, suppressing the rage within.

"Oh," he said again.

Louis and Constance came strolling by and stopped to ask if we would join them. Hawberk looked at his watch. At the same moment a puff of smoke shot from the casemates of Castle William, and the boom of the sunset gun rolled across the water and was re-echoed from the Highlands opposite. The flag came running down from the flag-pole, the bugles sounded on the white decks of the warships, and the first electric light sparkled out from the Jersey shore.

As I turned into the city with Hawberk I heard Constance murmur something to Louis which I did not understand; but Louis whispered "My darling," in reply; and again, walking ahead with Hawberk through the square I heard a murmur of "sweetheart," and "my own Constance," and I knew the time had nearly arrived when I should speak of important matters with my cousin Louis.

III

One morning early in May I stood before the steel safe in my bedroom, trying on the golden jewelled crown. The diamonds flashed fire as I turned to the mirror, and the heavy beaten gold burned like a halo about my head. I remembered Camilla's agonized scream and the awful words echoing through the dim streets of Carcosa. They were the last lines in the first act, and I dared not think of what followed—dared not, even in the spring sunshine, there in my own room, surrounded with familiar objects, reassured by the bustle from the street and the voices of the servants in the hallway outside. For those poisoned words had dropped slowly into my heart, as death-sweat drops upon a bed-sheet and is absorbed. Trembling, I put the diadem from my head and wiped my forehead, but I thought of Hastur and of my own rightful ambition, and I remembered Mr. Wilde as I had last left him, his face all torn and bloody from the claws of that devil's creature, and what he said—ah, what he said. The alarm bell in the safe began to whirr harshly, and I knew my time was up; but I would not heed it, and replacing the flashing circlet upon my head I turned defiantly to the mirror. I stood for a long time absorbed in the changing expression of my own eyes. The mirror reflected a face which was like my own, but whiter, and so thin that I hardly recognized it. And all the time I kept repeating between my clenched teeth, "The day has come! the day has come!" while the alarm in the safe whirred and clamored, and the diamonds sparkled and flamed above my brow. I heard a door open but did not heed it. It was only when I saw two faces in the mirror:—it was only when another face rose over my shoulder, and two other eyes met mine. I wheeled like a flash and seized a long knife from my dressing-table, and my cousin sprang back very pale, crying: "Hildred! for God's sake!" then as my hand fell, he said: "It is I, Louis, don't you know me?" I stood silent. I could not have spoken for my life. He walked up to me and took the knife from my hand.

"What is all this?" he inquired, in a gentle voice. "Are you ill?"

"No," I replied. But I doubt if he heard me.

"Come, come, old fellow," he cried, "take off that brass crown and toddle into the study. Are you going to a masquerade? What's all this theatrical tinsel anyway?"

I was glad he thought the crown was made of brass and paste, yet I didn't like him any the better for thinking so. I let him take it from my hand, knowing it was best to humor him. He tossed the splendid diadem in the air, and catching it, turned to me smiling.

"It's dear at fifty cents," he said. "What's it for?"

I did not answer, but took the circlet from his hands, and placing it in the safe shut the massive steel door. The alarm ceased its infernal din at once. He watched me curiously, but did not seem to notice the sudden ceasing of the alarm. He did, however, speak of the safe as a biscuit box. Fearing lest he might examine the combination I led the way into my study. Louis threw himself on the sofa and flicked at flies with his eternal riding-whip. He wore his fatigue uniform with the braided jacket and jaunty cap, and I noticed that his riding-boots were all splashed with red mud.

"Where have you been?" I inquired.

"Jumping mud creeks in Jersey," he said. "I haven't had time to change yet; I was rather in a hurry to see you. Haven't you got a glass of something? I'm dead tired; been in the saddle twenty-four hours."

I gave him some brandy from my medicinal store, which he drank with a grimace.

"Damned bad stuff," he observed. "I'll give you an address where they sell brandy that is brandy."

"It's good enough for my needs," I said indifferently. "I use it to rub my chest with." He stared and flicked at another fly.

"See here, old fellow," he began, "I've got something to suggest to you. It's four years now that you've shut yourself up here like an owl, never going anywhere, never taking any healthy exercise, never doing a damn thing but poring over those books up there on the mantelpiece."

He glanced along the row of shelves. "Napoleon, Napoleon, Napoleon!" he read. "For heaven's sake, have you nothing but Napoleons there?"

"I wish they were bound in gold," I said. "But wait, yes, there is another book, *The King in Yellow*." I looked him steadily in the eye.

"Have you never read it?" I asked.

"I? No, thank God! I don't want to be driven crazy."

I saw he regretted his speech as soon as he had uttered it. There is only one word which I loathe more than I do lunatic and that word is crazy. But I controlled myself and asked him why he thought *The King in Yellow* dangerous.

"Oh, I don't know," he said, hastily. "I only remember the excitement it created and the denunciations from pulpit and Press. I believe the author shot himself after bringing forth this monstrosity, didn't he?"

"I understand he is still alive," I answered.

"That's probably true," he muttered; "bullets couldn't kill a fiend like that."

"It is a book of great truths," I said.

"Yes," he replied, "of 'truths' which send men frantic and blast their lives. I don't care if the thing is, as they say, the very supreme essence of art. It's a crime to have written it, and I for one shall never open its pages."

"Is that what you have come to tell me?" I asked.

"No," he said, "I came to tell you that I am going to be married."

I believe for a moment my heart ceased to beat, but I kept my eyes on his face.

"Yes," he continued, smiling happily, "married to the sweetest girl on earth."

"Constance Hawberk," I said mechanically.

"How did you know?" he cried, astonished. "I didn't know it myself until that evening last April, when we strolled down to the embankment before dinner."

"When is it to be?" I asked.

"It was to have been next September, but an hour ago a despatch came ordering our regiment to the Presidio, San Francisco. We leave at noon tomorrow. Tomorrow," he repeated. "Just think, Hildred, tomorrow I shall be the happiest fellow that ever drew breath in this jolly world, for Constance will go with me."

I offered him my hand in congratulation, and he seized and shook it like the good-natured fool he was—or pretended to be.

"I am going to get my squadron as a wedding present," he rattled on. "Captain and Mrs. Louis Castaigne, eh, Hildred?"

Then he told me where it was to be and who were to be there, and made me promise to come and be best man. I set my teeth and listened to his boyish chatter without showing what I felt, but—

I was getting to the limit of my endurance, and when he jumped up, and, switching his spurs till they jingled, said he must go, I did not detain him.

"There's one thing I want to ask of you," I said quietly.

"Out with it, it's promised," he laughed.

"I want you to meet me for a quarter of an hour's talk tonight."

"Of course, if you wish," he said, somewhat puzzled. "Where?"

"Anywhere, in the park there."

"What time, Hildred?"

"Midnight."

"What in the name of—" he began, but checked himself and laughingly assented. I watched him go down the stairs and hurry away, his sabre banging at every stride. He turned into Bleecker Street, and I knew he was going to see Constance. I gave him ten minutes to disappear and then followed in his footsteps, taking with me the jewelled crown and the silken robe embroidered with the Yellow Sign. When I turned into Bleecker Street, and entered the doorway which bore the sign—

MR. WILDE,

REPAIRER OF REPUTATIONS.

Third Bell.

I saw old Hawberk moving about in his shop, and imagined I heard Constance's voice in the parlor; but I avoided them both and hurried up the trembling stairways to Mr. Wilde's apartment. I knocked and entered without ceremony. Mr. Wilde lay groaning on the floor, his face covered with blood, his clothes torn to shreds. Drops of blood were scattered about over the carpet, which had also been ripped and frayed in the evidently recent struggle.

"It's that cursed cat," he said, ceasing his groans, and turning his colorless eyes to me; "she attacked me while I was asleep. I believe she will kill me yet."

This was too much, so I went into the kitchen, and, seizing a hatchet from the pantry, started to find the infernal beast and settle her then and there. My search was fruitless, and after a while I gave it up and came back to find Mr. Wilde squatting on his high chair by the table. He had washed his face and changed his clothes. The great furrows which the cat's claws had ploughed up in his face he had filled with collodion, and a rag hid the wound in his throat. I told him I should kill the cat when I came across her, but he only shook his head and turned to the open ledger before him. He read name after name of the people who had come to him in regard to their reputation, and the sums he had amassed were startling.

"I put on the screws now and then," he explained.

"One day or other some of these people will assassinate you," I insisted.

"Do you think so?" he said, rubbing his mutilated ears.

It was useless to argue with him, so I took down the manuscript entitled *Imperial Dynasty of America*, for the last time I should ever take it down in Mr. Wilde's study. I read it through, thrilling and trembling with pleasure. When I had finished Mr. Wilde took the manuscript and, turning to the dark passage which leads from his study to his bed-chamber, called out in a loud voice, "Vance." Then for the first time, I noticed a man crouching there in the shadow. How I had overlooked him during my search for the cat, I cannot imagine.

"Vance, come in," cried Mr. Wilde.

The figure rose and crept towards us, and I shall never forget the face that he raised to mine, as the light from the window illuminated it.

"Vance, this is Mr. Castaigne," said Mr. Wilde. Before he had finished speaking, the man threw himself on the ground before the table, crying and grasping, "Oh, God! Oh, my God! Help me! Forgive me! Oh, Mr. Castaigne, keep that man away. You cannot, you cannot mean it! You are different—save me! I am broken down—I was in a madhouse and now—when all was coming right—when I had forgotten the King—the King in Yellow and—but I shall go mad again—I shall go mad—"

His voice died into a choking rattle, for Mr. Wilde had leapt on him and his right hand encircled the man's throat. When Vance fell in a heap on the floor, Mr. Wilde clambered nimbly into his chair again, and rubbing his mangled ears with the stump of his hand, turned to me and asked me for the ledger. I reached it down from the shelf and he opened it. After a moment's searching among the beautifully written pages, he coughed complacently, and pointed to the name Vance.

"Vance," he read aloud, "Osgood Oswald Vance." At the sound of his name, the man on the floor raised his head and turned a convulsed face to Mr. Wilde. His eyes were injected with blood, his lips tumefied. "Called April 28th," continued Mr. Wilde. "Occupation, cashier in the Seaforth National Bank; has served a term of forgery at Sing Sing, from whence he was transferred to the Asylum for the Criminal Insane. Pardoned by the Governor of New York, and discharged from the Asylum, January 19, 1918. Reputation damaged at Sheepshead Bay. Rumors that he lives beyond his income. Reputation to be repaired at once. Retainer $1,500.

"Note.—Has embezzled sums amounting to $30,000 since March 20, 1919, excellent family, and secured present position through uncle's influence. Father, President of Seaforth Bank."

I looked at the man on the floor.

"Get up, Vance," said Mr. Wilde in a gentle voice. Vance rose as if hypnotized. "He will do as we suggest now," observed Mr. Wilde, and opening the manuscript, he read the entire history of the Imperial Dynasty of America. Then in a kind and soothing murmur he ran over the important points with Vance, who stood like one stunned. His eyes were so blank and vacant that I imagined he had become half-witted, and remarked it to Mr. Wilde who replied that it was of no consequence anyway. Very patiently we pointed out to Vance what his share in the affair would be, and he seemed to understand after a while. Mr. Wilde explained the manuscript, using several volumes on Heraldry, to substantiate the result of his researches. He mentioned the establishment of the Dynasty in Carcosa, the lakes which connected Hastur, Aldebaran and the mystery of the Hyades. He spoke of Cassilda and Camilla, and sounded the cloudy depths of Demhe, and the Lake of Hali. "The scolloped tatters of the King in Yellow must hide Yhtill forever," he muttered, but I do not believe Vance heard him. Then by degrees he led Vance along the ramifications of the Imperial family, to Uoht and Thale, from Naotalba and Phantom of Truth, to Aldones, and then tossing aside his manuscript and notes, he began the wonderful story of the Last King. Fascinated and thrilled I watched him. He threw up his head, his long arms were stretched out in a magnificent gesture of pride and power, and his eyes blazed deep in their sockets like two emeralds. Vance listened stupefied. As for me, when at last Mr. Wilde had finished, and pointing to me, cried, "The cousin of the King!" my head swam with excitement.

Controlling myself with a superhuman effort, I explained to Vance why I alone was worthy of the crown and why my cousin must be exiled or die. I made him understand that my cousin must never marry, even after renouncing all his claims, and how that least of all he should marry the daughter of the Marquis of Avonshire and bring England into the question. I showed him a list of thousands of names which Mr. Wilde had drawn up; every man whose name was there had received the Yellow Sign which no living human being dared disregard. The city, the state, the whole land, were ready to rise and tremble before the Pallid Mask.

The time had come, the people should know the son of Hastur, and the whole world bow to the black stars which hang in the sky over Carcosa.

Vance leaned on the table, his head buried in his hands. Mr. Wilde drew a rough sketch on the margin of yesterday's *Herald* with a bit of lead pencil. It was a plan of Hawberk's rooms. Then he wrote out the order and affixed the seal, and shaking like a palsied man I signed my first writ of execution with my name Hildred-Rex.

Mr. Wilde clambered to the floor and, unlocking the cabinet, took a long square box from the first shelf. This he brought to the table and opened. A new knife lay in the tissue paper inside and I picked it up and handed it to Vance, along with the order and the plan of Hawberk's apartment. Then Mr. Wilde told Vance he could go; and he went, shambling like an outcast of the slums.

I sat for a while watching the daylight fade behind the square tower of the Judson Memorial Church, and finally, gathering up the manuscript and notes, took my hat and started for the door.

Mr. Wilde watched me in silence. When I had stepped into the hall I looked back. Mr. Wilde's small eyes were still fixed on me. Behind him, the shadows gathered in the fading light. Then I closed the door behind me and went out into the darkening streets.

I had eaten nothing since breakfast, but I was not hungry. A wretched, half-starved creature, who stood looking across the street at the Lethal Chamber, noticed me and came up to tell me a tale of misery. I gave him money, I don't know why, and he went away without thanking me. An hour later another outcast approached and whined his story. I had a blank bit of paper in my pocket, on which was traced the Yellow Sign, and I handed it to him. He looked at it stupidly for a moment, and then with an uncertain glance at me, folded it with what seemed to me exaggerated care and placed it in his bosom.

The electric lights were sparkling among the trees, and the new moon shone in the sky above the Lethal Chamber. It was tiresome waiting in the square; I wandered from the Marble Arch to the artillery stables and back again to the lotos fountain. The flowers and grass exhaled a fragrance which troubled me. The jet of the fountain played in the moonlight, and the musical splash of falling drops reminded me of the tinkle of chained mail in Hawberk's shop. But it was not so fascinating, and the dull sparkle of the moonlight on the water brought no such sensations of exquisite pleasure, as when the sunshine played over the polished steel of a corselet on Hawberk's knee. I watched the bats darting and turning above the water plants in the fountain basin, but their rapid, jerky flight set my nerves on edge, and I went away again to walk aimlessly to and fro among the trees.

The artillery stables were dark, but in the cavalry barracks the officers' windows were brilliantly lighted, and the sallyport was constantly filled with troopers in fatigue, carrying straw and harness and baskets filled with tin dishes.

Twice the mounted sentry at the gates was changed while I wandered up and down the asphalt walk. I looked at my watch. It was nearly time. The lights in the barracks went out one by one, the barred gate was closed, and every minute or two an officer passed in through the side wicket, leaving a rattle of accoutrements and a jingle of spurs on the night air. The square had become very silent. The last homeless loiterer had been driven away by the gray-coated park policeman, the car tracks along Wooster Street were deserted, and the only sound which broke the stillness was the stamping of the sentry's horse and the ring of his sabre against the saddle pommel. In the barracks, the officers' quarters were still lighted, and military servants passed and repassed before the bay windows. Twelve o'clock sounded from the new spire of St. Francis Xavier, and at the last stroke of the sad-toned bell a figure passed through the wicket beside the portcullis, returned the salute of the sentry, and crossing the street entered the square and advanced toward the Benedick apartment house.

"Louis," I called.

The man pivoted on his spurred heels and came straight toward me.

"Is that you, Hildred?"

"Yes, you are on time."

I took his offered hand, and we strolled toward the Lethal Chamber.

He rattled on about his wedding and the graces of Constance, and their future prospects, calling my attention to his captain's shoulder-straps, and the triple gold arabesque on his sleeve and fatigue cap. I believe I listened as much to the music of his spurs and sabre as I did to his boyish babble, and at last we stood under the elms on the Fourth Street corner of the square opposite the Lethal Chamber. Then he laughed and asked me what I wanted with him. I motioned him to a seat on a bench under the electric light, and sat down beside him. He looked at me curiously, with that same searching glance which I hate and fear so in doctors. I felt the insult of his look, but he did not know it, and I carefully concealed my feelings.

"Well, old chap," he inquired, "what can I do for you?"

I drew from my pocket the manuscript and notes of the *Imperial Dynasty of America*, and looking him in the eye said: "I will tell you. On your word as a soldier, promise me to read this manuscript from beginning to end, without asking me a question. Promise me to read these notes in the same way, and promise me to listen to what I have to tell later."

"I promise, if you wish it," he said pleasantly. "Give me the paper, Hildred."

He began to read, raising his eyebrows with a puzzled, whimsical air, which made me tremble with suppressed anger. As he advanced his, eyebrows contracted, and his lips seemed to form the word "rubbish."

Then he looked slightly bored, but apparently for my sake read, with an attempt at interest, which presently ceased to be an effort. He started when in the closely written pages he came to his own name, and when he came to mine he lowered the paper, and looked sharply at me for a moment. But he kept his word, and resumed his reading, and I let the half-formed question die on his lips unanswered. When he came to the end and read the signature of Mr. Wilde, he folded the paper carefully and returned it to me. I handed him the notes, and he settled back, pushing his fatigue cap up to his forehead, with a boyish gesture, which I remembered so well in school. I watched his face as he read, and when he finished I took the notes with the manuscript, and placed them in my pocket. Then I unfolded a scroll marked with the Yellow Sign. He saw the sign, but he did not seem to recognize it, and I called his attention to it somewhat sharply.

"Well," he said, "I see it. What is it?"

"It is the Yellow Sign," I said angrily.

"Oh, that's it, is it?" said Louis, in that flattering voice, which Doctor Archer used to employ with me, and would probably have employed again, had I not settled his affair for him.

I kept my rage down and answered as steadily as possible, "Listen, you have engaged your word?"

"I am listening, old chap," he replied soothingly.

I began to speak very calmly.

"Dr. Archer, having by some means become possessed of the secret of the Imperial Succession, attempted to deprive me of my right, alleging that because of a fall from my horse four years ago, I had become mentally deficient. He presumed to place me under restraint in his own house in hopes of either driving me insane or poisoning me. I have not forgotten it. I visited him last night and the interview was final."

Louis turned quite pale, but did not move. I resumed triumphantly, "There are yet three people to be interviewed in the interests of Mr. Wilde and myself. They are my cousin Louis, Mr. Hawberk, and his daughter Constance."

Louis sprang to his feet and I arose also, and flung the paper marked with the Yellow Sign to the ground.

"Oh, I don't need that to tell you what I have to say," I cried, with a laugh of triumph. "You must renounce the crown to me, do you hear, to *me*."

Louis looked at me with a startled air, but recovering himself said kindly, "Of course I renounce the—what is it I must renounce?"

"The crown," I said angrily.

"Of course," he answered, "I renounce it. Come, old chap, I'll walk back to your rooms with you."

"Don't try any of your doctor's tricks on me," I cried, trembling with fury. "Don't act as if you think I am insane."

"What nonsense," he replied. "Come, it's getting late, Hildred."

"No," I shouted, "you must listen. You cannot marry, I forbid it. Do you hear? I forbid it. You shall renounce the crown, and in reward I grant you exile, but if you refuse you shall die."

He tried to calm me, but I was roused at last, and drawing my long knife barred his way.

Then I told him how they would find Dr. Archer in the cellar with his throat open, and I laughed in his face when I thought of Vance and his knife, and the order signed by me.

"Ah, you are the King," I cried, "but I shall be King. Who are you to keep me from Empire over all the habitable earth! I was born the cousin of a king, but I shall be King!"

Louis stood white and rigid before me. Suddenly a man came running up Fourth Street, entered the gate of the Lethal Temple, traversed the path to the bronze doors at full speed, and plunged into the death chamber with the cry of one demented, and I laughed until I wept tears, for I had recognized Vance, and knew that Hawberk and his daughter were no longer in my way.

"Go," I cried to Louis, "you have ceased to be a menace. You will never marry Constance now, and if you marry anyone else in your exile, I will visit you as I did my doctor last night. Mr. Wilde takes charge of you tomorrow." Then I turned and darted into South Fifth Avenue, and with a cry of terror Louis dropped his belt and sabre and followed me like the wind. I heard him close behind me at the corner of Bleecker Street, and I dashed into the doorway under Hawberk's sign. He cried, "Halt, or I fire!" but when he saw that I flew up the stairs leaving Hawberk's shop below, he left me, and I heard him hammering and shouting at their door as though it were possible to arouse the dead.

Mr. Wilde's door was open, and I entered crying, "It is done, it is done! Let the nations rise and look upon their King!" but I could not find Mr. Wilde, so I went to the cabinet and took the splendid diadem from its case. Then I drew on the white silk robe, embroidered with the Yellow Sign, and placed the crown upon my head. At last I was King, King by my right in Hastur, King because I knew the mystery of the Hyades, and my mind had sounded the depths of the Lake of Hali. I was King! The first grey pencillings of dawn would raise a tempest which would shake two hemispheres. Then as I stood, my every nerve pitched to the highest tension, faint with the joy and splendor of my thought, without, in the dark passage, a man groaned.

I seized the tallow dip and sprang to the door. The cat passed me like a demon, and the tallow dip went out, but my long knife flew swifter than she, and I heard her screech, and I knew that my knife had found her. For a moment I listened to her tumbling and thumping about in the darkness, and then when her frenzy ceased, I lighted a lamp and raised it over my head. Mr. Wilde lay on the floor with his throat torn open. At first I thought he was dead, but as I looked, a green sparkle came into his sunken eyes, his mutilated hand trembled, and then a spasm stretched his mouth from ear to ear. For a moment my terror and despair gave place to hope, but as I bent over him his eyeballs rolled clean around in his head, and he died. Then while I stood, transfixed with rage and despair, seeing my crown, my empire, every hope and every ambition, my very life, lying prostrate there with the dead master, *they* came, seized me from behind, and bound me until my veins stood out like cords, and my voice failed with the paroxysms of my frenzied screams. But I still raged, bleeding and infuriated among them, and more than one policeman felt my sharp teeth. Then when I could no longer move they came nearer; I saw old Hawberk, and behind him my cousin Louis' ghastly face, and farther away, in the corner, a woman, Constance, weeping softly.

"Ah! I see it now!" I shrieked. "You have seized the throne and the empire. Woe! woe to you who are crowned with the crown of the King in Yellow!"

[EDITOR'S NOTE.—Mr. Castaigne died yesterday in the Asylum for Criminally Insane.]

THE MASK

Camilla: You, sir, should unmask.
Stranger: Indeed?
Cassilda: Indeed it's time. We all have laid aside
disguise but you.
Stranger: I wear no mask.
Camilla: (Terrified, aside to Cassilda.) No mask? No mask!

The King in Yellow, Act I, Scene 2.

I

Although I knew nothing of chemistry, I listened fascinated. He picked up an Easter lily which Geneviève had brought that morning from Notre Dame, and dropped it into the basin. Instantly the liquid lost its crystalline clearness. For a second the lily was enveloped in a milk-white foam, which disappeared, leaving the fluid opalescent. Changing tints of orange and crimson played over the surface, and then what seemed to be a ray of pure sunlight struck through from the bottom where the lily was resting. At the same instant he plunged his hand into the basin and drew out the flower. "There is no danger," he explained, "if you choose the right moment. That golden ray is the signal."

He held the lily toward me, and I took it in my hand. It had turned to stone, to the purest marble.

"You see," he said, "it is without a flaw. What sculptor could reproduce it?"

The marble was white as snow, but in its depths the veins of the lily were tinged with palest azure, and a faint flush lingered deep in its heart.

"Don't ask me the reason of that," he smiled, noticing my wonder. "I have no idea why the veins and heart are tinted, but they always are. Yesterday I tried one of Geneviève's gold-fish,—there it is."

The fish looked as if sculptured in marble. But if you held it to the light the stone was beautifully veined with a faint blue, and from somewhere within came a rosy light like the tint which slumbers in an opal. I looked into the basin. Once more it seemed filled with clearest crystal.

"If I should touch it now?" I demanded.

"I don't know," he replied, "but you had better not try."

"There is one thing I'm curious about," I said, "and that is where the ray of sunlight came from."

"It looked like a sunbeam true enough," he said. "I don't know, it always comes when I immerse any living thing. Perhaps," he continued, smiling, "perhaps it is the vital spark of the creature escaping to the source from whence it came."

I saw he was mocking, and threatened him with a mahl-stick, but he only laughed and changed the subject.

"Stay to lunch. Geneviève will be here directly."

"I saw her going to early mass," I said, "and she looked as fresh and sweet as that lily—before you destroyed it."

"Do you think I destroyed it?" said Boris gravely.

"Destroyed, preserved, how can we tell?"

We sat in the corner of a studio near his unfinished group of the "Fates." He leaned back on the sofa, twirling a sculptor's chisel and squinting at his work.

"By the way," he said, "I have finished pointing up that old academic Ariadne, and I suppose it will have to go to the Salon. It's all I have ready this year, but after the success the 'Madonna' brought me I feel ashamed to send a thing like that."

The "Madonna," an exquisite marble for which Geneviève had sat, had been the sensation of last year's Salon. I looked at the Ariadne. It was a magnificent piece of technical work, but I agreed with Boris that the world would expect something better of him than that. Still, it was impossible now to think of finishing in time for the Salon that splendid terrible group half shrouded in the marble behind me. The "Fates" would have to wait.

We were proud of Boris Yvain. We claimed him and he claimed

us on the strength of his having been born in America, although his father was French and his mother was a Russian. Every one in the Beaux Arts called him Boris. And yet there were only two of us whom he addressed in the same familiar way—Jack Scott and myself.

Perhaps my being in love with Geneviève had something to do with his affection for me. Not that it had ever been acknowledged between us. But after all was settled, and she had told me with tears in her eyes that it was Boris whom she loved, I went over to his house and congratulated him. The perfect cordiality of that interview did not deceive either of us, I always believed, although to one at least it was a great comfort. I do not think he and Geneviève ever spoke of the matter together, but Boris knew.

Geneviève was lovely. The Madonna-like purity of her face might have been inspired by the Sanctus in Gounod's Mass. But I was always glad when she changed that mood for what we called her "April Manœuvres." She was often as variable as an April day. In the morning grave, dignified and sweet, at noon laughing, capricious, at evening whatever one least expected. I preferred her so rather than in that Madonna-like tranquillity which stirred the depths of my heart. I was dreaming of Geneviève when he spoke again.

"What do you think of my discovery, Alec?"

"I think it wonderful."

"I shall make no use of it, you know, beyond satisfying my own curiosity so far as may be, and the secret will die with me."

"It would be rather a blow to sculpture, would it not? We painters lose more than we ever gain by photography."

Boris nodded, playing with the edge of the chisel.

"This new vicious discovery would corrupt the world of art. No, I shall never confide the secret to any one," he said slowly.

It would be hard to find any one less informed about such phenomena than myself; but of course I had heard of mineral springs so saturated with silica that the leaves and twigs which

fell into them were turned to stone after a time. I dimly comprehended the process, how the silica replaced the vegetable matter,
atom by atom, and the result was a duplicate of the object in
stone. This, I confess, had never interested me greatly, and as for
the ancient fossils thus produced, they disgusted me. Boris, it
appeared, feeling curiosity instead of repugnance, had investi-
gated the subject, and had accidentally stumbled on a solution
which, attacking the immersed object with a ferocity unheard
of, in a second did the work of years. This was all I could make
out of the strange story he had just been telling me. He spoke
again after along silence.

"I am almost frightened when I think what I have found.
Scientists would go mad over the discovery. It was so simple too;
it discovered itself. When I think of that formula, and that new
element precipitated in metallic scales—"

"What new element?"

"Oh, I haven't thought of naming it, and I don't believe I ever
shall. There are enough precious metals now in the world to cut
throats over."

I pricked up my ears. "Have you struck gold, Boris?"

"No, better;—but see here, Alec!" he laughed, starting up. "You
and I have all we need in this world. Ah! how sinister and
covetous you look already!" I laughed too, and told him I was
devoured by the desire for gold, and we had better talk of something else; so when Geneviève came in shortly after, we had
turned our backs on alchemy.

Geneviève was dressed in silvery gray from head to foot. The
light glinted along the soft curves of her fair hair as she turned
her cheek to Boris; then she saw me and returned my greeting.
She had never before failed to blow me a kiss from the tips of
her white fingers, and I promptly complained of the omission.
She smiled and held out her hand, which dropped almost before
it had touched mine; then she said, looking at Boris—

"You must ask Alec to stay for luncheon." This also was something new. She had always asked me herself until today.

"I did," said Boris shortly.

"And you said yes, I hope?" She turned to me with a charming conventional smile. I might have been an acquaintance of the day before yesterday. I made her a low bow. "*J'avais bien l'honneur, madame*," but refusing to take up our usual bantering tone, she murmured a hospitable commonplace and disappeared. Boris and I looked at one another.

"I had better go home, don't you think?" I asked.

"Hanged if I know," he replied frankly.

While we were discussing the advisability of my departure Geneviève reappeared in the doorway without her bonnet. She was wonderfully beautiful, but her color was too deep and her lovely eyes were too bright. She came straight up to me and took my arm.

"Luncheon is ready. Was I cross, Alec? I thought I had a headache, but I haven't. Come here, Boris;" and she slipped her other arm through his. "Alec knows that after you there is no one in the world whom I like as well as I like him, so if he sometimes feels snubbed it won't hurt him."

"*À la bonheur!*" I cried, "who says there are no thunderstorms in April?"

"Are you ready?" chanted Boris. "Aye ready;" and arm-in-arm we raced into the dining-room, scandalizing the servants. After all we were not so much to blame; Geneviève was eighteen, Boris was twenty-three, and I not quite twenty-one.

II

Some work that I was doing about this time on the decorations for Geneviève's boudoir kept me constantly at the quaint little hotel in the Rue Sainte-Cécile. Boris and I in those days labored hard but as we pleased, which was fitfully, and we all three, with Jack Scott, idled a great deal together.

One quiet afternoon I had been wandering alone over the house examining curios, prying into odd corners, bringing out sweetmeats and cigars from strange hiding-places, and at last I stopped in the bathing-room. Boris, all over clay, stood there washing his hands.

The room was built of rose-colored marble excepting the floor, which was tessellated in rose and gray. In the centre was a square pool sunken below the surface of the floor; steps led down into it, sculptured pillars supported a frescoed ceiling. A delicious marble Cupid appeared to have just alighted on his pedestal at the upper end of the room. The whole interior was Boris' work and mine. Boris, in his working-clothes of white canvas, scraped the traces of clay and red modelling wax from his handsome hands, and coquetted over his shoulder with the Cupid.

"I see you," he insisted, "don't try to look the other way and pretend not to see me. You know who made you, little humbug!"

It was always my rôle to interpret Cupid's sentiments in these conversations, and when my turn came I responded in such a manner, that Boris seized my arm and dragged me toward the pool, declaring he would duck me. Next instant he dropped my arm and turned pale. "Good God!" he said, "I forgot the pool is full of the solution!"

I shivered a little, and dryly advised him to remember better where he had stored the precious liquid.

"In Heaven's name, why do you keep a small lake of that gruesome stuff here of all places?" I asked.

"I want to experiment on something large," he replied.

"On me, for instance?"

"Ah! that came too close for jesting; but I do want to watch the action of that solution on a more highly organized living body; there is that big white rabbit," he said, following me into the studio.

Jack Scott, wearing a paint-stained jacket, came wandering in, appropriated all the Oriental sweetmeats he could lay his hands on, looted the cigarette case, and finally he and Boris disappeared together to visit the Luxembourg Gallery, where a new silver bronze by Rodin and a landscape of Monet's were claiming the exclusive attention of artistic France. I went back to the studio, and resumed my work. It was a Renaissance screen, which Boris wanted me to paint for Geneviève's boudoir. But the small boy who was unwillingly dawdling through a series of poses for it, today refused all bribes to be good. He never rested an instant in the same position, and inside of five minutes I had as many different outlines of the little beggar.

"Are you posing, or are you executing a song and dance, my friend?" I inquired.

"Whichever monsieur pleases," he replied, with an angelic smile.

Of course I dismissed him for the day, and of course I paid him for the full time, that being the way we spoil our models.

After the young imp had gone, I made a few perfunctory daubs at my work, but was so thoroughly out of humor, that it took me the rest of the afternoon to undo the damage I had done, so at last I scraped my palette, stuck my brushes in a bowl of black soap, and strolled into the smoking-room. I really believe that, excepting Geneviève's apartments, no room in the house was so free from the perfume of tobacco as this one. It was a queer chaos of odds and ends, hung with threadbare tapestry. A sweet-toned old spinet in good repair stood by the window. There were stands of weapons, some old and dull, others bright and modern, festoons of Indian and Turkish armor over the mantel, two or three good pictures, and a pipe-rack. It was here that we used to come for new sensations in smoking. I doubt if any type of pipe ever existed which was not represented in that rack. When we had selected one, we immediately carried it somewhere else and smoked it; for the place was, on the whole, more gloomy and less inviting than any in the house. But this afternoon, the twilight was very soothing, the rugs and skins on the floor looked brown and soft and drowsy; the big couch was piled with cushions—I found my pipe and curled up there for an unaccustomed smoke in the smoking-room. I had chosen one with a long flexible stem, and lighting it fell to dreaming. After a while it went out, but I did not stir. I dreamed on and presently fell asleep.

I awoke to the saddest music I had ever heard. The room was quite dark, I had no idea what time it was. A ray of moonlight silvered one edge of the old spinet, and the polished wood seemed to exhale the sounds as perfume floats above a box of sandalwood. Some one rose in the darkness, and came away weeping quietly, and I was fool enough to cry out "Geneviève!"

She dropped at my voice, and, I had time to curse myself while I made a light and tried to raise her from the floor. She shrank away with a murmur of pain. She was very quiet, and asked for Boris. I carried her to the divan, and went to look for him, but he was not in the house, and the servants were gone to bed. Perplexed and anxious, I hurried back to Geneviève. She lay where I had left her, looking very white.

"I can't find Boris nor any of the servants," I said.

"I know," she answered faintly, "Boris has gone to Ept with Mr. Scott. I did not remember when I sent you for him just now."

"But he can't get back in that case before tomorrow afternoon, and—are you hurt? Did I frighten you into falling? What an awful fool I am, but I was only half awake."

"Boris thought you had gone home before dinner. Do please excuse us for letting you stay here all this time."

"I have had a long nap," I laughed, "so sound that I did not know whether I was still asleep or not when I found myself staring at a figure that was moving toward me, and called out your name. Have you been trying the old spinet? You must have played very softly."

I would tell a thousand more lies worse than that one to see the look of relief that came into her face. She smiled adorably, and said in her natural voice: "Alec, I tripped on that wolf's head, and I think my ankle is sprained. Please call Marie, and then go home."

I did as she bade me, and left her there when the maid came in.

III

At noon next day when I called, I found Boris walking restlessly about his studio.

"Geneviève is asleep just now," he told me, "the sprain is nothing, but why should she have such a high fever? The doctor can't account for it; or else he will not," he muttered.

"Geneviève has a fever?" I asked.

"I should say so, and has actually been a little light-headed at intervals all night. The idea!—gay little Geneviève, without a care in the world,—and she keeps saying her heart's broken, and she wants to die!"

My own heart stood still.

Boris leaned against the door of his studio, looking down, his hands in his pockets, his kind, keen eyes clouded, a new line of trouble drawn "over the mouth's good mark, that made the smile." The maid had orders to summon him the instant Geneviève opened her eyes. We waited and waited, and Boris, growing restless, wandered about, fussing with modelling wax and red clay. Suddenly he started for the next room. "Come and see my rose-colored bath full of death!" he cried.

"Is it death?" I asked, to humor his mood.

"You are not prepared to call it life, I suppose," he answered. As he spoke he plucked a solitary gold-fish squirming and twisting out of its globe. "We'll send this one after the other— wherever that is," he said. There was feverish excitement in his voice. A dull weight of fever lay on my limbs and on my brain as I followed him to the fair crystal pool with its pink-tinted sides; and he dropped the creature in. Falling, its scales flashed with a hot orange gleam in its angry twistings and contortions; the moment it struck the liquid it became rigid and sank heavily to the bottom. Then came the milky foam, the splendid hues radiating on the surface and then the shaft of pure serene light broke through from seemingly infinite depths. Boris plunged in his hand and drew out an exquisite marble thing, blue-veined, rose-tinted, and glistening with opalescent drops.

"Child's play," he muttered, and looked wearily, longingly at me,—as if I could answer such questions! But Jack Scott came in and entered into the "game," as he called it, with ardor. Nothing would do but to try the experiment on the white rabbit then and there. I was willing that Boris should find distraction from his cares, but I hated to see the life go out of a warm, living creature and I declined to be present. Picking up a book at random, I sat down in the studio to read. Alas! I had found *The King in Yellow*. After a few moments, which seemed ages, I was putting it away with a nervous shudder, when Boris and Jack came in bringing their marble rabbit. At the same time the bell rang above, and a cry came from the sick-room. Boris was gone like a flash, and the next moment he called, "Jack, run for the doctor; bring him back with you. Alec, come here."

I went and stood at her door. A frightened maid came out in haste and ran away to fetch some remedy. Geneviève, sitting bolt upright, with crimson cheeks and glittering eyes, babbled incessantly and resisted Boris' gentle restraint. He called me to help. At my first touch she sighed and sank back, closing her eyes, and then—then—as we still bent above her, she opened them again, looked straight into Boris' face—poor fever-crazed girl!— and told her secret. At the same instant our three lives turned into new channels; the bond that held us so long together snapped for ever and a new bond was forged in its place, for she had spoken my name, and as the fever tortured her, her heart poured out its load of hidden sorrow. Amazed and dumb I bowed my head, while my face burned like a live coal, and the blood surged in my ears, stupefying me with its clamor. Incapable of movement, incapable of speech, I listened to her feverish words in an agony of shame and sorrow. I could not silence her, I could not look at Boris. Then I felt an arm upon my shoulder, and Boris turned a bloodless face to mine.

"It is not your fault, Alec; don't grieve so if she loves you—"
but he could not finish; and as the doctor stepped swiftly into
the room, saying—"Ah, the fever!" I seized Jack Scott and hurried
him to the street, saying, "Boris would rather be alone." We crossed
the street to our own apartments, and that night, seeing I was
going to be ill too, he went for the doctor again. The last thing
I recollect with any distinctness was hearing Jack say, "For
Heaven's sake, doctor, what ails him, to wear a face like that?"
and I thought of *The King in Yellow* and the Pallid Mask.

I was very ill, for the strain of two years which I had endured
since that fatal May morning when Geneviève murmured, "I love
you, but I think I love Boris best," told on me at last. I had never
imagined that it could become more than I could endure.
Outwardly tranquil, I had deceived myself. Although the inward
battle raged night after night, and I, lying alone in my room,
cursed myself for rebellious thoughts unloyal to Boris and
unworthy of Geneviève, the morning always brought relief, and
I returned to Geneviève and to my dear Boris with a heart washed
clean by the tempests of the night.

Never in word or deed or thought while with them had I
betrayed my sorrow even to myself.

The mask of self-deception was no longer a mask for me, it
was a part of me. Night lifted it, laying bare the stifled truth
below; but there was no one to see except myself, and when
the day broke the mask fell back again of its own accord. These
thoughts passed through my troubled mind as I lay sick, but they
were hopelessly entangled with visions of white creatures, heavy
as stone, crawling about in Boris' basin,—of the wolf's head on
the rug, foaming and snapping at Geneviève, who lay smiling
beside it. I thought, too, of the King in Yellow wrapped in the
fantastic colors of his tattered mantle, and that bitter cry of
Cassilda, "Not upon us, oh King, not upon us!" Feverishly I struggled to put it from me, but I saw the lake of Hali, thin and blank,
without a ripple or wind to stir it, and I saw the towers of
Carcosa behind the moon. Aldebaran, the Hyades, Alar, Hastur,

glided through the cloud-rifts which fluttered and flapped as they passed like the scolloped tatters of the King in Yellow. Among all these, one sane thought persisted. It never wavered, no matter what else was going on in my disordered mind, that my chief reason for existing was to meet some requirement of Boris and Geneviève. What this obligation was, its nature, was never clear; sometimes it seemed to be protection, sometimes support, through a great crisis. Whatever it seemed to be for the time, its weight rested only on me, and I was never so ill or so weak that I did not respond with my whole soul. There were always crowds of faces about me, mostly strange, but a few I recognized, Boris among them. Afterward they told me that this could not have been, but I know that once at least he bent over me. It was only a touch, a faint echo of his voice, then the clouds settled back on my senses, and I lost him, but he *did* stand there and bend over me *once* at least.

At last, one morning I awoke to find the sunlight falling across my bed, and Jack Scott reading beside me. I had not strength enough to speak aloud, neither could I think, much less remember, but I could smile feebly, as Jack's eye met mine, and when he jumped up and asked eagerly if I wanted anything, I could whisper, "Yes—Boris." Jack moved to the head of my bed, and leaned down to arrange my pillow: I did not see his face, but he answered heartily, "You must wait, Alec; you are too weak to see even Boris."

I waited and I grew strong; in a few days I was able to see whom I would, but meanwhile I had thought and remembered. From the moment when all the past grew clear again in my mind, I never doubted what I should do when the time came, and I felt sure that Boris would have resolved upon the same course so far as he was concerned; as for what pertained to me alone, I knew he would see that also as I did. I no longer asked for any one. I never inquired why no message came from them; why during the week I lay there, waiting and growing stronger, I never heard their name spoken. Preoccupied with my own searchings for the right way, and with my feeble but determined fight against despair, I simply acquiesced in Jack's reticence, taking for granted that he was afraid to speak of them, lest I should turn unruly and insist on seeing them. Meanwhile I said over and over to myself, how would it be when life began again for us all? We would take up our relations exactly as they were before Geneviève fell ill. Boris and I would look into each other's eyes, and there would be neither rancour nor cowardice nor mistrust in that glance. I would be with them again for a little while in the dear intimacy of their home, and then, without pretext or explanation, I would disappear from their lives for ever. Boris would know; Geneviève—the only comfort was that she would never know. It seemed, as I thought it over, that I had found the meaning of that sense of obligation which had persisted all through my delirium, and the only possible answer to it. So, when I was quite ready, I beckoned Jack to me one day, and said—

"Jack, I want Boris at once; and take my dearest greeting to Geneviève...."

When at last he made me understand that they were both dead, I fell into a wild rage that tore all my little convalescent strength to atoms. I raved and cursed myself into a relapse, from which I crawled forth some weeks afterward a boy of twenty-one who believed that his youth was gone for ever. I seemed to be past the capability of further suffering, and one day when Jack handed me a letter and the keys to Boris' house, I took them without a tremor and asked him to tell me all. It was cruel of me to ask him, but there was no help for it, and he leaned wearily on his thin hands, to reopen the wound which could never entirely heal. He began very quietly—

"Alec, unless you have a clue that I know nothing about, you will not be able to explain any more than I what has happened. I suspect that you would rather not hear these details, but you must learn them, else I would spare you the relation. God knows I wish I could be spared the telling. I shall use few words.

"That day when I left you in the doctor's care and came back to Boris, I found him working on the 'Fates.' Geneviève, he said, was sleeping under the influence of drugs. She had been quite out of her mind, he said. He kept on working, not talking any more, and I watched him. Before long, I saw that the third figure of the group—the one looking straight ahead, out over the world—bore his face; not as you ever saw it, but as it looked then and to the end. This is one thing for which I should like to find an explanation, but I never shall.

"Well, he worked and I watched him in silence, and we went on that way until nearly midnight. Then we heard the door open and shut sharply, and a swift rush in the next room. Boris sprang through the doorway and I followed; but we were too late. She lay at the bottom of the pool, her hands across her breast. Then Boris shot himself through the heart." Jack stopped speaking, drops of sweat stood under his eyes, and his thin cheeks twitched. "I carried Boris to his room. Then I went back and let that hellish fluid out of the pool, and turning on all the water, washed the marble clean of every drop. When at length I dared descend the steps, I found her lying there as white as snow. At last, when I had decided what was best to do, I went into the laboratory, and first emptied the solution in the basin into the waste-pipe; then I poured the contents of every jar and bottle after it. There was wood in the fireplace, so I built a fire, and breaking the locks of Boris' cabinet I burnt every paper, notebook and letter that I found there. With a mallet from the studio I smashed to pieces all the empty bottles, then loading them into a coal-scuttle, I carried them to the cellar and threw them over the red-hot bed of the furnace. Six times I made the journey, and at last, not a vestige remained of anything which might again aid in seeking for the formula which Boris had found. Then at last I dared call the doctor. He is a good man, and together we struggled to keep it from the public. Without him I never could have succeeded. At last we got the servants paid and sent away into the country, where old Rosier keeps them quiet with stories of Boris' and

Geneviève's travels in distant lands, from whence they will not return for years. We buried Boris in the little cemetery of Sèvres. The doctor is a good creature, and knows when to pity a man who can bear no more. He gave his certificate of heart disease and asked no questions of me."

Then, lifting his head from his hands, he said, "Open the letter, Alec; it is for us both."

I tore it open. It was Boris' will dated a year before. He left everything to Geneviève, and in case of her dying childless, I was to take control of the house in the Rue Sainte-Cécile, and Jack Scott the management at Ept. On our deaths the property reverted to his mother's family in Russia, with the exception of the sculptured marbles executed by himself. These he left to me.

The page blurred under our eyes, and Jack got up and walked to the window. Presently he returned and sat down again. I dreaded to hear what he was going to say, but he spoke with the same simplicity and gentleness.

"Geneviève lies before the Madonna in the marble room. The Madonna bends tenderly above her, and Geneviève smiles back into that calm face that never would have been except for her."

His voice broke, but he grasped my hand, saying, "Courage, Alec." Next morning he left for Ept to fulfil his trust.

IV

The same evening I took the keys and went into the house I had known so well. Everything was in order, but the silence was terrible. Though I went twice to the door of the marble room, I could not force myself to enter. It was beyond my strength. I went into the smoking-room and sat down before the spinet. A small lace handkerchief lay on the keys, and I turned away, choking. It was plain I could not stay, so I locked every door, every window, and the three front and back gates, and went away. Next morning Alcide packed my valise, and leaving him in charge of my apartments I took the Orient express for Constantinople. During the two years that I wandered through the East, at first, in our letters, we never mentioned Geneviève and Boris, but gradually their names crept in. I recollect particularly a passage in one of Jack's letters replying to one of mine—

"What you tell me of seeing Boris bending over you while you lay ill, and feeling his touch on your face, and hearing his voice, of course troubles me. This that you describe must have happened a fortnight after he died. I say to myself that you were dreaming, that it was part of your delirium, but the explanation does not satisfy me, nor would it you."

Toward the end of the second year a letter came from Jack to me in India so unlike anything that I had ever known of him that I decided to return at once to Paris. He wrote: "I am well, and sell all my pictures as artists do who have no need of money. I have not a care of my own, but I am more restless than if I had. I am unable to shake off a strange anxiety about you. It is not apprehension, it is rather a breathless expectancy—of what, God knows! I can only say it is wearing me out. Nights I dream always of you and Boris. I can never recall anything afterward, but I wake in the morning with my heart beating, and all day the excitement increases until I fall asleep at night to recall the same experience. I am quite exhausted by it, and have determined to break up this morbid condition. I must see you. Shall I go to Bombay, or will you come to Paris?"

I telegraphed him to expect me by the next steamer.

When we met I thought he had changed very little; I, he insisted, looked in splendid health. It was good to hear his voice again, and as we sat and chatted about what life still held for us, we felt that it was pleasant to be alive in the bright spring weather.

We stayed in Paris together a week, and then I went for a week to Ept with him, but first of all we went to the cemetery at Sèvres, where Boris lay.

"Shall we place the 'Fates' in the little grove above him?" Jack asked, and I answered—

"I think only the 'Madonna' should watch over Boris' grave." But Jack was none the better for my home-coming. The dreams of which he could not retain even the least definite outline continued, and he said that at times the sense of breathless expectancy was suffocating.

"You see I do you harm and not good," I said. "Try a change without me." So he started alone for a ramble among the Channel Islands, and I went back to Paris. I had not yet entered Boris' house, now mine, since my return, but I knew it must be done. It had been kept in order by Jack; there were servants there, so I gave up my own apartment and went there to live. Instead of the agitation I had feared, I found myself able to paint there tranquilly. I visited all the rooms—all but one. I could not bring myself to enter the marble room where Geneviève lay, and yet I felt the longing growing daily to look upon her face, to kneel beside her.

One April afternoon, I lay dreaming in the smoking-room, just as I had lain two years before, and mechanically I looked among the tawny Eastern rugs for the wolf-skin. At last I distinguished the pointed ears and flat cruel head, and I thought of my dream where I saw Geneviève lying beside it. The helmets still hung against the threadbare tapestry, among them the old Spanish morion which I remembered Geneviève had once put on when we were amusing ourselves with the ancient bits of mail. I turned my eyes to the spinet; every yellow key seemed eloquent of her caressing hand, and I rose, drawn by the strength of my life's passion to the sealed door of the marble room. The heavy doors swung inward under my trembling hands. Sunlight poured through the window, tipping with gold the wings of Cupid, and lingered like a nimbus over the brows of the Madonna. Her tender face bent in compassion over a marble form so exquisitely pure that I knelt and signed myself. Geneviève lay in the shadow under the Madonna, and yet, through her white arms, I saw the pale azure vein, and beneath her softly clasped hands the folds of her dress were tinged with rose, as if from some faint warm light within her breast.

Bending, with a breaking heart, I touched the marble drapery with my lips, then crept back into the silent house.

A maid came and brought me a letter, and I sat down in the little conservatory to read it; but as I was about to break the seal, seeing the girl lingering, I asked her what she wanted.

She stammered something about a white rabbit that had been caught in the house, and asked what should be done with it. I told her to let it loose in the walled garden behind the house, and opened my letter. It was from Jack, but so incoherent that I thought he must have lost his reason. It was nothing but a series of prayers to me not to leave the house until he could get back; he could not tell me why, there were the dreams, he said—he could explain nothing, but he was sure that I must not leave the house in the Rue Sainte-Cécile.

As I finished reading I raised my eyes and saw the same maid-servant standing in the doorway holding a glass dish in which two gold-fish were swimming: "Put them back into the tank and tell me what you mean by interrupting me," I said.

With a half-suppressed whimper she emptied water and fish into an aquarium at the end of the conservatory, and turning to me asked my permission to leave my service. She said people were playing tricks on her, evidently with a design of getting her into trouble; the marble rabbit had been stolen and a live one had been brought into the house; the two beautiful marble fish were gone, and she had just found those common live things flopping on the dining-room floor. I reassured her and sent her away, saying I would look about myself. I went into the studio; there was nothing there but my canvases and some casts, except the marble of the Easter lily. I saw it on a table across the room. Then I strode angrily over to it. But the flower I lifted from the table was fresh and fragile and filled the air with perfume.

Then suddenly I comprehended, and sprang through the hallway to the marble room. The doors flew open, the sunlight streamed into my face, and through it, in a heavenly glory, the Madonna smiled, as Geneviève lifted her flushed face from her marble couch and opened her sleepy eyes.

IN THE COURT OF THE DRAGON

"Oh, thou who burn'st in heart for those who burn
In Hell, whose fires thyself shall feed in turn;
How long be crying—'Mercy on them.' God!
Why, who art thou to teach and He to learn?"

In the Church of St. Barnabé vespers were over; the clergy left the altar; the little choir-boys flocked across the chancel and settled in the stalls. A Suisse in rich uniform marched down the south aisle, sounding his staff at every fourth step on the stone pavement; behind him came that eloquent preacher and good man, Monseigneur C——.

My chair was near the chancel rail, I now turned toward the west end of the church. The other people between the altar and the pulpit turned too. There was a little scraping and rustling while the congregation seated itself again; the preacher mounted the pulpit stairs, and the organ voluntary ceased.

I had always found the organ-playing at St. Barnabé highly interesting. Learned and scientific it was, too much so for my small knowledge, but expressing a vivid if cold intelligence. Moreover, it possessed the French quality of taste: taste reigned supreme, self-controlled, dignified and reticent.

Today, however, from the first chord I had felt a change for the worse, a sinister change. During vespers it had been chiefly the chancel organ which supported the beautiful choir, but now and again, quite wantonly as it seemed, from the west gallery where the great organ stands, a heavy hand had struck across the church at the serene peace of those clear voices. It was something more than harsh and dissonant, and it betrayed no lack of skill. As it recurred again and again, it set me thinking of what my architect's books say about the custom in early times to consecrate the choir as soon as it was built, and that the nave, being finished sometimes half a century later, often did not get any blessing at all: I wondered idly if that had been the case at St. Barnabé, and whether something not usually supposed to be at home in a Christian church might have entered undetected and taken possession of the west gallery. I had read of such things happening, too, but not in works on architecture.

Then I remembered that St. Barnabé was not much more than a hundred years old, and smiled at the incongruous association of mediaeval superstitions with that cheerful little piece of eighteenth-century rococo.

But now vespers were over, and there should have followed a few quiet chords, fit to accompany meditation, while we waited for the sermon. Instead of that, the discord at the lower end of the church broke out with the departure of the clergy, as if now nothing could control it.

I belong to those children of an older and simpler generation who do not love to seek for psychological subtleties in art; and I have ever refused to find in music anything more than melody and harmony, but I felt that in the labyrinth of sounds now issuing from that instrument there was something being hunted. Up and down the pedals chased him, while the manuals blared approval. Poor devil! whoever he was, there seemed small hope of escape!

My nervous annoyance changed to anger. Who was doing this? How dare he play like that in the midst of divine service? I glanced at the people near me: not one appeared to be in the least disturbed. The placid brows of the kneeling nuns, still turned towards the altar, lost none of their devout abstraction under the pale shadow of their white head-dress. The fashionable lady beside me was looking expectantly at Monseigneur C——. For all her face betrayed, the organ might have been singing an Ave Maria.

But now, at last, the preacher had made the sign of the cross, and commanded silence. I turned to him gladly. Thus far I had not found the rest I had counted on when I entered St. Barnabé that afternoon.

I was worn out by three nights of physical suffering and mental trouble: the last had been the worst, and it was an exhausted body, and a mind benumbed and yet acutely sensitive, which I had brought to my favorite church for healing. For I had been reading *The King in Yellow*.

> "The sun ariseth; they gather themselves together and lay them down in their dens." Monseigneur C—— delivered his text in a calm voice, glancing quietly over the congregation. My eyes turned, I knew not why, toward the lower end of the church. The organist was coming from behind his pipes, and passing along the gallery on his way out, I saw him disappear by a small door that leads to some stairs which descend directly to the street. He was a slender man, and his face was as white as his coat was black. "Good riddance!" I thought, "with your wicked music! I hope your assistant will play the closing voluntary."

With a feeling of relief—with a deep, calm feeling of relief, I turned back to the mild face in the pulpit and settled myself to listen. Here, at last, was the ease of mind I longed for.

"My children," said the preacher, "one truth the human soul finds hardest of all to learn: that it has nothing to fear. It can never be made to see that nothing can really harm it."

"Curious doctrine!" I thought, "for a Catholic priest. Let us see how he will reconcile that with the Fathers."

"Nothing can really harm the soul," he went on, in, his coolest, clearest tones, "because——"

But I never heard the rest; my eye left his face, I knew not for what reason, and sought the lower end of the church. The same man was coming out from behind the organ, and was passing along the gallery *the same way*. But there had not been time for him to return, and if he had returned, I must have seen him. I felt a faint chill, and my heart sank; and yet, his going and coming were no affair of mine. I looked at him: I could not look away from his black figure and his white face. When he was exactly opposite to me, he turned and sent across the church straight into my eyes, a look of hate, intense and deadly: I have never seen any other like it; would to God I might never see it again! Then he disappeared by the same door through which I had watched him depart less than sixty seconds before.

I sat and tried to collect my thoughts. My first sensation was like that of a very young child badly hurt, when it catches its breath before crying out.

To suddenly find myself the object of such hatred was exquisitely painful: and this man was an utter stranger. Why should he hate me so?—me, whom he had never seen before? For the moment all other sensation was merged in this one pang: even fear was subordinate to grief, and for that moment I never doubted; but in the next I began to reason, and a sense of the incongruous came to my aid.

As I have said, St. Barnabé is a modern church. It is small and well lighted; one sees all over it almost at a glance. The organ gallery gets a strong white light from a row of long windows in the clerestory, which have not even colored glass.

The pulpit being in the middle of the church, it followed that, when I was turned toward it, whatever moved at the west end could not fail to attract my eye. When the organist passed it was no wonder that I saw him: I had simply miscalculated the interval between his first and his second passing. He had come in that last time by the other side-door. As for the look which had so upset me, there had been no such thing, and I was a nervous fool.

I looked about. This was a likely place to harbor supernatural horrors! That clear-cut, reasonable face of Monseigneur C——, his collected manner and easy, graceful gestures, were they not just a little discouraging to the notion of a gruesome mystery? I glanced above his head, and almost laughed. That flyaway lady supporting one corner of the pulpit canopy, which looked like a fringed damask table-cloth in a high wind, at the first attempt of a basilisk to pose up there in the organ loft, she would point her gold trumpet at him, and puff him out of existence! I laughed to myself over this conceit, which, at the time, I thought very amusing, and sat and chaffed myself and everything else, from the

old harpy outside the railing, who had made me pay ten centimes
for my chair, before she would let me in (she was more like a
basilisk, I told myself, than was my organist with the anaemic
complexion): from that grim old dame, to, yes, alas! Monseigneur
C—— himself. For all devoutness had fled. I had never yet done
such a thing in my life, but now I felt a desire to mock.

As for the sermon, I could not hear a word of it for the jingle
in my ears of

> "The skirts of St. Paul has reached.
> Having preached us those six Lent lectures,
> More unctuous than ever he preached,"

keeping time to the most fantastic and irreverent thoughts.

It was no use to sit there any longer: I must get out of doors
and shake myself free from this hateful mood. I knew the rude-
ness I was committing, but still I rose and left the church.

A spring sun was shining on the Rue St. Honoré, as I ran
down the church steps. On one corner stood a barrow full of
yellow jonquils, pale violets from the Riviera, dark Russian violets,
and white Roman hyacinths in a golden cloud of mimosa. The
street was full of Sunday pleasure-seekers. I swung my cane and
laughed with the rest. Someone overtook and passed me. He
never turned, but there was the same deadly malignity in his
white profile that there had been in his eyes. I watched him as
long as I could see him. His lithe back expressed the same
menace; every step that carried him away from me seemed to
bear him on some errand connected with my destruction.

I was creeping along, my feet almost refusing to move. There
began to dawn in me a sense of responsibility for something
long forgotten. It began to seem as if I deserved that which he
threatened: it reached a long way back—a long, long way back.
It had lain dormant all these years: it was there, though, and
presently it would rise and confront me. But I would try to
escape; and I stumbled as best I could into the Rue de Rivoli,
across the Place de la Concorde and on to the Quai. I looked

with sick eyes upon the sun, shining through the white foam of the fountain, pouring over the backs of the dusky bronze river-gods, on the far-away Arc, a structure of amethyst mist, on the countless vistas of gray stems and bare branches faintly green. Then I saw him again coming down one of the chestnut alleys of the Cours la Reine.

I left the river-side, plunged blindly across to the Champs Elysées and turned toward the Arc. The setting sun was sending its rays along the green sward of the Rond-point: in the full glow he sat on a bench, children and young mothers all about him. He was nothing but a Sunday lounger, like the others, like myself. I said the words almost aloud, and all the while I gazed on the malignant hatred of his face. But he was not looking at me. I crept past and dragged my leaden feet up the Avenue. I knew that every time I met him brought him nearer to the accomplishment of his purpose and my fate. And still I tried to save myself.

The last rays of sunset were pouring through the great Arc. I passed under it, and met him face to face. I had left him far down the Champs Elysées, and yet he came in with a stream of people who were returning from the Bois de Boulogne. He came so close that he brushed me. His slender frame felt like iron inside its loose black covering. He showed no signs of haste, nor of fatigue, nor of any human feeling. His whole being expressed one thing: the will, and the power to work me evil.

In anguish I watched him where he went down the broad crowded Avenue, that was all flashing with wheels and the trappings of horses and the helmets of the Garde Republicaine.

He was soon lost to sight; then I turned and fled. Into the Bois, and far out beyond it—I know not where I went, but after a long while as it seemed to me, night had fallen, and I found myself sitting at a table before a small café. I had wandered back into the Bois. It was hours now since I had seen him. Physical fatigue and mental suffering had left me no power to think or feel. I was tired, so tired! I longed to hide away in my own den. I resolved to go home. But that was a long way off.

I live in the Court of the Dragon, a narrow passage that leads from the Rue de Rennes to the Rue du Dragon.

It is an "impasse"; traversable only for foot passengers. Over the entrance on the Rue de Rennes is a balcony, supported by an iron dragon. Within the court tall old houses rise on either side, and close the ends that give on the two streets. Huge gates, swung back during the day into the walls of the deep archways, close this court, after midnight, and one must enter then by ringing at certain small doors on the side. The sunken pavement collects unsavoury pools. Steep stairways pitch down to doors that open on the court. The ground floors are occupied by shops of second-hand dealers, and by iron workers. All day long the place rings with the clink of hammers and the clang of metal bars.

Unsavoury as it is below, there is cheerfulness, and comfort, and hard, honest work above.

Five flights up are the ateliers of architects and painters, and the hiding-places of middle-aged students like myself who want to live alone. When I first came here to live I was young, and not alone.

I had to walk a while before any conveyance appeared, but at last, when I had almost reached the Arc de Triomphe again, an empty cab came along and I took it.

From the Arc to the Rue de Rennes is a drive of more than half an hour, especially when one is conveyed by a tired cab horse that has been at the mercy of Sunday fête-makers.

There had been time before I passed under the Dragon's wings to meet my enemy over and over again, but I never saw him once, and now refuge was close at hand.

Before the wide gateway a small mob of children were playing. Our concierge and his wife walked among them, with their black poodle, keeping order; some couples were waltzing on the sidewalk. I returned their greetings and hurried in.

All the inhabitants of the court had trooped out into the street. The place was quite deserted, lighted by a few lanterns hung high up, in which the gas burned dimly.

My apartment was at the top of a house, halfway down the court, reached by a staircase that descended almost into the street, with only a bit of passage-way intervening, I set my foot on the threshold of the open door, the friendly old ruinous stairs rose before me, leading up to rest and shelter. Looking back over my right shoulder, I saw *him*, ten paces off. He must have entered the court with me.

He was coming straight on, neither slowly, nor swiftly, but straight on to me. And now he was looking at me. For the first time since our eyes encountered across the church they met now again, and I knew that the time had come.

Retreating backward, down the court, I faced him. I meant to escape by the entrance on the Rue du Dragon. His eyes told me that I never should escape.

It seemed ages while we were going, I retreating, he advancing, down the court in perfect silence; but at last I felt the shadow of the archway, and the next step brought me within it. I had meant to turn here and spring through into the street. But the shadow was not that of an archway; it was that of a vault. The great doors on the Rue du Dragon were closed. I felt this by the blackness which surrounded me, and at the same instant I read it in his face. How his face gleamed in the darkness, drawing swiftly nearer! The deep vaults, the huge closed doors, their cold iron clamps were all on his side. The thing which he had threatened had arrived: it gathered and bore down on me from the fathomless shadows; the point from which it would strike was his infernal eyes. Hopeless, I set my back against the barred doors and defied him.

There was a scraping of chairs on the stone floor, and a rustling as the congregation rose. I could hear the Suisse's staff in the south aisle, preceding Monseigneur C—— to the sacristy.

The kneeling nuns, roused from their devout abstraction, made their reverence and went away. The fashionable lady, my neighbor, rose also, with graceful reserve. As she departed her glance just flitted over my face in disapproval.

Half dead, or so it seemed to me, yet intensely alive to every trifle, I sat among the leisurely moving crowd, then rose too and went toward the door.

I had slept through the sermon. Had I slept through the sermon? I looked up and saw him passing along the gallery to his place. Only his side I saw; the thin bent arm in its black covering looked like one of those devilish, nameless instruments which lie in the disused torture-chambers of mediaeval castles.

But I had escaped him, though his eyes had said I should not. *Had* I escaped him? That which gave him the power over me came back out of oblivion, where I had hoped to keep it. For I knew him now. Death and the awful abode of lost souls, whither my weakness long ago had sent him—they had changed him for every other eye, but not for mine. I had recognized him almost from the first; I had never doubted what he was come to do; and now I knew while my body sat safe in the cheerful little church, he had been hunting my soul in the Court of the Dragon.

I crept to the door: the organ broke out overhead with a blare. A dazzling light filled the church, blotting the altar from my eyes. The people faded away, the arches, the vaulted roof vanished. I raised my seared eyes to the fathomless glare, and I saw the black stars hanging in the heavens: and the wet winds from the lake of Hali chilled my face.

And now, far away, over leagues of tossing cloud-waves, I saw the moon dripping with spray; and beyond, the towers of Carcosa rose behind the moon.

Death and the awful abode of lost souls, whither my weakness long ago had sent him, had changed him for every other eye but mine. And now I heard *his voice*, rising, swelling, thundering through the flaring light, and as I fell, the radiance increasing, increasing, poured over me in waves of flame. Then I sank into the depths, and I heard the King in Yellow whispering to my soul: "It is a fearful thing to fall into the hands of the living God!"

THE YELLOW SIGN

"Let the red dawn surmise
What we shall do,
When this blue starlight dies
And all is through."

I

There are so many things which are impossible to explain! Why should certain chords in music make me think of the brown and golden tints of autumn foliage? Why should the Mass of Sainte Cécile bend my thoughts wandering among caverns whose walls blaze with ragged masses of virgin silver? What was it in the roar and turmoil of Broadway at six o'clock that flashed before my eyes the picture of a still Breton forest where sunlight filtered through spring foliage and Sylvia bent, half curiously, half tenderly, over a small green lizard, murmuring: "To think that this also is a little ward of God!"

When I first saw the watchman his back was toward me. I looked at him indifferently until he went into the church. I paid no more attention to him than I had to any other man who lounged through Washington Square that morning, and when I shut my window and turned back into my studio I had forgotten him. Late in the afternoon, the day being warm, I raised the window again and leaned out to get a sniff of air. A man was standing in the courtyard of the church, and I noticed him again with as little interest as I had that morning. I looked across the square to where the fountain was playing and then, with my mind filled with vague impressions of trees, asphalt drives, and the moving groups of nursemaids and holiday-makers, I started to walk back to my easel. As I turned, my listless glance included the man below in the churchyard. His face was toward me now, and with a perfectly involuntary movement I bent to see it. At the same moment he raised his head and looked at me. Instantly I thought of a coffin-worm. Whatever it was about the man that repelled me I did not know, but the impression of a plump white grave-worm was so intense and nauseating that I must have shown it in my expression, for he turned his puffy face away with a movement which made me think of a disturbed grub in a chestnut.

I went back to my easel and motioned the model to resume her pose. After working a while I was satisfied that I was spoiling what I had done as rapidly as possible, and I took up a palette knife and scraped the color out again. The flesh tones were sallow and unhealthy, and I did not understand how I could have painted such sickly color into a study which before that had glowed with healthy tones.

I looked at Tessie. She had not changed, and the clear flush of health dyed her neck and cheeks as I frowned.

"Is it something I've done?" she said.

"No,—I've made a mess of this arm, and for the life of me I can't see how I came to paint such mud as that into the canvas," I replied.

"Don't I pose well?" she insisted.

"Of course, perfectly."

"Then it's not my fault?"

"No. It's my own."

"I am very sorry," she said.

I told her she could rest while I applied rag and turpentine to the plague spot on my canvas, and she went off to smoke a cigarette and look over the illustrations in the *Courrier Français*.

I did not know whether it was something in the turpentine or a defect in the canvas, but the more I scrubbed the more that gangrene seemed to spread. I worked like a beaver to get it out, and yet the disease appeared to creep from limb to limb of the study before me. Alarmed, I strove to arrest it, but now the color on the breast changed and the whole figure seemed to absorb the infection as a sponge soaks up water. Vigorously I plied palette-knife, turpentine, and scraper, thinking all the time what a *séance* I should hold with Duval who had sold me the canvas; but soon I noticed that it was not the canvas which was defective nor yet the colors of Edward. "It must be the turpentine," I thought angrily, "or else my eyes have become so blurred and confused by the afternoon light that I can't see straight." I called Tessie, the model. She came and leaned over my chair blowing rings of smoke into the air.

"What *have* you been doing to it?" she exclaimed

"Nothing," I growled, "it must be this turpentine!"

"What a horrible color it is now," she continued. "Do you think my flesh resembles green cheese?"

"No, I don't," I said angrily; "did you ever know me to paint like that before?"

"No, indeed!"

"Well, then!"

"It must be the turpentine, or something," she admitted.

She slipped on a Japanese robe and walked to the window. I scraped and rubbed until I was tired, and finally picked up my brushes and hurled them through the canvas with a forcible expression, the tone alone of which reached Tessie's ears.

Nevertheless she promptly began: "That's it! Swear and act silly and ruin your brushes! You have been three weeks on that study, and now look! What's the good of ripping the canvas? What creatures artists are!"

I felt about as much ashamed as I usually did after such an outbreak, and I turned the ruined canvas to the wall. Tessie helped me clean my brushes, and then danced away to dress. From the screen she regaled me with bits of advice concerning whole or partial loss of temper, until, thinking, perhaps, I had been tormented sufficiently, she came out to implore me to button her waist where she could not reach it on the shoulder.

"Everything went wrong from the time you came back from the window and talked about that horrid-looking man you saw in the churchyard," she announced.

"Yes, he probably bewitched the picture," I said, yawning. I looked at my watch.

"It's after six, I know," said Tessie, adjusting her hat before the mirror.

"Yes," I replied, "I didn't mean to keep you so long." I leaned out of the window but recoiled with disgust, for the young man with the pasty face stood below in the churchyard. Tessie saw my gesture of disapproval and leaned from the window.

"Is that the man you don't like?" she whispered.

I nodded.

"I can't see his face, but he does look fat and soft. Someway or other," she continued, turning to look at me, "he reminds me of a dream,—an awful dream I once had. Or," she mused, looking down at her shapely shoes, "was it a dream after all?"

"How should I know?" I smiled.

Tessie smiled in reply.

"You were in it," she said, "so perhaps you might know something about it."

"Tessie! Tessie!" I protested, "don't you dare flatter by saying that you dream about me!"

"But I did," she insisted; "shall I tell you about it?"

"Go ahead," I replied, lighting a cigarette.

Tessie leaned back on the open window-sill and began very seriously.

"One night last winter I was lying in bed thinking about nothing at all in particular. I had been posing for you and I was tired out, yet it seemed impossible for me to sleep. I heard the bells in the city ring ten, eleven, and midnight. I must have fallen asleep about midnight because I don't remember hearing the bells after that. It seemed to me that I had scarcely closed my eyes when I dreamed that something impelled me to go to the window. I rose, and raising the sash leaned out. Twenty-fifth Street was deserted as far as I could see. I began to be afraid; everything outside seemed so—so black and uncomfortable. Then the sound of wheels in the distance came to my ears, and it seemed to me as though that was what I must wait for. Very slowly the wheels approached, and, finally, I could make out a vehicle moving along the street. It came nearer and nearer, and when it passed beneath my window I saw it was a hearse. Then, as I trembled with fear, the driver turned and looked straight at me. When I awoke I was standing by the open window shivering with cold, but the black-plumed hearse and the driver were gone. I dreamed this dream again in March last, and again awoke beside the open window. Last night the dream came again. You remember how it was raining; when I awoke, standing at the open window, my night-dress was soaked."

"But where did I come into the dream?" I asked.

"You—you were in the coffin; but you were not dead."

"In the coffin?"

"Yes."

"How did you know? Could you see me?"

"No; I only knew you were there."

"Had you been eating Welsh rarebits, or lobster salad?" I began, laughing, but the girl interrupted me with a frightened cry.

"Hello! What's up?" I said, as she shrank into the embrasure by the window.

"The—the man below in the churchyard;—he drove the hearse."

"Nonsense," I said, but Tessie's eyes were wide with terror. I went to the window and looked out. The man was gone. "Come, Tessie," I urged, "don't be foolish. You have posed too long; you are nervous."

"Do you think I could forget that face?" she murmured. "Three times I saw the hearse pass below my window, and every time the driver turned and looked up at me. Oh, his face was so white and—and soft? It looked dead—it looked as if it had been dead a long time."

I induced the girl to sit down and swallow a glass of Marsala. Then I sat down beside her, and tried to give her some advice.

"Look here, Tessie," I said, "you go to the country for a week or two, and you'll have no more dreams about hearses. You pose all day, and when night comes your nerves are upset. You can't keep this up. Then again, instead of going to bed when your day's work is done, you run off to picnics at Sulzer's Park, or go to the Eldorado or Coney Island, and when you come down here next morning you are fagged out. There was no real hearse. There was a soft-shell crab dream."

She smiled faintly.

"What about the man in the churchyard?"

"Oh, he's only an ordinary unhealthy, everyday creature."

"As true as my name is Tessie Reardon, I swear to you, Mr. Scott, that the face of the man below in the churchyard is the face of the man who drove the hearse!"

"What of it?" I said. "It's an honest trade."

"Then you think I *did* see the hearse?"

"Oh," I said diplomatically, "if you really did, it might not be unlikely that the man below drove it. There is nothing in that."

Tessie rose, unrolled her scented handkerchief, and taking a bit of gum from a knot in the hem, placed it in her mouth. Then drawing on her gloves she offered me her hand, with a frank, "Good-night, Mr. Scott," and walked out.

II

The next morning, Thomas, the bell-boy, brought me the *Herald* and a bit of news. The church next door had been sold. I thanked Heaven for it, not that being a Catholic I had any repugnance for the congregation next door, but because my nerves were shattered by a blatant exhorter, whose every word echoed through the aisle of the church as if it had been my own rooms, and who insisted on his r's with a nasal persistence which revolted my every instinct. Then, too, there was a fiend in human shape, an organist, who reeled off some of the grand old hymns with an interpretation of his own, and I longed for the blood of a creature who could play the doxology with an amendment of minor chords which one hears only in a quartet of very young undergraduates. I believe the minister was a good man, but when he bellowed: "And the Lorrrrd said unto Moses, the Lorrrd is a man of war; the Lorrd is his name. My wrath shall wax hot and I will kill you with the sworrrrd!" I wondered how many centuries of purgatory it would take to atone for such a sin.

"Who bought the property?" I asked Thomas.

"Nobody that I knows, sir. They do say the gent wot owns this 'ere 'Amilton flats was lookin' at it. 'E might be a bildin' more studios."

I walked to the window. The young man with the unhealthy face stood by the churchyard gate, and at the mere sight of him the same overwhelming repugnance took possession of me.

"By the way, Thomas," I said, "who is that fellow down there?"

Thomas sniffed. "That there worm, sir? 'Es night-watchman of the church, sir. 'E maikes me tired a-sittin' out all night on them steps and lookin' at you insultin' like. I'd a punched 'is 'ed, sir—beg pardon, sir—"

"Go on, Thomas."

"One night a comin' 'ome with 'Arry, the other English boy, I sees 'im a sittin' there on them steps. We 'ad Molly and Jen with us, sir, the two girls on the tray service, an' 'e looks so insultin' at us that I up and sez: 'Wat you looking hat, you fat slug?'—beg pardon, sir, but that's 'ow I sez, sir. Then 'e don't say nothin' and I sez: 'Come out and I'll punch that puddin' 'ed.' Then I hopens the gate an' goes in, but 'e don't say nothin', only looks insultin' like. Then I 'its 'im one, but, ugh! 'is 'ed was that cold and mushy it ud sicken you to touch 'im."

"What did he do then?" I asked curiously.

"'Im? Nawthin'."

"And you, Thomas?"

The young fellow flushed with embarrassment and smiled uneasily.

"Mr. Scott, sir, I ain't no coward, an' I can't make it out at all why I run. I was in the 5th Lawncers, sir, bugler at Tel-el-Kebir, an' was shot by the wells."

"You don't mean to say you ran away?"

"Yes, sir; I run."

"Why?"

"That's just what I want to know, sir. I grabbed Molly an' run, an' the rest was as frightened as I."

"But what were they frightened at?"

Thomas refused to answer for a while, but now my curiosity was aroused about the repulsive young man below and I pressed him. Three years' sojourn in America had not only modified Thomas' cockney dialect but had given him the American's fear of ridicule.

"You won't believe me, Mr. Scott, sir?"

"Yes, I will."

"You will lawf at me, sir?"

"Nonsense!"

He hesitated. "Well, sir, it's Gawd's truth that when I 'it 'im 'e grabbed me wrists, sir, and when I twisted 'is soft, mushy fist one of 'is fingers come off in me 'and."

The utter loathing and horror of Thomas' face must have been reflected in my own, for he added:

"It's orful, an' now when I see 'im I just go away. 'E maikes me hill."

When Thomas had gone I went to the window. The man stood beside the church-railing with both hands on the gate, but I hastily retreated to my easel again, sickened and horrified, for I saw that the middle finger of his right hand was missing.

At nine o'clock Tessie appeared and vanished behind the screen with a merry "Good morning, Mr. Scott." When she had reappeared and taken her pose upon the model-stand I started a new canvas, much to her delight. She remained silent as long as I was on the drawing, but as soon as the scrape of the charcoal ceased and I took up my fixative she began to chatter.

"Oh, I had such a lovely time last night. We went to Tony Pastor's."

"Who are 'we'?" I demanded.

"Oh, Maggie, you know, Mr. Whyte's model, and Pinkie McCormick—we call her Pinkie because she's got that beautiful red hair you artists like so much—and Lizzie Burke."

I sent a shower of spray from the fixative over the canvas, and said: "Well, go on."

"We saw Kelly and Baby Barnes the skirt-dancer and—and all the rest. I made a mash."

"Then you have gone back on me, Tessie?"

She laughed and shook her head.

"He's Lizzie Burke's brother, Ed. He's a perfect gen'l'man."

I felt constrained to give her some parental advice concerning mashing, which she took with a bright smile.

"Oh, I can take care of a strange mash," she said, examining her chewing gum, "but Ed is different. Lizzie is my best friend."

Then she related how Ed had come back from the stocking mill in Lowell, Massachusetts, to find her and Lizzie grown up, and what an accomplished young man he was, and how he thought nothing of squandering half-a-dollar for ice-cream and oysters to celebrate his entry as clerk into the woollen department of Macy's. Before she finished I began to paint, and she resumed the pose, smiling and chattering like a sparrow. By noon I had the study fairly well rubbed in and Tessie came to look at it.

"That's better," she said.

I thought so too, and ate my lunch with a satisfied feeling that all was going well. Tessie spread her lunch on a drawing table opposite me and we drank our claret from the same bottle and lighted our cigarettes from the same match. I was very much attached to Tessie. I had watched her shoot up into a slender but exquisitely formed woman from a frail, awkward child. She had posed for me during the last three years, and among all my models she was my favorite. It would have troubled me very much indeed had she become "tough" or "fly," as the phrase goes, but I never noticed any deterioration of her manner, and felt at heart that she was all right. She and I never discussed morals at all, and I had no intention of doing so, partly because I had none myself, and partly because I knew she would do what she liked in spite of me. Still I did hope she would steer clear of complications, because I wished her well, and then also I had a selfish desire to retain the best model I had. I knew that mashing, as she termed it, had no significance with girls like Tessie, and that such things in America did not resemble in the least the same things in Paris. Yet, having lived with my eyes open, I also knew that somebody would take Tessie away some day, in one manner or another, and though I professed to myself that marriage was nonsense, I sincerely hoped that, in this case, there would be a priest at the end of the vista. I am a Catholic. When I listen to high mass, when I sign myself, I feel that everything, including myself, is more cheerful, and when I confess, it does me good. A man who lives as much alone as I do, must confess to somebody. Then, again, Sylvia was Catholic, and it was reason enough for me. But I was speaking of Tessie, which is very different. Tessie also was Catholic and much more devout than I, so, taking it all in all, I had little fear for my pretty model until she should fall in love. But *then* I knew that fate alone would decide her future for her, and I prayed inwardly that fate would keep her away from men like me and throw into her path nothing but Ed Burkes and Jimmy McCormicks, bless her sweet face!

Tessie sat blowing rings of smoke up to the ceiling and tinkling the ice in her tumbler.

"Do you know that I also had a dream last night?" I observed.

"Not about that man," she laughed.

"Exactly. A dream similar to yours, only much worse."

It was foolish and thoughtless of me to say this, but you know how little tact the average painter has. "I must have fallen asleep about ten o'clock," I continued, "and after a while I dreamt that I awoke. So plainly did I hear the midnight bells, the wind in the tree-branches, and the whistle of steamers from the bay, that even now I can scarcely believe I was not awake. I seemed to be lying in a box which had a glass cover. Dimly I saw the street lamps as I passed, for I must tell you, Tessie, the box in which I reclined appeared to lie in a cushioned wagon which jolted me over a stony pavement. After a while I became impatient and tried to move, but the box was too narrow. My hands were crossed on my breast, so I could not raise them to help myself. I listened and then tried to call. My voice was gone. I could hear the trample of the horses attached to the wagon, and even the breathing of the driver. Then another sound broke upon my ears like the raising of a window sash. I managed to turn my head a little, and found I could look, not only through the glass cover of my box, but also through the glass panes in the side of the covered vehicle. I saw houses, empty and silent, with neither light nor life about any of them excepting one. In that house a window was open on the first floor, and a figure all in white stood looking down into the street. It was you."

Tessie had turned her face away from me and leaned on the table with her elbow.

"I could see your face," I resumed, "and it seemed to me to be very sorrowful. Then we passed on and turned into a narrow black lane. Presently the horses stopped. I waited and waited, closing my eyes with fear and impatience, but all was silent as the grave. After what seemed to me hours, I began to feel uncomfortable. A sense that somebody was close to me made me unclose my eyes. Then I saw the white face of the hearse-driver looking at me through the coffin-lid—"

A sob from Tessie interrupted me. She was trembling like a leaf. I saw I had made an ass of myself and attempted to repair the damage.

"Why, Tess," I said, "I only told you this to show you what influence your story might have on another person's dreams. You don't suppose I really lay in a coffin, do you? What are you trembling for? Don't you see that your dream and my unreasonable dislike for that inoffensive watchman of the church simply set my brain working as soon as I fell asleep?"

She laid her head between her arms, and sobbed as if her heart would break. What a precious triple donkey I had made of myself! But I was about to break my record. I went over and put my arm about her.

"Tessie dear, forgive me," I said; "I had no business to frighten you with such nonsense. You are too sensible a girl, too good a Catholic to believe in dreams."

Her hand tightened on mine and her head fell back upon my shoulder, but she still trembled and I petted her and comforted her.

"Come, Tess, open your eyes and smile."

Her eyes opened with a slow languid movement and met mine, but their expression was so queer that I hastened to reassure her again.

"It's all humbug, Tessie; you surely are not afraid that any harm will come to you because of that."

"No," she said, but her scarlet lips quivered.

"Then, what's the matter? Are you afraid?"

"Yes. Not for myself."

"For me, then?" I demanded gaily.

"For you," she murmured in a voice almost inaudible. "I—I care for you."

At first I started to laugh, but when I understood her, a shock passed through me, and I sat like one turned to stone. This was the crowning bit of idiocy I had committed. During the moment which elapsed between her reply and my answer I thought of a thousand responses to that innocent confession. I could pass it by with a laugh, I could misunderstand her and assure her as to my health, I could simply point out that it was impossible she could love me. But my reply was quicker than my thoughts, and I might think and think now when it was too late, for I had kissed her on the mouth.

That evening I took my usual walk in Washington Park, pondering over the occurrences of the day. I was thoroughly committed. There was no back out now, and I stared the future straight in the face. I was not good, not even scrupulous, but I had no idea of deceiving either myself or Tessie. The one passion of my life lay buried in the sunlit forests of Brittany. Was it buried for ever? Hope cried "No!" For three years I had been listening to the voice of Hope, and for three years I had waited for a footstep on my threshold. Had Sylvia forgotten? "No!" cried Hope.

I said that I was no good. That is true, but still I was not exactly a comic opera villain. I had led an easy-going reckless life, taking what invited me of pleasure, deploring and sometimes bitterly regretting consequences. In one thing alone, except my painting, was I serious, and that was something which lay hidden if not lost in the Breton forests.

It was too late for me to regret what had occurred during the day. Whatever it had been, pity, a sudden tenderness for sorrow, or the more brutal instinct of gratified vanity, it was all the same now, and unless I wished to bruise an innocent heart, my path lay marked before me. The fire and strength, the depth of passion of a love which I had never even suspected, with all my imagined experience in the world, left me no alternative but to respond or send her away. Whether because I am so cowardly about giving pain to others, or whether it was that I have little of the gloomy Puritan in me, I do not know, but I shrank from disclaiming responsibility for that thoughtless kiss, and in fact had no time to do so before the gates of her heart opened and the flood poured forth. Others who habitually do their duty and find a sullen satisfaction in making themselves and everybody else unhappy, might have withstood it. I did not. I dared not. After the storm had abated I did tell her that she might better have loved Ed Burke and worn a plain gold ring, but she would not hear of it, and I thought perhaps as long as she had decided to love somebody she could not marry, it had better be me. I, at least, could treat her with an intelligent affection, and whenever she became tired of her infatuation she could go none the worse for it. For I was decided on that point although I knew how hard it would be. I remembered the usual termination of Platonic liaisons, and thought how disgusted I had been whenever I heard of one. I knew I was undertaking a great deal for so unscrupulous a man as I was, and I dreamed the future, but never for one moment did I doubt that she was safe with me. Had it been anybody but Tessie I should not have bothered my head about scruples. For it did not occur to me to sacrifice Tessie as I would have sacrificed a woman of the world. I looked the future squarely in the face and saw the several probable endings to the affair. She would either tire of the whole thing, or become so unhappy that I should have either to marry her or go away. If I married her we would be unhappy. I with a wife unsuited to me, and she with a husband unsuitable for any woman. For my past life could scarcely entitle me to marry. If I went away she might either fall ill, recover, and marry some Eddie Burke, or she might recklessly or deliberately go and do something foolish. On the other hand, if she tired of me, then her whole life would be before her with beautiful vistas of Eddie Burkes and marriage rings and twins and Harlem flats and Heaven knows what. As I strolled along through the trees by the Washington Arch, I decided that she should find a substantial friend in me, anyway, and the future could take care of itself. Then I went into the house and put on my evening dress, for the little faintly-perfumed note on my dresser said, "Have a cab at the stage door at eleven," and the note was signed "Edith Carmichel, Metropolitan Theatre."

I took supper that night, or rather we took supper, Miss Carmichel and I, at Solari's, and the dawn was just beginning to gild the cross on the Memorial Church as I entered Washington Square after leaving Edith at the Brunswick. There was not a soul in the park as I passed along the trees and took the walk which leads from the Garibaldi statue to the Hamilton Apartment House, but as I passed the churchyard I saw a figure sitting on the stone steps. In spite of myself a chill crept over me at the sight of the white puffy face, and I hastened to pass. Then he said something which might have been addressed to me or might merely have been a mutter to himself, but a sudden furious anger flamed up within me that such a creature should address me. For an instant I felt like wheeling about and smashing my stick over his head, but I walked on, and entering the Hamilton went to my apartment. For some time I tossed about the bed trying to get the sound of his voice out of my ears, but could not. It filled my head, that muttering sound, like thick oily smoke from a fat-rendering vat or an odor of noisome decay. And as I lay and tossed about, the voice in my ears seemed more distinct, and I began to understand the words he had muttered. They came to me slowly as if I had forgotten them, and at last I could make some sense out of the sounds. It was this:

"Have you found the Yellow Sign?"

"Have you found the Yellow Sign?"

"Have you found the Yellow Sign?"

I was furious. What did he mean by that? Then with a curse upon him and his I rolled over and went to sleep, but when I awoke later I looked pale and haggard, for I had dreamed the dream of the night before, and it troubled me more than I cared to think.

I dressed and went down into my studio. Tessie sat by the window, but as I came in she rose and put both arms around my neck for an innocent kiss. She looked so sweet and dainty that I kissed her again and then sat down before the easel.

"Hello! Where's the study I began yesterday?" I asked.

Tessie looked conscious, but did not answer. I began to hunt among the piles of canvases, saying, "Hurry up, Tess, and get ready; we must take advantage of the morning light."

When at last I gave up the search among the other canvases and turned to look around the room for the missing study I noticed Tessie standing by the screen with her clothes still on.

"What's the matter," I asked, "don't you feel well?"

"Yes."

"Then hurry."

"Do you want me to pose as—as I have always posed?"

Then I understood. Here was a new complication. I had lost, of course, the best nude model I had ever seen. I looked at Tessie. Her face was scarlet. Alas! Alas! We had eaten of the tree of knowledge, and Eden and native innocence were dreams of the past—I mean for her.

I suppose she noticed the disappointment on my face, for she said: "I will pose if you wish. The study is behind the screen here where I put it."

"No," I said, "we will begin something new;" and I went into my wardrobe and picked out a Moorish costume which fairly blazed with tinsel. It was a genuine costume, and Tessie retired to the screen with it enchanted. When she came forth again I was astonished. Her long black hair was bound above her forehead with a circlet of turquoises, and the ends, curled about her glittering girdle. Her feet were encased in the embroidered pointed slippers and the skirt of her costume, curiously wrought with arabesques in silver, fell to her ankles. The deep metallic blue vest embroidered with silver and the short Mauresque jacket spangled and sewn with turquoises became her wonderfully. She came up to me and held up her face smiling. I slipped my hand into my pocket, and drawing out a gold chain with a cross attached, dropped it over her head.

"It's yours, Tessie."

"Mine?" she faltered.

"Yours. Now go and pose." Then with a radiant smile she ran behind the screen and presently reappeared with a little box on which was written my name.

"I had intended to give it to you when I went home tonight," she said, "but I can't wait now."

I opened the box. On the pink cotton inside lay a clasp of black onyx, on which was inlaid a curious symbol or letter in gold. It was neither Arabic nor Chinese, nor, as I found afterwards, did it belong to any human script.

"It's all I had to give you for a keepsake," she said timidly.

I was annoyed, but I told her how much I should prize it, and promised to wear it always. She fastened it on my coat beneath the lapel.

"How foolish, Tess, to go and buy me such a beautiful thing as this," I said.

"I did not buy it," she laughed.

"Where did you get it?"

Then she told me how she had found it one day while coming from the Aquarium in the Battery, how she had advertised it and watched the papers, but at last gave up all hopes of finding the owner.

"That was last winter," she said, "the very day I had the first horrid dream about the hearse."

I remembered my dream of the previous night but said nothing, and presently my charcoal was flying over a new canvas, and Tessie stood motionless on the model-stand.

III

The day following was a disastrous one for me. While moving a framed canvas from one easel to another my foot slipped on the polished floor, and I fell heavily on both wrists. They were so badly sprained that it was useless to attempt to hold a brush, and I was obliged to wander about the studio, glaring at unfinished drawings and sketches, until despair seized me and I sat down to smoke and twiddle my thumbs with rage. The rain blew against the windows and rattled on the roof of the church, driving me into a nervous fit with its interminable patter. Tessie sat sewing by the window, and every now and then raised her head and looked at me with such innocent compassion that I began to feel ashamed of my irritation and looked about for something to occupy me. I had read all the papers and all the books in the library, but for the sake of something to do I went to the bookcases and shoved them open with my elbow. I knew every volume by its color and examined them all, passing slowly around the library and whistling to keep up my spirits. I was turning to go into the dining-room when my eye fell upon a book bound in serpent skin, standing in a corner of the top shelf of the last bookcase. I did not remember it, and from the floor could not decipher the pale lettering on the back, so I went to the smoking-room and called Tessie. She came in from the studio and climbed up to reach the book.

"What is it?" I asked.

"*The King in Yellow.*"

I was dumfounded. Who had placed it there? How came it in my rooms? I had long ago decided that I should never open that book, and nothing on earth could have persuaded me to buy it. Fearful lest curiosity might tempt me to open it, I had never even looked at it in book-stores. If I ever had had any curiosity to read it, the awful tragedy of young Castaigne, whom I knew, prevented me from exploring its wicked pages. I had always refused to listen to any description of it, and indeed, nobody ever ventured to discuss the second part aloud, so I had absolutely no knowledge of what those leaves might reveal. I stared at the poisonous mottled binding as I would at a snake.

"Don't touch it, Tessie," I said; "come down."

Of course my admonition was enough to arouse her curiosity, and before I could prevent it she took the book and, laughing, danced off into the studio with it. I called to her, but she slipped away with a tormenting smile at my helpless hands, and I followed her with some impatience.

"Tessie!" I cried, entering the library, "listen, I am serious. Put that book away. I do not wish you to open it!" The library was empty. I went into both drawing-rooms, then into the bedrooms, laundry, kitchen, and finally returned to the library and began a systematic search. She had hidden herself so well that it was half-an-hour later when I discovered her crouching white and silent by the latticed window in the store-room above. At the first glance I saw she had been punished for her foolishness. *The*

King in Yellow lay at her feet, but the book was open at the second part. I looked at Tessie and saw it was too late. She had opened *The King in Yellow*. Then I took her by the hand and led her into the studio. She seemed dazed, and when I told her to lie down on the sofa she obeyed me without a word. After a while she closed her eyes and her breathing became regular and deep, but I could not determine whether or not she slept. For a long while I sat silently beside her, but she neither stirred nor spoke, and at last I rose, and, entering the unused store-room, took the book in my least injured hand. It seemed heavy as lead, but I carried it into the studio again, and sitting down on the rug beside the sofa, opened it and read it through from beginning to end.

When, faint with excess of my emotions, I dropped the volume and leaned wearily back against the sofa, Tessie opened her eyes and looked at me....

We had been speaking for some time in a dull monotonous strain before I realized that we were discussing *The King in Yellow*. Oh the sin of writing such words,—words which are clear as crystal, limpid and musical as bubbling springs, words which sparkle and glow like the poisoned diamonds of the Medicis! Oh the wickedness, the hopeless damnation of a soul who could fascinate and paralyze human creatures with such words,—words understood by the ignorant and wise alike, words which are more precious than jewels, more soothing than music, more awful than death!

We talked on, unmindful of the gathering shadows, and she was begging me to throw away the clasp of black onyx quaintly inlaid with what we now knew to be the Yellow Sign. I never shall know why I refused, though even at this hour, here in my bedroom as I write this confession, I should be glad to know *what* it was that prevented me from tearing the Yellow Sign from my breast and casting it into the fire. I am sure I wished to do so, and yet Tessie pleaded with me in vain. Night fell and the hours dragged on, but still we murmured to each other of the King and the Pallid Mask, and midnight sounded from the misty spires in the fog-wrapped city. We spoke of Hastur and of Cassilda, while outside the fog rolled against the blank window-panes as the cloud waves roll and break on the shores of Hali.

The house was very silent now, and not a sound came up from the misty streets. Tessie lay among the cushions, her face a gray blot in the gloom, but her hands were clasped in mine, and I knew that she knew and read my thoughts as I read hers, for we had understood the mystery of the Hyades and the Phantom of Truth was laid. Then as we answered each other, swiftly, silently, thought on thought, the shadows stirred in the gloom about us, and far in the distant streets we heard a sound. Nearer and nearer it came, the dull crunching of wheels, nearer and yet nearer, and now, outside before the door it ceased, and I dragged myself to the window and saw a black-plumed hearse. The gate below opened and shut, and I crept shaking to my door and bolted it, but I knew no bolts, no locks, could keep that creature out who was coming for the Yellow Sign. And now I heard him moving very softly along the hall. Now he was at the door, and the bolts rotted at his touch. Now he had entered. With eyes starting from my head I peered into the darkness, but when he came into the room I did not see him. It was only when I felt him envelope me in his cold soft grasp that I cried out and struggled with deadly fury, but my hands were useless and he tore the onyx clasp from my coat and struck me full in the face. Then, as I fell, I heard Tessie's soft cry and her spirit fled: and even while falling I longed to follow her, for I knew that the King in Yellow had opened his tattered mantle and there was only God to cry to now.

I could tell more, but I cannot see what help it will be to the world. As for me, I am past human help or hope. As I lie here, writing, careless even whether or not I die before I finish, I can see the doctor gathering up his powders and phials with a vague gesture to the good priest beside me, which I understand.

They will be very curious to know the tragedy—they of the outside world who write books and print millions of newspapers, but I shall write no more, and the father confessor will seal my last words with the seal of sanctity when his holy office is done. They of the outside world may send their creatures into wrecked homes and death-smitten firesides, and their newspapers will batten on blood and tears, but with me their spies must halt before the confessional. They know that Tessie is dead and that I am dying. They know how the people in the house, aroused by an infernal scream, rushed into my room and found one living and two dead, but they do not know what I shall tell them now; they do not know that the doctor said as he pointed to a horrible decomposed heap on the floor—the livid corpse of the watchman from the church: "I have no theory, no explanation. That man must have been dead for months!"

~~~~~~~~~~

I think I am dying. I wish the priest would—

THE DEMOISELLE D'YS

"Mais je croy que je
Suis descendu on puiz
Ténébreux onquel disoit
Heraclytus estre Vereté cachée."

"There be three things which are too wonderful for
me, yea, four which I know not:

"The way of an eagle in the air; the way of a serpent
upon a rock; the way of a ship in the midst of the sea;
and the way of a man with a maid."

I

The utter desolation of the scene began to have its effect; I sat down to face the situation and, if possible, recall to mind some landmark which might aid me in extricating myself from my present position. If I could only find the ocean again all would be clear, for I knew one could see the island of Groix from the cliffs.

I laid down my gun, and kneeling behind a rock lighted a pipe. Then I looked at my watch. It was nearly four o'clock. I might have wandered far from Kerselec since daybreak.

Standing the day before on the cliffs below Kerselec with Goulven, looking out over the somber moors among which I had now lost my way, these downs had appeared to me level as a meadow, stretching to the horizon, and although I knew how deceptive is distance, I could not realize that what from Kerselec seemed to be mere grassy hollows were great valleys covered with gorse and heather, and what looked like scattered boulders were in reality enormous cliffs of granite.

"It's a bad place for a stranger," old Goulven had said: "you'd better take a guide;" and I had replied, "I shall not lose myself." Now I knew that I had lost myself, as I sat there smoking, with the sea-wind blowing in my face. On every side stretched the moorland, covered with flowering gorse and heath and granite boulders. There was not a tree in sight, much less a house. After a while, I picked up the gun, and turning my back on the sun tramped on again.

There was little use in following any of the brawling streams which every now and then crossed my path, for, instead of flowing into the sea, they ran inland to reedy pools in the hollows of the moors. I had followed several, but they all led me to swamps or silent little ponds from which the snipe rose peeping and wheeled away in an ecstasy of fright. I began to feel fatigued, and the gun galled my shoulder in spite of the double pads. The sun sank lower and lower, shining level across yellow gorse and the moorland pools.

As I walked my own gigantic shadow led me on, seeming to lengthen at every step. The gorse scraped against my leggings, crackled beneath my feet, showering the brown earth with blossoms, and the brake bowed and billowed along my path. From tufts of heath rabbits scurried away through the bracken, and among the swamp grass I heard the wild duck's drowsy quack. Once a fox stole across my path, and again, as I stooped to drink at a hurrying rill, a heron flapped heavily from the reeds beside me. I turned to look at the sun. It seemed to touch the edges of the plain. When at last I decided that it was useless to go on, and that I must make up my mind to spend at least one night on the moors, I threw myself down thoroughly fagged out. The evening sunlight slanted warm across my body, but the sea-winds began to rise, and I felt a chill strike through me from my wet shooting-boots. High overhead gulls were wheeling and tossing like bits of white paper; from some distant marsh a solitary curlew called. Little by little the sun sank into the plain, and the zenith flushed with the after-glow. I watched the sky change from palest gold to pink and then to smouldering fire. Clouds of midges danced above me, and high in the calm air a bat dipped and soared. My eyelids began to droop. Then as I shook off the drowsiness a sudden crash among the bracken roused me. I raised my eyes. A great bird hung quivering in the air above my face. For an instant I stared, incapable of motion; then something leaped past me in the ferns and the bird rose, wheeled, and pitched headlong into the brake.

I was on my feet in an instant peering through the gorse. There came the sound of a struggle from a bunch of heather close by, and then all was quiet. I stepped forward, my gun poised, but when I came to the heather the gun fell under my arm again, and I stood motionless in silent astonishment. A dead hare lay on the ground, and on the hare stood a magnificent falcon, one talon buried in the creature's neck, the other planted firmly on its limp flank. But what astonished me, was not the mere sight of a falcon sitting upon its prey. I had seen that more than once. It was that the falcon was fitted with a sort of leash about both talons, and from the leash hung a round bit of metal like a sleigh-bell. The bird turned its fierce yellow eyes on me, and then stooped and struck its curved beak into the quarry. At the same instant hurried steps sounded among the heather, and a girl sprang into the covert in front. Without a glance at me she walked up to the falcon, and passing her gloved hand under its breast, raised it from the quarry. Then she deftly slipped a small hood over the bird's head, and holding it out on her gauntlet, stooped and picked up the hare.

She passed a cord about the animal's legs and fastened the end of the thong to her girdle. Then she started to retrace her steps through the covert. As she passed me I raised my cap and she acknowledged my presence with a scarcely perceptible inclination. I had been so astonished, so lost in admiration of the scene before my eyes, that it had not occurred to me that here was my salvation. But as she moved away I recollected that unless I wanted to sleep on a windy moor that night I had better recover my speech without delay. At my first word she hesitated, and as

I stepped before her I thought a look of fear came into her beautiful eyes. But as I humbly explained my unpleasant plight, her face flushed and she looked at me in wonder.

"Surely you did not come from Kerselec!" she repeated.

Her sweet voice had no trace of the Breton accent nor of any accent which I knew, and yet there was something in it I seemed to have heard before, something quaint and indefinable, like the theme of an old song.

I explained that I was an American, unacquainted with Finistère, shooting there for my own amusement.

"An American," she repeated in the same quaint musical tones. "I have never before seen an American."

For a moment she stood silent, then looking at me she said. "If you should walk all night you could not reach Kerselec now, even if you had a guide."

This was pleasant news.

"But," I began, "if I could only find a peasant's hut where I might get something to eat, and shelter."

The falcon on her wrist fluttered and shook its head. The girl smoothed its glossy back and glanced at me.

"Look around," she said gently. "Can you see the end of these moors? Look, north, south, east, west. Can you see anything but moorland and bracken?"

"No," I said.

"The moor is wild and desolate. It is easy to enter, but sometimes they who enter never leave it. There are no peasants' huts here."

"Well," I said, "if you will tell me in which direction Kerselec lies, to-morrow it will take me no longer to go back than it has to come."

She looked at me again with an expression almost like pity.

"Ah," she said, "to come is easy and takes hours; to go is different—and may take centuries."

I stared at her in amazement but decided that I had misunderstood her. Then before I had time to speak she drew a whistle from her belt and sounded it.

"Sit down and rest," she said to me; "you have come a long distance and are tired."

She gathered up her pleated skirts and motioning me to follow picked her dainty way through the gorse to a flat rock among the ferns.

"They will be here directly," she said, and taking a seat at one end of the rock invited me to sit down on the other edge. The after-glow was beginning to fade in the sky and a single star twinkled faintly through the rosy haze. A long wavering triangle of water-fowl drifted southward over our heads, and from the swamps around plover were calling.

"They are very beautiful—these moors," she said quietly.

"Beautiful, but cruel to strangers," I answered.

"Beautiful and cruel," she repeated dreamily, "beautiful and cruel."

"Like a woman," I said stupidly.

"Oh," she cried with a little catch in her breath, and looked at me. Her dark eyes met mine, and I thought she seemed angry or frightened.

"Like a woman," she repeated under her breath, "How cruel to say so!" Then after a pause, as though speaking aloud to herself, "How cruel for him to say that!"

I don't know what sort of an apology I offered for my inane, though harmless speech, but I know that she seemed so troubled about it that I began to think I had said something very dreadful without knowing it, and remembered with horror the pitfalls and snares which the French language sets for foreigners. While I was trying to imagine what I might have said, a sound of voices came across the moor, and the girl rose to her feet.

"No," she said, with a trace of a smile on her pale face, "I will not accept your apologies, monsieur, but I must prove you wrong, and that shall be my revenge. Look. Here come Hastur and Raoul."

Two men loomed up in the twilight. One had a sack across his shoulders and the other carried a hoop before him as a waiter carries a tray. The hoop was fastened with straps to his shoulders, and around the edge of the circlet sat three hooded falcons fitted with tinkling bells. The girl stepped up to the falconer, and with a quick turn of her wrist transferred her falcon to the hoop, where it quickly sidled off and nestled among its mates, who shook their hooded heads and ruffled their feathers till the belled jesses tinkled again. The other man stepped forward and bowing respectfully took up the hare and dropped it into the game-sack.

"These are my piqueurs," said the girl, turning to me with a gentle dignity. "Raoul is a good fauconnier, and I shall some day make him grand veneur. Hastur is incomparable."

The two silent men saluted me respectfully.

"Did I not tell you, monsieur, that I should prove you wrong?" she continued. "This, then, is my revenge, that you do me the courtesy of accepting food and shelter at my own house."

Before I could answer she spoke to the falconers, who started instantly across the heath, and with a gracious gesture to me she followed. I don't know whether I made her understand how profoundly grateful I felt, but she seemed pleased to listen, as we walked over the dewy heather.

"Are you not very tired?" she asked.

I had clean forgotten my fatigue in her presence, and I told her so.

"Don't you think your gallantry is a little old-fashioned?" she said; and when I looked confused and humbled, she added quietly, "Oh, I like it, I like everything old-fashioned, and it is delightful to hear you say such pretty things."

The moorland around us was very still now under its ghostly sheet of mist. The plovers had ceased their calling; the crickets and all the little creatures of the fields were silent as we passed, yet it seemed to me as if I could hear them beginning again far behind us. Well in advance, the two tall falconers strode across the heather, and the faint jingling of the hawks' bells came to our ears in distant murmuring chimes.

Suddenly a splendid hound dashed out of the mist in front, followed by another and another until half-a-dozen or more were bounding and leaping around the girl beside me. She caressed and quieted them with her gloved hand, speaking to them in quaint terms which I remembered to have seen in old French manuscripts.

Then the falcons on the circlet borne by the falconer ahead began to beat their wings and scream, and from somewhere out of sight the notes of a hunting-horn floated across the moor. The hounds sprang away before us and vanished in the twilight, the falcons flapped and squealed upon their perch, and the girl, taking up the song of the horn, began to hum. Clear and mellow her voice sounded in the night air.

> *"Chasseur, chasseur, chassez encore,*
> *Quittez Rosette et Jeanneton,*
> *Tonton, tonton, tontaine, tonton,*
> *Ou, pour, rabattre, dès l'aurore,*
> *Que les Amours soient de planton,*
> *Tonton, tontaine, tonton."*

As I listened to her lovely voice a grey mass which rapidly grew more distinct loomed up in front, and the horn rang out joyously through the tumult of the hounds and falcons. A torch glimmered at a gate, a light streamed through an opening door, and we stepped upon a wooden bridge which trembled under our feet and rose creaking and straining behind us as we passed over the moat and into a small stone court, walled on every side. From an open doorway a man came and, bending in salutation, presented a cup to the girl beside me. She took the cup and touched it with her lips, then lowering it turned to me and said in a low voice, "I bid you welcome."

At that moment one of the falconers came with another cup, but before handing it to me, presented it to the girl, who tasted it. The falconer made a gesture to receive it, but she hesitated a moment, and then, stepping forward, offered me the cup with her own hands. I felt this to be an act of extraordinary gracious-ness, but hardly knew what was expected of me, and did not raise it to my lips at once. The girl flushed crimson. I saw that I must act quickly.

"Mademoiselle," I faltered, "a stranger whom you have saved from dangers he may never realize empties this cup to the gentlest and loveliest hostess of France."

"In His name," she murmured, crossing herself as I drained the cup. Then stepping into the doorway she turned to me with a pretty gesture and, taking my hand in hers, led me into the house, saying again and again: "You are very welcome, indeed you are welcome to the Château d'Ys."

II

I awoke next morning with the music of the horn in my ears, and leaping out of the ancient bed, went to a curtained window where the sunlight filtered through little deep-set panes. The horn ceased as I looked into the court below.

A man who might have been brother to the two falconers of the night before stood in the midst of a pack of hounds. A curved horn was strapped over his back, and in his hand he held a long-lashed whip. The dogs whined and yelped, dancing around him in anticipation; there was the stamp of horses, too, in the walled yard.

"Mount!" cried a voice in Breton, and with a clatter of hoofs the two falconers, with falcons upon their wrists, rode into the courtyard among the hounds. Then I heard another voice which sent the blood throbbing through my heart: "Piriou Louis, hunt the hounds well and spare neither spur nor whip. Thou Raoul and thou Gaston, see that the *epervier* does not prove himself *niais*, and if it be best in your judgment, *faites courtoisie à l'oiseau. Jardiner un oiseau*, like the *mué* there on Hastur's wrist, is not difficult, but thou, Raoul, mayest not find it so simple to govern that *hagard*. Twice last week he foamed *au vif* and lost the *beccade* although he is used to the *leurre*. The bird acts like a stupid *branchier. Paître un hagard n'est pas si facile.*"

Was I dreaming? The old language of falconry which I had read in yellow manuscripts—the old forgotten French of the middle ages was sounding in my ears while the hounds bayed and the hawks' bells tinkled accompaniment to the stamping horses. She spoke again in the sweet forgotten language:

"If you would rather attach the *longe* and leave thy *hagard au bloc*, Raoul, I shall say nothing; for it were a pity to spoil so fair a day's sport with an ill-trained *sors*. *Essimer abaisser*,—it is possibly the best way. *Ça lui donnera des reins.* I was perhaps hasty with the bird. It takes time to pass *à la filière* and the exercises *d'escap*."

Then the falconer Raoul bowed in his stirrups and replied: "If it be the pleasure of Mademoiselle, I shall keep the hawk."

"It is my wish," she answered. "Falconry I know, but you have yet to give me many a lesson in *Autourserie*, my poor Raoul. Sieur Piriou Louis mount!"

The huntsman sprang into an archway and in an instant returned, mounted upon a strong black horse, followed by a piqueur also mounted.

"Ah!" she cried joyously, "speed Glemarec René! speed! speed all! Sound thy horn, Sieur Piriou!"

The silvery music of the hunting-horn filled the courtyard, the hounds sprang through the gateway and galloping hoof-beats plunged out of the paved court; loud on the drawbridge, suddenly muffled, then lost in the heather and bracken of the moors. Distant and more distant sounded the horn, until it became so faint that the sudden carol of a soaring lark drowned it in my ears. I heard the voice below responding to some call from within the house.

"I do not regret the chase, I will go another time. Courtesy to the stranger, Pelagie, remember!"

And a feeble voice came quavering from within the house, "*Courtoisie*"

I stripped, and rubbed myself from head to foot in the huge earthen basin of icy water which stood upon the stone floor at the foot of my bed. Then I looked about for my clothes. They were gone, but on a settle near the door lay a heap of garments which I inspected with astonishment. As my clothes had vanished, I was compelled to attire myself in the costume which had evidently been placed there for me to wear while my own clothes dried. Everything was there, cap, shoes, and hunting doublet of silvery grey homespun; but the close-fitting costume and seamless shoes belonged to another century, and I remembered the strange costumes of the three falconers in the courtyard. I was sure that it was not the modern dress of any portion of France or Brittany; but not until I was dressed and stood before a mirror between the windows did I realize that I was clothed much more like a young huntsman of the middle ages than like a Breton of that day. I hesitated and picked up the cap. Should I go down and present myself in that strange guise? There seemed to be no help for it, my own clothes were gone and there was no bell in the ancient chamber to call a servant; so I contented myself with removing a short hawk's feather from the cap, and, opening the door, went downstairs.

By the fireplace in the large room at the foot of the stairs an old Breton woman sat spinning with a distaff. She looked up at me when I appeared, and, smiling frankly, wished me health in the Breton language, to which I laughingly replied in French. At the same moment my hostess appeared and returned my salutation with a grace and dignity that sent a thrill to my heart. Her lovely head with its dark curly hair was crowned with a head-dress which set all doubts as to the epoch of my own costume at rest. Her slender figure was exquisitely set off in the homespun hunting-gown edged with silver, and on her gauntlet-covered wrist she bore one of her petted hawks. With perfect simplicity she took my hand and led me into the garden in the court, and seating herself before a table invited me very sweetly to sit beside her. Then she asked me in her soft quaint accent how I had passed the night, and whether I was very much inconvenienced by wearing the clothes which old Pelagie had put there for me while I slept. I looked at my own clothes and shoes, drying in the sun by the garden-wall, and hated them. What horrors they were compared with the graceful costume which I now wore! I told her this laughing, but she agreed with me very seriously.

"We will throw them away," she said in a quiet voice. In my astonishment I attempted to explain that I not only could not think of accepting clothes from anybody, although for all I knew it might be the custom of hospitality in that part of the country, but that I should cut an impossible figure if I returned to France clothed as I was then.

She laughed and tossed her pretty head, saying something in old French which I did not understand, and then Pelagie trotted out with a tray on which stood two bowls of milk, a loaf of white bread, fruit, a platter of honey-comb, and a flagon of deep red wine. "You see I have not yet broken my fast because I wished you to eat with me. But I am very hungry," she smiled.

"I would rather die than forget one word of what you have said!" I blurted out, while my cheeks burned. "She will think me mad," I added to myself, but she turned to me with sparkling eyes.

"Ah!" she murmured. "Then Monsieur knows all that there is of chivalry—"

She crossed herself and broke bread. I sat and watched her white hands, not daring to raise my eyes to hers.

"Will you not eat?" she asked. "Why do you look so troubled?"

Ah, why? I knew it now. I knew I would give my life to touch with my lips those rosy palms—I understood now that from the moment when I looked into her dark eyes there on the moor last night I had loved her. My great and sudden passion held me speechless.

"Are you ill at ease?" she asked again.

Then, like a man who pronounces his own doom, I answered in a low voice: "Yes, I am ill at ease for love of you." And as she did not stir nor answer, the same power moved my lips in spite of me and I said, "I, who am unworthy of the lightest of your thoughts, I who abuse hospitality and repay your gentle courtesy with bold presumption, I love you."

She leaned her head upon her hands, and answered softly, "I love you. Your words are very dear to me. I love you."

"Then I shall win you."

"Win me," she replied.

But all the time I had been sitting silent, my face turned toward her. She, also silent, her sweet face resting on her upturned palm, sat facing me, and as her eyes looked into mine I knew that neither she nor I had spoken human speech; but I knew that her soul had answered mine, and I drew myself up feeling youth and joyous love coursing through every vein. She, with a bright colour in her lovely face, seemed as one awakened from a dream, and her eyes sought mine with a questioning glance which made me tremble with delight. We broke our fast, speaking of ourselves. I told her my name and she told me hers, the Demoiselle Jeanne d'Ys.

She spoke of her father and mother's death, and how the nineteen of her years had been passed in the little fortified farm alone with her nurse Pelagie, Glemarec René the piqueur, and the four falconers, Raoul, Gaston, Hastur, and the Sieur Piriou Louis, who had served her father. She had never been outside the moorland—never even had seen a human soul before, except the falconers and Pelagie. She did not know how she had heard of Kerselec; perhaps the falconers had spoken of it. She knew the legends of Loup Garou and Jeanne la Flamme from her nurse Pelagie. She embroidered and spun flax. Her hawks and hounds were her only distraction. When she had met me there on the moor she had been so frightened that she almost dropped at the sound of my voice. She had, it was true, seen ships at sea from the cliffs, but as far as the eye could reach the moors over which she galloped were destitute of any sign of human life. There was a legend which old Pelagie told, how anybody once lost in the unexplored moorland might never return, because the moors were enchanted. She did not know whether it was true, she never had thought about it until she met me. She did not know whether the falconers had even been outside, or whether they could go if they would. The books in the house which Pelagie, the nurse, had taught her to read were hundreds of years old.

All this she told me with a sweet seriousness seldom seen in any one but children. My own name she found easy to pronounce, and insisted, because my first name was Philip, I must have French blood in me. She did not seem curious to learn anything about the outside world, and I thought perhaps she considered it had forfeited her interest and respect from the stories of her nurse.

We were still sitting at the table, and she was throwing grapes to the small field birds which came fearlessly to our very feet.

I began to speak in a vague way of going, but she would not hear of it, and before I knew it I had promised to stay a week and hunt with hawk and hound in their company. I also obtained permission to come again from Kerselec and visit her after my return.

"Why," she said innocently, "I do not know what I should do if you never came back;" and I, knowing that I had no right to awaken her with the sudden shock which the avowal of my own love would bring to her, sat silent, hardly daring to breathe.

"You will come very often?" she asked.

"Very often," I said.

"Every day?"

"Every day."

"Oh," she sighed, "I am very happy. Come and see my hawks."

She rose and took my hand again with a childlike innocence of possession, and we walked through the garden and fruit trees to a grassy lawn which was bordered by a brook. Over the lawn were scattered fifteen or twenty stumps of trees—partially imbedded in the grass—and upon all of these except two sat falcons. They were attached to the stumps by thongs which were in turn fastened with steel rivets to their legs just above the talons. A little stream of pure spring water flowed in a winding course within easy distance of each perch.

The birds set up a clamour when the girl appeared, but she went from one to another, caressing some, taking others for an instant upon her wrist, or stooping to adjust their jesses.

"Are they not pretty?" she said. "See, here is a falcon-gentil. We call it 'ignoble,' because it takes the quarry in direct chase. This is a blue falcon. In falconry we call it 'noble' because it rises over the quarry, and wheeling, drops upon it from above. This white bird is a gerfalcon from the north. It is also 'noble!' Here is a merlin, and this tiercelet is a falcon-heroner."

I asked her how she had learned the old language of falconry. She did not remember, but thought her father must have taught it to her when she was very young.

Then she led me away and showed me the young falcons still in the nest. "They are termed *niais* in falconry," she explained. "A *branchier* is the young bird which is just able to leave the nest and hop from branch to branch. A young bird which has not yet moulted is called a *sors*, and a *mué* is a hawk which has moulted in captivity. When we catch a wild falcon which has changed its plumage we term it a *hagard*. Raoul first taught me to dress a falcon. Shall I teach you how it is done?"

She seated herself on the bank of the stream among the falcons and I threw myself at her feet to listen.

Then the Demoiselle d'Ys held up one rosy-tipped finger and began very gravely.

"First one must catch the falcon."

"I am caught," I answered.

She laughed very prettily and told me my *dressage* would perhaps be difficult, as I was noble.

"I am already tamed," I replied; "jessed and belled."

She laughed, delighted. "Oh, my brave falcon; then you will return at my call?"

"I am yours," I answered gravely.

She sat silent for a moment. Then the colour heightened in

her cheeks and she held up her finger again, saying, "Listen; I wish to speak of falconry—"

"I listen, Countess Jeanne d'Ys."

But again she fell into the reverie, and her eyes seemed fixed on something beyond the summer clouds.

"Philip," she said at last.

"Jeanne," I whispered.

"That is all,—that is what I wished," she sighed,—"Philip and Jeanne."

She held her hand toward me and I touched it with my lips.

"Win me," she said, but this time it was the body and soul which spoke in unison.

After a while she began again: "Let us speak of falconry."

"Begin," I replied; "we have caught the falcon."

Then Jeanne d'Ys took my hand in both of hers and told me how with infinite patience the young falcon was taught to perch upon the wrist, how little by little it became used to the belled jesses and the *chaperon à cornette*.

"They must first have a good appetite," she said; "then little by little I reduce their nourishment; which in falconry we call *pât*. When, after many nights passed *au bloc* as these birds are now, I prevail upon the *hagard* to stay quietly on the wrist, then the bird is ready to be taught to come for its food. I fix the *pât* to the end of a thong, or *leurre*, and teach the bird to come to me as soon as I begin to whirl the cord in circles about my head. At first I drop the *pât* when the falcon comes, and he eats the food on the ground. After a little he will learn to seize the *leurre* in motion as I whirl it around my head or drag it over the ground. After this it is easy to teach the falcon to strike at game, always remembering to *'faire courtoisie á l'oiseau'*, that is, to allow the bird to taste the quarry."

A squeal from one of the falcons interrupted her, and she arose to adjust the *longe* which had become whipped about the *bloc*, but the bird still flapped its wings and screamed.

"What *is* the matter?" she said. "Philip, can you see?"

I looked around and at first saw nothing to cause the commotion, which was now heightened by the screams and flapping of all the birds. Then my eye fell upon the flat rock beside the stream from which the girl had risen. A grey serpent was moving slowly across the surface of the boulder, and the eyes in its flat triangular head sparkled like jet.

"A couleuvre," she said quietly.

"It is harmless, is it not?" I asked.

She pointed to the black V-shaped figure on the neck.

"It is certain death," she said; "it is a viper."

We watched the reptile moving slowly over the smooth rock to where the sunlight fell in a broad warm patch.

I started forward to examine it, but she clung to my arm crying, "Don't, Philip, I am afraid."

"For me?"

"For you, Philip,—I love you."

Then I took her in my arms and kissed her on the lips, but all I could say was: "Jeanne, Jeanne, Jeanne." And as she lay trembling on my breast, something struck my foot in the grass below, but I did not heed it. Then again something struck my ankle, and a sharp pain shot through me. I looked into the sweet face of Jeanne d'Ys and kissed her, and with all my strength lifted her in my arms and flung her from me. Then bending, I tore the viper from my ankle and set my heel upon its head. I remember feeling weak and numb,—I remember falling to the ground. Through my slowly glazing eyes I saw Jeanne's white face bending close to mine, and when the light in my eyes went out I still felt her arms about my neck, and her soft cheek against my drawn lips.

When I opened my eyes, I looked around in terror. Jeanne was gone. I saw the stream and the flat rock; I saw the crushed viper in the grass beside me, but the hawks and *blocs* had disappeared. I sprang to my feet. The garden, the fruit trees, the drawbridge and the walled court were gone. I stared stupidly at a heap of crumbling ruins, ivy-covered and grey, through which great trees had pushed their way. I crept forward, dragging my numbed foot, and as I moved, a falcon sailed from the tree-tops among the ruins, and soaring, mounting in narrowing circles, faded and vanished in the clouds above.

"Jeanne, Jeanne," I cried, but my voice died on my lips, and I fell on my knees among the weeds. And as God willed it, I, not knowing, had fallen kneeling before a crumbling shrine carved in stone for our Mother of Sorrows. I saw the sad face of the Virgin wrought in the cold stone. I saw the cross and thorns at her feet, and beneath it I read:

> "PRAY FOR THE SOUL OF THE
> DEMOISELLE JEANNE D'Ys,
> WHO DIED
> IN HER YOUTH FOR LOVE OF
> PHILIP, A STRANGER.
> A.D. 1573."

But upon the icy slab lay a woman's glove still warm and fragrant.

THE PROPHET'S PARADISE

"If but the Vine and Love Abjuring Band
Are in the Prophets' Paradise to stand,
Alack, I doubt the Prophets' Paradise,
Were empty as the hollow of one's hand."

THE STUDIO

He smiled, saying, "Seek her throughout the world."

I said, "Why tell me of the world? My world is here, between these walls and the sheet of glass above; here among gilded flagons and dull jewelled arms, tarnished frames and canvasses, black chests and high-backed chairs, quaintly carved and stained in blue and gold."

"For whom do you wait?" he said, and I answered, "When she comes I shall know her."

On my hearth a tongue of flame whispered secrets to the whitening ashes. In the street below I heard footsteps, a voice, and a song.

"For whom then do you wait?" he said, and I answered, "I shall know her."

Footsteps, a voice, and a song in the street below, and I knew the song but neither the steps nor the voice.

"Fool!" he cried, "the song is the same, the voice and steps have but changed with years!"

On the hearth a tongue of flame whispered above the whitening ashes: "Wait no more; they have passed, the steps and the voice in the street below."

Then he smiled, saying, "For whom do you wait? Seek her throughout the world!"

I answered, "My world is here, between these walls and the sheet of glass above; here among gilded flagons and dull jewelled arms, tarnished frames and canvasses, black chests and high-backed chairs, quaintly carved and stained in blue and gold."

THE PHANTOM

The Phantom of the Past would go no further.

"If it is true," she sighed, "that you find in me a friend, let us turn back together. You will forget, here, under the summer sky."

I held her close, pleading, caressing; I seized her, white with anger, but she resisted.

"If it is true," she sighed, "that you find in me a friend, let us turn back together."

The Phantom of the Past would go no further.

THE SACRIFICE

I went into a field of flowers, whose petals are whiter than snow and whose hearts are pure gold.

Far afield a woman cried, "I have killed him I loved!" and from a jar she poured blood upon the flowers whose petals are whiter than snow and whose hearts are pure gold.

Far afield I followed, and on the jar I read a thousand names, while from within the fresh blood bubbled to the brim.

"I have killed him I loved!" she cried. "The world's athirst; now let it drink!" She passed, and far afield I watched her pouring blood upon the flowers whose petals are whiter than snow and whose hearts are pure gold.

DESTINY

I came to the bridge which few may pass.

"Pass!" cried the keeper, but I laughed, saying, "There is time;" and he smiled and shut the gates.

To the bridge which few may pass came young and old. All were refused. Idly I stood and counted them, until, wearied of their noise and lamentations, I came again to the bridge which few may pass.

Those in the throng about the gates shrieked out, "He comes too late!" But I laughed, saying, "There is time."

"Pass!" cried the keeper as I entered; then smiled and shut the gates.

THE THRONG

There, where the throng was thickest in the street, I stood with Pierrot. All eyes were turned on me.

"What are they laughing at?" I asked, but he grinned, dusting the chalk from my black cloak. "I cannot see; it must be something droll, perhaps an honest thief!"

All eyes were turned on me.

"He has robbed you of your purse!" they laughed.

"My purse!" I cried; "Pierrot—help! it is a thief!"

They laughed: "He has robbed you of your purse!"

Then Truth stepped out, holding a mirror. "If he is an honest thief," cried Truth, "Pierrot shall find him with this mirror!" but he only grinned, dusting the chalk from my black cloak.

"You see," he said, "Truth is an honest thief, she brings you back your mirror."

All eyes were turned on me.

"Arrest Truth!" I cried, forgetting it was not a mirror but a purse I lost, standing with Pierrot, there, where the throng was thickest in the street.

THE JESTER

"Was she fair?" I asked, but he only chuckled, listening to the bells jingling on his cap.

"Stabbed," he tittered. "Think of the long journey, the days of peril, the dreadful nights! Think how he wandered, for her sake, year after year, through hostile lands, yearning for kith and kin, yearning for her!"

"Stabbed," he tittered, listening to the bells jingling on his cap.

"Was she fair?" I asked, but he only snarled, muttering to the bells jingling on his cap.

"She kissed him at the gate," he tittered, "but in the hall his brother's welcome touched his heart."

"Was she fair?" I asked.

"Stabbed," he chuckled. "Think of the long journey, the days of peril, the dreadful nights! Think how he wandered, for her sake, year after year through hostile lands, yearning for kith and kin, yearning for her!"

"She kissed him at the gate, but in the hall his brother's welcome touched his heart."

"Was she fair?" I asked; but he only snarled, listening to the bells jingling in his cap.

THE GREEN ROOM

The Clown turned his powdered face to the mirror.

"If to be fair is to be beautiful," he said, "who can compare with me in my white mask?"

"Who can compare with him in his white mask?" I asked of Death beside me.

"Who can compare with me?" said Death, "for I am paler still."

"You are very beautiful," sighed the Clown, turning his powdered face from the mirror.

THE LOVE TEST

"If it is true that you love," said Love, "then wait no longer. Give her these jewels which would dishonour her and so dishonour you in loving one dishonoured. If it is true that you love," said Love, "then wait no longer."

I took the jewels and went to her, but she trod upon them, sobbing: "Teach me to wait—I love you!"

"Then wait, if it is true," said Love.

THE STREET OF
THE FOUR WINDS

"Ferme tes yeux à demi,
Croise tes bras sur ton sein,
Et de ton cœur endormi
Chasse à jamais tout dessein."

"Je chante la nature,
Les étoiles du soir, les larmes du matin,
Les couchers de soleil à l'horizon lointain,
Le ciel qui parle au cœur d'existence future!"

I

The animal paused on the threshold, interrogative alert, ready for flight if necessary. Severn laid down his palette, and held out a hand of welcome. The cat remained motionless, her yellow eyes fastened upon Severn.

"Puss," he said, in his low, pleasant voice, "come in."

The tip of her thin tail twitched uncertainly.

"Come in," he said again.

Apparently she found his voice reassuring, for she slowly settled upon all fours, her eyes still fastened upon him, her tail tucked under her gaunt flanks.

He rose from his easel smiling. She eyed him quietly, and when he walked toward her she watched him bend above her without a wince; her eyes followed his hand until it touched her head. Then she uttered a ragged mew.

It had long been Severn's custom to converse with animals, probably because he lived so much alone; and now he said, "What's the matter, puss?"

Her timid eyes sought his.

"I understand," he said gently, "you shall have it at once."

Then moving quietly about he busied himself with the duties of a host, rinsed a saucer, filled it with the rest of the milk from the bottle on the window-sill, and kneeling down, crumbled a roll into the hollow of his hand.

The creature rose and crept toward the saucer.

With the handle of a palette-knife he stirred the crumbs and milk together and stepped back as she thrust her nose into the mess. He watched her in silence. From time to time the saucer clinked upon the tiled floor as she reached for a morsel on the rim; and at last the bread was all gone, and her purple tongue travelled over every unlicked spot until the saucer shone like polished marble. Then she sat up, and coolly turning her back to him, began her ablutions.

"Keep it up," said Severn, much interested, "you need it."

She flattened one ear, but neither turned nor interrupted her toilet. As the grime was slowly removed Severn observed that nature had intended her for a white cat. Her fur had disappeared in patches, from disease or the chances of war, her tail was bony and her spine sharp. But what charms she had were becoming apparent under vigorous licking, and he waited until she had finished before re-opening the conversation. When at last she closed her eyes and folded her forepaws under her breast, he began again very gently: "Puss, tell me your troubles."

At the sound of his voice she broke into a harsh rumbling which he recognized as an attempt to purr. He bent over to rub her cheek and she mewed again, an amiable inquiring little mew, to which he replied, "Certainly, you are greatly improved, and when you recover your plumage you will be a gorgeous bird." Much flattered, she stood up and marched around and around his legs, pushing her head between them and making pleased remarks, to which he responded with grave politeness.

"Now, what sent you here," he said—"here into the Street of the Four Winds, and up five flights to the very door where you would be welcome? What was it that prevented your meditated flight when I turned from my canvas to encounter your yellow eyes? Are you a Latin Quarter cat as I am a Latin Quarter man? And why do you wear a rose-coloured flowered garter buckled about your neck?" The cat had climbed into his lap, and now sat purring as he passed his hand over her thin coat.

"Excuse me," he continued in lazy soothing tones, harmonizing with her purring, "if I seem indelicate, but I cannot help musing on this rose-coloured garter, flowered so quaintly and fastened with a silver clasp. For the clasp is silver; I can see the mint mark on the edge, as is prescribed by the law of the French Republic. Now, why is this garter woven of rose silk and delicately embroidered,—why is this silken garter with its silver clasp about your famished throat? Am I indiscreet when I inquire if its owner is your owner? Is she some aged dame living in memory of youthful vanities, fond, doting on you, decorating you with her intimate personal attire? The circumference of the garter would suggest this, for your neck is thin, and the garter fits you. But then again I notice—I notice most things—that the garter is capable of being much enlarged. These small silver-rimmed eyelets, of which I count five, are proof of that. And now I observe that the fifth eyelet is worn out, as though the tongue of the clasp were accustomed to lie there. That seems to argue a well-rounded form."

The cat curled her toes in contentment. The street was very still outside.

He murmured on: "Why should your mistress decorate you with an article most necessary to her at all times? Anyway, at most times. How did she come to slip this bit of silk and silver about your neck? Was it the caprice of a moment,—when you, before you had lost your pristine plumpness, marched singing into her bedroom to bid her good-morning? Of course, and she sat up among the pillows, her coiled hair tumbling to her shoulders, as you sprang upon the bed purring: 'Good-day, my lady.' Oh, it is very easy to understand," he yawned, resting his head on the back of the chair. The cat still purred, tightening and relaxing her padded claws over his knee.

"Shall I tell you all about her, cat? She is very beautiful—your mistress," he murmured drowsily, "and her hair is heavy as burnished gold. I could paint her,—not on canvas—for I should need shades and tones and hues and dyes more splendid than the iris of a splendid rainbow. I could only paint her with closed eyes, for in dreams alone can such colours as I need be found. For her eyes, I must have azure from skies untroubled by a cloud—the skies of dreamland. For her lips, roses from the palaces of slumberland, and for her brow, snow-drifts from mountains which tower in fantastic pinnacles to the moons;—oh, much higher than our moon here,—the crystal moons of dreamland. She is—very—beautiful, your mistress."

The words died on his lips and his eyelids drooped.

The cat, too, was asleep, her cheek turned up upon her wasted flank, her paws relaxed and limp.

II

"It is fortunate," said Severn, sitting up and stretching, "that we have tided over the dinner hour, for I have nothing to offer you for supper but what may be purchased with one silver franc."

The cat on his knee rose, arched her back, yawned, and looked up at him.

"What shall it be? A roast chicken with salad? No? Possibly you prefer beef? Of course,—and I shall try an egg and some white bread. Now for the wines. Milk for you? Good. I shall take a little water, fresh from the wood," with a motion toward the bucket in the sink.

He put on his hat and left the room. The cat followed to the door, and after he had closed it behind him, she settled down, smelling at the cracks, and cocking one ear at every creak from the crazy old building.

The door below opened and shut. The cat looked serious, for a moment doubtful, and her ears flattened in nervous expectation. Presently she rose with a jerk of her tail and started on a noiseless tour of the studio. She sneezed at a pot of turpentine, hastily retreating to the table, which she presently mounted, and having satisfied her curiosity concerning a roll of red modelling wax, returned to the door and sat down with her eyes on the crack over the threshold. Then she lifted her voice in a thin plaint.

When Severn returned he looked grave, but the cat, joyous and demonstrative, marched around him, rubbing her gaunt body against his legs, driving her head enthusiastically into his hand, and purring until her voice mounted to a squeal.

He placed a bit of meat, wrapped in brown paper, upon the table, and with a penknife cut it into shreds. The milk he took from a bottle which had served for medicine, and poured it into the saucer on the hearth.

The cat crouched before it, purring and lapping at the same time.

He cooked his egg and ate it with a slice of bread, watching her busy with the shredded meat, and when he had finished, and had filled and emptied a cup of water from the bucket in the sink, he sat down, taking her into his lap, where she at once curled up and began her toilet. He began to speak again, touching her caressingly at times by way of emphasis.

"Cat, I have found out where your mistress lives. It is not very far away;—it is here, under this same leaky roof, but in the north wing which I had supposed was uninhabited. My janitor tells me this. By chance, he is almost sober this evening. The butcher on the rue de Seine, where I bought your meat, knows you, and old Cabane the baker identified you with needless sarcasm. They tell me hard tales of your mistress which I shall not believe. They say she is idle and vain and pleasure-loving; they say she is hare-brained and reckless. The little sculptor on the ground floor, who was buying rolls from old Cabane, spoke to me to-night for the first time, although we have always bowed to each other. He said she was very good and very beautiful. He has only seen her once, and does not know her name. I thanked him;—I don't know why I thanked him so warmly. Cabane said, 'Into this cursed

Street of the Four Winds, the four winds blow all things evil.'The sculptor looked confused, but when he went out with his rolls, he said to me, 'I am sure, Monsieur, that she is as good as she is beautiful.'"

The cat had finished her toilet, and now, springing softly to the floor, went to the door and sniffed. He knelt beside her, and unclasping the garter held it for a moment in his hands. After a while he said: "There is a name engraved upon the silver clasp beneath the buckle. It is a pretty name, Sylvia Elven. Sylvia is a woman's name, Elven is the name of a town. In Paris, in this quarter, above all, in this Street of the Four Winds, names are worn and put away as the fashions change with the seasons. I know the little town of Elven, for there I met Fate face to face and Fate was unkind. But do you know that in Elven Fate had another name, and that name was Sylvia?"

He replaced the garter and stood up looking down at the cat crouched before the closed door.

"The name of Elven has a charm for me. It tells me of meadows and clear rivers. The name of Sylvia troubles me like perfume from dead flowers."

The cat mewed.

"Yes, yes," he said soothingly, "I will take you back. Your Sylvia is not my Sylvia; the world is wide and Elven is not unknown. Yet in the darkness and filth of poorer Paris, in the sad shadows of this ancient house, these names are very pleasant to me."

He lifted her in his arms and strode through the silent corridors to the stairs. Down five flights and into the moonlit court, past the little sculptor's den, and then again in at the gate of the north wing and up the worm-eaten stairs he passed, until he came to a closed door. When he had stood knocking for a long time, something moved behind the door; it opened and he went in. The room was dark. As he crossed the threshold, the cat sprang from his arms into the shadows. He listened but heard nothing. The silence was oppressive and he struck a match. At his elbow stood a table and on the table a candle in a gilded candlestick.

This he lighted, then looked around. The chamber was vast, the hangings heavy with embroidery. Over the fireplace towered a carved mantel, grey with the ashes of dead fires. In a recess by the deep-set windows stood a bed, from which the bedclothes, soft and fine as lace, trailed to the polished floor. He lifted the candle above his head. A handkerchief lay at his feet. It was faintly perfumed. He turned toward the windows. In front of them was a *canapé* and over it were flung, pell-mell, a gown of silk, a heap of lace-like garments, white and delicate as spiders' meshes, long, crumpled gloves, and, on the floor beneath, the stockings, the little pointed shoes, and one garter of rosy silk, quaintly flowered and fitted with a silver clasp. Wondering, he stepped forward and drew the heavy curtains from the bed. For a moment the candle flared in his hand; then his eyes met two other eyes, wide open, smiling, and the candle-flame flashed over hair heavy as gold.

She was pale, but not as white as he; her eyes were untroubled as a child's; but he stared, trembling from head to foot, while the candle flickered in his hand.

At last he whispered: "Sylvia, it is I."

Again he said, "It is I."

Then, knowing that she was dead, he kissed her on the mouth. And through the long watches of the night the cat purred on his knee, tightening and relaxing her padded claws, until the sky paled above the Street of the Four Winds.

THE STREET OF
THE FIRST SHELL

"Be of Good Cheer, the Sullen Month will die,
And a young Moon requite us by and by:
Look how the Old one, meagre, bent, and wan
With age and Fast, is fainting from the sky."

The room was already dark. The high roofs opposite cut off
what little remained of the December daylight. The girl drew
her chair nearer the window, and choosing a large needle,
threaded it, knotting the thread over her fingers. Then she
smoothed the baby garment across her knees, and bending, bit
off the thread and drew the smaller needle from where it rested
in the hem. When she had brushed away the stray threads and
bits of lace, she laid it again over her knees caressingly. Then she
slipped the threaded needle from her corsage and passed it
through a button, but as the button spun down the thread, her
hand faltered, the thread snapped, and the button rolled across
the floor. She raised her head. Her eyes were fixed on a strip of
waning light above the chimneys. From somewhere in the city
came sounds like the distant beating of drums, and beyond, far
beyond, a vague muttering, now growing, swelling, rumbling in
the distance like the pounding of surf upon the rocks, now like
the surf again, receding, growling, menacing. The cold had become
intense, a bitter piercing cold which strained and snapped at
joist and beam and turned the slush of yesterday to flint. From
the street below every sound broke sharp and metallic—the
clatter of sabots, the rattle of shutters or the rare sound of a
human voice. The air was heavy, weighted with the black cold
as with a pall. To breathe was painful, to move an effort.

In the desolate sky there was something that wearied, in the
brooding clouds, something that saddened. It penetrated the

freezing city cut by the freezing river, the splendid city with its towers and domes, its quays and bridges and its thousand spires. It entered the squares, it seized the avenues and the palaces, stole across bridges and crept among the narrow streets of the Latin Quarter, grey under the grey of the December sky. Sadness, utter sadness. A fine icy sleet was falling, powdering the pavement with a tiny crystalline dust. It sifted against the window-panes and drifted in heaps along the sill. The light at the window had nearly failed, and the girl bent low over her work. Presently she raised her head, brushing the curls from her eyes.

"Jack?"

"Dearest?"

"Don't forget to clean your palette."

He said, "All right," and picking up the palette, sat down upon the floor in front of the stove. His head and shoulders were in the shadow, but the firelight fell across his knees and glimmered red on the blade of the palette-knife. Full in the firelight beside him stood a colour-box. On the lid was carved,

J. TRENT.
École des Beaux Arts.
1870.

This inscription was ornamented with an American and a French flag.

The sleet blew against the window-panes, covering them with stars and diamonds, then, melting from the warmer air within, ran down and froze again in fern-like traceries.

A dog whined and the patter of small paws sounded on the zinc behind the stove.

"Jack, dear, do you think Hercules is hungry?"

The patter of paws was redoubled behind the stove.

"He's whining," she continued nervously, "and if it isn't because he's hungry it is because—"

Her voice faltered. A loud humming filled the air, the windows vibrated.

"Oh, Jack," she cried, "another—" but her voice was drowned in the scream of a shell tearing through the clouds overhead.

"That is the nearest yet," she murmured.

"Oh, no," he answered cheerfully, "it probably fell way over by Montmartre," and as she did not answer, he said again with exaggerated unconcern, "They wouldn't take the trouble to fire at the Latin Quarter; anyway they haven't a battery that can hurt it."

After a while she spoke up brightly: "Jack, dear, when are you going to take me to see Monsieur West's statues?"

"I will bet," he said, throwing down his palette and walking over to the window beside her, "that Colette has been here to-day."

"Why?" she asked, opening her eyes very wide. Then, "Oh, it's too bad!—really, men are tiresome when they think they know everything! And I warn you that if Monsieur West is vain enough to imagine that Colette—"

From the north another shell came whistling and quavering through the sky, passing above them with long-drawn screech which left the windows singing.

"That," he blurted out, "was too near for comfort."

They were silent for a while, then he spoke again gaily: "Go on, Sylvia, and wither poor West;" but she only sighed, "Oh, dear, I can never seem to get used to the shells."

He sat down on the arm of the chair beside her.

Her scissors fell jingling to the floor; she tossed the unfinished frock after them, and putting both arms about his neck drew him down into her lap.

"Don't go out to-night, Jack."

He kissed her uplifted face; "You know I must; don't make it hard for me."

"But when I hear the shells and—and know you are out in the city—"

"But they all fall in Montmartre—"

"They may all fall in the Beaux Arts; you said yourself that two struck the Quai d'Orsay—"

"Mere accident—"

"Jack, have pity on me! Take me with you!"

"And who will there be to get dinner?"

She rose and flung herself on the bed.

"Oh, I can't get used to it, and I know you must go, but I beg you not to be late to dinner. If you knew what I suffer! I—I—cannot help it, and you must be patient with me, dear."

He said, "It is as safe there as it is in our own house."

She watched him fill for her the alcohol lamp, and when he had lighted it and had taken his hat to go, she jumped up and clung to him in silence. After a moment he said: "Now, Sylvia, remember my courage is sustained by yours. Come, I must go!" She did not move, and he repeated: "I must go." Then she stepped back and he thought she was going to speak and waited, but she only looked at him, and, a little impatiently, he kissed her again, saying: "Don't worry, dearest."

When he had reached the last flight of stairs on his way to the street a woman hobbled out of the house-keeper's lodge waving a letter and calling: "Monsieur Jack! Monsieur Jack! this was left by Monsieur Fallowby!"

He took the letter, and leaning on the threshold of the lodge, read it:

"Dear Jack,

"I believe Braith is dead broke and I'm sure Fallowby is. Braith swears he isn't, and Fallowby swears he is, so you can draw your own conclusions. I've got a scheme for a dinner, and if it works, I will let you fellows in.

"Yours faithfully,
"WEST.

"P.S.—Fallowby has shaken Hartman and his gang, thank the Lord! There is something rotten there,—or it may be he's only a miser.

"P.P.S.—I'm more desperately in love than ever, but I'm
sure she does not care a straw for me."

"All right," said Trent, with a smile, to the concierge; "but tell me,
how is Papa Cottard?"

The old woman shook her head and pointed to the curtained
bed in the lodge.

"Père Cottard!" he cried cheerily, "how goes the wound to-day?"

He walked over to the bed and drew the curtains. An old
man was lying among the tumbled sheets.

"Better?" smiled Trent.

"Better," repeated the man wearily; and, after a pause, "Have
you any news, Monsieur Jack?"

"I haven't been out to-day. I will bring you any rumour I may
hear, though goodness knows I've got enough of rumours," he
muttered to himself. Then aloud: "Cheer up; you're looking better."

"And the sortie?"

"Oh, the sortie, that's for this week. General Trochu sent orders
last night."

"It will be terrible."

"It will be sickening," thought Trent as he went out into the
street and turned the corner toward the rue de Seine; "slaughter,
slaughter, phew! I'm glad I'm not going."

The street was almost deserted. A few women muffled in
tattered military capes crept along the frozen pavement, and a
wretchedly clad gamin hovered over the sewer-hole on the corner
of the Boulevard. A rope around his waist held his rags together.
From the rope hung a rat, still warm and bleeding.

"There's another in there," he yelled at Trent; "I hit him but
he got away."

Trent crossed the street and asked: "How much?"

"Two francs for a quarter of a fat one; that's what they give
at the St. Germain Market."

A violent fit of coughing interrupted him, but he wiped his
face with the palm of his hand and looked cunningly at Trent.

"Last week you could buy a rat for six francs, but," and here he swore vilely, "the rats have quit the rue de Seine and they kill them now over by the new hospital. I'll let you have this for seven francs; I can sell it for ten in the Isle St. Louis."

"You lie," said Trent, "and let me tell you that if you try to swindle anybody in this quarter the people will make short work of you and your rats."

He stood a moment eyeing the gamin, who pretended to snivel. Then he tossed him a franc, laughing. The child caught it, and thrusting it into his mouth wheeled about to the sewer-hole. For a second he crouched, motionless, alert, his eyes on the bars of the drain, then leaping forward he hurled a stone into the gutter, and Trent left him to finish a fierce grey rat that writhed squealing at the mouth of the sewer.

"Suppose Braith should come to that," he thought; "poor little chap;" and hurrying, he turned in the dirty passage des Beaux Arts and entered the third house to the left.

"Monsieur is at home," quavered the old concierge.

Home? A garret absolutely bare, save for the iron bedstead in the corner and the iron basin and pitcher on the floor.

West appeared at the door, winking with much mystery, and motioned Trent to enter. Braith, who was painting in bed to keep warm, looked up, laughed, and shook hands.

"Any news?"

The perfunctory question was answered as usual by: "Nothing but the cannon."

Trent sat down on the bed.

"Where on earth did you get that?" he demanded, pointing to a half-finished chicken nestling in a wash-basin.

West grinned.

"Are you millionaires, you two? Out with it."

Braith, looking a little ashamed, began, "Oh, it's one of West's exploits," but was cut short by West, who said he would tell the story himself.

"You see, before the siege, I had a letter of introduction to a '*type*' here, a fat banker, German-American variety. You know the species, I see. Well, of course I forgot to present the letter, but this morning, judging it to be a favourable opportunity, I called on him.

"The villain lives in comfort;—fires, my boy!—fires in the ante-rooms! The Buttons finally condescends to carry my letter and card up, leaving me standing in the hallway, which I did not like, so I entered the first room I saw and nearly fainted at the sight of a banquet on a table by the fire. Down comes Buttons, very insolent. No, oh, no, his master, 'is not at home, and in fact is too busy to receive letters of introduction just now; the siege, and many business difficulties—'

"I deliver a kick to Buttons, pick up this chicken from the table, toss my card on to the empty plate, and addressing Buttons as a species of Prussian pig, march out with the honours of war."

Trent shook his head.

"I forgot to say that Hartman often dines there, and I draw my own conclusions," continued West. "Now about this chicken, half of it is for Braith and myself, and half for Colette, but of course you will help me eat my part because I'm not hungry."

"Neither am I," began Braith, but Trent, with a smile at the pinched faces before him, shook his head saying, "What nonsense! You know I'm never hungry!"

West hesitated, reddened, and then slicing off Braith's portion, but not eating any himself, said good-night, and hurried away to number 470 rue Serpente, where lived a pretty girl named Colette, orphan after Sedan, and Heaven alone knew where she got the roses in her cheeks, for the siege came hard on the poor.

"That chicken will delight her, but I really believe she's in love with West," said Trent. Then walking over to the bed: "See here, old man, no dodging, you know, how much have you left?"

The other hesitated and flushed.

"Come, old chap," insisted Trent.

Braith drew a purse from beneath his bolster, and handed it to his friend with a simplicity that touched him.

"Seven sons," he counted; "you make me tired! Why on earth don't you come to me? I take it d——d ill, Braith! How many times must I go over the same thing and explain to you that because I have money it is my duty to share it, and your duty and the duty of every American to share it with me? You can't get a cent, the city's blockaded, and the American Minister has his hands full with all the German riff-raff and deuce knows what! Why don't you act sensibly?"

"I—I will, Trent, but it's an obligation that perhaps I can never even in part repay, I'm poor and—"

"Of course you'll pay me! If I were a usurer I would take your talent for security. When you are rich and famous—"

"Don't, Trent—"

"All right, only no more monkey business."

He slipped a dozen gold pieces into the purse, and tucking it again under the mattress smiled at Braith.

"How old are you?" he demanded.

"Sixteen."

Trent laid his hand lightly on his friend's shoulder. "I'm twenty-two, and I have the rights of a grandfather as far as you are concerned. You'll do as I say until you're twenty-one."

"The siège will be over then, I hope," said Braith, trying to laugh, but the prayer in their hearts: "How long, O Lord, how long!" was answered by the swift scream of a shell soaring among the storm-clouds of that December night.

II

West, standing in the doorway of a house in the rue Serpentine, was speaking angrily. He said he didn't care whether Hartman liked it or not; he was telling him, not arguing with him.

"You call yourself an American!" he sneered; "Berlin and hell are full of that kind of American. You come loafing about Colette with your pockets stuffed with white bread and beef, and a bottle of wine at thirty francs and you can't really afford to give a dollar to the American Ambulance and Public Assistance, which Braith does, and he's half starved!"

Hartman retreated to the curbstone, but West followed him, his face like a thunder-cloud. "Don't you dare to call yourself a countryman of mine," he growled,—"no,—nor an artist either! Artists don't worm themselves into the service of the Public Defence where they do nothing but feed like rats on the people's food! And I'll tell you now," he continued dropping his voice, for Hartman had started as though stung, "you might better keep away from that Alsatian Brasserie and the smug-faced thieves who haunt it. You know what they do with suspects!"

"You lie, you hound!" screamed Hartman, and flung the bottle in his hand straight at West's face. West had him by the throat in a second, and forcing him against the dead wall shook him wickedly.

"Now you listen to me," he muttered, through his clenched teeth. "You are already a suspect and—I swear—I believe you are a paid spy! It isn't my business to detect such vermin, and I don't intend to denounce you, but understand this! Colette don't like you and I can't stand you, and if I catch you in this street again I'll make it somewhat unpleasant. Get out, you sleek Prussian!"

Hartman had managed to drag a knife from his pocket, but West tore it from him and hurled him into the gutter. A gamin who had seen this burst into a peal of laughter, which rattled harshly in the silent street. Then everywhere windows were raised and rows of haggard faces appeared demanding to know why people should laugh in the starving city.

"Is it a victory?" murmured one.

"Look at that," cried West as Hartman picked himself up from the pavement, "look! you miser! look at those faces!" But Hartman gave *him* a look which he never forgot, and walked away without a word. Trent, who suddenly appeared at the corner, glanced curiously at West, who merely nodded toward his door saying, "Come in; Fallowby's upstairs."

"What are you doing with that knife?" demanded Fallowby, as he and Trent entered the studio.

West looked at his wounded hand, which still clutched the knife, but saying, "Cut myself by accident," tossed it into a corner and washed the blood from his fingers.

Fallowby, fat and lazy, watched him without comment, but Trent, half divining how things had turned, walked over to Fallowby smiling.

"I've a bone to pick with you!" he said.

"Where is it? I'm hungry," replied Fallowby with affected eagerness, but Trent, frowning, told him to listen.

"How much did I advance you a week ago?"

"Three hundred and eighty francs," replied the other, with a squirm of contrition.

"Where is it?"

Fallowby began a series of intricate explanations, which were soon cut short by Trent.

"I know; you blew it in;—you always blow it in. I don't care a rap what you did before the siege: I know you are rich and have a right to dispose of your money as you wish to, and I also know that, generally speaking, it is none of my business. But *now* it is my business, as I have to supply the funds until you get some more, which you won't until the siege is ended one way or another. I wish to share what I have, but I won't see it thrown out of the window. Oh, yes, of course I know you will reimburse me, but that isn't the question; and, anyway, it's the opinion of your friends, old man, that you will not be worse off for a little abstinence from fleshly pleasures. You are positively a freak in this famine-cursed city of skeletons!"

"I *am* rather stout," he admitted.

"Is it true you are out of money?" demanded Trent.

"Yes, I am," sighed the other.

"That roast sucking pig on the rue St. Honoré,—is it there yet?" continued Trent.

"Wh—at?" stammered the feeble one.

"Ah—I thought so! I caught you in ecstasy before that sucking pig at least a dozen times!"

Then laughing, he presented Fallowby with a roll of twenty franc pieces saying: "If these go for luxuries you must live on your own flesh," and went over to aid West, who sat beside the wash-basin binding up his hand.

West suffered him to tie the knot, and then said: "You remember, yesterday, when I left you and Braith to take the chicken to Colette."

"Chicken! Good heavens!" moaned Fallowby.

"Chicken," repeated West, enjoying Fallowby's grief;—"I—that is, I must explain that things are changed. Colette and I—are to be married—"

"What—what about the chicken?" groaned Fallowby.

"Shut up!" laughed Trent, and slipping his arm through West's, walked to the stairway.

"The poor little thing," said West, "just think, not a splinter of firewood for a week and wouldn't tell me because she thought I needed it for my clay figure. Whew! When I heard it I smashed that smirking clay nymph to pieces, and the rest can freeze and be hanged!" After a moment he added timidly: "Won't you call on your way down and say *bon soir*? It's No. 17."

"Yes," said Trent, and he went out softly closing the door behind.

He stopped on the third landing, lighted a match, scanned the numbers over the row of dingy doors, and knocked at No. 17.

"C'est toi Georges?" The door opened.

"Oh, pardon, Monsieur Jack, I thought it was Monsieur West," then blushing furiously, "Oh, I see you have heard! Oh, thank you so much for your wishes, and I'm sure we love each other very much,—and I'm dying to see Sylvia and tell her and—"

"And what?" laughed Trent.

"I am very happy," she sighed.

"He's pure gold," returned Trent, and then gaily: "I want you and George to come and dine with us to-night. It's a little treat,—

you see to-morrow is Sylvia's *fête*. She will be nineteen. I have written to Thorne, and the Guernalecs will come with their cousin Odile. Fallowby has engaged not to bring anybody but himself."

The girl accepted shyly, charging him with loads of loving messages to Sylvia, and he said good-night.

He started up the street, walking swiftly, for it was bitter cold, and cutting across the rue de la Lune he entered the rue de Seine. The early winter night had fallen, almost without warning, but the sky was clear and myriads of stars glittered in the heavens. The bombardment had become furious—a steady rolling thunder from the Prussian cannon punctuated by the heavy shocks from Mont Valérien.

The shells streamed across the sky leaving trails like shooting stars, and now, as he turned to look back, rockets blue and red flared above the horizon from the Fort of Issy, and the Fortress of the North flamed like a bonfire.

"Good news!" a man shouted over by the Boulevard St. Germain. As if by magic the streets were filled with people,—shivering, chattering people with shrunken eyes.

"Jacques!" cried one. "The Army of the Loire!"

"Eh! *mon vieux*, it has come then at last! I told thee! I told thee! To-morrow—to-night—who knows?"

"Is it true? Is it a sortie?"

Some one said: "Oh, God—a sortie—and my son?" Another cried: "To the Seine? They say one can see the signals of the Army of the Loire from the Pont Neuf."

There was a child standing near Trent who kept repeating: "Mamma, Mamma, then to-morrow we may eat white bread?" and beside him, an old man swaying, stumbling, his shrivelled hands crushed to his breast, muttering as if insane.

"Could it be true? Who has heard the news? The shoemaker on the rue de Buci had it from a Mobile who had heard a Franctireur repeat it to a captain of the National Guard."

Trent followed the throng surging through the rue de Seine to the river.

Rocket after rocket clove the sky, and now, from Montmartre, the cannon clanged, and the batteries on Montparnasse joined in with a crash. The bridge was packed with people.

Trent asked: "Who has seen the signals of the Army of the Loire?"

"We are waiting for them," was the reply.

He looked toward the north. Suddenly the huge silhouette of the Arc de Triomphe sprang into black relief against the flash of a cannon. The boom of the gun rolled along the quay and the old bridge vibrated.

Again over by the Point du Jour a flash and heavy explosion shook the bridge, and then the whole eastern bastion of the fortifications blazed and crackled, sending a red flame into the sky.

"Has any one seen the signals yet?" he asked again.

"We are waiting," was the reply.

"Yes, waiting," murmured a man behind him, "waiting, sick, starved, freezing, but waiting. Is it a sortie? They go gladly. Is it to starve? They starve. They have no time to think of surrender. Are they heroes,—these Parisians? Answer me, Trent!"

The American Ambulance surgeon turned about and scanned the parapets of the bridge.

"Any news, Doctor," asked Trent mechanically.

"News?" said the doctor; "I don't know any;—I haven't time to know any. What are these people after?"

"They say that the Army of the Loire has signalled Mont Valérien."

"Poor devils." The doctor glanced about him for an instant, and then: "I'm so harried and worried that I don't know what to do. After the last sortie we had the work of fifty ambulances on our poor little corps. To-morrow there's another sortie, and I wish you fellows could come over to headquarters. We may need volunteers. How is madame?" he added abruptly.

"Well," replied Trent, "but she seems to grow more nervous every day. I ought to be with her now."

"Take care of her," said the doctor, then with a sharp look at the people: "I can't stop now—good-night!" and he hurried away muttering, "Poor devils!"

Trent leaned over the parapet and blinked at the black river surging through the arches. Dark objects, carried swiftly on the breast of the current, struck with a grinding tearing noise against the stone piers, spun around for an instant, and hurried away into the darkness. The ice from the Marne.

As he stood staring into the water, a hand was laid on his shoulder. "Hello, Southwark!" he cried, turning around; "this is a queer place for you!"

"Trent, I have something to tell you. Don't stay here,—don't believe in the Army of the Loire:" and the *attaché* of the American Legation slipped his arm through Trent's and drew him toward the Louvre.

"Then it's another lie!" said Trent bitterly.

"Worse—we know at the Legation—I can't speak of it. But that's not what I have to say. Something happened this afternoon. The Alsatian Brasserie was visited and an American named Hartman has been arrested. Do you know him?"

"I know a German who calls himself an American;—his name is Hartman."

"Well, he was arrested about two hours ago. They mean to shoot him."

"What!"

"Of course we at the Legation can't allow them to shoot him off-hand, but the evidence seems conclusive."

"Is he a spy?"

"Well, the papers seized in his rooms are pretty damning proofs, and besides he was caught, they say, swindling the Public Food Committee. He drew rations for fifty, how, I don't know. He claims to be an American artist here, and we have been obliged to take notice of it at the Legation. It's a nasty affair."

"To cheat the people at such a time is worse than robbing the poor-box," cried Trent angrily. "Let them shoot him!"

"He's an American citizen."

"Yes, oh yes," said the other with bitterness. "American citizenship is a precious privilege when every goggle-eyed German—" His anger choked him.

Southwark shook hands with him warmly. "It can't be helped, we must own the carrion. I am afraid you may be called upon to identify him as an American artist," he said with a ghost of a smile on his deep-lined face; and walked away through the Cours la Reine.

Trent swore silently for a moment and then drew out his watch. Seven o'clock. "Sylvia will be anxious," he thought, and hurried back to the river. The crowd still huddled shivering on the bridge, a sombre pitiful congregation, peering out into the night for the signals of the Army of the Loire: and their hearts beat time to the pounding of the guns, their eyes lighted with each flash from the bastions, and hope rose with the drifting rockets.

A black cloud hung over the fortifications. From horizon to horizon the cannon smoke stretched in wavering bands, now capping the spires and domes with cloud, now blowing in streamers and shreds along the streets, now descending from the housetops, enveloping quays, bridges, and river, in a sulphurous mist. And through the smoke pall the lightning of the cannon played, while from time to time a rift above showed a fathomless black vault set with stars.

He turned again into the rue de Seine, that sad abandoned street, with its rows of closed shutters and desolate ranks of unlighted lamps. He was a little nervous and wished once or twice for a revolver, but the slinking forms which passed him in the darkness were too weak with hunger to be dangerous, he thought, and he passed on unmolested to his doorway. But there somebody sprang at his throat. Over and over the icy pavement he rolled with his assailant, tearing at the noose about his neck, and then with a wrench sprang to his feet.

"Get up," he cried to the other.

Slowly and with great deliberation, a small gamin picked himself out of the gutter and surveyed Trent with disgust.

"That's a nice clean trick," said Trent; "a whelp of your age! You'll finish against a dead wall! Give me that cord!"

The urchin handed him the noose without a word.

Trent struck a match and looked at his assailant. It was the rat-killer of the day before.

"H'm! I thought so," he muttered.

"Tiens, c'est toi?" said the gamin tranquilly.

The impudence, the overpowering audacity of the ragamuffin took Trent's breath away.

"Do you know, you young strangler," he gasped, "that they shoot thieves of your age?"

The child turned a passionless face to Trent. "Shoot, then."

That was too much, and he turned on his heel and entered his hotel.

Groping up the unlighted stairway, he at last reached his own landing and felt about in the darkness for the door. From his studio came the sound of voices, West's hearty laugh and Fallowby's chuckle, and at last he found the knob and, pushing back the door, stood a moment confused by the light.

"Hello, Jack!" cried West, "you're a pleasant creature, inviting people to dine and letting them wait. Here's Fallowby weeping with hunger—"

"Shut up," observed the latter, "perhaps he's been out to buy a turkey."

"He's been out garroting, look at his noose!" laughed Guernalec.

"So now we know where you get your cash!" added West; "vive le coup du Père François!"

Trent shook hands with everybody and laughed at Sylvia's pale face.

"I didn't mean to be late; I stopped on the bridge a moment to watch the bombardment. Were you anxious, Sylvia?"

She smiled and murmured, "Oh, no!" but her hand dropped

into his and tightened convulsively.

"To the table!" shouted Fallowby, and uttered a joyous whoop.

"Take it easy," observed Thorne, with a remnant of manners; "you are not the host, you know."

Marie Guernalec, who had been chattering with Colette, jumped up and took Thorne's arm and Monsieur Guernalec drew Odile's arm through his.

Trent, bowing gravely, offered his own arm to Colette, West took in Sylvia, and Fallowby hovered anxiously in the rear.

"You march around the table three times singing the Marseillaise," explained Sylvia, "and Monsieur Fallowby pounds on the table and beats time."

Fallowby suggested that they could sing after dinner, but his protest was drowned in the ringing chorus—

> "Aux armes!
> Formez vos bataillons!"

Around the room they marched singing,

> "Marchons! Marchons!"

with all their might, while Fallowby with very bad grace, hammered on the table, consoling himself a little with the hope that the exercise would increase his appetite. Hercules, the black and tan, fled under the bed, from which retreat he yapped and whined until dragged out by Guernalec and placed in Odile's lap.

"And now," said Trent gravely, when everybody was seated, "listen!" and he read the menu.

> Beef Soup à la Siège de Paris.
> —
> Fish.
> Sardines à la père Lachaise.
> (White Wine).
> —
> Rôti (Red Wine).

Fresh Beef à la sortie.

—

Vegetables.
Canned Beans à la chasse-pot,
Canned Peas Gravelotte,
Potatoes Irlandaises,
Miscellaneous.

—

Cold Corned Beef à la Thieis,
Stewed Prunes à la Garibaldi.

—

Dessert.
Dried prunes—White bread,
Currant Jelly,
Tea—Café,
Liqueurs,
Pipes and Cigarettes.

Fallowby applauded frantically, and Sylvia served the soup.

"Isn't it delicious?" sighed Odile.

Marie Guernalec sipped her soup in rapture.

"Not at all like horse, and I don't care what they say, horse doesn't taste like beef," whispered Colette to West. Fallowby, who had finished, began to caress his chin and eye the tureen.

"Have some more, old chap?" inquired Trent.

"Monsieur Fallowby cannot have any more," announced Sylvia; "I am saving this for the concierge." Fallowby transferred his eyes to the fish.

The sardines, hot from the grille, were a great success. While the others were eating Sylvia ran downstairs with the soup for the old concierge and her husband, and when she hurried back, flushed and breathless, and had slipped into her chair with a happy smile at Trent, that young man arose, and silence fell over the table. For an instant he looked at Sylvia and thought he had never seen her so beautiful.

"You all know," he began, "that to-day is my wife's nineteenth birthday—"

Fallowby, bubbling with enthusiasm, waved his glass in circles about his head to the terror of Odile and Colette, his neighbours, and Thorne, West and Guernalec refilled their glasses three times before the storm of applause which the toast of Sylvia had provoked, subsided.

Three times the glasses were filled and emptied to Sylvia, and again to Trent, who protested.

"This is irregular," he cried, "the next toast is to the twin Republics, France and America?"

"To the Republics! To the Republics!" they cried, and the toast was drunk amid shouts of "Vive la France! Vive l'Amérique! Vive la Nation!"

Then Trent, with a smile at West, offered the toast, "To a Happy Pair!" and everybody understood, and Sylvia leaned over and kissed Colette, while Trent bowed to West.

The beef was eaten in comparative calm, but when it was finished and a portion of it set aside for the old people below, Trent cried: "Drink to Paris! May she rise from her ruins and crush the invader!" and the cheers rang out, drowning for a moment the monotonous thunder of the Prussian guns.

Pipes and cigarettes were lighted, and Trent listened an instant to the animated chatter around him, broken by ripples of laughter from the girls or the mellow chuckle of Fallowby. Then he turned to West.

"There is going to be a sortie to-night," he said. "I saw the American Ambulance surgeon just before I came in and he asked me to speak to you fellows. Any aid we can give him will not come amiss."

Then dropping his voice and speaking in English, "As for me, I shall go out with the ambulance to-morrow morning. There is of course no danger, but it's just as well to keep it from Sylvia."

West nodded. Thorne and Guernalec, who had heard, broke in and offered assistance, and Fallowby volunteered with a groan.

"All right," said Trent rapidly,—"no more now, but meet me at Ambulance headquarters to-morrow morning at eight."

Sylvia and Colette, who were becoming uneasy at the conversation in English, now demanded to know what they were talking about.

"What does a sculptor usually talk about?" cried West, with a laugh.

Odile glanced reproachfully at Thorne, her *fiancé*.

"You are not French, you know, and it is none of your business, this war," said Odile with much dignity.

Thorne looked meek, but West assumed an air of outraged virtue.

"It seems," he said to Fallowby, "that a fellow cannot discuss the beauties of Greek sculpture in his mother tongue, without being openly suspected."

Colette placed her hand over his mouth and turning to Sylvia, murmured, "They are horridly untruthful, these men."

"I believe the word for ambulance is the same in both languages," said Marie Guernalec saucily; "Sylvia, don't trust Monsieur Trent."

"Jack," whispered Sylvia, "promise me—"

A knock at the studio door interrupted her.

"Come in!" cried Fallowby, but Trent sprang up, and opening the door, looked out. Then with a hasty excuse to the rest, he stepped into the hallway and closed the door.

When he returned he was grumbling.

"What is it, Jack?" cried West.

"What is it?" repeated Trent savagely; "I'll tell you what it is. I have received a dispatch from the American Minister to go at once and identify and claim, as a fellow-countryman and a brother artist, a rascally thief and a German spy!"

"Don't go," suggested Fallowby.

"If I don't they'll shoot him at once."

"Let them," growled Thorne.

"Do you fellows know who it is?"

"Hartman!" shouted West, inspired.

Sylvia sprang up deathly white, but Odile slipped her arm around her and supported her to a chair, saying calmly, "Sylvia has fainted,—it's the hot room,—bring some water."

Trent brought it at once.

Sylvia opened her eyes, and after a moment rose, and supported by Marie Guernalec and Trent, passed into the bedroom.

It was the signal for breaking up, and everybody came and shook hands with Trent, saying they hoped Sylvia would sleep it off and that it would be nothing.

When Marie Guernalec took leave of him, she avoided his eyes, but he spoke to her cordially and thanked her for her aid.

"Anything I can do, Jack?" inquired West, lingering, and then hurried downstairs to catch up with the rest.

Trent leaned over the banisters, listening to their footsteps and chatter, and then the lower door banged and the house was silent. He lingered, staring down into the blackness, biting his lips; then with an impatient movement, "I am crazy!" he muttered, and lighting a candle, went into the bedroom. Sylvia was lying on the bed. He bent over her, smoothing the curly hair on her forehead.

"Are you better, dear Sylvia?"

She did not answer, but raised her eyes to his. For an instant he met her gaze, but what he read there sent a chill to his heart and he sat down covering his face with his hands.

At last she spoke in a voice, changed and strained,—a voice which he had never heard, and he dropped his hands and listened, bolt upright in his chair.

"Jack, it has come at last. I have feared it and trembled,—ah! how often have I lain awake at night with this on my heart and prayed that I might die before you should ever know of it! For I love you, Jack, and if you go away I cannot live. I have deceived you;—it happened before I knew you, but since that first day when you found me weeping in the Luxembourg and spoke to me, Jack, I have been faithful to you in every thought and deed. I loved you from the first, and did not dare to tell you this—fearing that you would go away; and since then my love has grown—grown—and oh! I suffered!—but I dared not tell you. And now you know, but you do not know the worst. For him—now—what do I care? He was cruel—oh, so cruel!"

She hid her face in her arms.

"Must I go on? Must I tell you—can you not imagine, oh! Jack—"

He did not stir; his eyes seemed dead.

"I—I was so young, I knew nothing, and he said—said that he loved me—"

Trent rose and struck the candle with his clenched fist, and the room was dark.

The bells of St. Sulpice tolled the hour, and she started up, speaking with feverish haste,—"I must finish! When you told me you loved me—you—you asked me nothing; but then, even then, it was too late, and *that other life* which binds me to him, must stand for ever between you and me! For there *is another* whom he has claimed, and is good to. He must not die,—they cannot shoot him, for that *other's* sake!"

Trent sat motionless, but his thoughts ran on in an interminable whirl.

Sylvia, little Sylvia, who shared with him his student life,—who bore with him the dreary desolation of the siege without complaint,—this slender blue-eyed girl whom he was so quietly fond of, whom he teased or caressed as the whim suited, who sometimes made him the least bit impatient with her passionate devotion to him,—could this be the same Sylvia who lay weeping there in the darkness?

Then he clinched his teeth. "Let him die! Let him die!"—but then,—for Sylvia's sake, and,—for that *other's* sake,—Yes, he would go,—he *must* go,—his duty was plain before him. But Sylvia,—he could not be what he had been to her, and yet a vague terror seized him, now all was said. Trembling, he struck a light.

She lay there, her curly hair tumbled about her face, her small white hands pressed to her breast.

He could not leave her, and he could not stay. He never knew before that he loved her. She had been a mere comrade, this girl wife of his. Ah! he loved her now with all his heart and soul, and he knew it, only when it was too late. Too late? Why? Then he thought of that *other* one, binding her, linking her forever to the creature, who stood in danger of his life. With an oath he sprang to the door, but the door would not open,—or was it that he pressed it back,—locked it,—and flung himself on his knees beside the bed, knowing that he dared not for his life's sake leave what was his all in life.

III

It was four in the morning when he came out of the Prison of the Condemned with the Secretary of the American Legation. A knot of people had gathered around the American Minister's carriage, which stood in front of the prison, the horses stamping and pawing in the icy street, the coachman huddled on the box, wrapped in furs. Southwark helped the Secretary into the carriage, and shook hands with Trent, thanking him for coming.

"How the scoundrel did stare," he said; "your evidence was worse than a kick, but it saved his skin for the moment at least,—and prevented complications."

The Secretary sighed. "We have done our part. Now let them prove him a spy and we wash our hands of him. Jump in, Captain! Come along, Trent!"

"I have a word to say to Captain Southwark, I won't detain him," said Trent hastily, and dropping his voice, "Southwark, help *me* now. You know the story from the blackguard. You know the—the child is at his rooms. Get it, and take it to my own apartment, and if he is shot, I will provide a home for it."

"I understand," said the Captain gravely.

"Will you do this at once?"

"At once," he replied.

Their hands met in a warm clasp, and then Captain Southwark climbed into the carriage, motioning Trent to follow; but he shook his head saying, "Good-bye!" and the carriage rolled away.

He watched the carriage to the end of the street, then started toward his own quarter, but after a step or two hesitated, stopped, and finally turned away in the opposite direction. Something—perhaps it was the sight of the prisoner he had so recently confronted nauseated him. He felt the need of solitude and quiet to collect his thoughts. The events of the evening had shaken him terribly, but he would walk it off, forget, bury everything, and then go back to Sylvia. He started on swiftly, and for a time the bitter thoughts seemed to fade, but when he paused at last, breathless, under the Arc de Triomphe, the bitterness and the wretchedness of the whole thing—yes, of his whole misspent life came back with a pang. Then the face of the prisoner, stamped with the horrible grimace of fear, grew in the shadows before his eyes.

Sick at heart he wandered up and down under the great Arc, striving to occupy his mind, peering up at the sculptured cornices to read the names of the heroes and battles which he knew were engraved there, but always the ashen face of Hartman followed him, grinning with terror!—or was it terror?—was it not triumph?—At the thought he leaped like a man who feels a knife at his throat, but after a savage tramp around the square, came back again and sat down to battle with his misery.

The air was cold, but his cheeks were burning with angry shame. Shame? Why? Was it because he had married a girl whom chance had made a mother? *Did* he love her? Was this miserable bohemian existence, then, his end and aim in life? He turned his eyes upon the secrets of his heart, and read an evil story,—the story of the past, and he covered his face for shame, while, keeping time to the dull pain throbbing in his head, his heart beat out the story for the future. Shame and disgrace.

Roused at last from a lethargy which had begun to numb the bitterness of his thoughts, he raised his head and looked about. A sudden fog had settled in the streets; the arches of the Arc were choked with it. He would go home. A great horror of being alone seized him. *But he was not alone.* The fog was peopled with phantoms. All around him in the mist they moved, drifting through the arches in lengthening lines, and vanished, while from the fog others rose up, swept past and were engulfed. He was not alone, for even at his side they crowded, touched him, swarmed before him, beside him, behind him, pressed him back, seized, and bore him with them through the mist. Down a dim avenue, through lanes and alleys white with fog, they moved, and if they spoke their voices were dull as the vapour which shrouded them. At last in front, a bank of masonry and earth cut by a massive iron barred gate towered up in the fog. Slowly and more slowly they glided, shoulder to shoulder and thigh to thigh. Then all movement ceased. A sudden breeze stirred the fog. It wavered and eddied. Objects became more distinct. A pallor crept above the horizon, touching the edges of the watery clouds, and drew dull sparks from a thousand bayonets. Bayonets—they were everywhere, cleaving the fog or flowing beneath it in rivers of steel. High on the wall of masonry and earth a great gun loomed, and around it figures moved in silhouettes. Below, a broad torrent of bayonets swept through the iron barred gateway, out into the shadowy plain. It became lighter. Faces grew more distinct among the marching masses and he recognized one.

"You, Philippe!"

The figure turned its head.

Trent cried, "Is there room for me?" but the other only waved his arm in a vague adieu and was gone with the rest. Presently the cavalry began to pass, squadron on squadron, crowding out into the darkness; then many cannon, then an ambulance, then again the endless lines of bayonets. Beside him a cuirassier sat on his steaming horse, and in front, among a group of mounted officers he saw a general, with the astrakan collar of his dolman turned up about his bloodless face.

Some women were weeping near him and one was struggling to force a loaf of black bread into a soldier's haversack. The soldier tried to aid her, but the sack was fastened, and his rifle bothered him, so Trent held it, while the woman unbuttoned the sack and forced in the bread, now all wet with her tears. The rifle was not heavy. Trent found it wonderfully manageable. Was the bayonet sharp? He tried it. Then a sudden longing, a fierce, imperative desire took possession of him.

"*Chouette!*" cried a gamin, clinging to the barred gate, "*encore toi mon vieux*?"

Trent looked up, and the rat-killer laughed in his face. But when the soldier had taken the rifle again, and thanking him, ran hard to catch his battalion, he plunged into the throng about the gateway.

"Are you going?" he cried to a marine who sat in the gutter bandaging his foot.

"Yes."

Then a girl—a mere child—caught him by the hand and led him into the café which faced the gate. The room was crowded with soldiers, some, white and silent, sitting on the floor, others groaning on the leather-covered settees. The air was sour and suffocating.

"Choose!" said the girl with a little gesture of pity; "they can't go!"

In a heap of clothing on the floor he found a capote and képi.

She helped him buckle his knapsack, cartridge-box, and belt, and showed him how to load the chasse-pot rifle, holding it on her knees.

When he thanked her she started to her feet.

"You are a foreigner!"

"American," he said, moving toward the door, but the child barred his way.

"I am a Bretonne. My father is up there with the cannon of the marine. He will shoot you if you are a spy."

They faced each other for a moment. Then sighing, he bent over and kissed the child. "Pray for France, little one," he murmured, and she repeated with a pale smile: "For France and you, beau Monsieur."

He ran across the street and through the gateway. Once outside, he edged into line and shouldered his way along the road. A corporal passed, looked at him, repassed, and finally called an officer. "You belong to the 60th," growled the corporal looking at the number on his képi.

"We have no use for Franc-tireurs," added the officer, catching sight of his black trousers.

"I wish to volunteer in place of a comrade," said Trent, and the officer shrugged his shoulders and passed on.

Nobody paid much attention to him, one or two merely glancing at his trousers. The road was deep with slush and mud-ploughed and torn by wheels and hoofs. A soldier in front of him wrenched his foot in an icy rut and dragged himself to the edge of the embankment groaning. The plain on either side of them was grey with melting snow. Here and there behind dismantled hedge-rows stood wagons, bearing white flags with red crosses. Sometimes the driver was a priest in rusty hat and gown, sometimes a crippled Mobile. Once they passed a wagon driven by a Sister of Charity. Silent empty houses with great rents in their walls, and every window blank, huddled along the road. Further on, within the zone of danger, nothing of human habitation remained except here and there a pile of frozen bricks or a blackened cellar choked with snow.

For some time Trent had been annoyed by the man behind him, who kept treading on his heels. Convinced at last that it was intentional, he turned to remonstrate and found himself face to face with a fellow-student from the Beaux Arts. Trent stared.

"I thought you were in the hospital!"

The other shook his head, pointing to his bandaged jaw.

"I see, you can't speak. Can I do anything?"

The wounded man rummaged in his haversack and produced a crust of black bread.

"He can't eat it, his jaw is smashed, and he wants you to chew it for him," said the soldier next to him.

Trent took the crust, and grinding it in his teeth morsel by morsel, passed it back to the starving man.

From time to time mounted orderlies sped to the front, covering them with slush. It was a chilly, silent march through sodden meadows wreathed in fog. Along the railroad embankment across the ditch, another column moved parallel to their own. Trent watched it, a somber mass, now distinct, now vague, now blotted out in a puff of fog. Once for half-an-hour he lost it, but when again it came into view, he noticed a thin line detach itself from the flank, and, bellying in the middle, swing rapidly to the west. At the same moment a prolonged crackling broke out in the fog in front. Other lines began to slough off from the column, swinging east and west, and the crackling became continuous. A battery passed at full gallop, and he drew back with his comrades to give it way. It went into action a little to the right of his battalion, and as the shot from the first rifled piece boomed through the mist, the cannon from the fortifications opened with a mighty roar. An officer galloped by shouting something which Trent did not catch, but he saw the ranks in front suddenly part company with his own, and disappear in the twilight. More officers rode up and stood beside him peering into the fog. Away in front the crackling had become one prolonged crash. It was dreary waiting. Trent chewed some bread for the man behind, who tried to swallow it, and after a while shook his head, motioning Trent to eat the rest himself. A corporal offered him a little brandy and he drank it, but when he turned around to return the flask, the corporal was lying on the ground. Alarmed, he looked at the soldier next to him, who shrugged his shoulders and opened his mouth to speak, but something struck him and he rolled over and over into the ditch below. At that moment the horse of one of the officers gave a bound and backed into the battalion, lashing out with his heels. One man was ridden down; another was kicked in the chest and hurled through the ranks. The officer sank his spurs into the horse and forced him to the front again, where he stood trembling. The cannonade seemed to draw nearer. A staff-officer, riding slowly up and down the battalion suddenly collapsed in his saddle and clung to his horse's mane. One of his boots dangled, crimsoned and dripping, from the stirrup. Then out of the mist in front men came running. The roads, the fields, the ditches were full of them, and many of them fell. For an instant he imagined he saw horsemen riding about like ghosts in the vapours beyond, and a man behind him cursed horribly, declaring he too had seen them, and that they were Uhlans; but the battalion stood inactive, and the mist fell again over the meadows.

The colonel sat heavily upon his horse, his bullet-shaped head buried in the astrakan collar of his dolman, his fat legs sticking straight out in the stirrups.

The buglers clustered about him with bugles poised, and behind him a staff-officer in a pale blue jacket smoked a cigarette and chatted with a captain of hussars. From the road in front came the sound of furious galloping and an orderly reined up beside the colonel, who motioned him to the rear without turning his head. Then on the left a confused murmur arose which ended in a shout. A hussar passed like the wind, followed by another and another, and then squadron after squadron whirled by them into the sheeted mists. At that instant the colonel reared in his saddle, the bugles clanged, and the whole battalion scrambled down the embankment, over the ditch and started across the soggy meadow. Almost at once Trent lost his cap. Something snatched it from his head, he thought it was a tree branch. A good many of his comrades rolled over in the slush and ice, and he imagined that they had slipped. One pitched right across his path and he stopped to help him up, but the man screamed when he touched him and an officer shouted, "Forward! Forward!"

so he ran on again. It was a long jog through the mist, and he was often obliged to shift his rifle. When at last they lay panting behind the railroad embankment, he looked about him. He had felt the need of action, of a desperate physical struggle, of killing and crushing. He had been seized with a desire to fling himself among masses and tear right and left. He longed to fire, to use the thin sharp bayonet on his chasse-pot. He had not expected this. He wished to become exhausted, to struggle and cut until incapable of lifting his arm. Then he had intended to go home. He heard a man say that half the battalion had gone down in the charge, and he saw another examining a corpse under the embankment. The body, still warm, was clothed in a strange uniform, but even when he noticed the spiked helmet lying a few inches further away, he did not realize what had happened.

The colonel sat on his horse a few feet to the left, his eyes sparkling under the crimson képi. Trent heard him reply to an officer: "I can hold it, but another charge, and I won't have enough men left to sound a bugle."

"Were the Prussians here?" Trent asked of a soldier who sat wiping the blood trickling from his hair.

"Yes. The hussars cleaned them out. We caught their cross fire."

"We are supporting a battery on the embankment," said another.

Then the battalion crawled over the embankment and moved along the lines of twisted rails. Trent rolled up his trousers and tucked them into his woollen socks: but they halted again, and some of the men sat down on the dismantled railroad track. Trent looked for his wounded comrade from the Beaux Arts. He was standing in his place, very pale. The cannonade had become terrific. For a moment the mist lifted. He caught a glimpse of the first battalion motionless on the railroad track in front, of regiments on either flank, and then, as the fog settled again, the drums beat and the music of the bugles began away on the extreme left. A restless movement passed among the troops, the colonel threw up his arm, the drums rolled, and the

battalion moved off through the fog. They were near the front
now for the battalion was firing as it advanced. Ambulances
galloped along the base of the embankment to the rear, and
the hussars passed and repassed like phantoms. They were in
the front at last, for all about them was movement and turmoil,
while from the fog, close at hand, came cries and groans and
crashing volleys. Shells fell everywhere, bursting along the
embankment, splashing them with frozen slush. Trent was frightened. He began to dread the unknown, which lay there
crackling and flaming in obscurity. The shock of the cannon
sickened him. He could even see the fog light up with a dull
orange as the thunder shook the earth. It was near, he felt
certain, for the colonel shouted "Forward!" and the first battalion
was hastening into it. He felt its breath, he trembled, but hurried
on. A fearful discharge in front terrified him. Somewhere in the
fog men were cheering, and the colonel's horse, streaming with
blood plunged about in the smoke.

Another blast and shock, right in his face, almost stunned
him, and he faltered. All the men to the right were down. His
head swam; the fog and smoke stupefied him. He put out his
hand for a support and caught something. It was the wheel of
a gun-carriage, and a man sprang from behind it, aiming a blow
at his head with a rammer, but stumbled back shrieking with a
bayonet through his neck, and Trent knew that he had killed.
Mechanically he stooped to pick up his rifle, but the bayonet
was still in the man, who lay, beating with red hands against the
sod. It sickened him and he leaned on the cannon. Men were
fighting all around him now, and the air was foul with smoke
and sweat. Somebody seized him from behind and another in
front, but others in turn seized them or struck them solid blows.
The click! click! click! of bayonets infuriated him, and he grasped
the rammer and struck out blindly until it was shivered to pieces.

A man threw his arm around his neck and bore him to the
ground, but he throttled him and raised himself on his knees.
He saw a comrade seize the cannon, and fall across it with his

skull crushed in; he saw the colonel tumble clean out of his saddle into the mud; then consciousness fled.

When he came to himself, he was lying on the embankment among the twisted rails. On every side huddled men who cried out and cursed and fled away into the fog, and he staggered to his feet and followed them. Once he stopped to help a comrade with a bandaged jaw, who could not speak but clung to his arm for a time and then fell dead in the freezing mire; and again he aided another, who groaned: "Trent, c'est moi—Philippe," until a sudden volley in the midst relieved him of his charge.

An icy wind swept down from the heights, cutting the fog into shreds. For an instant, with an evil leer the sun peered through the naked woods of Vincennes, sank like a blood-clot in the battery smoke, lower, lower, into the blood-soaked plain.

IV

When midnight sounded from the belfry of St. Sulpice the gates of Paris were still choked with fragments of what had once been an army.

They entered with the night, a sullen horde, spattered with slime, faint with hunger and exhaustion. There was little disorder at first, and the throng at the gates parted silently as the troops tramped along the freezing streets. Confusion came as the hours passed. Swiftly and more swiftly, crowding squadron after squadron and battery on battery, horses plunging and caissons jolting, the remnants from the front surged through the gates, a chaos of cavalry and artillery struggling for the right of way. Close upon them stumbled the infantry; here a skeleton of a regiment marching with a desperate attempt at order, there a riotous mob of Mobiles crushing their way to the streets, then a turmoil of horsemen, cannon, troops without, officers, officers without men, then again a line of ambulances, the wheels groaning under their heavy loads.

Dumb with misery the crowd looked on.

All through the day the ambulances had been arriving, and all day long the ragged throng whimpered and shivered by the barriers. At noon the crowd was increased ten-fold, filling the squares about the gates, and swarming over the inner fortifications.

At four o'clock in the afternoon the German batteries suddenly wreathed themselves in smoke, and the shells fell fast on Montparnasse. At twenty minutes after four two projectiles struck a house in the rue de Bac, and a moment later the first shell fell in the Latin Quarter.

Braith was painting in bed when West came in very much scared.

"I wish you would come down; our house has been knocked into a cocked hat, and I'm afraid that some of the pillagers may take it into their heads to pay us a visit to-night."

Braith jumped out of bed and bundled himself into a garment which had once been an overcoat.

"Anybody hurt?" he inquired, struggling with a sleeve full of dilapidated lining.

"No. Colette is barricaded in the cellar, and the concierge ran away to the fortifications. There will be a rough gang there if the bombardment keeps up. You might help us—"

"Of course," said Braith; but it was not until they had reached the rue Serpente and had turned in the passage which led to West's cellar, that the latter cried: "Have you seen Jack Trent, to-day?"

"No," replied Braith, looking troubled, "he was not at Ambulance Headquarters."

"He stayed to take care of Sylvia, I suppose."

A bomb came crashing through the roof of a house at the end of the alley and burst in the basement, showering the street with slate and plaster. A second struck a chimney and plunged into the garden, followed by an avalanche of bricks, and another exploded with a deafening report in the next street.

They hurried along the passage to the steps which led to the cellar. Here again Braith stopped.

"Don't you think I had better run up to see if Jack and Sylvia are well entrenched? I can get back before dark."

"No. Go in and find Colette, and I'll go."

"No, no, let me go, there's no danger."

"I know it," replied West calmly; and, dragging Braith into the alley, pointed to the cellar steps. The iron door was barred.

"Colette! Colette!" he called. The door swung inward, and the girl sprang up the stairs to meet them. At that instant, Braith, glancing behind him, gave a startled cry, and pushing the two before him into the cellar, jumped down after them and slammed the iron door. A few seconds later a heavy jar from the outside shook the hinges.

"They are here," muttered West, very pale.

"That door," observed Colette calmly, "will hold for ever."

Braith examined the low iron structure, now trembling with the blows rained on it from without. West glanced anxiously at Colette, who displayed no agitation, and this comforted him.

"I don't believe they will spend much time here," said Braith; "they only rummage in cellars for spirits, I imagine."

"Unless they hear that valuables are buried there."

"But surely nothing is buried here?" exclaimed Braith uneasily.

"Unfortunately there is," growled West. "That miserly landlord of mine—"

A crash from the outside, followed by a yell, cut him short; then blow after blow shook the doors, until there came a sharp snap, a clinking of metal and a triangular bit of iron fell inwards, leaving a hole through which struggled a ray of light.

Instantly West knelt, and shoving his revolver through the aperture fired every cartridge. For a moment the alley resounded with the racket of the revolver, then absolute silence followed.

Presently a single questioning blow fell upon the door, and a moment later another and another, and then a sudden crack zigzagged across the iron plate.

"Here," said West, seizing Colette by the wrist, "you follow me, Braith!" and he ran swiftly toward a circular spot of light at the further end of the cellar. The spot of light came from a barred man-hole above. West motioned Braith to mount on his shoulders.

"Push it over. You *must*!"

With little effort Braith lifted the barred cover, scrambled out on his stomach, and easily raised Colette from West's shoulders.

"Quick, old chap!" cried the latter.

Braith twisted his legs around a fence-chain and leaned down again. The cellar was flooded with a yellow light, and the air reeked with the stench of petroleum torches. The iron door still held, but a whole plate of metal was gone, and now as they looked a figure came creeping through, holding a torch.

"Quick!" whispered Braith. "Jump!" and West hung dangling until Colette grasped him by the collar, and he was dragged out. Then her nerves gave way and she wept hysterically, but West threw his arm around her and led her across the gardens into the next street, where Braith, after replacing the man-hole cover and piling some stone slabs from the wall over it, rejoined them. It was almost dark. They hurried through the street, now only lighted by burning buildings, or the swift glare of the shells. They gave wide berth to the fires, but at a distance saw the flitting forms of pillagers among the *débris*. Sometimes they passed a female fury crazed with drink shrieking anathemas upon the world, or some slouching lout whose blackened face and hands betrayed his share in the work of destruction. At last they reached the Seine and passed the bridge, and then Braith said: "I must go back. I am not sure of Jack and Sylvia." As he spoke, he made way for a crowd which came trampling across the bridge, and along the river wall by the d'Orsay barracks. In the midst of it West caught the measured tread of a platoon. A lantern passed, a file of bayonets, then another lantern which glimmered on a deathly face behind, and Colette gasped, "Hartman!" and he was gone. They peered fearfully across the embankment, holding their breath. There was a shuffle of feet on the quay, and the gate of the barracks slammed. A lantern shone for a moment at the postern, the crowd pressed to the grille, then came the clang of the volley from the stone parade.

One by one the petroleum torches flared up along the embankment, and now the whole square was in motion. Down from the Champs Elysées and across the Place de la Concorde straggled the fragments of the battle, a company here, and a mob there. They poured in from every street followed by women and children, and a great murmur, borne on the icy wind, swept through the Arc de Triomphe and down the dark avenue,—"Perdus! perdus!"

A ragged end of a battalion was pressing past, the spectre of annihilation. West groaned. Then a figure sprang from the shadowy ranks and called West's name, and when he saw it was Trent he cried out. Trent seized him, white with terror.

"Sylvia?"

West stared speechless, but Colette moaned, "Oh, Sylvia! Sylvia!—and they are shelling the Quarter!"

"Trent!" shouted Braith; but he was gone, and they could not overtake him.

The bombardment ceased as Trent crossed the Boulevard St. Germain, but the entrance to the rue de Seine was blocked by a heap of smoking bricks. Everywhere the shells had torn great holes in the pavement. The café was a wreck of splinters and glass, the book-store tottered, ripped from roof to basement, and the little bakery, long since closed, bulged outward above a mass of slate and tin.

He climbed over the steaming bricks and hurried into the rue de Tournon. On the corner a fire blazed, lighting up his own street, and on the bank wall, beneath a shattered gas lamp, a child was writing with a bit of cinder.

"HERE FELL THE FIRST SHELL."

The letters stared him in the face. The rat-killer finished and stepped back to view his work, but catching sight of Trent's bayonet, screamed and fled, and as Trent staggered across the shattered street, from holes and crannies in the ruins fierce women fled from their work of pillage, cursing him.

At first he could not find his house, for the tears blinded him, but he felt along the wall and reached the door. A lantern burned in the concierge's lodge and the old man lay dead beside it. Faint with fright he leaned a moment on his rifle, then, snatching the lantern, sprang up the stairs. He tried to call, but his tongue hardly moved. On the second floor he saw plaster on the stairway, and on the third the floor was torn and the concierge lay in a pool of blood across the landing. The next floor was his, *theirs*. The door hung from its hinges, the walls gaped. He crept in and sank down by the bed, and there two arms were flung around his neck, and a tear-stained face sought his own.

"Sylvia!"

"O Jack! Jack! Jack!"

From the tumbled pillow beside them a child wailed.

"They brought it; it is mine," she sobbed.

"Ours," he whispered, with his arms around them both.

Then from the stairs below came Braith's anxious voice.

"Trent! Is all well?"

THE STREET OF OUR LADY
OF THE FIELDS

*"Et tout les jours passés dans la tristesse
Nous sont comptés comme des jours heureux!"*

I

The street is not fashionable, neither is it shabby. It is a pariah among streets—a street without a Quarter. It is generally understood to lie outside the pale of the aristocratic Avenue de l'Observatoire. The students of the Montparnasse Quarter consider it swell and will have none of it. The Latin Quarter, from the Luxembourg, its northern frontier, sneers at its respectability and regards with disfavour the correctly costumed students who haunt it. Few strangers go into it. At times, however, the Latin Quarter students use it as a thoroughfare between the rue de Rennes and the Bullier, but except for that and the weekly afternoon visits of parents and guardians to the Convent near the rue Vavin, the street of Our Lady of the Fields is as quiet as a Passy boulevard. Perhaps the most respectable portion lies between the rue de la Grande Chaumière and the rue Vavin, at least this was the conclusion arrived at by the Reverend Joel Byram, as he rambled through it with Hastings in charge. To Hastings the street looked pleasant in the bright June weather, and he had begun to hope for its selection when the Reverend Byram shied violently at the cross on the Convent opposite.

"Jesuits," he muttered.

"Well," said Hastings wearily, "I imagine we won't find anything better. You say yourself that vice is triumphant in Paris, and it seems to me that in every street we find Jesuits or something worse."

After a moment he repeated, "Or something worse, which of course I would not notice except for your kindness in warning me."

Dr. Byram sucked in his lips and looked about him. He was impressed by the evident respectability of the surroundings. Then frowning at the Convent he took Hastings' arm and shuffled across the street to an iron gateway which bore the number 201 *bis* painted in white on a blue ground. Below this was a notice printed in English:

1.   For Porter please oppress once.
2.   For Servant please oppress twice.
3.   For Parlour please oppress thrice.

Hastings touched the electric button three times, and they were ushered through the garden and into the parlour by a trim maid. The dining-room door, just beyond, was open, and from the table in plain view a stout woman hastily arose and came toward them. Hastings caught a glimpse of a young man with a big head and several snuffy old gentlemen at breakfast, before the door closed and the stout woman waddled into the room, bringing with her an aroma of coffee and a black poodle.

"It ees a plaisir to you receive!" she cried. "Monsieur is Anglish? No? Americain? Off course. My pension it ees for Americains surtout. Here all spik Angleesh, c'est à dire, ze personnel; ze sairvants do spik, plus ou moins, a little. I am happy to have you comme pensionnaires—"

"Madame," began Dr. Byram, but was cut short again.

"Ah, yess, I know, ah! mon Dieu! you do not spik Frainch but you have come to lairne! My husband does spik Frainch wiss ze pensionnaires. We have at ze moment a family Americaine who learn of my husband Frainch—"

Here the poodle growled at Dr. Byram and was promptly cuffed by his mistress.

"Veux tu!" she cried, with a slap, "veux tu! Oh! le vilain, oh! le vilain!"

"Mais, madame," said Hastings, smiling, "il n'a pas l'air très féroce."

The poodle fled, and his mistress cried, "Ah, ze accent charming! He does spik already Frainch like a Parisien young gentleman!"

Then Dr. Byram managed to get in a word or two and gathered more or less information with regard to prices.

"It ees a pension serieux; my clientèle ees of ze best, indeed a pension de famille where one ees at 'ome."

Then they went upstairs to examine Hastings' future quarters, test the bed-springs and arrange for the weekly towel allowance. Dr. Byram appeared satisfied.

Madame Marotte accompanied them to the door and rang for the maid, but as Hastings stepped out into the gravel walk, his guide and mentor paused a moment and fixed Madame with his watery eyes.

"You understand," he said, "that he is a youth of most careful bringing up, and his character and morals are without a stain. He is young and has never been abroad, never even seen a large city, and his parents have requested me, as an old family friend living in Paris, to see that he is placed under good influences. He is to study art, but on no account would his parents wish him to live in the Latin Quarter if they knew of the immorality which is rife there."

A sound like the click of a latch interrupted him and he raised his eyes, but not in time to see the maid slap the big-headed young man behind the parlour-door.

Madame coughed, cast a deadly glance behind her and then beamed on Dr. Byram.

"It ees well zat he come here. The pension more serious, il n'en existe pas, eet ees not any!" she announced with conviction.

So, as there was nothing more to add, Dr. Byram joined Hastings at the gate.

"I trust," he said, eyeing the Convent, "that you will make no acquaintances among Jesuits!"

Hastings looked at the Convent until a pretty girl passed before the gray façade, and then he looked at her. A young fellow with a paint-box and canvas came swinging along, stopped before the pretty girl, said something during a brief but vigorous hand-shake at which they both laughed, and he went his way, calling back, "À demain Valentine!" as in the same breath she cried, "À demain!"

"Valentine," thought Hastings, "what a quaint name;" and he started to follow the Reverend Joel Byram, who was shuffling towards the nearest tramway station.

II

"An' you are pleas wiz Paris, Monsieur 'Astang?" demanded Madame Marotte the next morning as Hastings came into the breakfast-room of the pension, rosy from his plunge in the limited bath above.

"I am sure I shall like it," he replied, wondering at his own depression of spirits.

The maid brought him coffee and rolls. He returned the vacant glance of the big-headed young man and acknowledged diffi-dently the salutes of the snuffy old gentlemen. He did not try to finish his coffee, and sat crumbling a roll, unconscious of the sympathetic glances of Madame Marotte, who had tact enough not to bother him.

Presently a maid entered with a tray on which were balanced two bowls of chocolate, and the snuffy old gentlemen leered at her ankles. The maid deposited the chocolate at a table near the window and smiled at Hastings. Then a thin young lady, followed by her counterpart in all except years, marched into the room and took the table near the window. They were evidently American, but Hastings, if he expected any sign of recognition, was disappointed. To be ignored by compatriots intensified his depression. He fumbled with his knife and looked at his plate.

The thin young lady was talkative enough. She was quite aware of Hastings' presence, ready to be flattered if he looked at her, but on the other hand she felt her superiority, for she had been three weeks in Paris and he, it was easy to see, had not yet unpacked his steamer-trunk.

Her conversation was complacent. She argued with her mother upon the relative merits of the Louvre and the Bon Marché, but her mother's part of the discussion was mostly confined to the observation, "Why, Susie!"

The snuffy old gentlemen had left the room in a body, outwardly polite and inwardly raging. They could not endure the Americans, who filled the room with their chatter.

The big-headed young man looked after them with a knowing cough, murmuring, "Gay old birds!"

"They look like bad old men, Mr. Bladen," said the girl.

To this Mr. Bladen smiled and said, "They've had their day," in a tone which implied that he was now having his.

"And that's why they all have baggy eyes," cried the girl. "I think it's a shame for young gentlemen—"

"Why, Susie!" said the mother, and the conversation lagged.

After a while Mr. Bladen threw down the *Petit Journal*, which he daily studied at the expense of the house, and turning to Hastings, started to make himself agreeable. He began by saying, "I see you are American."

To this brilliant and original opening, Hastings, deadly homesick, replied gratefully, and the conversation was judiciously nourished by observations from Miss Susie Byng distinctly addressed to Mr. Bladen. In the course of events Miss Susie, forgetting to address herself exclusively to Mr. Bladen, and Hastings replying to her general question, the *entente cordiale* was established, and Susie and her mother extended a protectorate over what was clearly neutral territory.

"Mr. Hastings, you must not desert the pension every evening as Mr. Bladen does. Paris is an awful place for young gentlemen, and Mr. Bladen is a horrid cynic."

Mr. Bladen looked gratified.

Hastings answered, "I shall be at the studio all day, and I

imagine I shall be glad enough to come back at night."

Mr. Bladen, who, at a salary of fifteen dollars a week, acted as agent for the Pewly Manufacturing Company of Troy, N.Y., smiled a sceptical smile and withdrew to keep an appointment with a customer on the Boulevard Magenta.

Hastings walked into the garden with Mrs. Byng and Susie, and, at their invitation, sat down in the shade before the iron gate.

The chestnut trees still bore their fragrant spikes of pink and white, and the bees hummed among the roses, trellised on the white-walled house.

A faint freshness was in the air. The watering carts moved up and down the street, and a clear stream bubbled over the spotless gutters of the rue de la Grande Chaumière. The sparrows were merry along the curb-stones, taking bath after bath in the water and ruffling their feathers with delight. In a walled garden across the street a pair of blackbirds whistled among the almond trees.

Hastings swallowed the lump in his throat, for the song of the birds and the ripple of water in a Paris gutter brought back to him the sunny meadows of Millbrook.

"That's a blackbird," observed Miss Byng; "see him there on the bush with pink blossoms. He's all black except his bill, and that looks as if it had been dipped in an omelet, as some Frenchman says—"

"Why, Susie!" said Mrs. Byng.

"That garden belongs to a studio inhabited by two Americans," continued the girl serenely, "and I often see them pass. They seem to need a great many models, mostly young and feminine—"

"Why, Susie!"

"Perhaps they prefer painting that kind, but I don't see why they should invite five, with three more young gentlemen, and all get into two cabs and drive away singing. This street," she continued, "is dull. There is nothing to see except the garden and a glimpse of the Boulevard Montparnasse through the rue de la Grande Chaumière. No one ever passes except a policeman. There is a convent on the corner."

"I thought it was a Jesuit College," began Hastings, but was at once overwhelmed with a Baedecker description of the place, ending with, "On one side stand the palatial hotels of Jean Paul Laurens and Guillaume Bouguereau, and opposite, in the little Passage Stanislas, Carolus Duran paints the masterpieces which charm the world."

The blackbird burst into a ripple of golden throaty notes, and from some distant green spot in the city an unknown wild-bird answered with a frenzy of liquid trills until the sparrows paused in their ablutions to look up with restless chirps.

Then a butterfly came and sat on a cluster of heliotrope and waved his crimson-banded wings in the hot sunshine. Hastings knew him for a friend, and before his eyes there came a vision of tall mulleins and scented milkweed alive with painted wings, a vision of a white house and woodbine-covered piazza,—a glimpse of a man reading and a woman leaning over the pansy bed,—and his heart was full. He was startled a moment later by Miss Byng.

"I believe you are homesick!" Hastings blushed. Miss Byng looked at him with a sympathetic sigh and continued:"Whenever I felt homesick at first I used to go with mamma and walk in the Luxembourg Gardens. I don't know why it is, but those old-fashioned gardens seemed to bring me nearer home than anything in this artificial city."

"But they are full of marble statues," said Mrs. Byng mildly; "I don't see the resemblance myself."

"Where is the Luxembourg?" inquired Hastings after a silence.

"Come with me to the gate," said Miss Byng. He rose and followed her, and she pointed out the rue Vavin at the foot of the street.

"You pass by the convent to the right," she smiled; and Hastings went.

III

The Luxembourg was a blaze of flowers. He walked slowly through the long avenues of trees, past mossy marbles and old-time columns, and threading the grove by the bronze lion, came upon the tree-crowned terrace above the fountain. Below lay the basin shining in the sunlight. Flowering almonds encircled the terrace, and, in a greater spiral, groves of chestnuts wound in and out and down among the moist thickets by the western palace wing. At one end of the avenue of trees the Observatory rose, its white domes piled up like an eastern mosque; at the other end stood the heavy palace, with every window-pane ablaze in the fierce sun of June.

Around the fountain, children and white-capped nurses armed with bamboo poles were pushing toy boats, whose sails hung limp in the sunshine. A dark policeman, wearing red epaulettes and a dress sword, watched them for a while and then went away to remonstrate with a young man who had unchained his dog. The dog was pleasantly occupied in rubbing grass and dirt into his back while his legs waved into the air.

The policeman pointed at the dog. He was speechless with indignation.

"Well, Captain," smiled the young fellow.

"Well, Monsieur Student," growled the policeman.

"What do you come and complain to me for?"

"If you don't chain him I'll take him," shouted the policeman.

"What's that to me, mon capitaine?"

"Wha—t! Isn't that bull-dog yours?"

"If it was, don't you suppose I'd chain him?"

The officer glared for a moment in silence, then deciding that as he was a student he was wicked, grabbed at the dog, who promptly dodged. Around and around the flower-beds they raced, and when the officer came too near for comfort, the bull-dog cut across a flower-bed, which perhaps was not playing fair.

The young man was amused, and the dog also seemed to enjoy the exercise.

The policeman noticed this and decided to strike at the fountain-head of the evil. He stormed up to the student and said, "As the owner of this public nuisance I arrest you!"

"But," objected the other, "I disclaim the dog."

That was a poser. It was useless to attempt to catch the dog until three gardeners lent a hand, but then the dog simply ran away and disappeared in the rue de Medici.

The policeman shambled off to find consolation among the white-capped nurses, and the student, looking at his watch, stood up yawning. Then catching sight of Hastings, he smiled and bowed. Hastings walked over to the marble, laughing.

"Why, Clifford," he said, "I didn't recognize you."

"It's my moustache," sighed the other. "I sacrificed it to humour a whim of—of—a friend. What do you think of my dog?"

"Then he is yours?" cried Hastings.

"Of course. It's a pleasant change for him, this playing tag with policemen, but he is known now and I'll have to stop it. He's gone home. He always does when the gardeners take a hand. It's a pity; he's fond of rolling on lawns." Then they chatted for a moment of Hastings' prospects, and Clifford politely offered to stand his sponsor at the studio.

"You see, old tabby, I mean Dr. Byram, told me about you before I met you," explained Clifford, "and Elliott and I will be glad to do anything we can." Then looking at his watch again, he muttered, "I have just ten minutes to catch the Versailles train; au revoir," and started to go, but catching sight of a girl advancing by the fountain, took off his hat with a confused smile.

"Why are you not at Versailles?" she said, with an almost imperceptible acknowledgment of Hastings' presence.

"I—I'm going," murmured Clifford.

For a moment they faced each other, and then Clifford, very red, stammered, "With your permission I have the honour of presenting to you my friend, Monsieur Hastings."

Hastings bowed low. She smiled very sweetly, but there was something of malice in the quiet inclination of her small Parisienne head.

"I could have wished," she said, "that Monsieur Clifford might spare me more time when he brings with him so charming an American."

"Must—must I go, Valentine?" began Clifford.

"Certainly," she replied.

Clifford took his leave with very bad grace, wincing, when she added, "And give my dearest love to Cécile!" As he disappeared in the rue d'Assas, the girl turned as if to go, but then suddenly remembering Hastings, looked at him and shook her head.

"Monsieur Clifford is so perfectly hare-brained," she smiled, "it is embarrassing sometimes. You have heard, of course, all about his success at the Salon?"

He looked puzzled and she noticed it.

"You have been to the Salon, of course?"

"Why, no," he answered, "I only arrived in Paris three days ago."

She seemed to pay little heed to his explanation, but continued: "Nobody imagined he had the energy to do anything good, but on varnishing day the Salon was astonished by the entrance of Monsieur Clifford, who strolled about as bland as you please with an orchid in his buttonhole, and a beautiful picture on the line."

She smiled to herself at the reminiscence, and looked at the fountain.

"Monsieur Bouguereau told me that Monsieur Julian was so astonished that he only shook hands with Monsieur Clifford in a dazed manner, and actually forgot to pat him on the back! Fancy," she continued with much merriment, "fancy papa Julian forgetting to pat one on the back."

Hastings, wondering at her acquaintance with the great Bouguereau, looked at her with respect. "May I ask," he said diffidently, "whether you are a pupil of Bouguereau?"

"I?" she said in some surprise. Then she looked at him curiously. Was he permitting himself the liberty of joking on such short acquaintance?

His pleasant serious face questioned hers.

"Tiens," she thought, "what a droll man!"

"You surely study art?" he said.

She leaned back on the crooked stick of her parasol, and looked at him. "Why do you think so?"

"Because you speak as if you did."

"You are making fun of me," she said, "and it is not good taste."

She stopped, confused, as he coloured to the roots of his hair.

"How long have you been in Paris?" she said at length.

"Three days," he replied gravely.

"But—but—surely you are not a nouveau! You speak French too well!"

Then after a pause, "Really are you a nouveau?"

"I am," he said.

She sat down on the marble bench lately occupied by Clifford, and tilting her parasol over her small head looked at him.

"I don't believe it."

He felt the compliment, and for a moment hesitated to declare himself one of the despised. Then mustering up his courage, he told her how new and green he was, and all with a frankness which made her blue eyes open very wide and her lips part in the sweetest of smiles.

"You have never seen a studio?"

"Never."

"Nor a model?"

"No."

"How funny," she said solemnly. Then they both laughed.

"And you," he said, "have seen studios?"

"Hundreds."

"And models?"

"Millions."

"And you know Bouguereau?"

"Yes, and Henner, and Constant and Laurens, and Puvis de Chavannes and Dagnan and Courtois, and—and all the rest of them!"

"And yet you say you are not an artist."

"Pardon," she said gravely, "did I say I was not?"

"Won't you tell me?" he hesitated.

At first she looked at him, shaking her head and smiling, then of a sudden her eyes fell and she began tracing figures with her parasol in the gravel at her feet. Hastings had taken a place on the seat, and now, with his elbows on his knees, sat watching the spray drifting above the fountain jet. A small boy, dressed as a sailor, stood poking his yacht and crying, "I won't go home! I won't go home!" His nurse raised her hands to Heaven.

"Just like a little American boy," thought Hastings, and a pang of homesickness shot through him.

Presently the nurse captured the boat, and the small boy stood at bay.

"Monsieur René, when you decide to come here you may have your boat."

The boy backed away scowling.

"Give me my boat, I say," he cried, "and don't call me René, for my name's Randall and you know it!"

"Hello!" said Hastings,—"Randall?—that's English."

"I am American," announced the boy in perfectly good English, turning to look at Hastings, "and she's such a fool she calls me René because mamma calls me Ranny—"

Here he dodged the exasperated nurse and took up his station behind Hastings, who laughed, and catching him around the waist lifted him into his lap.

"One of my countrymen," he said to the girl beside him. He smiled while he spoke, but there was a queer feeling in his throat.

"Don't you see the stars and stripes on my yacht?" demanded Randall. Sure enough, the American colours hung limply under the nurse's arm.

"Oh," cried the girl, "he is charming," and impulsively stooped to kiss him, but the infant Randall wriggled out of Hastings' arms, and his nurse pounced upon him with an angry glance at the girl.

She reddened and then bit her lips as the nurse, with eyes still fixed on her, dragged the child away and ostentatiously wiped his lips with her handkerchief.

Then she stole a look at Hastings and bit her lip again.

"What an ill-tempered woman!" he said. "In America, most nurses are flattered when people kiss their children."

For an instant she tipped the parasol to hide her face, then closed it with a snap and looked at him defiantly.

"Do you think it strange that she objected?"

"Why not?" he said in surprise.

Again she looked at him with quick searching eyes.

His eyes were clear and bright, and he smiled back, repeating, "Why not?"

"You *are* droll," she murmured, bending her head.

"Why?"

But she made no answer, and sat silent, tracing curves and circles in the dust with her parasol. After a while he said—"I am glad to see that young people have so much liberty here. I understood that the French were not at all like us. You know in America—or at least where I live in Milbrook, girls have every liberty,—go out alone and receive their friends alone, and I was afraid I should miss it here. But I see how it is now, and I am glad I was mistaken."

She raised her eyes to his and kept them there.

He continued pleasantly—"Since I have sat here I have seen a lot of pretty girls walking alone on the terrace there,—and then *you* are alone too. Tell me, for I do not know French customs,—do you have the liberty of going to the theatre without a chaperone?"

For a long time she studied his face, and then with a trembling smile said, "Why do you ask me?"

"Because you must know, of course," he said gaily.

"Yes," she replied indifferently, "I know."

He waited for an answer, but getting none, decided that perhaps she had misunderstood him.

"I hope you don't think I mean to presume on our short acquaintance," he began,—"in fact it is very odd but I don't know your name. When Mr. Clifford presented me he only mentioned mine. Is that the custom in France?"

"It is the custom in the Latin Quarter," she said with a queer light in her eyes. Then suddenly she began talking almost feverishly.

"You must know, Monsieur Hastings, that we are all *un peu sans gêne* here in the Latin Quarter. We are very Bohemian, and etiquette and ceremony are out of place. It was for that Monsieur Clifford presented you to me with small ceremony, and left us together with less,—only for that, and I am his friend, and I have many friends in the Latin Quarter, and we all know each other very well—and I am not studying art, but—but—"

"But what?" he said, bewildered.

"I shall not tell you,—it is a secret," she said with an uncertain smile. On both cheeks a pink spot was burning, and her eyes were very bright.

Then in a moment her face fell. "Do you know Monsieur Clifford very intimately?"

"Not very."

After a while she turned to him, grave and a little pale.

"My name is Valentine—Valentine Tissot. Might—might I ask a service of you on such very short acquaintance?"

"Oh," he cried, "I should be honoured."

"It is only this," she said gently, "it is not much. Promise me not to speak to Monsieur Clifford about me. Promise me that you will speak to no one about me."

"I promise," he said, greatly puzzled.

She laughed nervously. "I wish to remain a mystery. It is a caprice."

"But," he began, "I had wished, I had hoped that you might give Monsieur Clifford permission to bring me, to present me at your house."

"My—my house!" she repeated.

"I mean, where you live, in fact, to present me to your family." The change in the girl's face shocked him.

"I beg your pardon," he cried, "I have hurt you."

And as quick as a flash she understood him because she was a woman.

"My parents are dead," she said.

Presently he began again, very gently.

"Would it displease you if I beg you to receive me? It is the custom?"

"I cannot," she answered. Then glancing up at him, "I am sorry; I should like to; but believe me. I cannot."

He bowed seriously and looked vaguely uneasy.

"It isn't because I don't wish to. I—I like you; you are very kind to me."

"Kind?" he cried, surprised and puzzled.

"I like you," she said slowly, "and we will see each other sometimes if you will."

"At friends' houses."

"No, not at friends' houses."

"Where?"

"Here," she said with defiant eyes.

"Why," he cried, "in Paris you are much more liberal in your views than we are."

She looked at him curiously.

"Yes, we are very Bohemian."

"I think it is charming," he declared.

"You see, we shall be in the best of society," she ventured timidly, with a pretty gesture toward the statues of the dead queens, ranged in stately ranks above the terrace.

He looked at her, delighted, and she brightened at the success of her innocent little pleasantry.

"Indeed," she smiled, "I shall be well chaperoned, because you see we are under the protection of the gods themselves; look, there are Apollo, and Juno, and Venus, on their pedestals," counting them on her small gloved fingers, "and Ceres, Hercules, and—but I can't make out—"

Hastings turned to look up at the winged god under whose shadow they were seated.

"Why, it's Love," he said.

IV

"There is a nouveau here," drawled Laffat, leaning around his easel and addressing his friend Bowles, "there is a nouveau here who is so tender and green and appetizing that Heaven help him if he should fall into a salad bowl."

"Hayseed?" inquired Bowles, plastering in a background with a broken palette-knife and squinting at the effect with approval.

"Yes, Squeedunk or Oshkosh, and how he ever grew up among the daisies and escaped the cows, Heaven alone knows!"

Bowles rubbed his thumb across the outlines of his study to "throw in a little atmosphere," as he said, glared at the model, pulled at his pipe and finding it out struck a match on his neighbour's back to relight it.

"His name," continued Laffat, hurling a bit of bread at the hat-rack, "his name is Hastings. He *is* a berry. He knows no more about the world,"—and here Mr. Laffat's face spoke volumes for his own knowledge of that planet,—"than a maiden cat on its first moonlight stroll."

Bowles now having succeeded in lighting his pipe, repeated the thumb touch on the other edge of the study and said, "Ah!"

"Yes," continued his friend, "and would you imagine it, he seems to think that everything here goes on as it does in his d—d little backwoods ranch at home; talks about the pretty girls who walk alone in the street; says how sensible it is; and how

French parents are misrepresented in America; says that for his part he finds French girls,—and he confessed to only knowing one,—as jolly as American girls. I tried to set him right, tried to give him a pointer as to what sort of ladies walk about alone or with students, and he was either too stupid or too innocent to catch on. Then I gave it to him straight, and he said I was a vile-minded fool and marched off."

"Did you assist him with your shoe?" inquired Bowles, languidly interested.

"Well, no."

"He called you a vile-minded fool."

"He was correct," said Clifford from his easel in front.

"What—what do you mean?" demanded Laffat, turning red.

"*That*," replied Clifford.

"Who spoke to you? Is this your business?" sneered Bowles, but nearly lost his balance as Clifford swung about and eyed him.

"Yes," he said slowly, "it's my business."

No one spoke for some time.

Then Clifford sang out, "I say, Hastings!"

And when Hastings left his easel and came around, he nodded toward the astonished Laffat.

"This man has been disagreeable to you, and I want to tell you that any time you feel inclined to kick him, why, I will hold the other creature."

Hastings, embarrassed, said, "Why no, I don't agree with his ideas, nothing more."

Clifford said "Naturally," and slipping his arm through Hastings', strolled about with him, and introduced him to several of his own friends, at which all the nouveaux opened their eyes with envy, and the studio were given to understand that Hastings, although prepared to do menial work as the latest nouveau, was already within the charmed circle of the old, respected and feared, the truly great.

The rest finished, the model resumed his place, and work

went on in a chorus of songs and yells and every ear-splitting noise which the art student utters when studying the beautiful.

Five o'clock struck,—the model yawned, stretched and climbed into his trousers, and the noisy contents of six studios crowded through the hall and down into the street. Ten minutes later, Hastings found himself on top of a Montrouge tram, and shortly afterward was joined by Clifford.

They climbed down at the rue Gay Lussac.

"I always stop here," observed Clifford, "I like the walk through the Luxembourg."

"By the way," said Hastings, "how can I call on you when I don't know where you live?"

"Why, I live opposite you."

"What—the studio in the garden where the almond trees are and the blackbirds—"

"Exactly," said Clifford. "I'm with my friend Elliott."

Hastings thought of the description of the two American artists which he had heard from Miss Susie Byng, and looked blank.

Clifford continued, "Perhaps you had better let me know when you think of coming so,—so that I will be sure to—to be there," he ended rather lamely.

"I shouldn't care to meet any of your model friends there," said Hastings, smiling. "You know—my ideas are rather strait-laced,—I suppose you would say, Puritanical. I shouldn't enjoy it and wouldn't know how to behave."

"Oh, I understand," said Clifford, but added with great cordiality,—"I'm sure we'll be friends although you may not approve of me and my set, but you will like Severn and Selby because—because, well, they are like yourself, old chap."

After a moment he continued, "There is something I want to speak about. You see, when I introduced you, last week, in the Luxembourg, to Valentine—"

"Not a word!" cried Hastings, smiling; "you must not tell me a word of her!"

"Why—"

"No—not a word!" he said gaily. "I insist,—promise me upon your honour you will not speak of her until I give you permission; promise!"

"I promise," said Clifford, amazed.

"She is a charming girl,—we had such a delightful chat after you left, and I thank you for presenting me, but not another word about her until I give you permission."

"Oh," murmured Clifford.

"Remember your promise," he smiled, as he turned into his gateway.

Clifford strolled across the street and, traversing the ivy-covered alley, entered his garden.

He felt for his studio key, muttering, "I wonder—I wonder,—but of course he doesn't!"

He entered the hallway, and fitting the key into the door, stood staring at the two cards tacked over the panels.

FOXHALL CLIFFORD
RICHARD OSBORNE ELLIOTT

"Why the devil doesn't he want me to speak of her?"

He opened the door, and, discouraging the caresses of two brindle bull-dogs, sank down on the sofa.

Elliott sat smoking and sketching with a piece of charcoal by the window.

"Hello," he said without looking around.

Clifford gazed absently at the back of his head, murmuring, "I'm afraid, I'm afraid that man is too innocent. I say, Elliott," he said, at last, "Hastings,—you know the chap that old Tabby Byram came around here to tell us about—the day you had to hide Colette in the armoire—"

"Yes, what's up?"

"Oh, nothing. He's a brick."

"Yes," said Elliott, without enthusiasm.

"Don't you think so?" demanded Clifford.

"Why yes, but he is going to have a tough time when some of his illusions are dispelled."

"More shame to those who dispel 'em!"

"Yes,—wait until he comes to pay his call on us, unexpectedly, of course—"

Clifford looked virtuous and lighted a cigar.

"I was just going to say," he observed, "that I have asked him not to come without letting us know, so I can postpone any orgie you may have intended—"

"Ah!" cried Elliott indignantly, "I suppose you put it to him in that way."

"Not exactly," grinned Clifford. Then more seriously, "I don't want anything to occur here to bother him. He's a brick, and it's a pity we can't be more like him."

"I am," observed Elliott complacently, "only living with you—"

"Listen!" cried the other. "I have managed to put my foot in it in great style. Do you know what I've done? Well—the first time I met him in the street,—or rather, it was in the Luxembourg, I introduced him to Valentine!"

"Did he object?"

"Believe me," said Clifford, solemnly, "this rustic Hastings has no more idea that Valentine is—is—in fact is Valentine, than he has that he himself is a beautiful example of moral decency in a Quarter where morals are as rare as elephants. I heard enough in a conversation between that blackguard Loffat and the little immoral eruption, Bowles, to open my eyes. I tell you Hastings is a trump! He's a healthy, clean-minded young fellow, bred in a small country village, brought up with the idea that saloons are way-stations to hell—and as for women—"

"Well?" demanded Elliott

"Well," said Clifford, "his idea of the dangerous woman is probably a painted Jezabel."

"Probably," replied the other.

"He's a trump!" said Clifford, "and if he swears the world is as good and pure as his own heart, I'll swear he's right."

Elliott rubbed his charcoal on his file to get a point and turned to his sketch saying, "He will never hear any pessimism from Richard Osborne E."

"He's a lesson to me," said Clifford. Then he unfolded a small perfumed note, written on rose-coloured paper, which had been lying on the table before him.

He read it, smiled, whistled a bar or two from "Miss Helyett," and sat down to answer it on his best cream-laid note-paper. When it was written and sealed, he picked up his stick and marched up and down the studio two or three times, whistling.

"Going out?" inquired the other, without turning.

"Yes," he said, but lingered a moment over Elliott's shoulder, watching him pick out the lights in his sketch with a bit of bread.

"To-morrow is Sunday," he observed after a moment's silence.

"Well?" inquired Elliott.

"Have you seen Colette?"

"No, I will to-night. She and Rowden and Jacqueline are coming to Boulant's. I suppose you and Cécile will be there?"

"Well, no," replied Clifford. "Cécile dines at home to-night, and I—I had an idea of going to Mignon's."

Elliott looked at him with disapproval.

"You can make all the arrangements for La Roche without me," he continued, avoiding Elliott's eyes.

"What are you up to now?"

"Nothing," protested Clifford.

"Don't tell me," replied his chum, with scorn; "fellows don't rush off to Mignon's when the set dine at Boulant's. Who is it now?—but no, I won't ask that,—what's the use!" Then he lifted up his voice in complaint and beat upon the table with his pipe. "What's the use of ever trying to keep track of you? What will Cécile say,—oh, yes, what will she say? It's a pity you can't be constant two months, yes, by Jove! and the Quarter is indulgent, but you abuse its good nature and mine too!"

Presently he arose, and jamming his hat on his head, marched to the door.

"Heaven alone knows why any one puts up with your antics, but they all do and so do I. If I were Cécile or any of the other pretty fools after whom you have toddled and will, in all human probabilities, continue to toddle, I say, if I were Cécile I'd spank you! Now I'm going to Boulant's, and as usual I shall make excuses for you and arrange the affair, and I don't care a continental where you are going, but, by the skull of the studio skeleton! if you don't turn up to-morrow with your sketching-kit under one arm and Cécile under the other,—if you don't turn up in good shape, I'm done with you, and the rest can think what they please. Good-night."

Clifford said good-night with as pleasant a smile as he could muster, and then sat down with his eyes on the door. He took out his watch and gave Elliott ten minutes to vanish, then rang the concierge's call, murmuring, "Oh dear, oh dear, why the devil do I do it?"

"Alfred," he said, as that gimlet-eyed person answered the call, "make yourself clean and proper, Alfred, and replace your sabots with a pair of shoes. Then put on your best hat and take this letter to the big white house in the Rue de Dragon. There is no answer, *mon petit* Alfred."

The concierge departed with a snort in which unwillingness for the errand and affection for M. Clifford were blended. Then with great care the young fellow arrayed himself in all the beauties of his and Elliott's wardrobe. He took his time about it, and occasionally interrupted his toilet to play his banjo or make pleasing diversion for the bull-dogs by gambling about on all fours. "I've got two hours before me," he thought, and borrowed a pair of Elliott's silken foot-gear, with which he and the dogs played ball until he decided to put them on. Then he lighted a cigarette and inspected his dress-coat. When he had emptied it of four handkerchiefs, a fan, and a pair of crumpled gloves as long as his arm, he decided it was not suited to add *éclat* to his charms and cast about in his mind for a substitute. Elliott was too thin, and, anyway, his coats were now under lock and key.

Rowden probably was as badly off as himself. Hastings! Hastings was the man! But when he threw on a smoking-jacket and sauntered over to Hastings' house, he was informed that he had been gone over an hour.

"Now, where in the name of all that's reasonable could he have gone!" muttered Clifford, looking down the street.

The maid didn't know, so he bestowed upon her a fascinating smile and lounged back to the studio.

Hastings was not far away. The Luxembourg is within five minutes' walk of the rue Notre Dame des Champs, and there he sat under the shadow of a winged god, and there he had sat for an hour, poking holes in the dust and watching the steps which lead from the northern terrace to the fountain. The sun hung, a purple globe, above the misty hills of Meudon. Long streamers of clouds touched with rose swept low on the western sky, and the dome of the distant Invalides burned like an opal through the haze. Behind the Palace the smoke from a high chimney mounted straight into the air, purple until it crossed the sun, where it changed to a bar of smouldering fire. High above the darkening foliage of the chestnuts the twin towers of St. Sulpice rose, an ever-deepening silhouette.

A sleepy blackbird was carolling in some near thicket, and pigeons passed and repassed with the whisper of soft winds in their wings. The light on the Palace windows had died away, and the dome of the Pantheon swam aglow above the northern terrace, a fiery Valhalla in the sky; while below in grim array, along the terrace ranged, the marble ranks of queens looked out into the west.

From the end of the long walk by the northern façade of the Palace came the noise of omnibuses and the cries of the street. Hastings looked at the Palace clock. Six, and as his own watch agreed with it, he fell to poking holes in the gravel again. A constant stream of people passed between the Odéon and the fountain. Priests in black, with silver-buckled shoes; line soldiers, slouchy and rakish; neat girls without hats bearing milliners' boxes, students with black portfolios and high hats, students with bérets and big canes, nervous, quick-stepping officers, symphonies in turquoise and silver; ponderous jangling cavalrymen all over dust, pastry cooks' boys skipping along with utter disregard for the safety of the basket balanced on the impish head, and then the lean outcast, the shambling Paris tramp, slouching with shoulders bent and little eye furtively scanning the ground for smokers' refuse;—all these moved in a steady stream across the fountain circle and out into the city by the Odeon, whose long arcades were now beginning to flicker with gas-jets. The melancholy bells of St Sulpice struck the hour and the clock-tower of the Palace lighted up. Then hurried steps sounded across the gravel and Hastings raised his head.

"How late you are," he said, but his voice was hoarse and only his flushed face told how long had seemed the waiting.

She said, "I was kept—indeed, I was so much annoyed—and—and I may only stay a moment."

She sat down beside him, casting a furtive glance over her shoulder at the god upon his pedestal.

"What a nuisance, that intruding cupid still there?"

"Wings and arrows too," said Hastings, unheeding her motion to be seated.

"Wings," she murmured, "oh, yes—to fly away with when he's tired of his play. Of course it was a man who conceived the idea of wings, otherwise Cupid would have been insupportable."

"Do you think so?"

"*Ma foi*, it's what men think."

"And women?"

"Oh," she said, with a toss of her small head, "I really forget what we were speaking of."

"We were speaking of love," said Hastings.

"*I* was not," said the girl. Then looking up at the marble god, "I don't care for this one at all. I don't believe he knows how to shoot his arrows—no, indeed, he is a coward;—he creeps up like an assassin in the twilight. I don't approve of cowardice," she announced, and turned her back on the statue.

"I think," said Hastings quietly, "that he does shoot fairly—yes, and even gives one warning."

"Is it your experience, Monsieur Hastings?"

He looked straight into her eyes and said, "He is warning me."

"Heed the warning then," she cried, with a nervous laugh. As she spoke she stripped off her gloves, and then carefully proceeded to draw them on again. When this was accomplished she glanced at the Palace clock, saying, "Oh dear, how late it is!" furled her umbrella, then unfurled it, and finally looked at him.

"No," he said, "I shall not heed his warning."

"Oh dear," she sighed again, "still talking about that tiresome statue!" Then stealing a glance at his face, "I suppose—I suppose you are in love."

"I don't know," he muttered, "I suppose I am."

She raised her head with a quick gesture. "You seem delighted at the idea," she said, but bit her lip and trembled as his eyes met hers. Then sudden fear came over her and she sprang up, staring into the gathering shadows.

"Are you cold?" he said.

But she only answered, "Oh dear, oh dear, it is late—so late! I must go—good-night."

She gave him her gloved hand a moment and then withdrew it with a start.

"What is it?" he insisted. "Are you frightened?"

She looked at him strangely.

"No—no—not frightened,—you are very good to me—"

"By Jove!" he burst out, "what do you mean by saying I'm good to you? That's at least the third time, and I don't understand!"

The sound of a drum from the guard-house at the palace cut him short. "Listen," she whispered, "they are going to close. It's late, oh, so late!"

The rolling of the drum came nearer and nearer, and then the silhouette of the drummer cut the sky above the eastern terrace. The fading light lingered a moment on his belt and bayonet, then he passed into the shadows, drumming the echoes awake. The roll became fainter along the eastern terrace, then grew and grew and rattled with increasing sharpness when he passed the avenue by the bronze lion and turned down the western terrace walk. Louder and louder the drum sounded, and the echoes struck back the notes from the grey palace wall; and now the drummer loomed up before them—his red trousers a dull spot in the gathering gloom, the brass of his drum and bayonet touched with a pale spark, his epaulettes tossing on his shoulders. He passed leaving the crash of the drum in their ears, and far into the alley of trees they saw his little tin cup shining on his haversack. Then the sentinels began the monotonous cry: "On ferme! on ferme!" and the bugle blew from the barracks in the rue de Tournon.

"On ferme! on ferme!"

"Good-night," she whispered, "I must return alone to-night."

He watched her until she reached the northern terrace, and then sat down on the marble seat until a hand on his shoulder and a glimmer of bayonets warned him away.

She passed on through the grove, and turning into the rue de Medici, traversed it to the Boulevard. At the corner she bought a bunch of violets and walked on along the Boulevard to the rue des Écoles. A cab was drawn up before Boulant's, and a pretty girl aided by Elliott jumped out.

"Valentine!" cried the girl, "come with us!"

"I can't," she said, stopping a moment—"I have a rendezvous at Mignon's."

"Not Victor?" cried the girl, laughing, but she passed with a little shiver, nodding good-night, then turning into the Boulevard St. Germain, she walked a little faster to escape a gay party sitting before the Café Cluny who called to her to join them. At the door of the Restaurant Mignon stood a coal-black negro in buttons. He took off his peaked cap as she mounted the carpeted stairs.

"Send Eugene to me," she said at the office, and passing through the hallway to the right of the dining-room stopped before a row of panelled doors. A waiter passed and she repeated her demand for Eugene, who presently appeared, noiselessly skipping, and bowed murmuring, "Madame."

"Who is here?"

"No one in the cabinets, madame; in the half Madame Madelon and Monsieur Gay, Monsieur de Clamart, Monsieur Clisson, Madame Marie and their set." Then he looked around and bowing again murmured, "Monsieur awaits madame since half an hour," and he knocked at one of the panelled doors bearing the number six.

Clifford opened the door and the girl entered.

The garçon bowed her in, and whispering, "Will Monsieur have the goodness to ring?" vanished.

He helped her off with her jacket and took her hat and umbrella. When she was seated at the little table with Clifford opposite she smiled and leaned forward on both elbows looking him in the face.

"What are you doing here?" she demanded.

"Waiting," he replied, in accents of adoration.

For an instant she turned and examined herself in the glass. The wide blue eyes, the curling hair, the straight nose and short curled lip flashed in the mirror an instant only, and then its depths reflected her pretty neck and back. "Thus do I turn my back on vanity," she said, and then leaning forward again, "What are you doing here?"

"Waiting for you," repeated Clifford, slightly troubled.

"And Cécile."

"Now don't, Valentine—"

"Do you know," she said calmly, "I dislike your conduct?"

He was a little disconcerted, and rang for Eugene to cover his confusion.

The soup was bisque, and the wine Pommery, and the courses followed each other with the usual regularity until Eugene brought coffee, and there was nothing left on the table but a small silver lamp.

"Valentine," said Clifford, after having obtained permission to smoke, "is it the Vaudeville or the Eldorado—or both, or the Nouveau Cirque, or—"

"It is here," said Valentine.

"Well," he said, greatly flattered, "I'm afraid I couldn't amuse you—"

"Oh, yes, you are funnier than the Eldorado."

"Now see here, don't guy me, Valentine. You always do, and, and,—you know what they say,—a good laugh kills—"

"What?"

"Er—er—love and all that."

She laughed until her eyes were moist with tears. "Tiens," she cried, "he is dead, then!"

Clifford eyed her with growing alarm.

"Do you know why I came?" she said.

"No," he replied uneasily, "I don't."

"How long have you made love to me?"

"Well," he admitted, somewhat startled,—"I should say,—for about a year."

"It is a year, I think. Are you not tired?"

He did not answer.

"Don't you know that I like you too well to—to ever fall in love with you?" she said. "Don't you know that we are too good comrades,—too old friends for that? And were we not,—do you think that I do not know your history, Monsieur Clifford?"

"Don't be—don't be so sarcastic," he urged; "don't be unkind, Valentine."

"I'm not. I'm kind. I'm very kind,—to you and to Cécile."

"Cécile is tired of me."

"I hope she is," said the girl, "for she deserves a better fate. Tiens, do you know your reputation in the Quarter? Of the inconstant, the most inconstant,—utterly incorrigible and no more serious than a gnat on a summer night. Poor Cécile!"

Clifford looked so uncomfortable that she spoke more kindly.

"I like you. You know that. Everybody does. You are a spoiled child here. Everything is permitted you and every one makes allowance, but every one cannot be a victim to caprice."

"Caprice!" he cried. "By Jove, if the girls of the Latin Quarter are not capricious—"

"Never mind,—never mind about that! You must not sit in judgment—you of all men. Why are you here to-night? Oh," she cried, "I will tell you why! Monsieur receives a little note; he sends a little answer; he dresses in his conquering raiment—"

"I don't," said Clifford, very red.

"You do, and it becomes you," she retorted with a faint smile. Then again, very quietly, "I am in your power, but I know I am in the power of a friend. I have come to acknowledge it to you here,—and it is because of that that I am here to beg of you—a—a favour."

Clifford opened his eyes, but said nothing.

"I am in—great distress of mind. It is Monsieur Hastings."

"Well?" said Clifford, in some astonishment.

"I want to ask you," she continued in a low voice, "I want to ask you to—to—in case you should speak of me before him,— not to say,—not to say,—"

"I shall not speak of you to him," he said quietly.

"Can—can you prevent others?"

"I might if I was present. May I ask why?"

"That is not fair," she murmured; "you know how—how he considers me,—as he considers every woman. You know how different he is from you and the rest. I have never seen a man,— such a man as Monsieur Hastings."

He let his cigarette go out unnoticed.

"I am almost afraid of him—afraid he should know—what we all are in the Quarter. Oh, I do not wish him to know! I do not wish him to—to turn from me—to cease from speaking to me as he does! You—you and the rest cannot know what it has been to me. I could not believe him,—I could not believe he was so good and—and noble. I do not wish him to know—so soon. He will find out—sooner or later, he will find out for himself, and then he will turn away from me. Why!" she cried passionately, "why should he turn from me and not from *you*?"

Clifford, much embarrassed, eyed his cigarette.

The girl rose, very white. "He is your friend—you have a right to warn him."

"He is my friend," he said at length.

They looked at each other in silence.

Then she cried, "By all that I hold to me most sacred, you need not warn him!"

"I shall trust your word," he said pleasantly.

V

The month passed quickly for Hastings, and left few definite impressions after it. It did leave some, however. One was a painful impression of meeting Mr. Bladen on the Boulevard des Capucines in company with a very pronounced young person whose laugh dismayed him, and when at last he escaped from the café where Mr. Bladen had hauled him to join them in a *bock* he felt as if the whole boulevard was looking at him, and judging him by his company. Later, an instinctive conviction regarding the young person with Mr. Bladen sent the hot blood into his cheek, and he returned to the pension in such a miserable state of mind that Miss Byng was alarmed and advised him to conquer his homesickness at once.

Another impression was equally vivid. One Saturday morning, feeling lonely, his wanderings about the city brought him to the Gare St. Lazare. It was early for breakfast, but he entered the Hôtel Terminus and took a table near the window. As he wheeled about to give his order, a man passing rapidly along the aisle collided with his head, and looking up to receive the expected apology, he was met instead by a slap on the shoulder and a hearty, "What the deuce are you doing here, old chap?" It was Rowden, who seized him and told him to come along. So, mildly protesting, he was ushered into a private dining-room where Clifford, rather red, jumped up from the table and welcomed him with a startled air which was softened by the unaffected glee of Rowden and the extreme courtesy of Elliott. The latter presented him to three bewitching girls who welcomed him so charmingly and seconded Rowden in his demand that Hastings should make one of the party, that he consented at once. While Elliott briefly outlined the projected excursion to La Roche, Hastings delightedly ate his omelet, and returned the smiles of encouragement from Cécile and Colette and Jacqueline. Meantime Clifford in a bland whisper was telling Rowden what an ass he was. Poor Rowden looked miserable until Elliott, divining how affairs were turning, frowned on Clifford and found a moment to let Rowden know that they were all going to make the best of it.

"You shut up," he observed to Clifford, "it's fate, and that settles it."

"It's Rowden, and that settles it," murmured Clifford, concealing a grin. For after all he was not Hastings' wet nurse. So it came about that the train which left the Gare St. Lazare at 9.15 a.m. stopped a moment in its career towards Havre and deposited at the red-roofed station of La Roche a merry party, armed with sunshades, trout-rods, and one cane, carried by the non-combatant, Hastings. Then, when they had established their camp in a grove of sycamores which bordered the little river Ept, Clifford, the acknowledged master of all that pertained to sportsmanship, took command.

"You, Rowden," he said, "divide your flies with Elliott and keep an eye on him or else he'll be trying to put on a float and sinker. Prevent him by force from grubbing about for worms."

Elliott protested, but was forced to smile in the general laugh.

"You make me ill," he asserted; "do you think this is my first trout?"

"I shall be delighted to see your first trout," said Clifford, and dodging a fly hook, hurled with intent to hit, proceeded to sort and equip three slender rods destined to bring joy and fish to Cécile, Colette, and Jacqueline. With perfect gravity he ornamented each line with four split shot, a small hook, and a brilliant quill float.

"*I* shall never touch the worms," announced Cécile with a shudder.

Jacqueline and Colette hastened to sustain her, and Hastings pleasantly offered to act in the capacity of general baiter and taker-off of fish. But Cécile, doubtless fascinated by the gaudy flies in Clifford's book, decided to accept lessons from him in the true art, and presently disappeared up the Ept with Clifford in tow.

Elliott looked doubtfully at Colette.

"I prefer gudgeons," said that damsel with decision, "and you and Monsieur Rowden may go away when you please; may they not, Jacqueline?"

"Certainly," responded Jacqueline.

Elliott, undecided, examined his rod and reel.

"You've got your reel on wrong side up," observed Rowden.

Elliott wavered, and stole a glance at Colette.

"I—I—have almost decided to—er—not to flip the flies about just now," he began. "There's the pole that Cécile left—"

"Don't call it a pole," corrected Rowden.

"*Rod*, then," continued Elliott, and started off in the wake of the two girls, but was promptly collared by Rowden.

"No, you don't! Fancy a man fishing with a float and sinker when he has a fly rod in his hand! You come along!"

Where the placid little Ept flows down between its thickets to the Seine, a grassy bank shadows the haunt of the gudgeon, and on this bank sat Colette and Jacqueline and chattered and laughed and watched the swerving of the scarlet quills, while Hastings, his hat over his eyes, his head on a bank of moss, listened to their soft voices and gallantly unhooked the small and indignant gudgeon when a flash of a rod and a half-suppressed scream announced a catch. The sunlight filtered through the leafy thickets awaking to song the forest birds. Magpies in spotless black and white flirted past, alighting near by with a hop and bound and twitch of the tail. Blue and white jays with rosy breasts shrieked through the trees, and a low-sailing hawk wheeled among the fields of ripening wheat, putting to flight flocks of twittering hedge birds.

Across the Seine a gull dropped on the water like a plume. The air was pure and still. Scarcely a leaf moved. Sounds from a distant farm came faintly, the shrill cock-crow and dull baying. Now and then a steam-tug with big raking smoke-pipe, bearing the name "Guêpe 27," ploughed up the river dragging its interminable train of barges, or a sailboat dropped down with the current toward sleepy Rouen.

A faint fresh odour of earth and water hung in the air, and through the sunlight, orange-tipped butterflies danced above the marsh grass, soft velvety butterflies flapped through the mossy woods.

Hastings was thinking of Valentine. It was two o'clock when Elliott strolled back, and frankly admitting that he had eluded Rowden, sat down beside Colette and prepared to doze with satisfaction.

"Where are your trout?" said Colette severely.

"They still live," murmured Elliott, and went fast asleep.

Rowden returned shortly after, and casting a scornful glance at the slumbering one, displayed three crimson-flecked trout.

"And that," smiled Hastings lazily, "that is the holy end to which the faithful plod,—the slaughter of these small fish with a bit of silk and feather."

Rowden disdained to answer him. Colette caught another gudgeon and awoke Elliott, who protested and gazed about for the lunch baskets, as Clifford and Cécile came up demanding instant refreshment. Cécile's skirts were soaked, and her gloves torn, but she was happy, and Clifford, dragging out a two-pound trout, stood still to receive the applause of the company.

"Where the deuce did you get that?" demanded Elliott.

Cécile, wet and enthusiastic, recounted the battle, and then Clifford eulogized her powers with the fly, and, in proof, produced from his creel a defunct chub, which, he observed, just missed being a trout.

They were all very happy at luncheon, and Hastings was voted "charming." He enjoyed it immensely,—only it seemed to him at moments that flirtation went further in France than in Millbrook, Connecticut, and he thought that Cécile might be a little less enthusiastic about Clifford, that perhaps it would be quite as well if Jacqueline sat further away from Rowden, and that possibly Colette could have, for a moment at least, taken her eyes from Elliott's face. Still he enjoyed it—except when his thoughts drifted to Valentine, and then he felt that he was very far away from her. La Roche is at least an hour and a half from Paris. It is also true that he felt a happiness, a quick heart-beat when, at eight o'clock that night the train which bore them from La Roche rolled into the Gare St. Lazare and he was once more in the city of Valentine.

"Good-night," they said, pressing around him. "You must come with us next time!"

He promised, and watched them, two by two, drift into the darkening city, and stood so long that, when again he raised his eyes, the vast Boulevard was twinkling with gas-jets through which the electric lights stared like moons.

VI

It was with another quick heart-beat that he awoke next morning, for his first thought was of Valentine.

The sun already gilded the towers of Notre Dame, the clatter of workmen's sabots awoke sharp echoes in the street below, and across the way a blackbird in a pink almond tree was going into an ecstasy of trills.

He determined to awake Clifford for a brisk walk in the country, hoping later to beguile that gentleman into the American church for his soul's sake. He found Alfred the gimlet-eyed washing the asphalt walk which led to the studio.

"Monsieur Elliott?" he replied to the perfunctory inquiry, "*je ne sais pas.*"

"And Monsieur Clifford," began Hastings, somewhat astonished.

"Monsieur Clifford," said the concierge with fine irony, "will be pleased to see you, as he retired early; in fact he has just come in."

Hastings hesitated while the concierge pronounced a fine eulogy on people who never stayed out all night and then came battering at the lodge gate during hours which even a gendarme held sacred to sleep. He also discoursed eloquently upon the beauties of temperance, and took an ostentatious draught from the fountain in the court.

"I do not think I will come in," said Hastings.

"Pardon, monsieur," growled the concierge, "perhaps it would be well to see Monsieur Clifford. He possibly needs aid. Me he drives forth with hair-brushes and boots. It is a mercy if he has not set fire to something with his candle."

Hastings hesitated for an instant, but swallowing his dislike of such a mission, walked slowly through the ivy-covered alley and across the inner garden to the studio. He knocked. Perfect silence. Then he knocked again, and this time something struck the door from within with a crash.

"That," said the concierge, "was a boot." He fitted his duplicate key into the lock and ushered Hastings in. Clifford, in disordered evening dress, sat on the rug in the middle of the room. He held in his hand a shoe, and did not appear astonished to see Hastings.

"Good-morning, do you use Pears' soap?" he inquired with a vague wave of his hand and a vaguer smile.

Hastings' heart sank. "For Heaven's sake," he said, "Clifford, go to bed."

"Not while that—that Alfred pokes his shaggy head in here an' I have a shoe left."

Hastings blew out the candle, picked up Clifford's hat and cane, and said, with an emotion he could not conceal, "This is terrible, Clifford,—I—never knew you did this sort of thing."

"Well, I do," said Clifford.

"Where is Elliott?"

"Ole chap," returned Clifford, becoming maudlin, "Providence which feeds—feeds—er—sparrows an' that sort of thing watcheth over the intemperate wanderer—"

"Where is Elliott?"

But Clifford only wagged his head and waved his arm about. "He's out there,—somewhere about." Then suddenly feeling a desire to see his missing chum, lifted up his voice and howled for him.

Hastings, thoroughly shocked, sat down on the lounge without a word. Presently, after shedding several scalding tears, Clifford brightened up and rose with great precaution.

"Ole chap," he observed, "do you want to see er—er miracle? Well, here goes. I'm goin' to begin."

He paused, beaming at vacancy.

"Er miracle," he repeated.

Hastings supposed he was alluding to the miracle of his keeping his balance, and said nothing.

"I'm goin' to bed," he announced, "poor ole Clifford's goin' to bed, an' that's er miracle!"

And he did with a nice calculation of distance and equilibrium which would have rung enthusiastic yells of applause from Elliott had he been there to assist *en connaisseur*. But he was not. He had not yet reached the studio. He was on his way, however, and smiled with magnificent condescension on Hastings, who, half an hour later, found him reclining upon a bench in the Luxembourg. He permitted himself to be aroused, dusted and escorted to the gate. Here, however, he refused all further assistance, and bestowing a patronizing bow upon Hastings, steered a tolerably true course for the rue Vavin.

Hastings watched him out of sight, and then slowly retraced his steps toward the fountain. At first he felt gloomy and depressed, but gradually the clear air of the morning lifted the pressure from his heart, and he sat down on the marble seat under the shadow of the winged god.

The air was fresh and sweet with perfume from the orange flowers. Everywhere pigeons were bathing, dashing the water over their iris-hued breasts, flashing in and out of the spray or nestling almost to the neck along the polished basin. The sparrows, too, were abroad in force, soaking their dust-coloured feathers in the limpid pool and chirping with might and main. Under the sycamores which surrounded the duck-pond opposite the fountain of Marie de Medici, the water-fowl cropped the herbage, or waddled in rows down the bank to embark on some solemn aimless cruise.

Butterflies, somewhat lame from a chilly night's repose under the lilac leaves, crawled over and over the white phlox, or took a rheumatic flight toward some sun-warmed shrub. The bees were already busy among the heliotrope, and one or two grey flies with brick-coloured eyes sat in a spot of sunlight beside the marble seat, or chased each other about, only to return again to the spot of sunshine and rub their fore-legs, exulting.

The sentries paced briskly before the painted boxes, pausing at times to look toward the guard-house for their relief.

They came at last, with a shuffle of feet and click of bayonets, the word was passed, the relief fell out, and away they went, crunch, crunch, across the gravel.

A mellow chime floated from the clock-tower of the palace, the deep bell of St. Sulpice echoed the stroke. Hastings sat dreaming in the shadow of the god, and while he mused somebody came and sat down beside him. At first he did not raise his head. It was only when she spoke that he sprang up.

"You! At this hour?"

"I was restless, I could not sleep." Then in a low, happy voice—"And *you!* at this hour?"

"I—I slept, but the sun awoke me."

"*I* could not sleep," she said, and her eyes seemed, for a moment, touched with an indefinable shadow. Then, smiling, "I am so glad—I seemed to know you were coming. Don't laugh, I believe in dreams."

"Did you really dream of,—of my being here?"

"I think I was awake when I dreamed it," she admitted. Then for a time they were mute, acknowledging by silence the happiness of being together. And after all their silence was eloquent, for faint smiles, and glances born of their thoughts, crossed and recrossed, until lips moved and words were formed, which seemed almost superfluous. What they said was not very profound. Perhaps the most valuable jewel that fell from Hastings' lips bore direct reference to breakfast.

"I have not yet had my chocolate," she confessed, "but what a material man you are."

"Valentine," he said impulsively, "I wish,—I do wish that you would,—just for this once,—give me the whole day,—just for this once."

"Oh dear," she smiled, "not only material, but selfish!"

"Not selfish, hungry," he said, looking at her.

"A cannibal too; oh dear!"

"Will you, Valentine?"

"But my chocolate—"

"Take it with me."

"But *déjeuner*—"

"Together, at St. Cloud."

"But I can't—"

"Together,—all day,—all day long; will you, Valentine?"

She was silent.

"Only for this once."

Again that indefinable shadow fell across her eyes, and when it was gone she sighed. "Yes,—together, only for this once."

"All day?" he said, doubting his happiness.

"All day," she smiled; "and oh, I am so hungry!"

He laughed, enchanted.

"What a material young lady it is."

On the Boulevard St. Michel there is a Crémerie painted white and blue outside, and neat and clean as a whistle inside. The auburn-haired young woman who speaks French like a native, and rejoices in the name of Murphy, smiled at them as they entered, and tossing a fresh napkin over the zinc *tête-à-tête* table, whisked before them two cups of chocolate and a basket full of crisp, fresh croissons.

The primrose-coloured pats of butter, each stamped with a shamrock in relief, seemed saturated with the fragrance of Normandy pastures.

"How delicious!" they said in the same breath, and then laughed at the coincidence.

"With but a single thought," he began.

"How absurd!" she cried with cheeks all rosy. "I'm thinking I'd like a croisson."

"So am I," he replied triumphant, "that proves it."

Then they had a quarrel; she accusing him of behaviour unworthy of a child in arms, and he denying it, and bringing counter charges, until Mademoiselle Murphy laughed in sympathy, and the last croisson was eaten under a flag of truce. Then they rose, and she took his arm with a bright nod to Mlle. Murphy, who cried them a merry: "*Bonjour, madame! bonjour, monsieur!*" and watched them hail a passing cab and drive away. "*Dieu! qu'il est beau,*" she sighed, adding after a moment, "Do they be married, I dunno,—*ma foi ils ont bien l'air.*"

The cab swung around the rue de Medici, turned into the rue de Vaugirard, followed it to where it crosses the rue de Rennes, and taking that noisy thoroughfare, drew up before the Gare Montparnasse. They were just in time for a train and scampered up the stairway and out to the cars as the last note from the starting-gong rang through the arched station. The guard slammed the door of their compartment, a whistle sounded, answered by a screech from the locomotive, and the long train glided from the station, faster, faster, and sped out into the morning sunshine. The summer wind blew in their faces from the open window, and sent the soft hair dancing on the girl's forehead.

"We have the compartment to ourselves," said Hastings.

She leaned against the cushioned window-seat, her eyes bright and wide open, her lips parted. The wind lifted her hat, and fluttered the ribbons under her chin. With a quick movement she untied them, and, drawing a long hat-pin from her hat, laid it down on the seat beside her. The train was flying.

The colour surged in her cheeks, and, with each quick-drawn breath, her breath rose and fell under the cluster of lilies at her throat. Trees, houses, ponds, danced past, cut by a mist of telegraph poles.

"Faster! faster!" she cried.

His eyes never left her, but hers, wide open, and blue as the summer sky, seemed fixed on something far ahead,—something which came no nearer, but fled before them as they fled.

Was it the horizon, cut now by the grim fortress on the hill, now by the cross of a country chapel? Was it the summer moon, ghost-like, slipping through the vaguer blue above?

"Faster! faster!" she cried.

Her parted lips burned scarlet.

The car shook and shivered, and the fields streamed by like an emerald torrent. He caught the excitement, and his faced glowed.

"Oh," she cried, and with an unconscious movement caught his hand, drawing him to the window beside her. "Look! lean out with me!"

He only saw her lips move; her voice was drowned in the roar of a trestle, but his hand closed in hers and he clung to the sill. The wind whistled in their ears. "Not so far out, Valentine, take care!" he gasped.

Below, through the ties of the trestle, a broad river flashed into view and out again, as the train thundered along a tunnel, and away once more through the freshest of green fields. The wind roared about them. The girl was leaning far out from the window, and he caught her by the waist, crying, "Not too far!" but she only murmured, "Faster! faster! away out of the city, out of the land, faster, faster! away out of the world!"

"What are you saying all to yourself?" he said, but his voice was broken, and the wind whirled it back into his throat.

She heard him, and, turning from the window looked down at his arm about her. Then she raised her eyes to his. The car shook and the windows rattled. They were dashing through a forest now, and the sun swept the dewy branches with running flashes of fire. He looked into her troubled eyes; he drew her to him and kissed the half-parted lips, and she cried out, a bitter, hopeless cry, "Not that—not that!"

But he held her close and strong, whispering words of honest love and passion, and when she sobbed—"Not that—not that—I have promised! You must—you must know—I am—not—worthy—" In the purity of his own heart her words were, to him, meaningless then, meaningless for ever after. Presently her voice ceased, and her head rested on his breast. He leaned against the window, his ears swept by the furious wind, his heart in a joyous tumult. The forest was passed, and the sun slipped from behind the trees, flooding the earth again with brightness. She raised her eyes and looked out into the world from the window. Then she began to speak, but her voice was faint, and he bent his head close to hers and listened. "I cannot turn from you; I am too weak. You were long ago my master—master of my heart and soul. I have broken my word to one who trusted me, but I have told you all;—what matters the rest?" He smiled at her innocence and she worshipped his. She spoke again: "Take me or cast me away;—what matters it? Now with a word you can kill me, and it might be easier to die than to look upon happiness as great as mine."

He took her in his arms, "Hush, what are you saying? Look,—look out at the sunlight, the meadows and the streams. We shall be very happy in so bright a world."

She turned to the sunlight. From the window, the world below seemed very fair to her.

Trembling with happiness, she sighed: "Is this the world? Then I have never known it."

"Nor have I, God forgive me," he murmured.

Perhaps it was our gentle Lady of the Fields who forgave them both.

RUE BARRÉE

"For let Philosopher and Doctor preach
Of what they will and what they will not,—each
Is but one link in an eternal chain
That none can slip nor break nor over-reach."

~~~~~~~~~~~~~

"Crimson nor yellow roses nor
The savour of the mounting sea
Are worth the perfume I adore
That clings to thee.

The languid-headed lilies tire,
The changeless waters weary me;
I ache with passionate desire
Of thine and thee.

There are but these things in the world—
Thy mouth of fire,
Thy breasts, thy hands, thy hair upcurled
And my desire."

I

One morning at Julian's, a student said to Selby, "That is Foxhall Clifford," pointing with his brushes at a young man who sat before an easel, doing nothing.

Selby, shy and nervous, walked over and began: "My name is Selby,—I have just arrived in Paris, and bring a letter of introduction—" His voice was lost in the crash of a falling easel, the owner of which promptly assaulted his neighbour, and for a time the noise of battle rolled through the studios of MM. Boulanger and Lefebvre, presently subsiding into a scuffle on the stairs outside. Selby, apprehensive as to his own reception in the studio, looked at Clifford, who sat serenely watching the fight.

"It's a little noisy here," said Clifford, "but you will like the fellows when you know them." His unaffected manner delighted Selby. Then with a simplicity that won his heart, he presented him to half a dozen students of as many nationalities. Some were cordial, all were polite. Even the majestic creature who held the position of Massier, unbent enough to say: "My friend, when a man speaks French as well as you do, and is also a friend of Monsieur Clifford, he will have no trouble in this studio. You expect, of course, to fill the stove until the next new man comes?"

"Of course."

"And you don't mind chaff?"

"No," replied Selby, who hated it.

Clifford, much amused, put on his hat, saying, "You must expect lots of it at first."

Selby placed his own hat on his head and followed him to the door.

As they passed the model stand there was a furious cry of "Chapeau! Chapeau!" and a student sprang from his easel menacing Selby, who reddened but looked at Clifford.

"Take off your hat for them," said the latter, laughing.

A little embarrassed, he turned and saluted the studio.

"Et moi?" cried the model.

"You are charming," replied Selby, astonished at his own audacity, but the studio rose as one man, shouting: "He has done well! he's all right!" while the model, laughing, kissed her hand to him and cried: "*À demain beau jeune homme!*"

All that week Selby worked at the studio unmolested. The French students christened him "*l'Enfant Prodigue*," which was freely translated, "The Prodigious Infant," "The Kid," "Kid Selby," and "Kidby." But the disease soon ran its course from "Kidby" to "Kidney," and then naturally to "Tidbits," where it was arrested by Clifford's authority and ultimately relapsed to "Kid."

Wednesday came, and with it M. Boulanger. For three hours the students writhed under his biting sarcasms,—among the others Clifford, who was informed that he knew even less about a work of art than he did about the art of work. Selby was more fortunate. The professor examined his drawing in silence, looked at him sharply, and passed on with a non-committal gesture. He presently departed arm in arm with Bouguereau, to the relief of Clifford, who was then at liberty to jam his hat on his head and depart.

The next day he did not appear, and Selby, who had counted on seeing him at the studio, a thing which he learned later it was vanity to count on, wandered back to the Latin Quarter alone.

Paris was still strange and new to him. He was vaguely troubled by its splendour. No tender memories stirred his American bosom at the Place du Châtelet, nor even by Notre Dame. The Palais de Justice with its clock and turrets and stalking sentinels in blue and vermilion, the Place St. Michel with its jumble of omnibuses and ugly water-spitting griffins, the hill of the Boulevard St. Michel, the tooting trams, the policemen dawdling two by two, and the table-lined terraces of the Café Vacehett were nothing to him, as yet, nor did he even know, when he stepped from the stones of the Place St. Michel to the asphalt of the Boulevard, that he had crossed the frontier and entered the student zone,—the famous Latin Quarter.

A cabman hailed him as "bourgeois," and urged the superiority of driving over walking. A gamin, with an appearance of great concern, requested the latest telegraphic news from London, and then, standing on his head, invited Selby to feats of strength. A pretty girl gave him a glance from a pair of violet eyes. He did not see her, but she, catching her own reflection in a window, wondered at the colour burning in her cheeks. Turning to resume her course, she met Foxhall Clifford, and hurried on. Clifford, open-mouthed, followed her with his eyes; then he looked after Selby, who had turned into the Boulevard St. Germain toward

the rue de Seine. Then he examined himself in the shop window.
The result seemed to be unsatisfactory.

"I'm not a beauty," he mused, "but neither am I a hobgoblin.
What does she mean by blushing at Selby? I never before saw
her look at a fellow in my life,—neither has any one in the
Quarter. Anyway, I can swear she never looks at me, and goodness
knows I have done all that respectful adoration can do."

He sighed, and murmuring a prophecy concerning the salvation of his immortal soul swung into that graceful lounge which
at all times characterized Clifford. With no apparent exertion, he
overtook Selby at the corner, and together they crossed the sunlit
Boulevard and sat down under the awning of the Café du Cercle.
Clifford bowed to everybody on the terrace, saying, "You shall
meet them all later, but now let me present you to two of the
sights of Paris, Mr. Richard Elliott and Mr. Stanley Rowden."

The "sights" looked amiable, and took vermouth.

"You cut the studio to-day," said Elliott, suddenly turning on
Clifford, who avoided his eyes.

"To commune with nature?" observed Rowden.

"What's her name this time?" asked Elliott, and Rowden
answered promptly, "Name, Yvette; nationality, Breton—"

"Wrong," replied Clifford blandly, "it's Rue Barrée."

The subject changed instantly, and Selby listened in surprise
to names which were new to him, and eulogies on the latest
Prix de Rome winner. He was delighted to hear opinions boldly
expressed and points honestly debated, although the vehicle was
mostly slang, both English and French. He longed for the time
when he too should be plunged into the strife for fame.

The bells of St. Sulpice struck the hour, and the Palace of the
Luxembourg answered chime on chime. With a glance at the
sun, dipping low in the golden dust behind the Palais Bourbon,
they rose, and turning to the east, crossed the Boulevard St.
Germain and sauntered toward the École de Médecine. At the
corner a girl passed them, walking hurriedly. Clifford smirked,
Elliott and Rowden were agitated, but they all bowed, and, without

raising her eyes, she returned their salute. But Selby, who had lagged behind, fascinated by some gay shop window, looked up to meet two of the bluest eyes he had ever seen. The eyes were dropped in an instant, and the young fellow hastened to overtake the others.

"By Jove," he said, "do you fellows know I have just seen the prettiest girl—" An exclamation broke from the trio, gloomy, foreboding, like the chorus in a Greek play.

"Rue Barrée!"

"What!" cried Selby, bewildered.

The only answer was a vague gesture from Clifford.

Two hours later, during dinner, Clifford turned to Selby and said, "You want to ask me something; I can tell by the way you fidget about."

"Yes, I do," he said, innocently enough; "it's about that girl. Who is she?"

In Rowden's smile there was pity, in Elliott's bitterness.

"Her name," said Clifford solemnly, "is unknown to any one, at least," he added with much conscientiousness, "as far as I can learn. Every fellow in the Quarter bows to her and she returns the salute gravely, but no man has ever been known to obtain more than that. Her profession, judging from her music-roll, is that of a pianist. Her residence is in a small and humble street which is kept in a perpetual process of repair by the city authorities, and from the black letters painted on the barrier which defends the street from traffic, she has taken the name by which we know her,—Rue Barrée. Mr. Rowden, in his imperfect knowledge of the French tongue, called our attention to it as Roo Barry—"

"I didn't," said Rowden hotly.

"And Roo Barry, or Rue Barrée, is to-day an object of adoration to every rapin in the Quarter—"

"We are not rapins," corrected Elliott.

"*I* am not," returned Clifford, "and I beg to call to your attention, Selby, that these two gentlemen have at various and

apparently unfortunate moments, offered to lay down life and
limb at the feet of Rue Barrée. The lady possesses a chilling smile
which she uses on such occasions and," here he became gloomily
impressive, "I have been forced to believe that neither the schol-
arly grace of my friend Elliott nor the buxom beauty of my friend
Rowden have touched that heart of ice."

Elliott and Rowden, boiling with indignation, cried out, "And
you!"

"I," said Clifford blandly, "do fear to tread where you rush in."

II

Twenty-four hours later Selby had completely forgotten Rue
Barrée. During the week he worked with might and main at the
studio, and Saturday night found him so tired that he went to
bed before dinner and had a nightmare about a river of yellow
ochre in which he was drowning. Sunday morning, apropos of
nothing at all, he thought of Rue Barrée, and ten seconds afterwards he saw her. It was at the flower-market on the marble
bridge. She was examining a pot of pansies. The gardener had
evidently thrown heart and soul into the transaction, but Rue
Barrée shook her head.

It is a question whether Selby would have stopped then and
there to inspect a cabbage-rose had not Clifford unwound for
him the yarn of the previous Tuesday. It is possible that his curiosity was piqued, for with the exception of a hen-turkey, a boy
of nineteen is the most openly curious biped alive. From twenty
until death he tries to conceal it. But, to be fair to Selby, it is also
true that the market was attractive. Under a cloudless sky the
flowers were packed and heaped along the marble bridge to the
parapet. The air was soft, the sun spun a shadowy lacework
among the palms and glowed in the hearts of a thousand roses.
Spring had come,—was in full tide. The watering carts and
sprinklers spread freshness over the Boulevard, the sparrows had

become vulgarly obtrusive, and the credulous Seine angler anxiously followed his gaudy quill floating among the soapsuds of the lavoirs. The white-spiked chestnuts clad in tender green vibrated with the hum of bees. Shoddy butterflies flaunted their winter rags among the heliotrope. There was a smell of fresh earth in the air, an echo of the woodland brook in the ripple of the Seine, and swallows soared and skimmed among the anchored river craft. Somewhere in a window a caged bird was singing its heart out to the sky.

Selby looked at the cabbage-rose and then at the sky. Something in the song of the caged bird may have moved him, or perhaps it was that dangerous sweetness in the air of May.

At first he was hardly conscious that he had stopped, then he was scarcely conscious why he had stopped, then he thought he would move on, then he thought he wouldn't, then he looked at Rue Barrée.

The gardener said, "Mademoiselle, this is undoubtedly a fine pot of pansies."

Rue Barrée shook her head.

The gardener smiled. She evidently did not want the pansies. She had bought many pots of pansies there, two or three every spring, and never argued. What did she want then? The pansies were evidently a feeler toward a more important transaction. The gardener rubbed his hands and gazed about him.

"These tulips are magnificent," he observed, "and these hyacinths—" He fell into a trance at the mere sight of the scented thickets.

"That," murmured Rue, pointing to a splendid rose-bush with her furled parasol, but in spite of her, her voice trembled a little. Selby noticed it, more shame to him that he was listening, and the gardener noticed it, and, burying his nose in the roses, scented a bargain. Still, to do him justice, he did not add a centime to the honest value of the plant, for after all, Rue was probably poor, and any one could see she was charming.

"Fifty francs, Mademoiselle."

The gardener's tone was grave. Rue felt that argument would
be wasted. They both stood silent for a moment. The gardener
did not eulogize his prize,—the rose-tree was gorgeous and any
one could see it.

"I will take the pansies," said the girl, and drew two francs
from a worn purse. Then she looked up. A tear-drop stood in the
way refracting the light like a diamond, but as it rolled into a
little corner by her nose a vision of Selby replaced it, and when
a brush of the handkerchief had cleared the startled blue eyes,
Selby himself appeared, very much embarrassed. He instantly
looked up into the sky, apparently devoured with a thirst for
astronomical research, and as he continued his investigations for
fully five minutes, the gardener looked up too, and so did a
policeman. Then Selby looked at the tips of his boots, the gardener
looked at him and the policeman slouched on. Rue Barrée had
been gone some time.

"What," said the gardener, "may I offer Monsieur?"

Selby never knew why, but he suddenly began to buy flowers.
The gardener was electrified. Never before had he sold so many
flowers, never at such satisfying prices, and never, never with
such absolute unanimity of opinion with a customer. But he
missed the bargaining, the arguing, the calling of Heaven to
witness. The transaction lacked spice.

"These tulips are magnificent!"

"They are!" cried Selby warmly.

"But alas, they are dear."

"I will take them."

"Dieu!" murmured the gardener in a perspiration, "he's madder
than most Englishmen."

"This cactus—"

"Is gorgeous!"

"Alas—"

"Send it with the rest."

The gardener braced himself against the river wall.

"That splendid rose-bush," he began faintly.

"That is a beauty. I believe it is fifty francs—"

He stopped, very red. The gardener relished his confusion. Then a sudden cool self-possession took the place of his momentary confusion and he held the gardener with his eye, and bullied him.

"I'll take that bush. Why did not the young lady buy it?"

"Mademoiselle is not wealthy."

"How do you know?"

"*Dame*, I sell her many pansies; pansies are not expensive."

"Those are the pansies she bought?"

"These, Monsieur, the blue and gold."

"Then you intend to send them to her?"

"At mid-day after the market."

"Take this rose-bush with them, and"—here he glared at the gardener—"don't you dare say from whom they came." The gardener's eyes were like saucers, but Selby, calm and victorious, said: "Send the others to the Hôtel du Sénat, 7 rue de Tournon. I will leave directions with the concierge."

Then he buttoned his glove with much dignity and stalked off, but when well around the corner and hidden from the gardener's view, the conviction that he was an idiot came home to him in a furious blush. Ten minutes later he sat in his room in the Hôtel du Sénat repeating with an imbecile smile: "What an ass I am, what an ass!"

An hour later found him in the same chair, in the same position, his hat and gloves still on, his stick in his hand, but he was silent, apparently lost in contemplation of his boot toes, and his smile was less imbecile and even a bit retrospective.

III

About five o'clock that afternoon, the little sad-eyed woman who fills the position of concierge at the Hôtel du Sénat held up her hands in amazement to see a wagon-load of flower-bearing shrubs draw up before the doorway. She called Joseph, the intemperate garçon, who, while calculating the value of the flowers in *petits verres*, gloomily disclaimed any knowledge as to their destination.

"*Voyons*," said the little concierge, "*cherchons la femme*!"

"You?" he suggested.

The little woman stood a moment pensive and then sighed. Joseph caressed his nose, a nose which for gaudiness could vie with any floral display.

Then the gardener came in, hat in hand, and a few minutes later Selby stood in the middle of his room, his coat off, his shirt-sleeves rolled up. The chamber originally contained, besides the furniture, about two square feet of walking room, and now this was occupied by a cactus. The bed groaned under crates of pansies, lilies and heliotrope, the lounge was covered with hyacinths and tulips, and the washstand supported a species of young tree warranted to bear flowers at some time or other.

Clifford came in a little later, fell over a box of sweet peas, swore a little, apologized, and then, as the full splendour of the floral *fête* burst upon him, sat down in astonishment upon a geranium. The geranium was a wreck, but Selby said, "Don't mind," and glared at the cactus.

"Are you going to give a ball?" demanded Clifford.

"N—no,—I'm very fond of flowers," said Selby, but the statement lacked enthusiasm.

"I should imagine so." Then, after a silence, "That's a fine cactus."

Selby contemplated the cactus, touched it with the air of a connoisseur, and pricked his thumb.

Clifford poked a pansy with his stick. Then Joseph came in with the bill, announcing the sum total in a loud voice, partly to impress Clifford, partly to intimidate Selby into disgorging a *pourboire* which he would share, if he chose, with the gardener. Clifford tried to pretend that he had not heard, while Selby paid bill and tribute without a murmur. Then he lounged back into the room with an attempt at indifference which failed entirely when he tore his trousers on the cactus.

Clifford made some commonplace remark, lighted a cigarette and looked out of the window to give Selby a chance. Selby tried to take it, but getting as far as—"Yes, spring is here at last," froze solid. He looked at the back of Clifford's head. It expressed volumes. Those little perked-up ears seemed tingling with suppressed glee. He made a desperate effort to master the situation, and jumped up to reach for some Russian cigarettes as an incentive to conversation, but was foiled by the cactus, to whom again he fell a prey. The last straw was added.

"Damn the cactus." This observation was wrung from Selby against his will,—against his own instinct of self-preservation, but the thorns on the cactus were long and sharp, and at their repeated prick his pent-up wrath escaped. It was too late now; it was done, and Clifford had wheeled around.

"See here, Selby, why the deuce did you buy those flowers?"

"I'm fond of them," said Selby.

"What are you going to do with them? You can't sleep here."

"I could, if you'd help me take the pansies off the bed."

"Where can you put them?"

"Couldn't I give them to the concierge?"

As soon as he said it he regretted it. What in Heaven's name would Clifford think of him! He had heard the amount of the bill. Would he believe that he had invested in these luxuries as a timid declaration to his concierge? And would the Latin Quarter comment upon it in their own brutal fashion? He dreaded ridicule and he knew Clifford's reputation.

Then somebody knocked.

Selby looked at Clifford with a hunted expression which touched that young man's heart. It was a confession and at the same time a supplication. Clifford jumped up, threaded his way through the floral labyrinth, and putting an eye to the crack of the door, said, "Who the devil is it?"

This graceful style of reception is indigenous to the Quarter.

"It's Elliott," he said, looking back, "and Rowden too, and their bulldogs." Then he addressed them through the crack.

"Sit down on the stairs; Selby and I are coming out directly."

Discretion is a virtue. The Latin Quarter possesses few, and discretion seldom figures on the list. They sat down and began to whistle.

Presently Rowden called out, "I smell flowers. They feast within!"

"You ought to know Selby better than that," growled Clifford behind the door, while the other hurriedly exchanged his torn trousers for others.

"*We* know Selby," said Elliott with emphasis.

"Yes," said Rowden, "he gives receptions with floral decorations and invites Clifford, while we sit on the stairs."

"Yes, while the youth and beauty of the Quarter revel," suggested Rowden; then, with sudden misgiving; "Is Odette there?"

"See here," demanded Elliott, "is Colette there?"

Then he raised his voice in a plaintive howl, "Are you there, Colette, while I'm kicking my heels on these tiles?"

"Clifford is capable of anything," said Rowden; "his nature is soured since Rue Barrée sat on him."

Elliott raised his voice: "I say, you fellows, we saw some flowers carried into Rue Barrée's house at noon."

"Posies and roses," specified Rowden.

"Probably for her," added Elliott, caressing his bulldog.

Clifford turned with sudden suspicion upon Selby. The latter hummed a tune, selected a pair of gloves and, choosing a dozen cigarettes, placed them in a case. Then walking over to the cactus, he deliberately detached a blossom, drew it through his buttonhole, and picking up hat and stick, smiled upon Clifford, at which the latter was mightily troubled.

IV

Monday morning at Julian's, students fought for places; students with prior claims drove away others who had been anxiously squatting on coveted tabourets since the door was opened in hopes of appropriating them at roll-call; students squabbled over palettes, brushes, portfolios, or rent the air with demands for Ciceri and bread. The former, a dirty ex-model, who had in palmier days posed as Judas, now dispensed stale bread at one sou and made enough to keep himself in cigarettes. Monsieur Julian walked in, smiled a fatherly smile and walked out. His disappearance was followed by the apparition of the clerk, a foxy creature who flitted through the battling hordes in search of prey.

Three men who had not paid dues were caught and summoned. A fourth was scented, followed, outflanked, his retreat towards the door cut off, and finally captured behind the stove. About that time, the revolution assuming an acute form, howls rose for "Jules!"

Jules came, umpired two fights with a sad resignation in his big brown eyes, shook hands with everybody and melted away in the throng, leaving an atmosphere of peace and good-will. The lions sat down with the lambs, the massiers marked the best places for themselves and friends, and, mounting the model stands, opened the roll-calls.

The word was passed, "They begin with C this week."

They did.

"Clisson!"

Clisson jumped like a flash and marked his name on the floor in chalk before a front seat.

"Caron!"

Caron galloped away to secure his place. Bang! went an easel. "*Nom de Dieu*!" in French,—"Where in h—l are you goin'!" in English. Crash! a paintbox fell with brushes and all on board. "*Dieu de Dieu de—*" spat! A blow, a short rush, a clinch and scuffle, and the voice of the massier, stern and reproachful:

"Cochon!"

Then the roll-call was resumed.

"Clifford!"

The massier paused and looked up, one finger between the leaves of the ledger.

"Clifford!"

Clifford was not there. He was about three miles away in a direct line and every instant increased the distance. Not that he was walking fast,—on the contrary, he was strolling with that leisurely gait peculiar to himself. Elliott was beside him and two bulldogs covered the rear. Elliott was reading the "Gil Blas," from which he seemed to extract amusement, but deeming boisterous mirth unsuitable to Clifford's state of mind, subdued his amusement to a series of discreet smiles. The latter, moodily aware of this, said nothing, but leading the way into the Luxembourg Gardens installed himself upon a bench by the northern terrace and surveyed the landscape with disfavour. Elliott, according to the Luxembourg regulations, tied the two dogs and then, with an interrogative glance toward his friend, resumed the "Gil Blas" and the discreet smiles.

The day was perfect. The sun hung over Notre Dame, setting the city in a glitter. The tender foliage of the chestnuts cast a shadow over the terrace and flecked the paths and walks with tracery so blue that Clifford might here have found encouragement for his violent "impressions" had he but looked; but as usual in this period of his career, his thoughts were anywhere except in his profession. Around about, the sparrows quarrelled and chattered their courtship songs, the big rosy pigeons sailed from tree to tree, the flies whirled in the sunbeams and the flowers exhaled a thousand perfumes which stirred Clifford with languorous wistfulness. Under this influence he spoke.

"Elliott, you are a true friend—"

"You make me ill," replied the latter, folding his paper. "It's just as I thought,—you are tagging after some new petticoat again. And," he continued wrathfully, "if this is what you've kept me away from Julian's for,—if it's to fill me up with the perfections of some little idiot—"

"Not idiot," remonstrated Clifford gently.

"See here," cried Elliott, "have you the nerve to try to tell me that you are in love again?"

"Again?"

"Yes, again and again and again and—by George have you?"

"This," observed Clifford sadly, "is serious."

For a moment Elliott would have laid hands on him, then he laughed from sheer helplessness. "Oh, go on, go on; let's see, there's Clémence and Marie Tellec and Cosette and Fifine, Colette, Marie Verdier—"

"All of whom are charming, most charming, but I never was serious—"

"So help me, Moses," said Elliott, solemnly, "each and every one of those named have separately and in turn torn your heart with anguish and have also made me lose my place at Julian's in this same manner; each and every one, separately and in turn. Do you deny it?"

"What you say may be founded on facts—in a way—but give me the credit of being faithful to one at a time—"

"Until the next came along."

"But this,—this is really very different. Elliott, believe me, I am all broken up."

Then there being nothing else to do, Elliott gnashed his teeth and listened.

"It's—it's Rue Barrée."

"Well," observed Elliott, with scorn, "if you are moping and moaning over *that* girl,—the girl who has given you and myself every reason to wish that the ground would open and engulf us,—well, go on!"

"I'm going on,—I don't care; timidity has fled—"

"Yes, your native timidity."

"I'm desperate, Elliott. Am I in love? Never, never did I feel so d—n miserable. I can't sleep; honestly, I'm incapable of eating properly."

"Same symptoms noticed in the case of Colette."

"Listen, will you?"

"Hold on a moment, I know the rest by heart. Now let me ask you something. Is it your belief that Rue Barrée is a pure girl?"

"Yes," said Clifford, turning red.

"Do you love her,—not as you dangle and tiptoe after every pretty inanity—I mean, do you honestly love her?"

"Yes," said the other doggedly, "I would—"

"Hold on a moment; would you marry her?"

Clifford turned scarlet. "Yes," he muttered.

"Pleasant news for your family," growled Elliott in suppressed fury. "'Dear father, I have just married a charming grisette whom I'm sure you'll welcome with open arms, in company with her mother, a most estimable and cleanly washlady.' Good heavens! This seems to have gone a little further than the rest. Thank your stars, young man, that my head is level enough for us both. Still, in this case, I have no fear. Rue Barrée sat on your aspirations in a manner unmistakably final."

"Rue Barrée," began Clifford, drawing himself up, but he suddenly ceased, for there where the dappled sunlight glowed in spots of gold, along the sun-flecked path, tripped Rue Barrée. Her gown was spotless, and her big straw hat, tipped a little from the white forehead, threw a shadow across her eyes.

Elliott stood up and bowed. Clifford removed his head-covering with an air so plaintive, so appealing, so utterly humble that Rue Barrée smiled.

The smile was delicious and when Clifford, incapable of sustaining himself on his legs from sheer astonishment, toppled slightly, she smiled again in spite of herself. A few moments later she took a chair on the terrace and drawing a book from her music-roll, turned the pages, found the place, and then placing it open downwards in her lap, sighed a little, smiled a little, and looked out over the city. She had entirely forgotten Foxhall Clifford.

After a while she took up her book again, but instead of reading began to adjust a rose in her corsage. The rose was big and red. It glowed like fire there over her heart, and like fire it warmed her heart, now fluttering under the silken petals. Rue Barrée sighed again. She was very happy. The sky was so blue, the air so soft and perfumed, the sunshine so caressing, and her heart sang within her, sang to the rose in her breast. This is what it sang: "Out of the throng of passers-by, out of the world of yesterday, out of the millions passing, one has turned aside to me."

So her heart sang under his rose on her breast. Then two big mouse-coloured pigeons came whistling by and alighted on the terrace, where they bowed and strutted and bobbed and turned until Rue Barrée laughed in delight, and looking up beheld Clifford before her. His hat was in his hand and his face was wreathed in a series of appealing smiles which would have touched the heart of a Bengal tiger.

For an instant Rue Barrée frowned, then she looked curiously at Clifford, then when she saw the resemblance between his bows and the bobbing pigeons, in spite of herself, her lips parted in the most bewitching laugh. Was this Rue Barrée? So changed, so changed that she did not know herself; but oh! that song in her heart which drowned all else, which trembled on her lips, struggling for utterance, which rippled forth in a laugh at nothing,—at a strutting pigeon,—and Mr. Clifford.

"And you think, because I return the salute of the students in the Quarter, that you may be received in particular as a friend? I do not know you, Monsieur, but vanity is man's other name;— be content, Monsieur Vanity, I shall be punctilious—oh, most punctilious in returning your salute."

"But I beg—I implore you to let me render you that homage which has so long—"

"Oh dear; I don't care for homage."

"Let me only be permitted to speak to you now and then,— occasionally—very occasionally."

"And if *you*, why not another?"

"Not at all,—I will be discretion itself."

"Discretion—why?"

Her eyes were very clear, and Clifford winced for a moment, but only for a moment. Then the devil of recklessness seizing him, he sat down and offered himself, soul and body, goods and chattels. And all the time he knew he was a fool and that infatuation is not love, and that each word he uttered bound him in honour from which there was no escape. And all the time Elliott was scowling down on the fountain plaza and savagely checking both bulldogs from their desire to rush to Clifford's rescue,—for even they felt there was something wrong, as Elliott stormed within himself and growled maledictions.

When Clifford finished, he finished in a glow of excitement, but Rue Barrée's response was long in coming and his ardour cooled while the situation slowly assumed its just proportions. Then regret began to creep in, but he put that aside and broke out again in protestations. At the first word Rue Barrée checked him.

"I thank you," she said, speaking very gravely. "No man has ever before offered me marriage." She turned and looked out over the city. After a while she spoke again. "You offer me a great deal. I am alone, I have nothing, I am nothing." She turned again and looked at Paris, brilliant, fair, in the sunshine of a perfect day. He followed her eyes.

"Oh," she murmured, "it is hard,—hard to work always—always alone with never a friend you can have in honour, and the love that is offered means the streets, the boulevard—when passion is dead. I know it,—*we* know it,—we others who have nothing,—have no one, and who give ourselves, unquestioning—when we love,—yes, unquestioning—heart and soul, knowing the end."

She touched the rose at her breast. For a moment she seemed to forget him, then quietly—"I thank you, I am very grateful." She opened the book and, plucking a petal from the rose, dropped it between the leaves. Then looking up she said gently, "I cannot accept."

V

It took Clifford a month to entirely recover, although at the end of the first week he was pronounced convalescent by Elliott, who was an authority, and his convalescence was aided by the cordiality with which Rue Barrée acknowledged his solemn salutes. Forty times a day he blessed Rue Barrée for her refusal, and thanked his lucky stars, and at the same time, oh, wondrous heart of ours!—he suffered the tortures of the blighted.

Elliott was annoyed, partly by Clifford's reticence, partly by the unexplainable thaw in the frigidity of Rue Barrée. At their frequent encounters, when she, tripping along the rue de Seine, with music-roll and big straw hat would pass Clifford and his familiars steering an easterly course to the Café Vachette, and at the respectful uncovering of the band would colour and smile at Clifford, Elliott's slumbering suspicions awoke. But he never found out anything, and finally gave it up as beyond his comprehension, merely qualifying Clifford as an idiot and reserving his opinion of Rue Barrée. And all this time Selby was jealous. At first he refused to acknowledge it to himself, and cut the studio for a day in the country, but the woods and fields of course aggravated his case, and the brooks babbled of Rue Barrée and the mowers calling to each other across the meadow ended in a quavering "Rue Bar-rée-e!" That day spent in the country made him angry for a week, and he worked sulkily at Julian's, all the time tormented by a desire to know where Clifford was and what he might be doing. This culminated in an erratic stroll on Sunday which ended at the flower-market on the Pont au Change, began again, was gloomily extended to the morgue, and again ended at the marble bridge. It would never do, and Selby felt it, so he went to see Clifford, who was convalescing on mint juleps in his garden.

They sat down together and discussed morals and human happiness, and each found the other most entertaining, only Selby failed to pump Clifford, to the other's unfeigned amusement. But the juleps spread balm on the sting of jealousy, and trickled hope to the blighted, and when Selby said he must go, Clifford went too, and when Selby, not to be outdone, insisted on accompanying Clifford back to his door, Clifford determined to see Selby back half way, and then finding it hard to part, they decided to dine together and "flit." To flit, a verb applied to Clifford's nocturnal prowls, expressed, perhaps, as well as anything, the gaiety proposed. Dinner was ordered at Mignon's, and while Selby interviewed the chef, Clifford kept a fatherly eye on the butler. The dinner was a success, or was of the sort generally termed a success. Toward the dessert Selby heard some one say as at a great distance, "Kid Selby, drunk as a lord."

A group of men passed near them; it seemed to him that he shook hands and laughed a great deal, and that everybody was very witty. There was Clifford opposite swearing undying confidence in his chum Selby, and there seemed to be others there, either seated beside them or continually passing with the swish of skirts on the polished floor. The perfume of roses, the rustle of fans, the touch of rounded arms and the laughter grew vaguer and vaguer. The room seemed enveloped in mist. Then, all in a moment each object stood out painfully distinct, only forms and visages were distorted and voices piercing. He drew himself up, calm, grave, for the moment master of himself, but very drunk. He knew he was drunk, and was as guarded and alert, as keenly suspicious of himself as he would have been of a thief at his elbow. His self-command enabled Clifford to hold his head safely under some running water, and repair to the street considerably the worse for wear, but never suspecting that his companion was drunk. For a time he kept his self-command. His face was only a bit paler, a bit tighter than usual; he was only a trifle slower and more fastidious in his speech. It was midnight when he left Clifford peacefully slumbering in somebody's arm-chair, with a long suede glove dangling in his hand and a plumy boa twisted about his neck to protect his throat from drafts. He walked through the hall and down the stairs, and found himself on the sidewalk in a quarter he did not know. Mechanically he looked up at the name of the street. The name was not familiar. He turned and steered his course toward some lights clustered at the end of the street. They proved farther away than he had anticipated, and after a long quest he came to the conclusion that his eyes had been mysteriously removed from their proper places and had been reset on either side of his head like those of a bird. It grieved him to think of the inconvenience this transformation might occasion him, and he attempted to cock up his head, hen-like, to test the mobility of his neck. Then an immense despair stole over him,—tears gathered in the tear-ducts, his heart melted, and he collided with a tree. This shocked him into comprehension; he stifled the violent tenderness in his breast, picked up his hat and moved on more briskly. His mouth was white and drawn, his teeth tightly clinched. He held his course pretty well and strayed but little, and after an apparently interminable length of time found himself passing a line of cabs. The brilliant lamps, red, yellow, and green annoyed him, and he felt it might be pleasant to demolish them with his cane, but mastering this impulse he passed on. Later an idea struck him that it would save fatigue to take a cab, and he started back with that intention, but the cabs seemed already so far away and the lanterns were so bright and confusing that he gave it up, and pulling himself together looked around.

A shadow, a mass, huge, undefined, rose to his right. He recognized the Arc de Triomphe and gravely shook his cane at it. Its size annoyed him. He felt it was too big. Then he heard something fall clattering to the pavement and thought probably it was his cane but it didn't much matter. When he had mastered himself and regained control of his right leg, which betrayed symptoms of insubordination, he found himself traversing the Place de la Concorde at a pace which threatened to land him at the Madeleine. This would never do. He turned sharply to the right and crossing the bridge passed the Palais Bourbon at a trot and wheeled into the Boulevard St. Germain. He got on well enough although the size of the War Office struck him as a personal insult, and he missed his cane, which it would have been pleasant to drag along the iron railings as he passed. It occurred to him, however, to substitute his hat, but when he found it he forgot what he wanted it for and replaced it upon his head with gravity.

Then he was obliged to battle with a violent inclination to sit down and weep. This lasted until he came to the rue de Rennes, but there he became absorbed in contemplating the dragon on the balcony overhanging the Cour du Dragon, and time slipped away until he remembered vaguely that he had no business there, and marched off again. It was slow work. The inclination to sit down and weep had given place to a desire for solitary and deep reflection. Here his right leg forgot its obedience and attacking the left, outflanked it and brought him up against a wooden board which seemed to bar his path. He tried to walk around it, but found the street closed. He tried to push it over, and found he couldn't. Then he noticed a red lantern standing on a pile of paving-stones inside the barrier. This was pleasant. How was he to get home if the boulevard was blocked? But he was not on the boulevard. His treacherous right leg had beguiled him into a detour, for there, behind him lay the boulevard with its endless line of lamps,—and here, what was this narrow dilapidated street piled up with earth and mortar and heaps of stone? He looked up. Written in staring black letters on the barrier was

RUE BARRÉE.

He sat down. Two policemen whom he knew came by and advised him to get up, but he argued the question from a standpoint of personal taste, and they passed on, laughing. For he was at that moment absorbed in a problem. It was, how to see Rue Barrée. She was somewhere or other in that big house with the iron balconies, and the door was locked, but what of that? The simple idea struck him to shout until she came. This idea was replaced by another equally lucid,—to hammer on the door until she came; but finally rejecting both of these as too uncertain, he decided to climb into the balcony, and opening a window politely inquire for Rue Barrée. There was but one lighted window in the house that he could see. It was on the second floor, and toward this he cast his eyes. Then mounting the wooden barrier and clambering over the piles of stones, he reached the sidewalk and looked up at the façade for a foothold. It seemed impossible. But a sudden fury seized him, a blind, drunken obstinacy, and the blood rushed to his head, leaping, beating in his ears like the dull thunder of an ocean. He set his teeth, and springing at a window-sill, dragged himself up and hung to the iron bars. Then reason fled; there surged in his brain the sound of many voices, his heart leaped up beating a mad tattoo, and gripping at cornice and ledge he worked his way along the façade, clung to pipes and shutters, and dragged himself up, over and into the balcony by the lighted window. His hat fell off and rolled against the pane. For a moment he leaned breathless against the railing—then the window was slowly opened from within.

They stared at each other for some time. Presently the girl took two unsteady steps back into the room. He saw her face,— all crimsoned now,—he saw her sink into a chair by the lamplit table, and without a word he followed her into the room, closing the big door-like panes behind him. Then they looked at each other in silence.

The room was small and white; everything was white about it,—the curtained bed, the little wash-stand in the corner, the bare walls, the china lamp,—and his own face,—had he known it, but the face and neck of Rue were surging in the colour that dyed the blossoming rose-tree there on the hearth beside her. It did not occur to him to speak. She seemed not to expect it. His mind was struggling with the impressions of the room. The whiteness, the extreme purity of everything occupied him— began to trouble him. As his eye became accustomed to the light, other objects grew from the surroundings and took their places in the circle of lamplight. There was a piano and a coal-scuttle and a little iron trunk and a bath-tub. Then there was a row of wooden pegs against the door, with a white chintz curtain covering the clothes underneath. On the bed lay an umbrella and a big straw hat, and on the table, a music-roll unfurled, an ink-stand, and sheets of ruled paper. Behind him stood a wardrobe faced with a mirror, but somehow he did not care to see his own face just then. He was sobering.

The girl sat looking at him without a word. Her face was expressionless, yet the lips at times trembled almost imperceptibly. Her eyes, so wonderfully blue in the daylight, seemed dark and soft as velvet, and the colour on her neck deepened and whitened with every breath. She seemed smaller and more slender than when he had seen her in the street, and there was now something in the curve of her cheek almost infantine. When at last he turned and caught his own reflection in the mirror behind him, a shock passed through him as though he had seen a shameful thing, and his clouded mind and his clouded thoughts grew clearer. For a moment their eyes met then his sought the floor, his lips tightened, and the struggle within him bowed his head and strained every nerve to the breaking. And now it was over, for the voice within had spoken. He listened, dully interested but already knowing the end,—indeed it little mattered;—the end would always be the same for him;—he understood now—always the same for him, and he listened, dully interested, to a voice which grew within him. After a while he stood up, and she rose at once, one small hand resting on the table. Presently he opened the window, picked up his hat, and shut it again. Then he went over to the rose-bush and touched the blossoms with his face. One was standing in a glass of water on the table and mechanically the girl drew it out, pressed it with her lips and laid it on the table beside him. He took it without a word and crossing the room, opened the door. The landing was dark and silent, but the girl lifted the lamp and gliding past him slipped down the polished stairs to the hallway. Then unchaining the bolts, she drew open the iron wicket.

Through this he passed with his rose.

THE MAKER OF MOONS

I am myself just as much evil as good, and my nation is—
And I say there is in fact no evil;
(Or if there is, I say it is just as important to you,
to the land, or to me, as anything else.)

Each is not for its own sake;
I say the whole earth, and all the stars in the sky
are for Religion's sake.
I say no man has ever yet been half devout enough;
None has ever adored or worshipped half enough;
None has begun to think how divine he himself is, and
how certain the future is.

—*Walt Whitman*

I have heard what the Talkers were talking,—the talk
Of the beginning and the end;
But I do not talk of the beginning or the end.

CHAPTER I

Concerning Yue-Laou and the Xin I know nothing more than you shall know. I am miserably anxious to clear the matter up. Perhaps what I write may save the United States Government money and lives, perhaps it may arouse the scientific world to action; at any rate it will put an end to the terrible suspense of two people. Certainty is better than suspense.

If the Government dares to disregard this warning and refuses to send a thoroughly equipped expedition at once, the people of the State may take swift vengeance on the whole region and leave a blackened devastated waste where today forest and flowering meadow land border the lake in the Cardinal Woods.

You already know part of the story; the New York papers have been full of alleged details.

This much is true: Barris caught the "Shiner," red handed, or rather yellow handed, for his pockets and boots and dirty fists were stuffed with lumps of gold. I say gold, advisedly. You may call it what you please. You also know how Barris was—but unless I begin at the beginning of my own experiences you will be none the wiser after all.

On the third of August of this present year I was standing in Tiffany's, chatting with George Godfrey of the designing department. On the glass counter between us lay a coiled serpent, an exquisite specimen of chiselled gold.

"No," replied Godfrey to my question, "it isn't my work; I wish it was. Why, man, it's a masterpiece!"

"Whose?" I asked... "Now I should be very glad to know also," said Godfrey. "We bought it from an old jay who says he lives in the country somewhere about the Cardinal Woods. That's near Starlit Lake, I believe—"

"Lake of the Stars?" I suggested.

"Some call it Starlit Lake,—it's all the same. Well, my rustic Reuben says that he represents the sculptor of this snake for all practical and business purposes. He got his price too. We hope he'll bring us something more. We have sold this already to the Metropolitan Museum."

I was leaning idly on the glass case, watching the keen eyes of the artist in precious metals as he stooped over the gold serpent.

"A masterpiece!" he muttered to himself fondling the glittering coil; "look at the texture! whew!" But I was not looking at the serpent. Something was moving,—crawling out of Godfrey's coat pocket,—the pocket nearest to me,—something soft and yellow with crab-like legs all covered with coarse yellow hair.

"What in Heaven's name," said I, "have you got in your pocket? It's crawling out—it's trying to creep up your coat, Godfrey!"

He turned quickly and dragged the creature out with his left hand.

I shrank back as he held the repulsive object dangling before me, and he laughed and placed it on the counter.

"Did you ever see anything like that?" he demanded.

"No," said I truthfully, "and I hope I never shall again. What is it?"

"I don't know. Ask them at the Natural History Museum—they can't tell you. The Smithsonian is all at sea too. It is, I believe, the connecting link between a sea-urchin, a spider, and the devil. It looks venomous but I can't find either fangs or mouth. Is it blind? These things may be eyes but they look as if they were painted. A Japanese sculptor might have produced such an impossible beast, but it is hard to believe that God did. It looks unfinished too. I have a mad idea that this creature is only one of the parts of some larger and more grotesque organism,—it looks so lonely, so hopelessly dependent, so cursedly unfinished. I'm going to use it as a model. If I don't out-Japanese the Japs my name isn't Godfrey."

The creature was moving slowly across the glass case towards me. I drew back.

"Godfrey," I said, "I would execute a man who executed any such work as you propose. What do you want to perpetuate such a reptile for? I can stand the Japanese grotesque but I can't stand that—spider—"

"It's a crab."

"Crab or spider or blind-worm—ugh! What do you want to do it for? It's a nightmare—it's unclean!"

I hated the thing. It was the first living creature that I had ever hated.

For some time I had noticed a damp acrid odor in the air, and Godfrey said it came from the reptile.

"Then kill it and bury it," I said; "and by the way, where did it come from?"

"I don't know that either," laughed Godfrey; "I found it clinging to the box that this gold serpent was brought in. I suppose my old Reuben is responsible."

"If the Cardinal Woods are the lurking places for things like this," said I, "I am sorry that I am going to the Cardinal Woods."

"Are you?" asked Godfrey; "for the shooting?"

"Yes, with Barris and Pierpont. Why don't you kill that creature?"

"Go off on your shooting trip, and let me alone," laughed Godfrey...I shuddered at the "crab," and bade Godfrey good-bye until December.

That night, Pierpont, Barris, and I sat chatting in the smoking-car of the Quebec Express when the long train pulled out of the Grand Central Depot. Old David had gone forward with the dogs; poor things, they hated to ride in the baggage car, but the Quebec and Northern road provides no sportsman's cars, and David and the three Gordon setters were in for an uncomfortable night.

Except for Pierpont, Barris, and myself, the car was empty. Barris, trim, stout, ruddy, and bronzed, sat drumming on the window ledge, puffing a short fragrant pipe. His gun-case lay beside him on the floor.

"When I have white hair and years of discretion," said Pierpont languidly, "I'll not flirt with pretty serving-maids; will you, Roy?"

"No," said I, looking at Barris.

"You mean the maid with the cap in the Pullman car?" asked Barris.

"Yes," said Pierpont.

I smiled, for I had seen it also.

Barris twisted his crisp gray moustache, and yawned.

"You children had better be toddling off to bed," he said. "That lady's-maid is a member of the Secret Service."

"Oh," said Pierpont, "one of your colleagues?"

"You might present us, you know," I said; "the journey is monotonous."

Barris had drawn a telegram from his pocket, and as he sat turning it over and over between his fingers he smiled. After a moment or two he handed it to Pierpont who read it with slightly raised eyebrows.

"It's rot,—I suppose it's cipher," he said; "I see it's signed by General Drummond—"

"Drummond, Chief of the Government Secret Service," said Barris.

"Something interesting?" I enquired, lighting a cigarette.

"Something so interesting," replied Barris, "that I'm going to look into it myself—"

"And break up our shooting trio—"

"No. Do you want to hear about it? Do you, Billy Pierpont?"

"Yes," replied that immaculate young man.

Barris rubbed the amber mouth-piece of his pipe on his handkerchief, cleared the stem with a bit of wire, puffed once or twice, and leaned back in his chair.

"Pierpont," he said, "do you remember that evening at the United States Club when General Miles, General Drummond, and I were examining that gold nugget that Captain Mahan had? You examined it also, I believe."

"I did," said Pierpont.

"Was it gold?" asked Barris, drumming on the window.

"It was," replied Pierpont.

"I saw it too," said I; "of course, it was gold."

"Professor La Grange saw it also," said Barris; "he said it was gold."

"Well?" said Pierpont.

"Well," said Barris, "it was not gold."

After a silence Pierpont asked what tests had been made.

"The usual tests," replied Barris. "The United States Mint is satisfied that it is gold, so is every jeweller who has seen it. But it is not gold,—and yet—it is gold."

Pierpont and I exchanged glances.

"Now," said I, "for Barris' usual coup-de-théâtre: what was the nugget?"

"Practically it was pure gold; but," said Barris, enjoying the situation intensely, "really it was not gold. Pierpont, what is gold?"

"Gold's an element, a metal—"

"Wrong! Billy Pierpont," said Barris coolly.

"Gold was an element when I went to school," said I.

"It has not been an element for two weeks," said Barris; "and, except General Drummond, Professor La Grange, and myself, you two youngsters are the only people, except one, in the world who know it,—or have known it."

"Do you mean to say that gold is a composite metal?" said Pierpont slowly.

"I do. La Grange has made it. He produced a scale of pure gold day before yesterday. That nugget was manufactured gold."

Could Barris be joking? Was this a colossal hoax? I looked at Pierpont. He muttered something about that settling the silver question, and turned his head to Barris, but there was that in Barris' face which forbade jesting, and Pierpont and I sat silently pondering.

"Don't ask me how it's made," said Barris, quietly; "I don't know. But I do know that somewhere in the region of the Cardinal Woods there is a gang of people who do know how gold is made, and who make it. You understand the danger this is to every civilized nation. It's got to be stopped of course. Drummond and I have decided that I am the man to stop it. Wherever and whoever these people are—these gold-makers,—they must be caught, every one of them,—caught or shot."

"Or shot," repeated Pierpont, who was owner of the Cross-Cut Gold Mine and found his income too small; "Professor La Grange will of course be prudent;—science need not know things that would upset the world!"

"Little Willy," said Barris laughing, "your income is safe."

"I suppose," said I, "some flaw in the nugget gave Professor La Grange the tip."

"Exactly. He cut the flaw out before sending the nugget to be tested. He worked on the flaw and separated gold into its three elements."

"He is a great man," said Pierpont, "but he will be the greatest man in the world if he can keep his discovery to himself."

"Who?" said Barris.

"Professor La Grange."

"Professor La Grange was shot through the heart two hours ago," replied Barris slowly.

CHAPTER II

We had been at the shooting box in the Cardinal Woods five days when a telegram was brought to Barris by a mounted messenger from the nearest telegraph station, Cardinal Springs, a hamlet on the lumber railroad which joins the Quebec and Northern at Three Rivers Junction, thirty miles below.

Pierpont and I were sitting out under the trees, loading some special shells as experiments; Barris stood beside us, bronzed, erect, holding his pipe carefully so that no sparks should drift into our powder box. The beat of hoofs over the grass aroused us, and when the lank messenger drew bridle before the door, Barris stepped forward and took the sealed telegram. When he had torn it open he went into the house and presently reappeared, reading something that he had written.

"This should go at once," he said, looking the messenger full in the face..."At once, Colonel Barris," replied the shabby countryman.

Pierpont glanced up and I smiled at the messenger who was gathering his bridle and settling himself in his stirrups. Barris handed him the written reply and nodded goodbye: there was a thud of hoofs on the greensward, a jingle of bit and spur across the gravel, and the messenger was gone. Barris' pipe went out and he stepped to windward to relight it.

"It is queer," said I, "that your messenger—a battered native,— should speak like a Harvard man."

"He is a Harvard man," said Barris.

"And the plot thickens," said Pierpont; "are the Cardinal Woods full of your Secret Service men, Barris?"

"No," replied Barris, "but the telegraph stations are. How many ounces of shot are you using, Roy?"

I told him, holding up the adjustable steel measuring cup. He nodded. After a moment on two he sat down on a camp-stool beside us and picked up a crimper.

"That telegram was from Drummond," he said; "the messenger was one of my men as you two bright little boys divined. Pooh! If he had spoken the Cardinal County dialect you wouldn't have known."

"His make-up was good," said Pierpont.

Barris twirled the crimper and looked at the pile of loaded shells. Then he picked up one and crimped it.

"Let 'em alone," said Pierpont, "you crimp too tight."

"Does his little gun kick when the shells are crimped too tight?" enquired Barris tenderly; "well, he shall crimp his own shells then,—where's his little man?"

"His little man" was a weird English importation, stiff, very carefully scrubbed, tangled in his aspirates, named Howlett. As valet, gilly, gun-bearer, and crimper, he aided Pierpont to endure the ennui of existence, by doing for him everything except breathing. Lately, however, Barris' taunts had driven Pierpont to do a few things for himself. To his astonishment he found that cleaning his own gun was not a bore, so he timidly loaded a shell or two, was much pleased with himself, loaded some more, crimped them, and went to breakfast with an appetite. So when Barris asked where "his little man" was, Pierpont did not reply but dug a cupful of shot from the bag and poured it solemnly into the half filled shell.

Old David came out with the dogs and of course there was a pow-wow when "Voyou," my Gordon, wagged his splendid rail across the loading table and sent a dozen unstopped cartridges rolling over the grass, vomiting powder and shot.

"Give the dogs a mile or two," said I; "we will shoot over the Sweet Fern Covert about four o'clock, David."

"Two guns, David," added Barris.

"Are you not going?" asked Pierpont, looking up, as David disappeared with the dogs.

"Bigger game," said Barris shortly. He picked up a mug of ale from the tray which Howlett had just set down beside us and took a long pull. We did the same, silently. Pierpont set his mug on the turf beside him and returned to his loading.

We spoke of the murder of Professor La Grange, of how it had been concealed by the authorities in New York at Drummond's request, of the certainty that it was one of the gang of gold-makers who had done it, and of the possible alertness of the gang.

"Oh, they know that Drummond will be after them sooner on later," said Barris, "but they don't know that the mills of the gods have already begun to grind. Those smart New York papers builded better than they knew when their ferret-eyed reporter poked his red nose into the house on 58th Street and sneaked off with a column on his cuffs about the 'suicide' of Professor La Grange. Billy Pierpont, my revolver is hanging in your room; I'll take yours too—" "Help yourself," said Pierpont.

"I shall be gone over night," continued Barris; "my poncho and some bread and meat are all I shall take except the 'barkers.'"

"Will they bark to-night?" I asked.

"No, I trust not for several weeks yet. I shall nose about a bit. Roy, did it even strike you how queer it is that this wonderfully beautiful country should contain no inhabitants?"

"It's like those splendid stretches of pools and rapids which one finds on every trout river and in which one never finds a fish," suggested Pierpont.

"Exactly,—and Heaven alone knows why," said Barris; "I suppose this country is shunned by human beings for the same mysterious reasons."

"The shooting is the better for it," I observed.

"The shooting is good," said Barris, "have you noticed the snipe on the meadow by the lake? Why it's brown with them! That's a wonderful meadow."

"It's a natural one," said Pierpont, "no human being even cleaned that land."

"Then it's supernatural," said Barris; "Pierpont, do you want to come with me?"

Pierpont's handsome face flushed as he answered slowly, "It's awfully good of you,—if I may."

"Bosh," said I, piqued because he had asked Pierpont, "what use is little Willy without his man?"

"True," said Barris gravely, "you can't take Howlett, you know."

Pierpont muttered something which ended in "d—n."

"Then," said I, "there will be but one gun on the Sweet Fern Covent this afternoon. Very well, I wish you joy of your cold supper and colder bed. Take your night-gown, Willy, and don't sleep on the damp ground."

"Let Pierpont alone," retorted Barris, "you shall go next time, Roy."

"Oh, all right,—you mean when there's shooting going on?"

"And I?" demanded Pierpont, grieved.

"You too, my son; stop quarrelling! Will you ask Howlett to pack our kits—lightly mind you,—no bottles,—they clink."

"My flask doesn't," said Pierpont, and went off to get ready for a night's stalking of dangerous men.

"It is strange," said I, "that nobody ever settles in this region. How many people live in Cardinal Springs, Barris?"

"Twenty counting the telegraph operator and not counting the lumbermen; they are always changing and shifting. I have six men among them."

"Where have you no men? In the Four Hundred?"

"I have men there also,—chums of Billy's only he doesn't know it. David tells me that there was a strong flight of woodcock last night. You ought to pick up some this afternoon."

Then we chatted about alder-coven and swamp until Pierpont came out of the house and it was time to part.

"Au revoir," said Barris, buckling on his kit, "come along, Pierpont, and don't walk in the damp grass."

"If you are not back by tomorrow noon," said I, "I will take Howlett and David and hunt you up. You say your course is due north?"

"Due north." replied Barris, consulting his compass.

"There is a trail for two miles and a spotted lead for two more," said Pierpont.

"Which we won't use for various reasons," added Barris pleasantly; "don't worry, Roy, and keep your confounded expedition out of the way; there's no danger."

He knew, of course, what he was talking about and I held my peace.

When the tip end of Pierpont's shooting coat had disappeared in the Long Covert, I found myself standing alone with Howlett. He bore my gaze for a moment and then politely lowered his eyes.

"Howlett," said I, "take these shells and implements to the gun room, and drop nothing. Did Voyou come to any harm in the briers this morning?"

"No 'arm, Mr. Cardenhe, sir," said Howlett.

"Then be careful not no drop anything else," said I, and walked away leaving him decorously puzzled. For he had dropped no cartridges. Poor Howlett!

CHAPTER III

About four o'clock that afternoon I men David and the dogs at the spinney which leads into the Sweet Fern Covent. The three setters, Voyou, Gamin, and Mioche, were in fine feather,— David had killed a woodcock and a brace of grouse over them that morning,—and they were thrashing about the spinney an short range when I came up, gun under arm and pipe lighted.

"What's the prospect, David," I asked, trying to keep my feet in the tangle of wagging, whining dogs; "hello, what's amiss with Mioche?"

"A brier in his foot sir; I drew it and stopped the wound but I guess the gravel's got in. If you have no objection, sin, I might take him back with me."

"It's safer," I said; "take Gamin too, I only want one dog this afternoon. What is the situation?"

"Fair sir; the grouse lie within a quarter of a mile of the oak second-growth. The woodcock are mostly on the alders. I saw any number of snipe on the meadows. There's something else in by the lake,—I can't just tell what, but the wood-duck set up a clatter when I was in the thicket and they come dashing through the wood as if a dozen foxes was snappin' on their tail feathers."

"Probably a fox," I said; "leash those dogs,—they must learn to stand in. I'll be back by dinner time."

"There is one more thing sir," said David, lingering with his gun under his arm.

"Well," said I.

"I saw a man in the woods by the Oak Covern,—at least I think I did."

"A lumberman?"

"I think not sir—at least,—do they have Chinamen among them?"

"Chinese? No. You didn't see a Chinaman in the woods here?"

"I—I think I did sir,—I can't say positively. He was gone when I ran into the covert."

"Did the dogs notice it?"

"I can't say—exactly. They acted queer like. Gamin here lay down an' whined—it may have been colic—and Mioche whimpered,—perhaps it was the brier."

"And Voyou?"

"Voyou, he was most remarkable sir, and the hair on his back stood up, I did see a groundhog makin' for a tree near by."

"Then no wonder Voyou bristled. David, your Chinaman was a stump or tussock. Take the dogs now."

"I guess it was sir; good afternoon sir," said David, and walked away with the Gordons leaving me alone with Voyou in the spinney.

I looked at the dog and he looked at me.

"Voyou!"

The dog sat down and danced with his fore feet, his beautiful brown eyes sparkling.

"You're a fraud," I said; "which shall it be, the alders or the upland? Upland? Good!—now for the grouse,—heel, my friend, and show your miraculous self-restraint."

Voyou wheeled into my tracks and followed close, nobly refusing to notice the impudent chipmunks and the thousand and one alluring and important smells which an ordinary dog would have lost no time in investigating.

The brown and yellow autumn woods were crisp with drifting heaps of leaves and twigs that crackled under foot as we turned from the spinney into the forest. Every silent little stream hurrying toward the lake was gay with painted leaves afloat, scarlet maple or yellow oak. Spots of sunlight fell upon the pools, searching the brown depths, illuminating the gravel bottom where shoals of minnows swam to and fro, and to and fro again, busy with the purpose of their little lives. The crickets were chirping in the long brittle grass on the edge of the woods, but we left them far behind in the silence of the deeper forest.

"Now!" said I to Voyou.

The dog sprang to the front, circled once, zigzagged through the ferns around us and, all in a moment, stiffened stock still, rigid as sculptured bronze. I stepped forward, raising my gun, two paces, three paces, ten perhaps, before a great cock-grouse blundered up from the brake and burst through the thicket fringe toward the deeper growth. There was a flash and puff from my gun, a crash of echoes among the low wooded cliffs, and through the faint veil of smoke something dark dropped from mid-air amid a cloud of feathers, brown as the brown leaves under foot.

"Fetch!"

Up from the ground sprang Voyou, and in a moment he came galloping back, neck arched, tail stiff but waving, holding tenderly in his pink mouth a mass of mottled bronzed feathers. Very gravely he laid the bird at my feet and crouched close beside in, his silky ears across his paws, his muzzle on the ground.

I dropped the grouse into my pocket, held for a moment a silent caressing communion with Voyou, then swung my gun under my arm and motioned the dog on.

It must have been five o'clock when I walked into a little opening in the woods and sat down to breathe. Voyou came and sat down in front of me.

"Well?" I enquired.

Voyou gravely presented one paw which I took.

"We will never get back in time for dinner," said I, "so we might as well take it easy. It's all your fault, you know. Is there a brier in your foot?—let's see,—there! it's out my friend and you are free to nose about and lick it. If you loll your tongue out you'll get it all over twigs and moss."

"Can't you lie down and try to pant less? No, there is no use in sniffing and looking at that fern patch, for we are going to smoke a little, doze a little, and go home by moonlight. Think what a big dinner we will have! Think of Howlett's despair when we are not in time! Think of all the stories you will have to tell to Gamin and Mioche! Think what a good dog you have been!"

"There—you are tired old chap; take forty winks with me."

Voyou was a little tired. He stretched out on the leaves at my feet but whether or not he really slept I could not be certain, until his hind legs twitched and I knew he was dreaming of mighty deeds.

Now I may have taken forty winks, but the sun seemed to be no lower when I sat up and unclosed my lids. Voyou raised his head, saw in my eyes that I was not going yet, thumped his tail half a dozen times on the dried leaves, and settled back with a sigh.

I looked lazily around, and for the first time noticed what a wonderfully beautiful spot I had chosen for a nap. It was an oval glade in the heart of the forest, level and carpeted with green grass. The trees that surrounded it were gigantic; they formed one towering circular wall of verdure, blotting out all except the turquoise blue of the sky-oval above. And now I noticed that in the centre of the greensward lay a pool of water, crystal clear, glimmering like a mirror in the meadow grass, beside a block of granite. It scarcely seemed possible than the symmetry of tree and lawn and lucent pool could have been one of nature's accidents. I had never before seen this glade nor had I ever heard it spoken of by either Pierpont or Barris. It was a marvel, this diamond clean basin, regular and graceful as a Roman fountain, set in the gem of turf. And these great trees,—they also belonged, not in America but in some legend-haunted forest of France, where moss-grown marbles stand neglected in dim glades, and the twilight of the forest shelters fairies and slender shapes from shadow-land.

I lay and watched the sunlight showering the tangled thicket where masses of crimson Cardinal-flowers glowed, or where one long dusty sunbeam tipped the edge of the floating leaves in the pool, running them to palest gilt. There were birds too, passing through the dim avenues of trees like jets of flame,—the gorgeous Cardinal-Bind in his deep stained crimson robe,—the bird that gave to the woods, to the village fifteen miles away, to the whole country, the name of Cardinal.

I rolled over on my back and looked up at the sky. How pale,—paler than a robin's egg,—it was. I seemed to be lying at the bottom of a well, walled with verdure, high towering on every side. And, as I lay, all about me the air became sweet scented. Sweeter and sweeter and more penetrating grew the perfume, and I wondered what stray breeze, blowing over acres of lilies, could have brought in. But there was no breeze; the air was still. A gilded fly alighted on my hand,—a honey-fly. It was as troubled as I by the scented silence.

Then, behind me, my dog growled.

I sat quite still at first, hardly breathing, but my eyes were fixed on a shape that moved along the edge of the pool among the meadow grasses. The dog had ceased growling and was now snarling, alert and trembling.

At last I rose and walked rapidly down to the pool, my dog following close to heel.

The figure, a woman's, turned slowly toward us.

CHAPTER IV

She was standing still when I approached the pool. The forest around us was so silent that when I spoke the sound of my own voice startled me.

"No," she said,—and her voice was smooth as flowing water, "I have not lost my way. Will he come to me, your beautiful dog?"

Before I could speak, Voyou crept to her and laid his silky head against her knees.

"But surely," said I, "you did not come here alone."

"Alone? I did come alone."

"But the nearest settlement is Cardinal, probably nineteen miles from where we are standing."

"I do not know Cardinal," she said.

"Ste. Croix in Canada is forty miles at least,—how did you come into the Cardinal Woods?" I asked amazed.

"Into the woods?" she repeated a little impatiently.

"Yes."

She did not answer at first but stood caressing Voyou with gentle phrase and gesture.

"Your beautiful dog I am fond of, but I am not fond of being questioned," she said quietly.

"My name is Ysonde and I came to the fountain here to see your dog."

I was properly quenched. After a moment or two I did say that in another hour in would be growing dusky, but she neither replied nor looked at me.

"This," I ventured, "is a beautiful pool,—you call it a fountain,—a delicious fountain: I have never before seen it. It is hard to imagine that nature did all this."

"Is it?" she said.

"Don't you think so?" I asked.

"I haven't thought; I wish when you go you would leave me your dog."

"My—my dog?"

"If you don't mind," she said sweetly, and looked at me for the first time in the face.

For an instant our glances met, then she grew grave, and I saw that her eyes were fixed on my forehead. Suddenly she rose and drew nearer, looking intently at my forehead. There was a faint mark there, a tiny crescent, just over my eyebrow. It was a birthmark.

"Is that a scar?" she demanded drawing nearer.

"That crescent shaped mark? No."

"No? Are you sure?" she insisted.

"Perfectly," I replied, astonished.

"A—a birthmark?"

"Yes,—may I ask why?"

As she drew away from me, I saw that the color had fled from her cheeks. For a second she clasped both hands over her eyes as if to shut out my face, then slowly dropping her hands, she sat down on a long square block of stone which half encircled the basin, and on which to my amazement I saw carving. Voyou went to her again and laid his head in her lap.

"What is your name?" she asked at length.

"Roy Cardenhe."

"Mine is Ysonde. I carved these dragon-flies on the stone, these fishes and shells and butterflies you see."

"You! They are wonderfully delicate,—but those are not American dragon-flies—"

"No—they are more beautiful. See, I have my hammer and chisel with me."

She drew from a queer pouch at her side a small hammer and chisel and held them toward me.

"You are very talented," I said, "where did you study?"

"I? I never studied,—I knew how. I saw things and cut them out of stone. Do you like them? Some time I will show you other things that I have done. If I had a great lump of bronze I could make your dog, beautiful as he is."

Her hammer fell into the fountain and I leaned over and plunged my arm into the water to find it.

"It is there, shining on the sand," she said, leaning over the pool with me... "Where," said I, looking at our reflected faces in the water. For it was only in the water that I had dared, as yet, to look her long in the face.

The pool mirrored the exquisite oval of her head, the heavy hair, the eyes. I heard the silken rustle of her girdle, I caught the flash of a white arm, and the hammer was drawn up dripping with spray.

The troubled surface of the pool grew calm and again I saw her eyes reflected.

"Listen," she said in a low voice, "do you think you will come again to my fountain?"

"I will come," I said. My voice was dull; the noise of water filled my ears.

Then a swift shadow sped across the pool; I rubbed my eyes. Where her reflected face had bent beside mine there was nothing mirrored but the rosy evening sky with one pale star glimmering.

I drew myself up and turned. She was gone. I saw the faint star twinkling above me in the afterglow, I saw the tall trees motionless in the still evening air, I saw my dog slumbering at my feet.

The sweet scent in the air had faded, leaving in my nostrils the heavy odor of fern and forest mould. A blind fear seized me, and I caught up my gun and sprang into the darkening woods.

The dog followed me, crashing through the undergrowth at my side. Duller and duller grew the light, but I strode on, the sweat pouring from my face and hair, my mind a chaos. How I reached the spinney I can hardly tell. As I turned up the path I caught a glimpse of a human face peering at me from the darkening thicket,—a horrible human face, yellow and drawn with high-boned cheeks and narrow eyes.

Involuntarily I halted; the dog at my heels snarled. Then I sprang straight at it, floundering blindly through the thicket, but the night had fallen swiftly and I found myself panting and struggling in a maze of twisted shrubbery and twining vines, unable to see the very undergrowth that ensnared me.

It was a pale face, and a scratched one that I carried to a late dinner that night. Howlett served me, dumb reproach in his eyes, for the soup had been standing and the grouse was juiceless.

David brought the dogs in after they had had their supper, and I drew my chair before the blaze and set my ale on a table beside me. The dogs curled up at my feet, blinking gravely at the sparks that snapped and flew in eddying showers from the heavy birch logs.

"David," said I, "did you say you saw a Chinaman today?"

"I did sir."

"What do you think about it now?"

"I may have been mistaken sir—".

"But you think not. What sort of whiskey did you put in my flask today?"

"The usual sir."

"Is there much gone?"

"About three swallows sir, as usual."

"You don't suppose there could have been any mistake about that whiskey,—no medicine could have gotten into it for instance."

David smiled and said, "No sir."

"Well," said I, "I have had an extraordinary dream."

When I said "dream," I felt comforted and reassured. I had scarcely dared to say it before, even to myself.

"An extraordinary dream," I repeated; "I fell asleep in the woods about five o'clock, in that pretty glade where the fountain—I mean the pool is. You know the place?"

"I do not sir."

I described it minutely, twice, but David shook his head.

"Carved stone did you say sir? I never chanced on it. You don't mean the New Spring—"

"No, no! This glade is way beyond that. Is it possible that any people inhabit the forest between here and the Canada line?"

"Nobody short of Ste. Croix; at least I have no knowledge of any.

"Of course," said I, "when I thought I saw a Chinaman, it was imagination. Of course I had been more impressed than I was aware of by your adventure. Of course you saw no Chinaman, David."

"Probably not sir," replied David dubiously.

I sent him off to bed, saying I should keep the dogs with me all night; and when he was gone, I took a good long draught of ale, "just to shame the devil," as Pierpont said, and lighted a cigar.

Then I thought of Barris and Pierpont, and their cold bed, for I knew they would not dare build a fire, and, in spite of the hot chimney corner and the crackling blaze, I shivered in sympathy.

"I'll tell Barris and Pierpont the whole story and take them to see the carved stone and the fountain," I thought to myself; "what a marvelous dream it was—Ysonde,—if it was a dream."

Then I went to the mirror and examined the faint white mark above my eyebrow.

CHAPTER V

About eight o'clock next morning, as I sat listlessly eyeing my coffee cup which Howlett was filling, Gamin and Mioche set up a howl, and in a moment more I heard Barris' step on the porch.

"Hello, Roy," said Pierpont, stamping into the dining room, "I want my breakfast by jingo! Where's Howlett,—none of your café au lait for me,—I want a chop and some eggs. Look at that dog, he'll wag the hinge off his tail in a moment—" "Pierpont," said I, "this loquacity is astonishing but welcome. Where's Barris? You are soaked from neck to ankle."

Pierpont sat down and tore off his stiff muddy leggings.

"Barris is telephoning to Cardinal Springs,—I believe he wants some of his men,—down! Gamin, you idiot! Howlett, three eggs poached and more toast,—what was I saying? Oh, about Barris; he's struck something or other which he hopes will locate these gold-making fellows. I had a jolly time,—-he'll tell you about it."

"Billy! Billy!" I said in pleased amazement, "you are learning to talk! Dear me! You load your own shells and you carry your own gun and you fire it yourself—hello! here's Barris all over mud. You fellows really ought to change your rig—whew! what a frightful odor!"

"It's probably this," said Barris tossing something onto the hearth where it shuddered for a moment and then began to writhe; "I found it in the woods by the lake. Do you know what it can be, Roy?"

To my disgust I saw it was another of those spidery wormy crablike creatures that Godfrey had in Tiffany's.

"I thought I recognized that acrid odor," I said; "for the love of the Saints take it away from the breakfast table, Barris!"

"But what is it?" he persisted, unslinging his field-glass and revolver.

"I'll tell you what I know after breakfast," I replied firmly. "Howlett, get a broom and sweep that thing into the road.—What are you laughing at, Pierpont?" Howlett swept the repulsive creature out and Barris and Pierpont went to change their dew-soaked clothes for dryer raiment. David came to take the dogs for an airing and in a few minutes Barris reappeared and sat down in his place at the head of the table.

"Well," said I, "is there a story to tell?"

"Yes, not much. They are near the lake on the other side of the woods,—I mean these gold-makers. I shall collar one of them this evening. I haven't located the main gang with any certainty,—

shove the toast rack this way will you, Roy,—no, I am not at all certain, but I've nailed one anyway. Pierpont was a great help, really,—and, what do you think, Roy? He wants to join the Secret Service!"

"Little Willy!"

"Exactly. Oh I'll dissuade him. What sort of a reptile was that I brought in? Did Howlett sweep it away?"

"He can sweep it back again for all I care," I said indifferently. "I've finished my breakfast."

"No," said Barris, hastily swallowing his coffee, "it's of no importance; you can tell me about the beast—"

"Serve you right if I had it brought in on toast," I returned.

Pierpont came in radiant, fresh from the bath.

"Go on with your story, Roy," he said; and I told them about Godfrey and his reptile pet.

"Now what in the name of common sense can Godfrey find interesting in that creature?" I ended, tossing my cigarette into the fireplace.

"It's Japanese, don't you think?" said Pierpont.

"No," said Barris, "it is non artistically grotesque, it's vulgar and horrible,—it looks cheap and unfinished—"

"Unfinished,—exactly," said I, "like an American humorist—"

"Yes," said Pierpont, "cheap. What about that gold serpent?"

"Oh, the Metropolitan Museum bought it; you must see it, it's marvellous."

Barris and Pierpont had lighted their cigarettes and, after a moment, we all rose and strolled out to the lawn, where chains and hammocks were placed under the maple trees.

David passed, gun under arm, dogs heeling.

"Three guns on the meadows at four this afternoon," said Pierpont.

"Roy," said Barris as David bowed and started on, "what did you do yesterday?"

This was the question that I had been expecting. All night long I had dreamed of Ysonde and the glade in the woods, where, at the bottom of the crystal fountain, I saw the reflection of her eyes. All the morning while bathing and dressing I had been persuading myself that the dream was not worth recounting and than a search for the glade and the imaginary stone carving would be ridiculous. But now, as Barris asked the question, I suddenly decided to tell him the whole story.

"See here, you fellows," I said abruptly, "I am going to tell you something queer. You can laugh as much as you please too, but first I want to ask Barris a question or two. You have been in China, Barris?"

"Yes," said Barris, looking straight into my eyes.

"Would a Chinaman be likely to turn lumberman?"

"Have you seen a Chinaman?" he asked in a quiet voice.

"I don't know; David and I both imagined we did."

Barris and Pierpont exchanged glances.

"Have you seen one also?" I demanded, turning to include Pierpont... "No," said Barris slowly; "but I know that there is, or has been, a Chinaman in these woods."

"The devil!" said I.

"Yes," said Barris gravely; "the devil, if you like,—a devil,—a member of the Kuen-Yuin."

I drew my chair close to the hammock where Pierpont lay at full length, holding out to me a ball of pure gold.

"Well?" said I, examining the engraving on its surface, which represented a mass of twisted creatures,—dragons, I supposed.

"Well," repeated Barris, extending his hand to take the golden ball, "this globe of gold engraved with reptiles and Chinese hieroglyphics is the symbol of the Kuen-Yuin."

"Where did you get it?" I asked, feeling that something startling was impending.

Pierpont found it by the lake at sunrise this morning. "It is the symbol of the Kuen-Yuin," he repeated, "the terrible Kuen-Yuin, the sorcerers of China, and the most murderously diabolical sect on earth."

We puffed our cigarettes in silence until Barris rose, and began to pace backward and forward among the trees, twisting his gray moustache.

"The Kuen-Yuin are sorcerers," he said, pausing before the hammock where Pierpont lay watching him; "I mean exactly what I say,—sorcerers. I've seen them,—I've seen them at their devilish business, and I repeat to you solemnly, that as there are angels above, there is a race of devils on earth, and they are sorcerers. Bah!" he cried, "talk to me of Indian magic and Yogis and all that clap-trap! Why, Roy, I tell you than the Kuen-Yuin have absolute control of a hundred millions of people, mind and body, body and soul. Do you know what goes on in the interior of China? Does Europe know,—could any human being conceive of the condition of that gigantic hell-pit? You read the papers, you hear diplomatic twaddle about Li-Hung-Chang and the Emperor, you see accounts of battles on sea and land, and you know that Japan has raised a toy tempest along the jagged edge of the great unknown. But you never before heard of the Kuen-Yuin; no, nor has any European except a stray missionary or two, and yet I tell you that when the fires from this pit of hell have eaten through the continent to the coast, the explosion will inundate half a world,—and God help the other half."

Pierpont's cigarette went out; he lighted another, and looked hard at Barris.

"But," resumed Barris quietly, "'sufficient unto the day,' you know,—I didn't intend to say as much as I did,—it would do no good,—even you and Pierpont will forget it,—it seems so impossible and so far away,—like the burning out of the sun. What I want to discuss is the possibility or probability of a Chinaman,—a member of the Kuen-Yuin, being here, at this moment, in the forest."

"If he is," said Pierpont, "possibly the gold-makers owe their discovery to him."

"I do not doubt it for a second," said Barris earnestly.

I took the little golden globe in my hand, and examined the characters engraved upon it.

"Barris," said Pierpont, "I can't believe in sorcery while I am wearing one of Sanford's shooting suits in the pocket of which rests an uncut volume of the 'Duchess.'"

"Neither can I," I said, "for I read the *Evening Post*, and I know Mr. Godkin would not allow it. Hello! What's the matter with this gold ball?"

"What is the matter?" said Barris grimly.

"Why—why—it's changing color—purple, no, crimson—no, it's green I mean—good Heavens! these dragons are twisting under my fingers—"

"Impossible!" muttered Pierpont, leaning over me; "those are not dragons—"

"No!" I cried excitedly; "they are pictures of that reptile that Barris brought back—see—see how they crawl and turn—"

"Drop it!" commanded Barris; and I threw the ball on the turf. In an instant we had all knelt down on the grass beside it, but the globe was again golden, grotesquely wrought with dragons and strange signs.

Pierpont, a little red in the face, picked it up, and handed it to Barris. He placed it on a chair, and sat down beside me.

"Whew!" said I, wiping the perspiration from my face, "how did you play us that trick, Barris?"

"Trick?" said Barris contemptuously.

I looked at Pierpont, and my heart sank. If this was not a trick, what was it? Pierpont returned my glance and colored, but all he said was, "It's devilish queer," and Barris answered, "Yes, devilish." Then Barris asked me again to tell my story, and I did, beginning from the time I met David in the spinney to the moment when I sprang into the darkening thicket where that yellow mask had grinned like a phantom skull.

"Shall we try to find the fountain?" I asked after a pause.

"Yes,—and—er—the lady," suggested Pierpont vaguely.

"Don't be an ass," I said a little impatiently, "you need not come, you know."

"Oh, I'll come," said Pierpont, "unless you think I am indiscreet—"

"Shut up, Pierpont," said Barris, "this thing is serious; I never heard of such a glade or such a fountain, but it's true that nobody knows this forest thoroughly. It's worth while trying for; Roy, can you find your way back to it?"

"Easily," I answered; "when shall we go?"

"It will knock our snipe shooting on the head," said Pierpont, "but then when one has the opportunity of finding a live dream-lady—"

I rose, deeply offended, but Pierpont was not very penitent and his laughter was irresistible.

"The lady's yours by right of discovery," he said. "I'll promise not to infringe on your dreams,—I'll dream about other ladies—"

"Come, come," said I, "I'll have Howlett put you to bed in a minute. Barris, if you are ready—-we can get back to dinner—"

Barris had risen and was gazing at me earnestly.

"What's the matter?" I asked nervously, for I saw that his eyes were fixed on my forehead, and I thought of Ysonde and the white crescent scar.

"Is that a birthmark?" said Barris.

"Yes—why, Barris?"

"Nothing,—an interesting coincidence—"

"What!—for Heaven's sake!"

"The scar,—or rather the birthmark. It is the print of the dragon's claw,—the crescent symbol of Yue-Laou—"

"And who the devil is Yue-Laou?" I said crossly.

"Yue-Laou, the Moon Maker, Dzil-Nbu of the Kuen-Yuin;—it's Chinese mythology, but it is believed that Yue-Laou has returned to rule the Kuen-Yuin—"

"The conversation," interrupted Pierpont, "smacks of peacock's feathers and yellow-jackets. The chicken-pox has left its card on Roy, and Barris is guying us. Come on, you fellows, and make your call on the dream-lady. Barris, I hear galloping; here come your men."

Two mud splashed riders clattered up to the porch and dismounted at a motion from Barris. I noticed that both of them carried repeating rifles and heavy Colt's revolvers.

They followed Barris, deferentially, into the dining-room, and presently we heard the tinkle of plates and bottles and the low hum of Barris' musical voice.

Half an hour later they came out again, saluted Pierpont and me, and galloped away in the direction of the Canadian frontier. Ten minutes passed, and, as Barris did not appear, we rose and went into the house, to find him. He was sitting silently before the table, watching the small golden globe, now glowing with scarlet and orange fire, brilliant as a live coal. Howlett, mouth ajar, and eyes starting from the sockets, stood petrified behind him.

"Are you coming," asked Pierpont, a little startled. Barris did not answer. The globe slowly turned to pale gold again,—but the face that Barris raised to ours was white as a sheet. Then he stood up, and smiled with an effort which was painful to us all.

"Give me a pencil and a bit of paper," he said.

Howlett brought it. Barris went to the window and wrote rapidly. He folded the paper, placed it in the top drawer of his desk, locked the drawer, handed me the key, and motioned us to precede him.

When again we stood under the maples, he turned to me with an impenetrable expression.

"You will know when to use the key," he said:

"Come, Pierpont, we must try to find Roy's fountain."

CHAPTER VI

At two o'clock that afternoon, at Barris' suggestion, we gave up the search for the fountain in the glade and cut across the forest to the spinney where David and Howlett were waiting with our guns and the three dogs.

Pierpont guyed me unmercifully about the "dream-lady" as he called her, and, but for the significant coincidence of Ysonde's and Barris' questions concerning the white scar on my forehead, I should long ago have been perfectly persuaded that I had dreamed the whole thing.

As it was, I had no explanation to offer. We had not been able to find the glade although fifty times I came to landmarks which convinced me that we were just about to enter it. Barris was quiet, scarcely uttering a word to either of us during the entire search. I had never before seen him depressed in spirits. However, when we came in sight of the spinney where a cold bit of grouse and a bottle of Burgundy awaited each, Barris seemed no recover his habitual good humor.

"Here's to the dream-lady!" said Pierpont, raising his glass and standing up.

I did not like it. Even if she was only a dream, it irritated me to hear Pierpont's mocking voice.

Perhaps Barris understood,—I don't know, but he bade Pierpont drink his wine without further noise, and that young man obeyed with a childlike confidence which almost made Barris smile.

"What about the snipe, David," I asked; "the meadows should be in good condition."

"There is not a snipe on the meadows, sir," said David solemnly.

"Impossible," exclaimed Barris, "they can't have left."

"They have, sir," said David in a sepulchral voice which I hardly recognized. We all three looked at the old man curiously, waiting for his explanation of this disappointing but sensational report.

David looked at Howlett and Howlett examined the sky... "I was going," began the old man, with his eyes fastened on Howlett, "I was going along by the spinney with the dogs when I heard a noise in the covert and I seen Howlett come walkin' very fast toward me. In fact," continued David, "I may say he was runnin'. Was you runnin', Howlett?"

Howlett said "Yes," with a decorous cough.

"I beg pardon," said David, "but I'd rather Howlett told the rest. He saw things which I did not."

"Go on, Howlett," commanded Pierpont, much interested.

Howlett coughed again behind his large red hand.

"What David says is true sir," he began; "I h'observed the dogs at a distance 'ow they was a workin' sir, and David stood a lightin' of 's pipe be'ind the spotted beech when I see a 'ead pop up in the covert 'oldin a stick like 'e was h'aimin' at the dogs sir"—"A head holding a stick?" said Pierpont severely.

"The 'ead 'ad 'ands, sir," explained Howlent, "'ands that 'eld a painted stick,—like that, sir. 'Owlett, thinks I to meself this 'ere's queer, so I jumps it an' runs, but the beggar 'e seen me an' w'en I comes alongside of David, 'e was gone. "'Ello 'Owlett,' sez David, 'what the 'ell—I beg pardon, sir,—'ow did you come 'ere,' sez 'e very loud. 'Run!' sez I, 'the Chinaman is harrnyin' the dawgs!' 'For Gawd's sake wot Chinaman?' sez David, h'aimin' 'is gun at every bush. Then I thinks I see 'im an' we run an' run, the dawgs a boundin' close to heel sir, but we don't see no Chinaman."

"I'll tell the rest," said David, as Howlett coughed and stepped in a modest corner behind the dogs.

"Go on," said Barris in a strange voice.

"Well sir, when Howlett and I stopped chasin', we was on the cliff overlooking the south meadow. I noticed that there was hundreds of birds there, mostly yellow-legs and plover, and Howlett seen them too. Then before I could say a word to Howlett, something out in the lake gave a splash—a splash as if the whole cliff had fallen into the water. I was that scared that I jumped straight into the bush and Howlett he sat down quick, and all those snipe wheeled up—-there was hundreds,—all a squeelin' with fright, and the wood-duck came bowlin' over the meadows as if the old Nick was behind."

David paused and glanced meditatively at the dogs.

"Go on," said Barris in the same strained voice.

"Nothing more sir. The snipe did not come back."

"But that splash in the lake?"

"I don't know what it was sir."

"A salmon? A salmon couldn't have frightened the duck and the snipe that way?"

"No—oh no, sir. If fifty salmon had jumped they couldn't have made that splash. Couldn't they, Howlett?"

"No 'ow," said Howlett.

"Roy," said Barris at length, "what David tells us settles the snipe shooting for today. I am going to take Pierpont up to the house. Howlett and David will follow with the dogs,—I have something to say to them. If you care to come, come along; if not, go and shoot a brace of grouse for dinner and be back by eight if you want to see what Pierpont and I discovered last night."

David whistled Gamin and Mioche to heel and followed Howlett and his hamper toward the house. I called Voyou to my side, picked up my gun and turned to Barris... "I will be back by eight," I said; "you are expecting to catch one of the gold-makers, are you not?"

"Yes," said Barris listlessly.

Pierpont began to speak about the Chinaman but Barris motioned him to follow, and, nodding to me, took the path that Howlett and David had followed toward the house. When they disappeared I tucked my gun under my arm and turned sharply into the forest, Voyou trotting close to my heels.

In spite of myself the continued apparition of the Chinaman made me nervous. If he troubled me again I had fully decided to get the drop on him and find out what he was doing in the Cardinal Woods. If he could give no satisfactory account of himself I would march him in to Barris as a gold-making suspect,—I would march him in anyway, I thought, and rid the forest of his ugly face. I wondered what it was that David had heard in the lake. It must have been a big fish, a salmon, I thought; probably David's and Howlett's nerves were overwrought after their Celestial chase.

A whine from the dog broke the thread of my meditation and I raised my head. Then I stopped short in my tracks.

The lost glade lay straight before me.

Already the dog had bounded into it, across the velvet turf to the carved stone where a slim figure sat. I saw my dog lay his silky head lovingly against her silken kirtle; I saw her face bend above him, and I caught my breath and slowly entered the sun-lit glade.

Half timidly she held out one white hand.

"Now than you have come," she said, "I can show you more of my work. I told you that I could do other things besides these dragon-flies and moths carved here in stone. Why do you stare at me so? Are you ill?"

"Ysonde," I stammered.

"Yes," she said, with a faint color under her eyes.

"I—I never expected to see you again," I blurted out, "—you—I—I—thought I had dreamed—"

"Dreamed, of me? Perhaps you did, is that strange?"

"Strange? N—no—but—where did you go when—when we were leaning over the fountain together? I saw your face,—your face reflected beside mine and then—then suddenly I saw the blue sky and only a star twinkling."

"It was because you fell asleep," she said, "was it not?"

"I—asleep?"

"You slept—I thought you were very tired and I went back—"

"Back?—where?"

"Back to my home where I carve my beautiful images; see, here is one I brought to show you today."

I took the sculptured creature that she held toward me, a massive golden lizard with frail claw-spread wings of gold so thin that the sunlight burned through and fell on the ground in flaming gilded patches.

"Good Heavens!" I exclaimed, "this is astounding! Where did you learn to do such work? Ysonde, such a thing is beyond price!"

"Oh, I hope so," she said earnestly, "I can't bear to sell my work, but my step-father takes it and sends it away. This is the second thing I have done and yesterday he said I must give it to him. I suppose he is poor."

"I don't see how he can be poor if he gives you gold to model in," I said, astonished.

"Gold!" she exclaimed, "gold! He has a room full of gold! He makes it." I sat down on the turf at her feet completely unnerved.

"Why do you look at me so?" she asked, a little troubled.

"Where does your step-father live?" I said at last.

"Here."

"Here!"

"In the woods near the lake. You could never find our house."

"A house!"

"Of course. Did you think I lived in a tree? How silly. I live with my step-father in a beautiful house,—a small house, but very beautiful. He makes his gold there but the men who carry it away never come to the house, for they don't know where it is and if they did they could not get in. My step-father carries the gold in lumps to a canvas satchel. When the satchel is full he takes it out into the woods where the men live and I don't know what they do with it. I wish he could sell the gold and become rich for then I could go back to Yian where all the gardens are sweet and the river flows under the thousand bridges."

"Where is this city?" I asked faintly.

"Yian? I don't know. It is sweet with perfume and the sound of silver bells all day long. Yesterday I carried a blossom of dried lotus buds from Yian, in my breast, and all the woods were fragrant. Did you smell it?"

"Yes."

"I wondered, last night, whether you did. How beautiful your dog is; I love him. Yesterday I thought most about your dog but last night—"

"Last night," I repeated below my breath.

"I thought of you. Why do you wear the dragon-claw?"

I raised my hand impulsively to my forehead, covering the scar.

"What do you know of the dragon-claw?" I muttered.

"In is the symbol of Yue-Laou, and Yue-Laou rules the Kuen-Yuin, my step-father says. My step-father tells me everything than I know. We lived in Yian until I was sixteen years old. I am eighteen now; that is two years we have lived in the forest. Look!—see those scarlet birds! What are they? There are birds of the same color in Yian."

"Where is Yian, Ysonde?" I asked with deadly calmness.

"Yian? I don't know."

"But you have lived there?"

"Yes, a very long time."

"Is it across the ocean, Ysonde?"

"It is across seven oceans and the great river which is longer than from the earth to the moon."

"Who told you that?"

"Who? My step-father; he tells me everything."

"Will you tell me his name, Ysonde?"

"I don't know it, he is my step-father, that is all."

"And what is your name?"

"You know it, Ysonde."

"Yes, but what other name.

"Than is all, Ysonde. Have you two names? Why do you look at me so impatiently?"

"Does your step-father make gold? Have you seen him make it?"

"Oh yes. He made it also in Yian and I loved to watch the sparks at night whirling like golden bees. Yian is lovely,—if it is all like our garden and the gardens around. I can see the thousand bridges from my garden and the white mountain beyond—"

"And the people—tell me of the people, Ysonde" I urged gently.

"The people of Yian? I could see them in swarms like ants—oh! many, many millions crossing and recrossing the thousand bridges."

"But how did they look? Did they dress as I do?"

"I don't know. They were very far away, moving specks on the thousand bridges. For sixteen years I saw them every day from my garden but I never went out of my garden into the streets of Yian, for my step-father forbade me."

"You never saw a living creature near by in Yian?" I asked in despair.

"My birds, oh such tall, wise-looking birds, all over gray and rose color."

She leaned over the gleaming water and drew her polished hand across the surface.

"Why do you ask me these questions," she murmured; "are you displeased?"

"Tell me about your step-father," I insisted. "Does he look as I do? Does he dress, does he speak as I do? Is he American?"

"American? I don't know. He does not dress as you do and he does not look as you do. He is old, very, very old. He speaks sometimes as you do, sometimes as they do in Yian. I speak also in both manners."

"Then speak as they do in Yian," I urged impatiently, "speak as—why, Ysonde! why are you crying? Have I hurt you?—I did not intend,—I did not dream of your caring! There Ysonde, forgive me,—see, I beg you on my knees here at your feet."

I stopped, my eyes fastened on a small golden ball which hung from her waist by a golden chain. I saw it trembling against her thigh, I saw it change color, now crimson, now purple, now flaming scarlet. It was the symbol of the Kuen-Yuin.

She bent over me and laid her fingers gently on my arm.

"Why do you ask me such things?" she said, while the tears glistened on her lashes. "It hurts me here,—" she pressed her hand to her breast,— "in pains.—I don't know why. Ah, now your eyes are hard and cold again; you are looking at the golden globe which hangs from my waist. Do you wish to know also what that is?"

"Yes," I muttered, my eyes fixed on the infernal color flames which subsided as I spoke, leaving the ball a pale gilt again.

"It is the symbol of the Kuen-Yuin," she said in a trembling voice; "why do you ask?"

"Is it yours?"

"Y—yes."

"Where did you get in?" I cried harshly.

"My—my step-fa—"

Then she pushed me away from her with all the strength of her slender wrists and covered her face.

If I slipped my arm about her and drew her to me,—if I kissed away the tears that fell slowly between her fingers,—if I told her how I loved her—how it cut me to the heart to see her unhappy,—after all that is my own business. When she smiled through her tears, the pure love and sweetness in her eyes lifted my soul higher than the high moon vaguely glimmering through the sun-lit blue above. My happiness was so sudden, so fierce and overwhelming that I only knelt there, her fingers clasped in mine, my eyes raised to the blue vault and the glimmering moon.. Then something in the long grass beside me moved close to my knees and a damp acrid odor filled my nostrils.

"Ysonde!" I cried, but the touch of her hand was already gone and my two clenched fists were cold and damp with dew.

"Ysonde!" I called again, my tongue stiff with fright;—but I called as one awaking from a dream—a horrid dream, for my nostrils quivered with the damp acrid odor and I felt the crab-reptile clinging to my knee. Why had the night fallen so swiftly,—and where was I—where?—-stiff, chilled, torn, and bleeding, lying flung like a corpse over my own threshold with Voyou licking my face and Barris snooping above me in the light of a lamp that flared and smoked in the night breeze like a torch. Faugh! the choking stench of the lamp aroused me and I cried out:

"Ysonde!"

"What the devil's the matter with him?" muttered Pierpont, lifting me in his arms like a child, "has he been stabbed, Barris?"

CHAPTER VII

In a few minutes I was able to stand and walk stiffly into my bedroom where Howlett had a hot bath ready and a hotter tumbler of Scotch. Pierpont sponged the blood from my throat where it had coagulated. The cut was slight, almost invisible, a mere puncture from a thorn. A shampoo cleaned my mind, and a cold plunge and alcohol friction did the rest.

"Now," said Pierpont, "swallow your hot Scotch and lie down. Do you want a broiled woodcock? Good, I fancy you are coming about."

Barris and Pierpont watched me as I sat on the edge of the bed, solemnly chewing on the woodcock's wishbone and sipping my Bordeaux, very much an my ease.

Pierpont sighed his relief.

"So," he said pleasantly, "it was a mere case of ten dollars or ten days. I thought you had been stabbed—"

"I was not intoxicated," I replied, serenely picking up a bit of celery.

"Only jagged?" enquired Pierpont, full of sympathy.

"Nonsense," said Barris, "let him alone. Want some more celery, Roy?—it will make you sleep."

"I don't want to sleep," I answered; "when are you and Pierpont going to catch your gold-maker?"

Barris looked at his watch and closed it with a snap.

"In an hour; you don't propose to go with us?"

"But I do,—toss me a cup of coffee, Pierpont, will you,—that's just what I propose to do. Howlett, bring the new box of Panatellas,—the mild imported;—and leave the decanter. Now Barris, I'll be dressing, and you and Pierpont keep still and listen to what I have to say. Is that door shut night?"

Barris locked it and sat down.

"Thanks," said I. "Barris, where is the city of Yian?"

An expression akin to terror flashed into Barris' eyes and I saw him stop breathing for a moment.

"There is no such city," he said at length, "have I been talking in my sleep?"

"It is a city," I continued, calmly, "where the river winds under the thousand bridges, where the gardens are sweet scented and the air is filled with the music of silver bells—"

"Stop!" gasped Barris, and rose trembling from his chair. He had grown ten years older.

"Roy," interposed Pierpont coolly, "what the deuce are you harrying Barris for?"

I looked at Barris and he looked at me. After a second or two he sat down again.

"Go on, Roy," he said.

"I must," I answered, "for now I am certain that I have not dreamed."

I told them everything; but, even as I told it, the whole thing seemed so vague, so unreal, that at times I stopped with the hot blood tingling in my ears, for it seemed impossible that sensible men, in the year of our Lord 1896, could seriously discuss such manners.

I feared Pierpont, but he did not even smile. As for Barris, he sat with his handsome head sunk on his breast, his unlighted pipe clasped tight in both hands.

When I had finished, Pierpont turned slowly and looked at Barris. Twice he moved his lips as if about to ask something and then remained mute.

"Yian is a city," said Barris, speaking dreamily; "was that why you wished to know, Pierpont?"

We nodded silently.

"Yian is a city," repeated Barris, "where the great river winds under the thousand bridges,—where the gardens are sweet scented, and the air is filled with the music of silver bells."

My lips formed the question, "Where is this city?"

"It lies," said Barris, almost querulously, "across the seven oceans and the river which is longer than from the earth to the moon."

"What do you mean?" said Pierpont.

"Ah," said Barris, rousing himself with an effort and raising his sunken eyes, "I am using the allegories of another land; let it pass. Have I not told you of the Kuen-Yuin? Yian is the centre of the Kuen-Yuin. It lies hidden in that gigantic shadow called China, vague and vast as the midnight Heavens,—a continent unknown, impenetrable."

"Impenetrable," repeated Pierpont below his breath.

"I have seen it," said Barris dreamily. "I have seen the dead plains of Black Cathay and I have crossed the mountains of Death, whose summits are above the atmosphere. I have seen the shadow of Xangi cast across Abaddon. Better to die a million miles from Yezd and Ater Quedah than to have seen the white water-lotus close in the shadow of Xangi! I have slept among the ruins of Xaindu where the winds never cease and the Wulwulleh is wailed by the dead."

"And Yian," I urged gently.

There was an unearthly look on his face as he turned slowly toward me.

"Yian,—I have lived there—and loved there. When the breath of my body shall cease, when the dragon's claw shall fade from my arm,"—he tore up his sleeve, and we saw a white crescent shining above his elbow,—"when the light of my eyes has faded forever, then, even then I shall not forget the city of Yian. Why, it is my home,—mine! The river and the thousand bridges, the white peak beyond, the sweet-scented gardens, the lilies, the pleasant noise of the summer wind laden with bee music and the music of bells,—all these are mine. Do you think because the Kuen-Yuin feared the dragon's claw on my arm that my work with them is ended? Do you think than because Yue-Laou could give, that I acknowledge his right to take away? Is he Xangi in whose shadow the white water-lotus dares not raise its head? No! No!" he cried violently, "it was not from Yue-Laou, the sorcerer, the Maker of Moons, that my happiness came! It was real, it was not a shadow to vanish like a tinted bubble! Can a sorcerer create and give a man the woman he loves? Is Yue-Laou as great as Xangi then? Xangi is God. In His own time, in His infinite goodness and mercy He will bring me again to the woman I love. And I know she waits for me at God's feet."

In the strained silence that followed I could hear my heart's double beat and I saw Pierpont's face, blanched and pitiful. Barris shook himself and raised his head. The change in his ruddy face frightened me.

"Heed!" he said, with a terrible glance at me; "the print of the dragon's claw is on your forehead and Yue-Laou knows in. If you must love, then love like a man, for you will suffer like a soul in hell, in the end. What is her name again?"

"Ysonde," I answered simply.

CHAPTER VIII

At nine o'clock that night we caught one of the gold-makers. I do not know how Barris had laid his trap; all I saw of the affair can be told in a minute or two.

We were posted on the Cardinal road about a mile below the house, Pierpont and I with drawn revolvers on one side, under a butternut tree, Barris on the other, a Winchester across his knees.

I had just asked Pierpont the hour, and he was feeling for his watch when far up the road we heard the sound of a galloping horse, nearer, nearer, clattering, thundering past. Then Barris' rifle spat flame and the dark mass, horse and rider, crashed into the dust. Pierpont had the half stunned horseman by the collar in a second,—the horse was stone dead,—and, as we lighted a pine knot to examine the fellow, Barris' two riders galloped up and drew bridle beside us.

"Hm!" said Barris with a scowl, "it's the 'Shiner,' or I'm a moonshiner."

We crowded curiously around to see the "Shiner." He was red-headed, fat and filthy, and his little red eyes burned in his head like the eyes of an angry pig.

Barris went through his pockets methodically while Pierpont held him and I held the torch. The Shiner was a gold mine; pockets, shirt, bootlegs, hat, even his dirty fists, clutched tight and bleeding, were bursting with lumps of soft yellow gold. Barris dropped this "moonshine gold" as we had come to call it, into the pockets of his shooting-coat, and withdrew to question the prisoner. He came back again in a few minutes and motioned his mounted men to take the Shiner in charge. We watched them, rifle on thigh, walking their horses slowly away into the darkness, the Shiner, tightly bound, shuffling sullenly between them.

"Who is the Shiner?" asked Pierpont, slipping the revolver into his pocket again.

"A moonshiner, counterfeiter, forger, and highwayman," said Barris, "and probably a murderer. Drummond will be glad to see him, and I think it likely he will be persuaded to confess to him what he refuses to confess no me."

"Wouldn't he talk?" I asked.

"Not a syllable. Pierpont, there is nothing more for you to do."

"For me to do? Are you not coming back with us, Barris?"

"No," said Barris.

We walked along the dark road in silence for a while, I wondering what Barris intended to do, but he said nothing more until we reached our own verandah. Here he held out his hand, first to Pierpont, then to me, saying good-bye as though he were going on a long journey.

"How soon will you be back?" I called out to him as he turned away toward the gate. He came across the lawn again and again took our hands with a quiet affection that I had never imagined him capable of.

"I am going," he said, "to put an end to his gold-making tonight. I know that you fellows have never suspected what I was about on my little solitary evening strolls after dinner. I will tell you.

Already I have unobtrusively killed four of these gold-makers,—my men put them underground just below the new wash-out at the four mile stone. There are three left alive,—the Shiner whom we have, another criminal named 'Yellow,' or 'Yaller' in the vernacular, and the third—"

"The third," repeated Pierpont, excitedly.

"The third I have never yet seen. But I know who and what he is,—I know; and if he is of human flesh and blood, his blood will flow tonight."

As he spoke a slight noise across the turf attracted my attention. A mounted man was advancing silently in the starlight over the spongy meadowland. When he came nearer Barris struck a match, and we saw that he bore a corpse across his saddle bow.

"Yaller, Colonel Barris," said the man, touching his slouched hat in salute.

This grim introduction to the corpse made me shudder, and, after a moment's examination of the stiff, wide-eyed dead man, I drew back.

"Identified," said Barris, "take him to the four mile post and carry his effects to Washington,—under seal, mind, Johnstone."

Away cantered the rider with his ghastly burden, and Barris took our hands once more for the last time. Then he went away, gaily, with a jest on his lips, and Pierpont and I turned back into the house.

For an hour we sat moodily smoking in the hall before the fire, saying little until Pierpont burst out with: "I wish Barris had taken one of us with him tonight!"

The same thought had been running in my mind, but I said: "Barris knows what he's about."

This observation neither comforted us nor opened the lane to further conversation, and after a few minutes Pierpont said good night and called for Howlett and hot water. When he had been warmly tucked away by Howlett, I turned out all but one lamp, sent the dogs away with David and dismissed Howlett for the night.

I was not inclined to retire for I knew I could not sleep. There was a book lying open on the table beside the fire and I opened it and read a page or two, but my mind was fixed on other things.

The window shades were raised and I looked out at the star-set firmament. There was no moon that night but the sky was dusted all over with sparkling stars and a pale radiance, brighter even than moonlight, fell over meadow and wood. Far away in the forest I heard the voice of the wind, a soft warm wind that whispered a name, Ysonde.

"Listen," sighed the voice of the wind, and "listen" echoed the swaying trees with every little leaf a-quiver. I listened.

Where the long grasses trembled with the cricket's cadence I heard her name, Ysonde; I heard it in the rustling woodbine where gray moths hovered; I heard it in the drip, drip, drip of the dew from the porch. The silent meadow brook whispered her name, the rippling woodland streams repeated it, Ysonde, Ysonde, until all earth and sky were filled with the soft thrill, Ysonde, Ysonde, Ysonde.

A night-thrush sang in a thicket by the porch and I stole to the verandah to listen. After a while it began again, a little further on. I ventured out into the road. Again I heard it far away in the forest and I followed it, for I knew it was singing of Ysonde.

When I came to the path that leaves the main road and enters the Sweet-Fern Covert below the spinney, I hesitated; but the beauty of the night lured me on and the night-thrushes called me from every thicket. In the starry radiance, shrubs, grasses, field flowers, stood out distinctly, for there was no moon to cast shadows. Meadow and brook, grove and stream, were illuminated by the pale glow. Like great lamps lighted the planets hung from the high domed sky and through their mysterious rays the fixed stars, calm, serene, stared from the heavens like eyes...I waded on waist deep through fields of dewy golden-red, through late clover and wild-oat wastes, through crimson fruited sweetbrier, blueberry, and wild plum, until the low whisper of the Wier Brook warned me that the path had ended.

But I would not stop, for the night air was heavy with the perfume of water-lilies and far away, across the low wooded cliffs and the wet meadowland beyond, there was a distant gleam of silver, and I heard the murmur of sleepy waterfowl. I would go to the lake. The way was clear except for the dense young growth and the snares of the moose-bush.

The night-thrushes had ceased but I did not want for the company of living creatures. Slender, quick darting forms crossed my path at intervals, sleek mink, that fled like shadows at my step, wiry weasels and fat muskrats, hurrying onward to some tryst or killing.

I never had seen so many little woodland creatures on the move at night. I began to wonder where they all were going so fast, why they all hurried on in the same direction. Now I passed a hare hopping through the brushwood, now a rabbit scurrying by, flag hoisted. As I entered the beech second-growth two foxes glided by me; a little further on a doe crashed out of the under-brush, and close behind her stole a lynx, eyes shining like coals.

He neither paid attention to the doe nor to me, but loped away toward the north.

The lynx was in flight.

"From what?" I asked myself, wondering. There was no forest fine, no cyclone, no flood.

If Barris had passed that way could he have stirred up this sudden exodus? Impossible; even a regiment in the forest could scarcely have put to rout these frightened creatures.

"What on earth," thought I, turning to watch the headlong flight of a fisher-cat, "what on earth has started the beasts out at this time of night?"

I looked up into the sky. The placid glow of the fixed stars comforted me and I stepped on through the narrow spruce belt that leads down to the borders of the Lake of the Stars.

Wild cranberry and moose-bush entwined my feet, dewy branches spattered me with moisture, and the thick spruce needles scraped my face as I threaded my way over mossy logs and deep spongy tussocks down to the level gravel of the lake shore.

Although there was no wind the little waves were hurrying in from the lake and I heard them splashing among the pebbles. In the pale star glow thousands of water-lilies lifted their half-closed chalices toward the sky.

I threw myself full length upon the shore, and, chin on hand, looked out across the lake.

Splash, splash, came the waves along the shore, higher, nearer, until a film of water, thin and glittering as a knife blade, crept up to my elbows. I could not understand it; the lake was rising, but there had been no rain. All along the shore the water was running up; I heard the waves among the sedge grass; the weeds at my side were awash in the ripples. The lilies rocked on the tiny waves, every wet pad rising on the swells, sinking, rising again until the whole lake was glimmering with undulating blossoms. How sweet and deep was the fragrance from the lilies.

And now the water was ebbing, slowly, and the waves receded, shrinking from the shore rim until the white pebbles appeared again, shining like froth on a brimming glass.

No animal swimming out in the darkness along the shore, no heavy salmon surging, could have set the whole shore aflood as though the wash from a great boat were rolling in. Could it have been the overflow, through the Weir Brook, of some cloud-burst far back in the forest? This was the only way I could account for it, and yet when I had crossed the Weir Brook I had not noticed that it was swollen.

And as I lay there thinking, a faint breeze sprang up and I saw the surface of the lake whiten with lifted lily pads. All around me the alders were sighing; I heard the forest behind me stir; the crossed branches rubbing softly, bark against bark. Something— it may have been an owl—sailed out of the night, dipped, soared, and was again engulfed, and far across the water I heard its faint cry, Ysonde.

Then first, for my heart was full, I cast myself down upon my face, calling on her name. My eyes were wet when I raised my head,—for the spray from the shore was drifting in again,—and my heart beat heavily; "No more, no more." But my heart lied, for even as I raised my face to the calm stars, I saw her standing still, close beside me; and very gently I spoke her name, Ysonde.

She held out both hands.

"I was lonely," she said, "and I went to the glade, but the forest is full of frightened creatures and they frightened me. Has anything happened in the woods? The deer are running toward the heights."

Her hand still lay in mine as we moved along the shore, and the lapping of the water on rock and shallow was no lower than our voices.

"Why did you leave me without a word, there at the fountain in the glade?" she said.

"I leave you!—"

"Indeed you did, running swiftly with your dog, plunging through thickens and brush,—oh—-you frightened me."

"Did I leave you so?"

"Yes—after—"

"After?"

"You had kissed me—"

Then we leaned down together and looked into the black water set with stars, just as we had bent together over the fountain in the glade.

"Do you remember?" I asked.

"Yes. See, the water is inlaid with silver stars,—everywhere white lilies floating and the stars below, deep, deep down."

"What is the flower you hold in your hand?"

"White water-lotus."

"Tell me about Yue-Laou, Dzil-Nbu of the Kuen-Yuin," I whispered, lifting her head so I could see her eyes.

"Would it please you to hear?"

"Yes, Ysonde."

"All that I know is yours, now, as I am yours, all than I am. Bend closer. Is it of Yue-Laou you would know? Yue-Laou is Dzil-Nhu of the Kuen-Yuin. He lived in the Moon. He is old—very, very old, and once, before he came to rule the Kuen-Yuin, he was the old man who unites with a silken cord all predestined couples, after which nothing can prevent their union. But all that is changed since he came to rule the Kuen-Yuin. Now he has perverted the Xin,—the good genii of China,—and has fashioned from their warped bodies a monster which he calls the Xin. This monster is horrible, for it not only lives in its own body, but it has thousands of loathsome satellites,—living creatures without mouths, blind, that move when the Xin moves, like a mandarin and his escort. They are part of the Xin although they are not attached. Yet if one of these satellites is injured the Xin writhes with agony. It is fearful—this huge living bulk and these creatures spread out like severed fingers that wriggle around a hideous hand."

"Who told you this?"

"My step-father."

"Do you believe it?"

"Yes. I have seen one of the Xin's creatures."

"Where, Ysonde?"

"Here in the woods."

"Then you believe there is a Xin here?"

"There must be,—perhaps in the lake—"

"Oh, Xins inhabit lakes?"

"Yes, and the seven seas. I am not afraid here."

"Why?"

"Because I wear the symbol of the Kuen-Yuin."

"Then I am not safe," I smiled.

"Yes you are, for I hold you in my arms. Shall I tell you more about the Xin? When the Xin is about to do to death a man, the Yeth-hounds gallop through the night—"

"What are the Yeth-hounds, Ysonde?"

"The Yeth-hounds are dogs without heads. They are the spirits of murdered children, which pass through the woods at night, making a wailing noise."

"Do you believe this?"

"Yes, for I have worn the yellow lotus—"

"The yellow lotus—"

"Yellow is the symbol of faith—"

"Where?"

"In Yian," she said faintly.

After a while I said, "Ysonde, you know there is a God?"

"God and Xangi are one."

"Have you ever heard of Christ?"

"No," she answered softly.

The wind began again among the tree tops. I felt her hands closing in mine.

"Ysonde," I asked again, "do you believe in sorcerers?"

"Yes, the Kuen-Yuin are sorcerers; Yue-Laou is a sorcerer."

"Have you seen sorcery?"

"Yes, the reptile satellite of the Xin—"

"Anything else?"

"My charm,—the golden ball, the symbol of the Kuen-Yuin. Have you seen it change,—have you seen the reptiles writhe—?"

"Yes," I said shortly, and then remained silent, for a sudden shiver of apprehension had seized me. Barris also had spoken gravely, ominously of the sorcerers, the Kuen-Yuin, and I had seen with my own eyes the graven reptiles turning and twisting on the glowing globe.

"Still," said I aloud, "God lives and sorcery is but a name."

"Ah," murmured Ysonde, drawing closer no me, "they say, in Yian, the Kuen-Yuin live; God is but a name."

"They lie," I whispered fiercely.

"Be careful," she pleaded, "they may hear you. Remember that you have the mark of the dragon's claw on your brow."

"What of it?" I asked, thinking also of the white mark on Barris' arm.

"Ah don't you know that those who are marked with the dragon's claw are followed by Yue-Laou, for good or for evil,—and the evil means death if you offend him?"

"Do you believe that!" I asked impatiently... "I know it," she sighed.

"Who told you all this? Your step-father? What in Heaven's name is he then,—a Chinaman!"

"I don't know; he is not like you."

"Have—have you told him anything about me?"

"He knows about you—no, I have told him nothing,—ah what is this—see—it is a cord, a cord of silk about your neck—and about mine!"

"Where did that come from?" I asked astonished.

"It must be—it must be Yue-Laou who binds me to you,—it is as my step-father said—he said Yue-Laou would bind us—"

"Nonsense," I said almost roughly, and seized the silken cord, but to my amazement it melted in my hand like smoke.

"What is all this damnable jugglery!" I whispered angrily, but my anger vanished as the words were spoken, and a convulsive shudder shook me to the feet. Standing on the shore of the lake, a stone's throw away, was a figure, twisted and bent,—a little old man, blowing sparks from a live coal which he held in his naked hand. The coal glowed with increasing radiance, lighting up the skull-like face above it, and threw a red glow over the sands at his feet. But the face!—the ghastly Chinese face on which the light flickered,—and the snaky slitted eyes, sparkling as the coal glowed hotter. Coal! It was not a coal but a golden globe staining the night with crimson flames—it was the symbol of the Kuen-Yuin.

"See! See!" gasped Ysonde, trembling violently, "see the moon rising from between his fingers! Oh I thought it was my step-father and it is Yue-Laou the Maker of Moons—no! no! it is my step-father—ah God! they are the same!"

Frozen with terror I stumbled to my knees, groping for my revolver which bulged in my coat pocket; but something held me—something which bound me like a web in a thousand strong silky meshes. I struggled and turned but the web grew tighter; it was over us—all around us, drawing, pressing us into each other's arms until we lay side by side, bound hand and body and foot, palpitating, panting like a pair of netted pigeons.

And the creature on the shore below! What was my horror to see a moon, huge, silvery, rise like a bubble from between his fingers, mount higher, higher into the still air and hang aloft in the midnight sky, while another moon rose from his fingers, and another and yet another until the vast span of Heaven was set with moons and the earth sparkled like a diamond in the white glare.

A great wind began to blow from the east and it bore to our ears a long mournful howl,—a cry so unearthly that for a moment our hearts stopped.

"The Yeth-hounds!" sobbed Ysonde, "do you hear!—they are passing through the forest! The Xin is near!"

Then all around us in the dry sedge grasses came a rustle as if some small animals were creeping, and a damp acrid odor filled the air. I knew the smell, I saw the spidery crablike creatures swarm out around me and drag their soft yellow hairy bodies across the shrinking grasses. They passed, hundreds of them, poisoning the air, rumbling, writhing, crawling with their blind mouthless heads raised. Birds, half asleep and confused by the darkness, fluttered away before them in helpless fright, rabbits sprang from their forms, weasels glided away like flying shadows. What remained of the forest creatures rose and fled from the loathsome invasion; I heard the squeak of a terrified hare, the snort of stampeding deer, and the lumbering gallop of a bear; and all the time I was choking, half suffocated by the poisoned air.

Then, as I struggled to free myself from the silken snare about me, I cast a glance of deadly fear at the sorcerer below, and at the same moment I saw him turn in his tracks... "Halt!" cried a voice from the bushes.

"Barris!" I shouted, half leaping up in my agony.

I saw the sorcerer spring forward, I heard the bang! bang! bang! of a revolver, and, as the sorcerer fell on the water's edge, I saw Barris jump out into the white glare and fire again, once, twice, three times, into the writhing figure at his feet.

Then an awful thing occurred. Up out of the black lake reared a shadow, a nameless shapeless mass, headless, sightless, gigantic, gaping from end to end.

A great wave struck Barris and he fell, another washed him up on the pebbles, another whirled him back into the water and then,—and then the thing fell over him,—and I fainted.

~~~~~~~~~~

This, then, is all that I know concerning Yue-Laou and the Xin. I do not fear the ridicule of scientists or of the press for I have told the truth. Barris is gone and the thing that killed him is alive today in the Lake of the Stars while the spider-like satellites roam through the Cardinal Woods. The game has fled, the forests around the lake are empty of any living creatures save the reptiles than creep when the Xin moves in the depths of the lake.

General Drummond knows what he has lost in Barris, and we, Pierpont and I, know what we have lost also. His will we found in the drawer, the key of which he had handed me. It was wrapped in a bit of paper on which was written:

"Yue-Laou the sorcerer is here in the Cardinal Woods. I must kill him or he will kill me. He made and gave to me the woman I loved,—he made her,—I saw him,—he made her out of a white water-lotus bud. When our child was born, he came again before me and demanded from me the woman I loved. Then, when I refused, he went away, and that night my wife and child vanished from my side, and I found upon her pillow a white lotus bud. Roy, the woman of your dream, Ysonde, may be my child. God help you if you love her for Yue-Laou will give,—and take away, as though he were Xangi, which is God. I will kill Yue-Laou before I leave this forest,—or he will kill me.

"FRANKLYN BARRIS."

Now the world knows what Barris thought of the Kuen-Yuin and of Yue-Laou. I see that the newspapers are just becoming excited over the glimpses that Li-Hung-Chang has afforded them of Black Cathay and the demons of the Kuen-Yuin. The Kuen-Yuin are on the move.

Pierpont and I have dismantled the shooting box in the Cardinal Woods. We hold ourselves ready at a moment's notice to join and lead the first Government party to drag the Lake of Stars and cleanse the forest of the crab reptiles. But it will be necessary that a large force assembles, and a well-armed force, for we never have found the body of Yue-Laou, and, living or dead, I fear him. Is he living?

Pierpont, who found Ysonde and myself lying unconscious on the lake shore, the morning after, saw no trace of corpse or blood on the sands. He may have fallen into the lake, but I fear and Ysonde fears that he is alive. We never were able to find either her dwelling place or the glade and the fountain again. The only thing that remains to her of her former life is the gold serpent in the Metropolitan Museum and her golden globe, the symbol of the Kuen-Yuin; but the latter no longer changes color.

David and the dogs are waiting for me in the court yard as I write. Pierpont is in the gun room loading shells, and Howlett brings him mug after mug of my ale from the wood. Ysonde bends over my desk,—I feel her hand on my arm, and she is saying, "Don't you think you have done enough today, dear? How can you write such silly nonsense without a shadow of truth or foundation.

THE HARBOUR-MASTER

CHAPTER I

BECAUSE it all seems so improbable—so horridly impossible to me now, sitting here safe and sane in my own library—I hesitate to record an episode which already appears to me less horrible than grotesque. Yet, unless the story is written now, I know I shall never have the courage to tell the truth about the matter, not from fear of ridicule, but because I myself shall soon cease to credit what I now know to be true. Yet scarcely a month has elapsed since I heard the stealthy purring of what I believed to be the shoaling undertow—scarcely a month ago with my own eyes I saw that which, even now, I am beginning to believe never existed. As for the Harbor-Master, and the blow I am now striking at the old order of things— But of that I shall not speak now or later. I shall try to tell the story simply and truthfully, and let my employers testify as to my probity, and the editor of this magazine corroborate them.

On Feb. 29 of the present year I resigned my position under the Government and left Washington to accept an offer from Professor Farrago—whose name he kindly permits me to use in this article—and on the first day of April I entered upon my new and congenial duties as general superintendent of the water-fowl department connected with the Zoological Gardens now in course of erection at Bronx Park, New York.

For a week I followed the routine, examining the new foundations, studying the architect's plans, following the surveyors through the Bronx thickets, suggesting arrangements for water-courses and pools destined to be included in the enclosures for swans, geese, pelicans, herons, and such of the waders and swimmers as we might expect to acclimate in Bronx Park.

It was, and is, the policy of the trustees and officers of the Zoological Gardens not to employ collectors, nor to send out expeditions in search of specimens. The Society decided to depend upon voluntary contributions, and I was always busy, part of the day, in dictating answers to correspondents who wrote offering their services as hunters of big game, collectors of all sorts of fauna, trappers, snarers, and also to those who offered specimens for sale, usually at exorbitant rates.

To the proprietors of five-legged kittens, mangy lynxes, moth-eaten coyotes, and dancing bears I returned courteous but uncompromising refusals—of course, first submitting all such letters, together with my replies, to Professor Farrago.

One day towards the end of May, however, just as I was leaving Bronx Park to return to town, Professor Lesard, of the Reptilian Department, called out to me that Professor Farrago wanted to see me a moment; so I put my pipe into my pocket again, and retraced my steps to the temporary wooden building occupied by Professor Farrago, General Superintendent of the Zoological Gardens. The Professor, who was sitting at his desk before a pile of letters and replies submitted for approval by me, pushed his glasses down and looked over them at me with a whimsical smile that suggested amusement, impatience, annoyance, and perhaps a faint trace of apology.

"Now, here's a letter," he said, with a deliberate gesture toward a sheet of paper impaled on a file—"a letter that I suppose you remember." He disengaged the sheet of paper and handed it to me.

"Oh, yes," I replied with a shrug; "of course, the man is mistaken, or—"

"Or what?" demanded Professor Farrago, tranquilly wiping his glasses.

"Or a liar," I replied.

After a silence he leaned back in his chair and bade me read the letter to him again, and I did so with a contemptuous tolerance for the writer, who must have been either a very innocent victim or a very stupid swindler. I said as much to Professor Farrago, but to my surprise he appeared to waver.

"I suppose," he said, with his near-sighted embarrassed smile, "that nine hundred and ninety-nine men in a thousand would throw that letter aside and condemn the writer as a liar or a fool."

"In my opinion," said I, "he's one or the other."

"He isn't—in mine," said the Professor placidly.

"What!" I exclaimed; "here is a man living all alone on a strip of rock and sand between the wilderness and the sea, who wants you to send somebody to take charge of a bird that doesn't exist!"

"How do you know," asked Professor Farrago, "that the bird in question does not exist?"

"It is generally accepted," I replied sarcastically, "that the Great Auk has been extinct for years. Therefore I may be pardoned for doubting that our correspondent possesses a pair of them alive."

"Oh, you young fellows!" said the Professor, smiling wearily, "you embark on a theory for destinations that don't exist."

He leaned back in his chair, amused eyes searching space for the imagery that made him smile.

"Like swimming squirrels, you navigate with the help of Heaven and a stiff breeze, but you never land where you hope to—do you?"

Rather red in the face, I said, "Don't you believe the Great Auk to be extinct?"

"Audubon saw the Great Auk."

"Who has seen a single specimen since?"

"Nobody—except our correspondent here," he replied, laughing.

I laughed too, considering the interview at an end, but the Professor went on coolly—

"Whatever it is that our correspondent has—and I am daring to believe that it is the Great Auk itself—I want you to secure it for the Society."

When my astonishment subsided, my first conscious sentiment was one of pity. Clearly Professor Farrago was on the verge of dotage—ah! what a loss to the world!

I believe now that Professor Farrago perfectly interpreted my thoughts, but he betrayed neither resentment nor impatience. I drew a chair up beside his desk—there was nothing to do but to obey, and this fool's errand was none of my conceiving.

Together we made out a list of articles necessary for me, and itemized the expenses I might incur; and I set a date for my return, allowing no margin for a successful termination to the expedition.

"Never mind that," said the Professor; "what I want you to do is to get those birds here safely. Now, how many men will you take?"

"None," I replied bluntly; "it's a useless expense unless there is something to bring back. If there is, I'll wire you, you may be sure."

"Very well," said Professor Farrago good-humoredly, "you shall have all the assistance you may require. Can you leave tonight?"

The old gentleman was certainly prompt. I nodded half sulkily, aware of his amusement.

"So," I said, picking up my hat, "I am to start north to find a place called Black Harbor, where there is a man named Halyard who possesses, among other household utensils, two extinct Great Auks—"

We were both laughing by this time. I asked him why on earth he credited the assertion of a man he had never before heard of.

"I suppose," he replied, with the same half-apologetic, half-humorous smile, "it is instinct. I feel, somehow, that this man Halyard *has* got an auk—perhaps two. I can't get away from the idea that we are on the eve of acquiring the rarest of living creatures. It's odd for a scientist to talk as I do; doubtless, you're shocked—admit it now!"

But I was not shocked; on the contrary. I was conscious that the same strange hope that Professor Farrago cherished was beginning, in spite of me, to stir my pulses too.

"If he has—" I began, then stopped.

The Professor and I looked hard at each other in silence.

"Go on," he said encouragingly.

But I had nothing more to say, for the prospect of beholding with my own eyes a living specimen of the Great Auk produced a series of conflicting emotions within me which rendered speech profanely superfluous.

As I took my leave Professor Farrago came to the door of the temporary wooden office and handed me the letter written by the man Halyard. I folded it and put it into my pocket, as Halyard might require it for my own identification.

"How much does he want for the pair?" I asked.

"Ten thousand dollars. Don't demur—if the birds are really—"

"I know," I said hastily, not daring to hope too much.

"One thing more," said Professor Farrago gravely; "You know, in that last paragraph of his letter. Halyard speaks of something else in the way of specimens—an undiscovered species of amphibious biped. Just read that paragraph again, will you?"

I drew the letter from my pocket and read as he directed—

When you have seen the two living specimens of the Great Auk, and have satisfied yourself that I tell the truth, you may be wise enough to listen without prejudice to a statement I shall make concerning the existence of the strangest creature ever fashioned. I will merely say, at this time, that the creature referred to is an amphibious biped, and inhabits the ocean near this coast. More I cannot say, for I personally have not seen the animal, but I have a witness who has, and there are many who affirm that they have seen the creature. You will naturally say that my statement amounts to nothing; but when your representative arrives, if he be free from prejudice, I expect his reports to you concerning this sea-biped will confirm the solemn statements of a witness I *know* to be un-impeachable.

> —Yours truly,
> Burton Halyard.
> Black Harbour.

"Well," I said, after a moment's thought, "here goes for the wild-goose chase—"

"Wild auk, you mean," said Professor Farrago, shaking hands with me. "You will start tonight, won't you?"

"Yes; but Heaven knows how I'm ever going to land in this man Halyard's door-yard! Good-bye."

"About that sea-biped—" began Professor Farrago shyly.

"Oh, don't!" I said. "I can swallow the auks, feathers and claws, but if this fellow Halyard is hinting he's seen an amphibious creature resembling a man—"

"Or a woman—" said the Professor cautiously.

I retired disgusted, my faith shaken in the mental vigor of Professor Farrago.

CHAPTER II

The three days' voyage by boat and rail was irksome. I bought my kit at Sainte Croix on the C.P.R., and on June 1 I began the last stage of my journey via the Sainte Isole broad-gauge, arriving in the wilderness by daylight. A tedious forced march by blazed trail, freshly spotted on the wrong side, of course, brought me to the northern terminus of the rusty narrow-gauge lumber railway which runs from the heart of the hushed pine wilderness to the sea.

Already a long train of battered flat cars, piled with sluice props and roughly hewn sleepers, was moving slowly off into the brooding forest gloom when I came in sight of the track;

but I developed a gratifying and unexpected burst of speed, shouting all the while. The train stopped; I swung myself aboard the last car, where a pleasant young fellow was sitting on the rear brake, chewing spruce and reading a letter.

"Come aboard, Sir," he said, looking up with a smile; "I guess you're the man in a hurry."

"I'm looking for a man named Halyard," I said, dropping rifle and knapsack on the fresh-cut fragrant pile of pine. "Are you Halyard?"

"No, I'm Francis Lee, bossing the mica-pit at Port-of-Waves," he replied; "but this letter is from Halyard, asking me to look out for a man in a hurry from Bronx Park, New York."

"I'm that man," said I, filling my pipe and offering him a share of the weed-of-peace; and we sat side by side smoking very amiably, until a signal from the locomotive sent him forward and I was left alone, lounging at ease, head pillowed on both arms, watching the blue sky flying through the branches overhead.

Long before we came in sight of the ocean I smelled it; the fresh salt aroma stole into my senses, drowsy with the heated odor of pine and hemlock, and I sat up, peering ahead into the dusky sea of pines.

Fresher and fresher came the wind from the sea, in puffs, in mild sweet breezes, in steady freshening currents, blowing the feathery crowns of the pines, setting the balsam's blue tufts rocking.

Lee wandered back over the long line of flats, balancing himself nonchalantly, as the cars swung around a sharp curve where water dripped from a newly propped sluice that suddenly emerged from the depths of the forest to run parallel to the railroad track.

"Built it this spring," he said, surveying his handiwork, which seemed to undulate as the cars swept past. "It runs to the cove, or ought to." He stopped abruptly, with a thoughtful glance at me.

"So you're going over to Halyard's?" he continued, as though answering a question asked by himself.

I nodded.

"You've never been there, of course?"

"No," I said, "and I'm not likely to go again."

I would have told him why I was going if I had not already begun to feel ashamed of my idiotic errand.

"I guess you're going to look at those birds of his," continued Lee placidly.

"I guess I am," I said sulkily, glancing askance to see whether he was smiling.

But he only asked me quite seriously whether a Great Auk was really a very rare bird, and I told him that the last one ever seen had been found dead off Labrador in January 1870. Then I asked him whether these birds of Halyard's were really Great Auks, and he replied somewhat indifferently that he supposed they were—at least, nobody had ever before seen such birds near Port-of-Waves.

"There's something else," he said, running a pine-sliver through his pipe-stem; "something that interests us all here more than auks, big or little. I suppose I might as well speak about it, as you are bound to hear about it sooner or later."

He hesitated, and I could see that he was embarrassed, searching for the exact words to convey his meaning.

"If," said I, "you have anything in this region more important to science than the Great Auk, I should be very glad to know about it."

Perhaps there was the faintest tinge of sarcasm in my voice, for he shot a sharp glance at me and then turned slightly. After a moment, however, he put his pipe into his pocket, laid hold of the brake with both hands, vaulted to his perch aloft, and glanced down at me.

"Did you ever hear of the Harbor-Master?" he asked maliciously.

"Which Harbor-Master?" I inquired.

"You'll know before long," he observed, with a satisfied glance into perspective.

This rather extraordinary observation puzzled me. I waited for him to resume. and, as he did not, I asked him what he meant.

"If I knew," he said, "I'd tell you. But, come to think of it. I'd be a fool to go into details with a scientific man. You'll hear about the Harbor-Master—perhaps you will see the Harbour-Master. In that event I should be glad to converse with you on the subject."

I could not help laughing at his prim and precise manner, and, after a moment, he also laughed, saying—

"It hurts a man's vanity to know he knows a thing that some-body else knows he doesn't know. I'm damned if I say another word about the Harbor-Master until you've been to Halyard's!"

"A Harbor-Master," I persisted, "is an official who superintends the moorings of ships—isn't he?"

But he refused to be tempted into conversation, and we lounged silently on the lumber until a long, thin whistle from the locomotive and a rush of stinging salt wind brought us to our feet.

Through the trees I could see the bluish-black ocean stretching out beyond black headlands to meet the clouds; a great wind was roaring among the trees as the train slowly came to a stand-still on the edge of the primeval forest.

Lee jumped to the ground and aided me with my rifle and pack, and then the train began to back away along a curved side-track, which, Lee said, led to the mica-pit and company stores.

"Now, what will you do?" he asked pleasantly. "I can give you a good dinner and a decent bed tonight if you like; and I'm sure Mrs. Lee would be very glad to have you stop with us as long as you choose."

I thanked him, but said that I was anxious to reach Halyard's before dark, and he very kindly led me along the cliffs and pointed out the path.

"This man Halyard," he said, "is an invalid. He lives at a cove called Black Harbor, and all his truck goes through to him over the company's road. We receive it here, and send a pack-mule through once a month. I've met him. He's a bad-tempered hypo-chondriac, a cynic at heart, and a man whose word is never doubted. If he says he has a Great Auk you may be satisfied he has."

My heart was beating with excitement at the prospect; I looked out across the wooded headlands and tangled stretches of dune and hollow, trying to realize what it might mean to me, to Professor Farrago, to the world, if I should lead back to New York a live auk.

"He's a crank," said Lee; "frankly, I don't like him. If you find it unpleasant there, come back to us."

"Does Halyard live alone?" I asked.

"Yes—except for a professional trained nurse—poor thing!"

"A man?"

"No," said Lee disgustedly.

Presently he gave me a peculiar glance, hesitated, and finally said; "Ask Halyard to tell you about his nurse and—the Harbor-Master. Good-bye—I'm due at the quarry! Come and stay with us whenever you care to; you will find a welcome at Port-of-Waves."

We shook hands and parted on the cliff, he turning back into the forest along the railway, I starting northward, pack slung, rifle over my shoulder. Once I met a group of quarrymen, faces burned brick-red, scarred hands swinging as they walked. And, as I passed them with a nod, turning, I saw that they also had turned to look after me, and I caught a word or two of their conversation, whirled back to me on the sea-wind.

They were speaking of the Harbor-Master.

CHAPTER III

Toward sunset I came out on a sheer granite cliff where the sea-birds were whirling and clamoring and the great breakers dashed, rolling in double-thundered reverberations on the sun-dyed crimson sands below the bedded rock.

Across the half-moon of beach towered another cliff, and,

behind this, I saw a column of smoke rising in the still air. It certainly came from Halyard's chimney, although the opposite cliff prevented me from seeing the house itself.

I rested a moment to refill my pipe, then resumed rifle and pack and cautiously started to skirt the cliffs. I had descended half-way toward the beach, and was examining the cliff opposite, when something on the very top of the rock arrested my attention—a man darkly outlined against the sky. The next moment, however, I knew it could not be a man, for the object suddenly glided over the face of the cliff and slid down the sheer smooth face like a lizard. Before I could get a square look at it, the thing crawled into the surf—or, at least, it seemed to—but the whole episode occurred so suddenly, so unexpectedly, that I was not sure I had seen anything at all.

However, I was curious enough to climb the cliff on the land side and make my way toward the spot where I imagined I saw the man. Of course there was nothing there—not a trace of a human being, I mean. Something *had* been there—a sea-otter possibly; for the remains of a freshly killed fish lay on the rock, eaten to the backbone and tail.

The next moment, below me, I saw the house, a freshly painted, trim, flimsy structure, modern, and very much out of harmony with the splendid savagery surrounding it. It struck a nasty, cheap note in the noble gray monotony of headland and sea.

The descent was easy enough. I crossed the crescent beach, hard as pink marble, and found a little trodden path among the rocks that led to the front porch of the house.

There were two people on the porch—I heard their voices before I saw them—and when I set my foot upon the wooden steps I saw one of them, a woman, rise from her chair and step hastily toward me.

"Come back!" cried the other, a man with a smooth-shaven, deeply lined face, and a pair of angry blue eyes; and the woman stepped back quietly, acknowledging my lifted hat with a silent inclination. The man, who was reclining in an invalid's rolling-chair, clapped both large pale hands to the wheels, and pushed himself out along the porch. He had shawls pinned about him, an untidy drab-colored hat on his head, and when he looked down at me he scowled.

"I know who you are," he said in his acid voice, "You're one of the Zoological men from Bronx Park. You look like it, anyway."

"It is easy to recognize you from your reputation," I replied, irritated at his discourtesy.

"Really." he replied, with something between a sneer and a laugh, "I'm obliged for your frankness. You're after my Great Auks, are you not?"

"Nothing else would have tempted me into this place," I replied sincerely.

"Thank Heaven for that!" he said. "Sit down a moment; you've interrupted us." Then, turning to the young woman, who wore the neat gown and tiny cap of a professional nurse, he bade her resume what she had been saying. She did so with deprecating glance at me, which made the old man sneer again.

"It happened so suddenly," she said in her low voice, "that I had no chance to get back. The boat was drifting in the cove; I sat in the stern, reading, both oars shipped and tiller swinging. Then I heard a scratching under the boat, but thought it might be seaweed; and the next moment came those soft thumpings, like the sound of a big fish rubbing its nose against a float."

Halyard clutched the wheels of his chair and stared at the girl in grim displeasure.

"Didn't you know enough to be frightened?" he demanded.

"No—not then," she said, coloring faintly; "but when, after a few moments, I looked up and saw the Harbor-Master running up and down the beach, I was horribly frightened."

"Really?" said Halyard sarcastically, "it was about time." Then, turning to me, he rasped out: "And that young lady was obliged to row all the way to Port-of-Waves, and call to Lee's quarrymen to take her boat in."

Completely mystified, I looked from Halyard to the girl, not in the least comprehending what all this meant.

"That will do," said Halyard ungraciously, which curt phrase was apparently the usual dismissal for the nurse.

She rose, and I rose, and she passed me with an inclination, stepping noiselessly into the house.

"I want beef-tea!" bawled Halyard after her; then he gave me an unamiable glance.

"I was a well-bred man," he sneered. "I'm a Harvard graduate, too; but I live as I like, and I do what I like, and I say what I like."

"You certainly are not reticent," I said, disgusted.

"Why should I be?" he rasped; "I pay that young woman for my irritability, it's a bargain between us."

"In your domestic affairs," I said, "there is nothing that interests me. I came to see those auks—"

"You probably believe them to be razor-billed auks," he said contemptuously; "but they're not; they're Great Auks."

I suggested that he permit me to examine them, and he replied indifferently that they were in a pen in his back-yard, and that I was free to step around the house when I cared to.

I laid my rifle and pack on the verandah, and hastened off with mixed emotions, among which hope no longer predominated. No man in his senses would keep two such precious prizes in a pen in his back-yard, I argued, and I was perfectly prepared to find anything from a puffin to a penguin in that pen.

I shall never forget as long as I live my stupor of amazement when I came to the wire-covered enclosure. Not only were there two Great Auks in the pen, alive, breathing, squatting in bulky majesty on their seaweed bed, but one of them was gravely contemplating two newly hatched chicks, all bill and feet, which nestled sedately at the edge of a puddle of salt water, where some small fish were swimming.

For a while excitement blinded, nay, deafened me. I tried to realize that I was gazing upon the last two individuals of an all but extinct race—the sole survivors of the gigantic auk which, for thirty years, has been accounted an extinct creature.

I believe that I did not move muscle or limb until the sun had gone down and the crowding darkness blurred my straining eyes and blotted the great silent bright-eyed birds from sight.

Even then I could not tear myself away from the enclosure; I listened to the strange drowsy note of the male bird, the fainter responses of the female, the thin plaints of the chicks, huddling under her breast; I heard their flipper-like embryotic wings beating drowsily as the birds stretched and yawned their beaks and clacked them, preparing for sleep.

"If you please," came a soft voice from the door, "Mr. Halyard awaits your company to dinner."

CHAPTER IV

I dined well—or, rather, I might have enjoyed my dinner if Mr. Halyard had been eliminated; and the feast consisted exclusively of a joint of beef, the pretty nurse, and myself. She was exceedingly attractive, with a disturbing fashion of lowering her head and raising her dark eyes when spoken to.

As for Halyard, he was unspeakable, bundled up in his snuffy shawls and making uncouth noises over his gruel. But it is only just to say that his table was worth sitting down to, and his wine was sound as a bell.

"Yah!" he snapped. "I'm sick of this cursed soup—and I'll trouble you to fill my glass—"

"It is dangerous for you to touch claret," said the pretty nurse.

"I might as well die at dinner as anywhere," he observed.

"Certainly," said I, cheerfully passing the decanter; but he did not appear over-pleased with the attention.

"I can't smoke, either," he snarled, hitching the shawls around until he looked like Richard III.

However, he was good enough to shove a box of cigars at me, and I took one and stood up as the pretty nurse slipped past and vanished into the little parlor beyond.

We sat there for a while without speaking. He picked irritably at the bread-crumbs on the cloth, never glancing in my direction; and I, tired from my long foot-tour, lay back in my chair, silently appreciating one of the best cigars I ever smoked.

"Well," he rasped out at length, "what do you think of my auks—and my veracity?"

I told him that both were unimpeachable.

"Didn't they call me a swindler down there at your Museum?" he demanded. I admitted that I had heard the term applied. Then I made a clean breast of the matter, telling him that it was I who had doubted; that my chief, Professor Farrago, had sent me against my will, and that I was ready and glad to admit that he, Mr. Halyard, was a benefactor of the human race.

"Bosh!" he said; "what good does a confounded wobbly, bandy-toed bird do to the human race?"

But he was pleased nevertheless; and presently he asked me, not unamiably, to punish his claret again.

"I'm done for," he said; "good things to eat and drink are no use to me. Some day I'll get mad enough to have a fit, and then—"

He paused to yawn.

"Then," he continued, "that little nurse of mine will drink up my claret and go back to civilization, where people are polite."

Somehow or other, in spite of the fact that Halyard was an old pig, what he said touched me. There was certainly not much left in life for him—as he regarded life.

"I'm going to leave her this house," he said, arranging his shawls. "She doesn't know it. I'm going to leave her my money too. She doesn't know that. Good Lord! What kind of a woman can she be to stand my bad temper for a few dollars a month!"

"I think," said I, "that it's partly because she's poor, partly because she's sorry for you."

He looked up with a ghastly smile.

"You think she really is sorry?"

Before I could answer he went on: "I'm no mawkish senti-
mentalist, and I won't allow anybody to be sorry for me; do you
hear?"

"Oh, I'm not sorry for you!" I said hastily, and for the first
time since I had seen him he laughed heartily without a sneer.

We both seemed to feel better after that; I drank his wine
and smoked his cigars, and he appeared to take a certain grim
pleasure in watching me.

"There's no fool like a young fool," he observed presently.

As I had no doubt he referred to me I paid him no attention.

After fidgetting with his shawls, he gave me an oblique scowl
and asked me my age.

"Twenty-four," I replied.

"Sort of a tadpole, aren't you?" he said.

As I took no offence he repeated the remark.

"Oh, come," said I, "there's no use in trying to irritate me. I
see through you; a row acts like a cocktail on you; but you'll
have to stick to gruel in my company."

"I call that impudence!" he rasped out wrathfully.

"I don't care what you call it," I replied, undisturbed. "I am
not going to be worried by you. Anyway," I ended, "it is my
opinion that you could be very good company if you chose."

The proposition appeared to take his breath away—at least
he said nothing more; and I finished my cigar in peace and tossed
the stump into a saucer.

"Now," said I, "what price do you set upon your birds, Mr.
Halyard?"

"Ten thousand dollars," he snapped with an evil smile.

"You will receive a certified cheque when the birds are deliv-
ered," I said quietly.

"You don't mean to say you agree to that outrageous
bargain?—and I won't take a cent less either. Good Lord!
haven't you any spirit left?" he cried, half rising from his pile
of shawls.

His piteous eagerness for a dispute sent me into laughter impossible to control, and he eyed me, mouth open, animosity rising visibly.

Then he seized the wheels of his invalid chair and trundled away, too mad to speak, and I strolled out into the parlour, still laughing.

The pretty nurse was there, sewing under a hanging lamp.

"If I am not indiscreet—" I began.

"Indiscretion is the better part of valor," said she, dropping her head but raising her eyes.

So I sat down with a frivolous smile peculiar to the appreciated.

"Doubtless," said I, "you are hemming a kerchief."

"Doubtless I am not," she said; "this is a night-cap for Mr. Halyard."

A mental vision of Halyard in a night-cap, very mad, nearly sent me laughing again.

"Like the King of Yvetot, he wears his crown in bed." I said flippantly.

"The King of Yvetot might have made that remark," she observed, re-threading her needle.

It is unpleasant to be reproved. How large and red and hot a man's ears feel.

To cool them, I strolled out to the porch; and after a while the pretty nurse came out, too, and sat down in a chair not far away. She probably regretted her lost opportunity to be flirted with.

"I have so little company—it is a great relief to see somebody from the world," she said. "If you can be agreeable I wish you would."

The idea that she had come out to see me was so agreeable that I remained speechless until she said: "Do tell me what people are doing in New York."

So I seated myself on the steps and talked about the portion of the world inhabited by me, while she sat sewing in the dull light that straggled out from the parlor windows.

She had a certain coquetry of her own, using the usual methods with an individuality that was certainly fetching. For instance, when she lost her needle—and, another time, when we both, on hands and knees, hunted for her thimble.

However, directions for these pastimes may be found in contemporary classics.

I was as entertaining as I could be—perhaps not quite as entertaining as a young man usually thinks he is. However, we got on very well together until I asked her tenderly who the Harbor-Master might be whom they all spoke of so mysteriously.

"I do not care to speak about it," she said, with a primness of which I had not suspected her capable.

Of course I could scarcely pursue the subject after that—and, indeed, I did not intend to; so I began to tell her how I fancied I had seen a man on the cliff that afternoon, and how the creature slid over the sheer rock like a snake.

To my amazement she asked me to kindly discontinue the account of my adventures in an icy tone, which left no room for protest.

"It was only a sea-otter," I tried to explain, thinking perhaps she did not care for snake stories.

But the explanation did not appear to interest her, and I was mortified to observe that my impression upon her was anything but pleasant.

"She doesn't seem to like me and my stories," thought I; "but she is too young, perhaps, to appreciate them."

So I forgave her—for she was even prettier than I had thought her at first—and I took my leave, saying that Mr. Halyard would doubtless direct me to my room.

Halyard was in his library, cleaning a revolver, when I entered.

"Your room is next to mine," he said; "pleasant dreams, and kindly refrain from snoring."

"May I venture an absurd hope that you will do the same?" I replied politely.

That maddened him, so I hastily withdrew.

I had been asleep for at least two hours, when a movement by my bedside and a light in my eyes awakened me. I sat bolt upright in bed, blinking at Halyard, who, clad in a dressing-gown and wearing a night-cap, had wheeled himself into my room with one hand, while with the other he solemnly waved a candle over my head.

"I'm so cursed lonely," he said; "come, there's a good fellow—talk to me in your own original impudent way."

I objected strenuously, but he looked so worn and thin, so lonely and bad-tempered, so lovelessly grotesque, that I got out of bed and passed a spongeful of cold water over my head.

Then I returned to bed and propped the pillows up for a back-rest, ready to quarrel with him if it might bring some little pleasure into his morbid existence.

"No," he said amiably; "I'm too worried to quarrel, but I'm much obliged for your kindly offer. I want to tell you something."

"What?" I asked suspiciously.

"I want to ask you if you ever saw a man with gills like a fish?"

"Gills?" I repeated.

"Yes, gills! Did you?"

"No," I replied angrily; "and neither did you."

"No, I never did," he said in a curiously placid voice; "but there's a man with gills like a fish who lives in the ocean out there. Oh, you needn't look that way: nobody ever thinks of doubting my word, and I tell you that there's a man—or a thing that looks like a man—as big as you are, too, all slate-colored, with nasty red gills like a fish; and I've a witness to prove what I say."

"Who?" I asked sarcastically.

"The witness? My nurse."

"Oh! She saw a slate-colored man with gills?"

"Yes, she did. So did Francis Lee, superintendent of the Mica Quarry Company at Port-of-Waves. So have a dozen men who work in the quarry. Oh, you needn't laugh, young man. It's an old story here, and anybody can tell you about the Harbor-Master."

"The Harbor-Master!" I exclaimed.

"Yes; that slate-coloured thing with gills that looks like a man—and, by Heaven, *is* a man!—that's the Harbor-Master. Ask any quarryman at Port-of-Waves what it is that comes purring around their boats at the wharf, and unties painters and changes the mooring of every catboat in the cove at night! Ask Francis Lee what it was he saw running and leaping up and down the shoal at sunset last Friday! Ask anybody along the coast what sort of a thing moves about the cliffs like a man, and slides over them into the sea like an otter!"

"I saw it do that!" I burst out.

"Oh, did you? Well, *what was it?*"

Something kept me silent, although a dozen explanations flew to my lips.

After a pause, Halyard said: "You saw the Harbor-Master—that's what you saw!"

I looked at him without a word.

"Don't mistake me," he said pettishly; "I don't think that the Harbor-Master is a spirit, or a sprite, or a hobgoblin, or any sort of damned rot. Neither do I believe it to be an optical illusion."

"What do you think it is?" I asked.

"I think it's a man; I think it's a branch of the human race—that's what I think. Let me tell you something. The deepest spot in the Atlantic Ocean is a trifle over five miles deep; and I suppose you know that this place lies only about a quarter of a mile off this headland. The British exploring vessel, *Gull*, Captain Marotte, discovered and sounded it, I believe. Anyway, it's there, and it's my belief that the profound depths are inhabited by the remnants of the last race of amphibious human beings."

This was childish; I did not bother to reply.

"Believe it or not, as you will," he said angrily; "one thing I know, and that is this: the Harbor-Master has taken to hanging round my cove, and he is attracted by my nurse! I won't have it! I'll blow his fishy gills out of his head if I ever get a shot at him! I don't care whether it's homicide or not—anyway, it's a new kind of murder, and it attracts me!"

I gazed at him incredulously, but he was working himself into a passion, and I did not choose to say what I thought.

"Yes, this slate-colored thing with gills goes purring and grinning and spitting about after my nurse—when she walks, when she rows, when she sits on the beach! Gad! It drives me nearly frantic. I won't tolerate it, I tell you!"

"No," said I; "I wouldn't either." And I rolled over in bed convulsed with laughter.

The next moment I heard my door slam. I smothered my mirth, and rose to close the window, for the land wind blew cold from the forest, and a drizzle was sweeping the carpet as far as my bed.

That luminous glare which sometimes lingers after the stars go out threw a trembling nebulous radiance over sand and cove. I heard the seething currents under the breakers' softened thunder louder than I ever heard it. Then, as I closed my window, lingering for a last look at the crawling tide, I saw a man standing ankle-deep in the surf, all alone there in the night. But—was it a man? For the figure suddenly began running over the beach on all fours, like a beetle, waving its limbs like feelers. Before I could throw open the window again it darted into the surf, and when I leaned out into the chilling drizzle, I saw nothing save the flat ebb crawling on the coast—I heard nothing save the purring of bubbles on seething sands.

CHAPTER V

It took me a week to perfect my arrangements for transporting the Great Auks by water to Port-of-Waves, where a lumber-schooner was to be sent from Petite-Sainte-Isole, chartered by me for a voyage to New York.

I had constructed a cage made of osiers, in which my auks were to squat until they arrived at Bronx Park. My telegrams to Professor Farrago were brief; one merely said "Victory!" another explained that I wanted no assistance; and a third read, "Schooner *Borogrove* chartered. Arrive New York July I. Send furniture-van to foot of Bluff Street."

My week as a guest of Mr. Halyard proved interesting. I wrangled with that invalid to his heart's content, I worked all day on my osier-cage, I hunted the thimble in the moonlight with the pretty nurse. We sometimes found it.

As for the thing they called the Harbor-Master, I saw it a dozen times, but always either at night or so far away and so close to the sea that of course no trace of it remained when I reached the spot, rifle in hand.

1 had quite made up my mind that the so-called Harbor-Master was a demented darky—wandered from Heaven knows where—perhaps shipwrecked and gone mad from his sufferings. Still, it was far from pleasant to know that the creature was strongly attracted by the pretty nurse.

She, however, persisted in regarding the Harbor-Master as a sea-creature; she earnestly affirmed that it had gills, like a fish's gills, that it only had a soft, fleshy hole for a mouth, and its eyes were luminous and lidless and fixed.

"Besides," she said, with a shudder, "it's all slate-color, like a porpoise, and it looks as wet as a sheet of india-rubber in a dissecting-room."

The day before I was to set sail with my auks in a cat-boat bound for Port-of-Waves, Halyard trundled up to me in his chair, and announced his intention of going with me.

"Going where?" I asked.

"To Port-of-Waves and then to New York," he replied tranquilly.

I was doubtful, and my lack of cordiality hurt his feelings.

"Oh, of course, if you need the sea-voyage," I began.

"I don't, I need you," he said savagely; "I need the stimulus of our daily quarrel. I never disagreed so pleasantly with anybody in my life; it agrees with me; I am a hundred per cent better than I was last week."

I was inclined to resent this, but something in the deep-lined face of the invalid softened me. Besides, I had taken a hearty liking to the old pig.

"I don't want any mawkish sentiment about it," he said, observing me closely; "I won't permit anybody to feel sorry for me—do you understand?"

"I'll trouble you to use a different tone in addressing me," I replied hotly. "I'll feel sorry for you if I choose to!" And our usual quarrel proceeded, to his deep satisfaction.

By six o'clock next evening I had Halyard's luggage stowed away in the cat-boat, and the pretty nurse's effects corded down. She and I placed the ozier-cage aboard, securing it firmly, and then, throwing tablecloths over the auks' heads, we led those simple and dignified birds down the path and across the plank at the little wooden pier. Together, we locked up the house, while Halyard stormed at us both and wheeled himself furiously up and down the beach below. At the last moment she forgot her thimble. But we found it; I forget where.

"Come on!" shouted Halyard, waving his shawls furiously. "What the devil are you about up there!"

He received our explanation with a sniff, and we trundled him aboard without further ceremony.

"Don't run me across the plank like a steamer-trunk!" he shouted, as I shot him dexterously into the cockpit.

But the wind was dying away, and I had no time to dispute with him then.

The sun was setting above the pine-clad ridge as our skiff flapped and partly filled, and I cast off, and began a long tack, east by south, to avoid the spouting rocks on our starboard bow.

The sea-birds rose in clouds as we swung across the shoal; the black surf-ducks scuttered out to sea; the gulls tossed their sun-tipped wings in the ocean, riding the rollers like bits of froth.

Already we were sailing slowly out across that great hole in the ocean, five miles deep, the most profound sounding ever taken in the Atlantic. The presence of great heights or great depths, seen or unseen, always impresses the human mind— perhaps oppresses it. We were very silent; the sunlight stain on cliff and beach deepened to crimson, then faded into a sombre purple bloom that lingered long after the rose tint died out in the zenith.

Our progress was slow; at times, although the sail filled with the rising land breeze, we scarcely seemed to move at all.

"Of course," said the pretty nurse, "we wouldn't be aground in the deepest hole in the Atlantic."

"Scarcely," said Halyard sarcastically, "unless we're grounded on a whale."

"What's that soft thumping?" I asked; "have we run afoul of a barrel or log?"

It was almost too dark to see, but I leaned over the rail and swept the water with my hand. Instantly something smooth glided under it, like the back of a great fish, and I jerked my hand back to the tiller. At the same moment the whole surface of the water seemed to begin to purr, with a sound like the breaking of froth in a champagne-glass.

"What's the matter with you?" asked Halyard sharply.

"A fish came up under my hand," I said: "a porpoise or some- thing—"

With a low cry the pretty nurse clasped my arm in both her hands.

"Listen!" she whispered; "it's purring around the boat!"

"What the devil's purring?" shouted Halyard. "I won't have anything purring around me."

At that moment, to my amazement, I saw that the boat had stopped entirely, although the sail was full and the small pennant fluttered from the mast-head. Something, too, was tugging at the rudder, twisting and jerking it until the tiller strained and creaked in my hand. All at once it snapped; the tiller swung useless, and the boat whirled around, heeling in the stiffening wind, and drove shoreward.

It was then that I, ducking to escape the boom, caught a glimpse of something ahead—something that a sudden wave seemed to toss on deck and leave there, wet and flapping—a man with round, fixed, fishy eyes and soft, slaty skin.

But the horror of the thing were the two gills that swelled and relaxed spasmodically, emitting a rasping, purring sound—two gasping blood-red gills, all fluted and scolloped and distended.

Frozen with amazement and repugnance, I stared at the creature; I felt the hair stirring on my head, and the icy sweat on my forehead.

"It's the Harbor-Master!" screamed Halyard.

The Harbor-Master had gathered himself into a wet lump, squatting motionless in the bows under the mast; his lidless eyes were phosphorescent, like eyes of living codfish. After a while I felt that either terror or disgust was going to strangle me where I sat, but it was only the arms of the pretty nurse clasped around me in a frenzy of terror.

There was not a firearm aboard that we could get at. Halyard's hand crept backward where a steel-shod boat-hook lay, and I also made a clutch at it. The next moment I had it in my hand and staggered forward, but the boat was already tumbling shoreward among the breakers, and the next I knew the Harbor-Master ran at me like a colossal rat, just as the boat rolled over and over through the surf, spilling freight and passengers among the seaweed-covered rocks.

When I came to myself I was thrashing about knee-deep in a rocky pool, blinded by the water and half suffocated, while under my feet, like a stranded porpoise, the Harbor-Master made the water boil in his efforts to upset me. But his limbs seemed soft and boneless; he had no nails, no teeth, and he bounced and thumped and flapped and splashed like a fish, while I rained blows on him with the boat-hook that sounded like blows on a football. And all the while his gills were blowing out, and frothing, and purring, and his lidless eyes looked into mine, until, nauseated and trembling, I dragged myself back to the beach, where already the pretty nurse alternately wrung her hands and her petticoats in ornamental despair.

Beyond the cove, Halyard was bobbing up and down, afloat in his invalid's chair, trying to steer shoreward. He was the maddest man I ever saw.

"Have you killed that rubber-headed thing yet?" he roared.

"I can't kill it," I shouted breathlessly; "I might as well try to kill a football!"

"Can't you punch a hole in it?" he bawled. "If I can only get at him—"

His words were drowned in a thunderous splashing, a roar of great broad flippers beating the sea, and I saw the gigantic forms of my two Great Auks blundering past in a shower of spray, driving headlong out into the ocean.

"Oh, Lord!" I said, "I can't stand that!" and for the first time in my life I fainted peacefully—and appropriately—at the feet of the pretty nurse.

~~~~~~~~~~

It is within the range of possibility that this story may be doubted. It doesn't matter; nothing can add to the despair of a man who has lost two Great Auks.

As for Halyard, nothing affects him, except his involuntary sea-bath, and that did him so much good that he writes me from the south that he's going on a walking tour through Switzerland, if I'll join him. I might have joined him if he had not married the pretty nurse. I wonder whether— But, of course, this is no place for speculation.

In regard to the Harbor-Master, you may believe it or not, as you choose. But if you hear of any Great Auks being found, kindly throw a tablecloth over their heads and notify the authorities at the new Zoological Gardens in Bronx Park, New York. The reward is ten thousand dollars.